Tolkien's Mythic Meaning

Tolkien's Mythic Meaning

Personal Encounters Through *The Lord of the Rings*

Quinn A. J. Gervel

PICKWICK *Publications* • Eugene, Oregon

TOLKIEN'S MYTHIC MEANING
Personal Encounters Through *The Lord of the Rings*

Pickwick Publications
An Imprint of Wipf and Stock Publishers
199 W. 8th Ave., Suite 3
Eugene, OR 97401

www.wipfandstock.com

PAPERBACK ISBN: 978-1-7252-7198-2
HARDCOVER ISBN: 978-1-7252-7199-9
EBOOK ISBN: 978-1-7252-7200-2

Cataloguing-in-Publication data:

Names: Gervel, Quinn A. J., author.

Title: Tolkien's mythic meaning : personal encounters through *The Lord of the Rings* / by Quinn A. J. Gervel.

Description: Eugene, OR : Pickwick Publications, 2025 | Includes bibliographical references and index.

Identifiers: ISBN 978-1-7252-7198-2 (paperback) | ISBN 978-1-7252-7199-9 (hardcover) | ISBN 978-1-7252-7200-2 (ebook)

Subjects: LCSH: Tolkien, J. R. R. (John Ronald Reuel), 1892–1973. Lord of the rings. | Tolkien, J. R. R. (John Ronald Reuel), 1892–1973—Religion. | Christianity and literature—England—History—20th century. | Christian fiction, English—History and criticism. | Fantasy fiction, English—History and criticism.

Classification: PR6039.O32 .G47 2025 (paperback) | PR6039.O32 .G47 (ebook)

VERSION NUMBER 05/22/25

The Letters of J. R. R. Tolkien. 1981. Edited by Humphrey Carpenter. Boston: Houghton Mifflin, 2000.

The Hobbit. 1937. Boston: Houghton Mifflin, 2001.

The Lord of the Rings. 1954. Boston: Houghton Mifflin, 1994.

The Tolkien Reader. New York: Ballantine, 1966.

"Mythopoeia." In *Tree and Leaf*. 1964. London: HarperCollins, 2001.

Tolkien On Fairy-Stories. Edited by Verlyn Flieger and Douglas A. Anderson. London: HarperCollins, 2008.

Smith of Wootton Major. First edition, 1967. Extended edition, 2005. Edited by Verlyn Flieger. London: HarperCollins, 2015.

The Monsters and the Critics and Other Essays. 1983. Edited by Christopher Tolkien. London: HarperCollins, 2006.

For mom, who I know is proud of me

For dad, who I know would be

For Kate, my very own Rosie Cotton,
and our three beautiful halflings

Contents

Preface

As I WAS PREPARING this manuscript, the Bodleian Libraries showcased its *Tolkien: Maker of Middle-earth* exhibition at Oxford. It opened in June 2018 and ended five months later. A thirty-two-page summary was prepared by the Libraries for The Tolkien Trust afterward, from which I would like to highlight a few things relevant to the theme of this book.

One of the purposes of the exhibition was to attract a broader, more diverse audience than just Tolkien enthusiasts—the "casual visitor," along with anyone unfamiliar with Tolkien altogether.[1] To say the event was successful is an understatement. The Bodleian never had a more successful showing. Nearly 139,000 visitors experienced it for themselves, greater than any exhibit in Oxford's long history.[2] It was headline news from media outlets throughout the United Kingdom and internationally and generated sales revenues of over £1,030,000 from new publications and retail items showcasing Tolkien's creativity.[3] Why is this relevant? The curator remained true to the exhibition's name: More than Middle-earth was on display; attendees were also encountering Tolkien as a person.

Tolkien died in 1973, but long before and ever since, Tolkien's admirers have continued to find new ways to make him and his world accessible to future generations. In the past few years alone, highly dedicated researchers have published about Tolkien's character, imagination, interests, inspirations, and concerns and how these shaped his creativity.[4] Also

1. Bodleian Libraries, *Tolkien*, 4, 5.

2. Bodleian Libraries, *Tolkien*, 4, 5.

3. Bodleian Libraries, *Tolkien*, 5, 10. £1,030,000 is roughly $1,285,000.

4. See Ordway, *Tolkien's Faith*; Tolkien, *Nature*; Freeman, *Tolkien Dogmatics*—to name a few.

noteworthy are HarperCollins's revised and expanded edition of Tolkien's letters,[5] the *Tolkien* biographical film inspired by the earlier years of his life,[6] and Amazon's streaming debut of *The Lord of the Rings: The Rings of Power* in 2022. Publishers keep Tolkien's works in print because his name is profitable, and Amazon would not have spent $715 million making *The Rings of Power* if executives did not think the monetary returns would well surpass the expenses.[7] But this would all not be possible unless Tolkien provided access to his world in the first place. *Maker of Middle-earth* continued the trend of providing access, while also demonstrating why Middle-earth is still meaningful to so many.

Attendees left the exhibition enlightened, moved, and fulfilled by the J. R. R. Tolkien they had encountered, many of whom expressed their appreciation about what they loved and learned through personal testimonials.[8] Having been introduced to the story behind the "maker," they understood that Tolkien was more than just another author who merely introduced readers to half-sized, human-like fictional beings with large appetites, good humor, and hairy feet. With Tolkien's personhood on display, they were given an in-depth look at the various ways he used art, language, and life experience to forge a mythological history bred from an intimate understanding of how to share this creatively with others. It was a matter of such great importance to its trustees that The Tolkien Trust contributed £470,000 to give people the opportunity to get to know Tolkien in the most seamless way possible, free of charge.[9]

This book concentrates on Tolkien as *myth*maker, best understood by becoming acquainted with who he was. The meaning instilled in *The Lord of the Rings* is capable of awakening fundamental sensibilities of readers in deeply personal ways, and my focus on the methods of its making provide insights into how and why. I do not concentrate much on the intricate details within the story because I do not find these as interesting as exploring the reasons the story's meaning is mythically capable of enlarging a person's comprehension of reality. Of course, Tolkien would not claim that the world upheld in his story should *supersede* reality, but he was determined to bring readers a clearer recognition

5. Tolkien, *Letters* [2023].
6. Karukoski, *Tolkien*.
7. Schwartzel, "How Amazon."
8. Bodleian Libraries, *Tolkien*, 5.
9. Bodleian Libraries, *Tolkien*, 4. £470,000 is roughly $586,000.

of reality. This was, after all, what he perceived his readers to be longing for, and this is what I hope you will appreciate in what follows.

Acknowledgments

To THOSE WHO SPENT time and energy in kindly answering my inquiries along the way: Tom Shippey, Thomas W. Smith, Michael Drout, David Lyle Jeffrey, Philip Tallon, Alan Jacobs, Edmund Weiner, Jeremy Marshall, Chris Matocha, Brian Murdoch, John Walsh, Allan Turner, Douglas Anderson, Michael Elam, Robin Reid, Cathleen Blackburn.

To those through Nazarene Theological College who were so supportive and available throughout my first leg of the journey: Peter Rae, Kent Brower, Andrew Brower Latz, Tom Noble, Geordan Hammond, Stephen Wright, Julie Lunn, Carol Blessing.

To those whose confidence and assistance helped me begin this endeavor: David Setran, Jim Wilhoit, Joseph Dongell.

To those whose expertise aided me in the research process: Laura Schmidt, Alexandra Duenow, Bonnie Temple.

Special thanks to those who encouraged me to take this project one step further. For all your kindness, I am in your debt:

—Dwight Swanson, Robert Pelfrey, Ben Pugh, William Fliss: You kindly endured all my questions and provided helpful feedback.

—Paul A. Hoffman, Deirdre Brower Latz, Joseph Coleson: I wouldn't have made it without you.

Lastly, much love and gratitude to Kate, Nancy, Shannon, Brian, and Bonnie—Each of you bring light to my life in all the ways I need it.

Abbreviations of Tolkien Works

"Aman"	"The Annals of Aman"
"Appendix"	"The Appendix on Languages"
"Beowulf"	"Beowulf: The Monsters and the Critics"
Bombadil	*The Adventures of Tom Bombadil*
"Draft"	"Tolkien's Draft Introduction to *The Golden Key*"
"Essay"	"Smith of Wootton Major Essay"
"Genesis"	"'Genesis of the story' Tolkien's Note to Clyde Kilby"
Hobbit	*The Hobbit*
"Istari"	"The Istari"
"LaterQS1"	"The Later Quenta Silmarillion, Phase 1"
Leaf	*Leaf by Niggle*
Letters	*The Letters of J. R. R. Tolkien*
Lost Tales	*The Book of Lost Tales 1*
LOTR	*The Lord of the Rings*
"Making"	The Making of Appendix A
"Manuscript"	"Manuscript B"
"Names"	"Guide to the Names in *The Lord of the Rings*"
OFS	"On Fairy-stories"

"Papers"	"Notion Club Papers"
Peoples	*The Peoples of Middle-earth*
"Power"	"Of the Rings of Power and the Third Age"
Reader	*The Tolkien Reader*
Sauron	*Sauron Defeated*
Shadow	*The Return of the Shadow*
Silmarillion	*The Silmarillion*
SWM	*Smith of Wootton Major*
"Vice"	"A Secret Vice"
War	*The War of the Ring*
"Welsh"	"English and Welsh"

Introduction

J. R. R. Tolkien's *The Lord of the Rings* (*LOTR*) is a book of some six hundred thousand words that is popular throughout the world.[1] Millions read *LOTR* because of its social and personal significance, not because they have to.[2] It has remained in print every year since first publication,[3] been translated into eighty-seven languages,[4] and proved its staying power with multigenerational appeal.[5] *LOTR* attracts no exact type of reader[6] and has continued to captivate countless imaginations thus far into the twenty-first century.

1. Tolkien, *Letters*, 160. Note: For all Tolkien primary sources, his name is used in the first citation only. In all subsequent references, only the source and page number are cited.

2. Shippey, *JRRT: Author*, xxvii–xxiii.

3. Hammond and Scull, "*LOTR*" *Companion*, xxxix. Since initial publication, nearly 250 editions of *LOTR* have been published in various languages (see "*LOTR* > Editions"). One of the latest editions from HarperCollins (2021) includes more of Tolkien's artwork, adding sales to the 150 million copies already sold internationally.

4. From 1956 into Dutch; most recently into Georgian in 2016 and Sinhala (Sri Lankan) in 2018 (Strelzyk, "Chronology").

5. The edition marking the one-hundred-year anniversary of Tolkien's birth (1992) sold out immediately (Bailey, *JRRT*). As of 1999, Tolkien's books had "increased every year since his death in 1973" (Unwin, "Tolkien," 210). Peter Jackson's film adaptations—released as three separate films in December 2001, 2002, and 2003—boosted book sales prior to the first film's release (Bell, "*LOTR*," 166). Anticipation of the first film alone allowed readers to experience *LOTR* directly with their own imaginations before seeing the dramatic imagery of Jackson's films. Anticipation for the second film spiked sales again (335), and after the final film's release, there was a new wave of *LOTR* intrigue, inspiring a new generation of readers internationally (277–79).

6. In addition to C. S. Lewis, Charles Williams, and Tolkien's son Christopher, among those demanding more of *LOTR* while it was being written were enthusiasts

Christopher Tolkien stated his father's world reveals what otherwise "cannot be seen, cannot be found" unless imagined through Tolkien's "extraordinary power of compelling literary belief."[7] This book explores how inducing such belief can lead to personal transformation in a reader. Central to this argument is Tolkien's unique method of creativity in deriving *mythos*, "the regenerative power of story."[8] Throughout the book, *mythos* is used to highlight how stories effectively mediate experience, whether they be told, read, or heard. There is no telling how stories will resonate, but their lastingness affirms their significance to the human imagination. *LOTR* was meant to instill a certain kind of experience. I contend that how Tolkien presented it as a literary *Secondary World* is instrumental to residual effects in a reader's actual *Primary World* experience.[9]

Many of us perceive life as a living narrative and use our imaginations in the process. We are also impacted by forms of meaning over time. Such natural ways of experiencing our own narratives elevate the significance of what imaginary worlds show us as they are revealed. Tolkien's world introduces "participatory realism" into the imagination "by which we learn to share in divine creativity by awakening the world beyond itself to its own reality."[10] If one participates in God's creativity through reading, the possibility arises that a reader's character may be affected by observing character transformation happening within the story. If so, it stands to reason that personal responses are reactions to the literary world as constructed—not theoretically, but actually.[11] This book deals

from a wide array of professional disciplines (see *Letters*, 122).

7. Bailey, *JRRT*. This was in the 1990s, prior to Peter Jackson's film adaptations. Literary narrative compels the reader's imagination differently than cinematic narrative because the imagination participates with them differently. However closely films adhere to texts, someone *else's* interpretations and imageries are projected into viewers' minds. The point here is that the films caused audiences to want to experience *LOTR* in its original format.

8. Zaleski and Zaleski, *Fellowship*, 4.

9. Tolkien used Primary and Secondary to emphasize the difference between actuality and a literary world. See Tolkien, "On Fairy-stories" (OFS), 52, 63.

10. Milbank, "Apologetics," 44.

11. I am not specifically engaging with modern reader-response theories where the reader is seen as maker of the meaning apart from the "achieved structure of the meanings" imbibed from texts that appeared in the 1960s (Abrams, *Glossary*, 265), at least five years after *LOTR* hit bookshops. Reader-response theories are relevant and may be utilized and applied to examine the effects of *LOTR*. For an example of interpreting *LOTR* using reader-response theory, see Bowman, "Story," 272–93. I have not engaged further with reader-response theories, however, because my book argues that readers' responses are always actual responses: personal real-world affects

with Tolkien's response to the demand for more of his Secondary World after *The Hobbit* (*Hobbit*) was published and the extent to which he mined the depths of the greater reality of this world to write *LOTR*. To discern how *LOTR* exercises its own reality beyond itself—the world to which it belongs within the narrative—and translate it to personal experience, I will articulate how reading *LOTR* enables divine encounters.

Tolkien said *LOTR*'s mythological history is relevant to its *mythos* because he was "fundamentally concerned with the problem of the relation of Art (and Sub-creation) and Primary Reality."[12] *Sub-creation* is Tolkien's term for both actively producing *mythos* with inner consistency to its own secondary plane and the result, the completed work. Distinguishing art and sub-creation from reality and emphasizing a like relationship between them indicates this fundamental concern was analogical in nature, yet damaged. Therefore, I discuss how Tolkien attempted to address the problem and restore the relation between art (and sub-creation) and Primary Reality. By coming to an understanding of Tolkien's creativity and how it relates to the reader's, I interpret how Tolkien instilled *LOTR* with meaning to awaken religious sensibility, which then creates conditions for belief that can be interpreted as an ontological encounter with God outside, or apart from, the story. How can *LOTR* sub-creatively bridge into Primary World experience? I am using language about the analogical relation to explore this question.[13]

Tolkien described himself as "the most reckless user of coincidence and chance-connexions in story-telling," which, he admitted, "cannot

via encounters with the text. Insofar as narrative is a mediatory medium readers experience from beginning to end, their responses are based on the fact that narrative induces anticipation through linear progression and subsequently projects new visualizations into the imagination from the locale contextualized by the writer (see Ward, "Narrative," 447). Tolkien believed external meanings should not detract from life inside the story (see *Letters*, 379–87, for examples). Therefore, to focus on Tolkien's particular way of meaning-making, and to amplify that he attempted to show readers a specific kind of imaginary world through his unique creativity, I have restricted my argument to the *author-determined approach* to focus on meanings of origination and intent. The author-determined approach is "commonsense . . . to all communication. . . . Any act of communication can progress only on the assumption that someone is trying to convey meaning to us and we then respond to that meaning intended by the speaker or writer" (Plummer, *Forty Questions*, 130).

12. *Letters*, 145n.

13. Drawn from Boersma, *Heavenly*; Przywara, *Analogia*; McGrath, *Order of Things*; *Theory*; Poythress, *Chance*; Wolf, *Building*; Oliver, *Creation*; Giussani, *Religious Sense*; Williams, Series Introduction; *Grace*; Di Fuccia, *Owen Barfield*; Ward, "How Literature"; Taylor, *Language Animal*; *Secular*.

rival what actually happens."[14] This stresses that although an analogical relationship exists between stories and actual experience, stories should be regarded to a lesser extent. But if storytelling adheres to a quality of its own plane that coheres with a lifelikeness that enlightens readers' Primary World experiences, it gives new meaning to their lives as they live them. Therefore, reading can affect personal being parallel to our growing conscious understanding of the world.

Even if readers have not determined that God plays an active part in the world, experiencing narratives can bring them into a growing realization of divinity through texts that might cause them to recognize this possibility. Therefore, I intend to show how Tolkien meant *LOTR* to be conceived as a likeness to historical reality through a feigned secondary parallel reality, always based on meaning within that world, which involves the projection of a divine mind. I maintain that a bridge exists as a reminder that Primary and Secondary Worlds always remain "two worlds in action,"[15] ever distinct. Primarily, language depicts "what otherwise would have remained hidden" prior to what the writer has revealed through it.[16] Consequently, because *LOTR* pre-exists the reader's participation in it, reading authenticates meaning to the reader's experience in the Primary World through the context of the narrative as written. Throughout the book, I build and support this point. Chapter-by-chapter, various threads are interwoven until a full tapestry of the kind of experience Tolkien posited through *LOTR* becomes clear.

Chapter 1 lays groundwork for how and why sub-creative *mythos* establishes itself as a personalized form of meaning that becomes a shared ontological experience. We will see how Tolkien established this in Bilbo Baggins, a character thrust into Tolkien's mythological history unplanned, and how this proves instrumental in *LOTR*'s profound capability of relating to actual needs of readership.

Chapter 2 constructs a specific framework of Tolkien's view of Primary Reality in anticipation of the kind of world to which *LOTR* is analogous. This provides a lens for experiencing the cosmos as sacramental based on the gift of creativity each person shares with each other, from God. Throughout the chapter, I analyze how Tolkien's sub-creativity is seen as shaped through a Christian, *logos*-centric lens that engaged his sacramental imagination. Consequently, I discuss how Tolkien's reading

14. Tolkien, Letter to Nancy Smith.

15. Flieger, "Time," 649.

16. MacQuarrie, *Principles*, 126.

of reality provided ways for him to use language, myth, and narrative to give meaning to personal experience.

Chapters 3 and 4 narrow the scope of Tolkien's personal sub-creative particularity based on his belief that God is ever involved in the world and on his desire for mythopoesis (mythmaking) in conjunction with his own "linguistic predilections."[17] Secondary Worlds establish their own historical concreteness based on their own rules and meaning. *LOTR* projects something imaginative that is contextually true based on the way its narrative unfolds, which is how we also try to understand our own lives: interpreted through contextual experience. If meaning stems from the uniqueness of the world's construction, this keeps *LOTR* from being an allegory of life events and circumstances. The more firmly the bridge between worlds is established, the more the meaning of the Secondary World freely transmits meaning on its own grounds. I expound upon such meaning on the other side of the bridge by accentuating two ways Tolkien provided for experiencing the action of *mythos*. Through Tolkien's depiction of human encounters with an otherworld in *Smith of Wootton Major*, I discuss how *LOTR* compares to observing a stage play unfold before our eyes, like how we might read two parallel planes of history. Each has its own plane of narrative linearity that brings about distinct contexts of experience. I use "The Notion Club Papers"[18] to enhance how the literary credibility of Tolkien's *mythos* intensifies participation inside *LOTR*. Tolkien's perception of the power of fantasy gives the impression that the *mythos* has transported us to another time, which is contingent on the language-making that bred Tolkien's mythology.

Chapters 5 and 6 deepen the meaning of the kind of Primary World lens *LOTR* parallels. *LOTR* presents an imaginative world that echoes a particular kind of real-world ontological space filled with signs signifying the greater reality of a divine mind to whom religious awakening may be attributed. This requires feeling grounded in a real sense of transcendent presence, which is not necessarily common to a present-day reading of the Primary World. Therefore, I articulate the kind of cosmic experience *LOTR* was meant to echo. Charles Taylor's notion of secularization is used to explain the challenges that may hinder North Atlantic (or Western)[19] readers from an awareness of participating in the divine. This elevates the importance of how reading can telescope people into

17. Tolkien, Interview with Gueroult.

18. Tolkien, *Sauron*, 145–327.

19. Western European and North American.

seeing the action of Tolkien's *mythos* close-up, as if they have travelled into that world. Such an experience is not escaping reality but offering a lens that mediates secondary truths that bring clarity about Primary World ambiguities and concerns. *LOTR* offers a window through which readers can clearly see and experience everything within the story because of what is implied beyond the window's frame. I then discuss how *LOTR* contrasts the "immanent frame" presented through secular naturalism.[20] The fantasy of *LOTR* rivals the fantasy of naturalism by offering an alternative way of imagining through *mythos* that beckons what Luigi Giussani termed the *religious sense*.[21]

Chapter 7 draws attention to the impact of *mythos*'s inner consistency through feigned history as a means of enchantment. If readers are influenced by secularity and affected by the immanent frame lens, *LOTR* provides a way to imagine otherwise. Even if a reader maintains a secularized vantage point, the operative virtue of a story localizes readers in its own imaginative plane. If feigned history affirms something relevant to readers presently through enchantment, and if the tale awakens readers through an inherent causality through the narrative as constructed, *LOTR* can mythically affect the reader based upon what is dramatized. The discussion then investigates how a perceptible immaterial causality involved in-and-beyond the narrative can have effects that may lead to a greater sense of purpose and fullness only possible if also verifiable in Primary World experience.

Chapter 8 explores how a reading of *LOTR* effectively resonates with a participatory ontology orchestrated by a divine mind. Tolkien projected meaning through *LOTR*, including character development in hobbit characters through Gandalf, Aragorn, and the "manager" of Tolkien's world. Its narrative implies divine involvement in the lives of characters and analogically resounds with how divine involvement may occur in readers' personal narratives. Thus, if readers are awakened to the possibility of God through sub-creation, God can use it to mediate divine presence and affirm teleological significance to the uniqueness of personal being.

To arrive at a conclusion involves accepting mysteriousness about *LOTR*'s lifelikeness. *LOTR* portrays a perceptibly happenstance way characters encounter and experience everyday life set against the

20. Taylor, *Secular*, 542.

21. Giussani, "Religious Sense and Faith"; *Religious Sense*; López, "Growing Human."

backdrop of a rich mythological history. As the narrative unfolds, they demonstrate how its participatory realism bespeaks of a greater reality into which they are absorbed. Upheld by the medieval modus operandi of *interlacement*, *LOTR* presents "a profound sense of reality, of . . . *the way things are*. There *is* a pattern in Tolkien's story, but his characters can never see it (naturally, because they are in it)."[22] Interlacing allowed Tolkien to weave strands of history, characters, and events into a structure that proved he knew what he was doing, even though the real-time of the narrative impresses continuous uncertainty and disorder.[23] Readers have the advantage of viewing this detached from the events and decision-making. We are *shown* as characters *act*. If there are narratives of life grounded in the divine inside *LOTR*, they offer a parallel means through which readers can recognize how divine reality can impact the trajectory of the reader's life. The task is to ascertain why any mysterious meaning *LOTR* engenders might evidence a greater mystery in the Primary World that awakens readers to the existing relation they have with the Judeo-Christian God.

"Fairyland is not the road to heaven or hell," Tolkien said,[24] but fairy-stories have the capacity to affect those who experience the truth represented in their literary planes. Because of the real-world affinity *LOTR* instills and because of the literary belief it compels, I conclude that it can direct sensibilities to a greater awareness of personal identity in the divine and a taste of salvation unique to individual living narratives, regardless of belief system. Analogical participation in *LOTR* can awaken the sense for how God can be seen as present in our own lives if we are grounded in divine reality. If God can be made real to us through characters transformed through participation in the divine mind of *LOTR*, this highlights the significance of the kind of participation Tolkien induces through his *mythos*.

As the book advances, I take an interdisciplinary approach that weaves together doctrine of creation, imagination, analogy of being, myth, fairy-stories, and secularization in Western cultures to accentuate how Tolkien produced meaning through *LOTR* that affects individual lives in a Christian way. Primarily, it draws from and complements

22. Shippey, *JRRT: Author*, 107.

23. Shippey, *Road*, 163.

24. OFS, 28.

arguments made by Alison Milbank and Colin Duriez concerning Tolkien's creativity and its effects.[25]

Milbank acknowledges the contemporary need for people to comprehend and articulate how to live and be in the most fundamental sense, that the basis of this is religious, and that being able to imagine differently apart from the self can offer a means of coming to this realization.[26] Human creativity echoes God's creativity by making works that are new and distinct and offers alternative views of imagining apart from the normalities that may stultify and stunt present experience.[27] Tolkien's "work seeks to accord transcendent significance to human life and activity,"[28] and my argument progressively shows how, in Tolkien's making of *LOTR*'s "narrative ontology,"[29] he authenticates an awareness of transcendent sensibilities whose potential "opens the way to God and the way to encounters with the world."[30]

Duriez notes how Tolkien helps readers identify an inner "sense of disenchantment with their secular cultures" which might prompt them to seek answers to unanswered questions about the meaning of existence.[31] Since in secular time God is often no longer seen as the source by which meaning is interpreted, *LOTR* challenges readers to intuit otherwise. I develop how Tolkien re-enchants readers through the "attractive spirituality"[32] of *LOTR*. The better portrayed in the Secondary World, the better it can analogically direct readers "to a reality other than itself"[33] in the Primary World. Tolkien enables this by grounding *LOTR* in its own secondary context which introduces readers to its own "particular way of seeing."[34]

The secular culture suggested by Duriez differs from the medieval world Tolkien spent his academic career teaching about. The pre-secular

25. Milbank, *Chesterton*; "Apologetics"; Duriez, "Sub-Creation"; "JRRT for the Ages."

26. Milbank, "Apologetics," 32–33, 42.

27. Milbank, "Apologetics," 34.

28. Milbank, *Chesterton*, ix.

29. Milbank, *Chesterton*, 156.

30. Milbank, *Chesterton*, 166.

31. Duriez, "JRRT for the Ages," 322–23.

32. Duriez, "JRRT for the Ages," 324.

33. Duriez, "JRRT for the Ages," 327.

34. Duriez, "JRRT for the Ages," 332. The basis for this was Tolkien's own languages and original myth (329–31) which fortifies a better comprehension of *LOTR*'s meaning in the author-determined approach (see note 11 above).

Western envisioning of reality saw nature and grace as conjoined by divine involvement in the cosmos, and Tolkien still viewed reality this way.[35] I develop the manner by which Tolkien's creativity utilized natural theology to derive meaning via God's revelatory mediation through the created order.[36] Therefore, since humanity is creative like God, it is possible that God may also mediate grace through creative storytelling, and this may lead to "contact with [the] reality" of the divine[37] through a subcreated form of "religious experience."[38]

These foundations help me ground this study of Tolkien in the Christian tradition similar to other Tolkien scholars. Craig Bernthal, Bradley Birzer, Stratford Caldecott, Matthew Dickerson, and Ralph Wood each acknowledge how Catholic Christianity shaped Tolkien's outlook and influenced his creativity.[39] Of these, this book is closely aligned with Bernthal. Milbank maintains that "to invent a world at all . . . is to commit to metaphysics,"[40] and Bernthal similarly argues how the "religious and metaphysical" serve as the "underpinning[s]" of Tolkien's world.[41] Each accounts for the sense of "providential depth"[42] and "rhythm"[43] readers can appreciate in *LOTR*, which reincorporates a divine sensibility denied by writers who deem God as inconsequential in storytelling because irrelevant in their perception of actuality.[44] Bernthal particularly emphasizes how Tolkien as a Catholic saw all creation through a sacramental lens: all forms of being participate in the divine presence in an analogical way, which is meant to direct attention to God, the creator and sustainer of the cosmos.[45] I complement this interpretation of Tolkien's reading of reality and explore how he set *LOTR*

35. See Duriez, "Sub-Creation," 133–35.

36. Duriez, "Sub-Creation," 136–38.

37. Duriez, "Sub-Creation," 139.

38. Duriez, "Sub-Creation," 147.

39. Bernthal, *Sacramental Vision*; Birzer, *JRRT's Sanctifying*; Caldecott, *Power*; "Over the Chasm"; Dickerson, *Hobbit Journey*; Wood, *Gospel*.

40. Milbank, *Chesterton*, 18.

41. Bernthal, *Sacramental Vision*, 5.

42. Bernthal, *Sacramental Vision*, 5.

43. Bernthal, *Sacramental Vision*, 7.

44. Bernthal, *Sacramental Vision*, 6.

45. Bernthal, *Sacramental Vision*, 1–90. For Caldecott on Tolkien's reading of the "sacramental universe," see *Power*, 59–62.

within a particular world of Faërie, an independent sub-created literary cosmos with its own sacramental meaning.[46]

Like Bernthal, Birzer emphasizes Faërie as a separate sacramental world derived from Tolkien's view of creation and creativity, through which God's transcendence is perceptible by means of grace.[47] Thus, Faërie itself is a "gift of grace" from a sub-creator through which God may mediate divine grace to humanity.[48] Faërie, then, provides humanity with a whole new picture of an otherworld, one that allows for a reader not only to perceive the imagery inside of its frame, but also implies that meaning derives from unseen sources outside the frame.[49] The mystery of the whole of this, what Caldecott called "mythic space,"[50] is "an imaginal dimension where dramatic action 'interprets eternity to time and time to eternity'" for making sense of encounters with God through story.[51] Birzer's study argues for the mythic appreciation of Tolkien's world developed throughout this book, one that underscores how myth can "transcend time and space" and provide a way to understand how meaning affects personal being.[52] Thus, God's constant presence can still sanctify humanity via "*anamnesis*," a formerly common way to understand truths and "recall encounters with transcendence that had helped to order [peoples'] souls and their society."[53]

Like Wood, but developing beyond him, I argue how *LOTR* can have a formative impact on readers mythically via "the Christian dimension" that becomes "accessible to the ordinary interested reader" through *LOTR*.[54] Consequently, I show how readers are gradually immersed into a world of its own religious significance through a "divine self-disclosure" like Christianity, but true to the religiousness of its own plane.[55] Thus, *LOTR* may be a means through which "theological mediation" is possible, based on sub-created "transcendent moral reality" that shapes characters

46. See Bernthal, *Sacramental Vision*, 67, 69.
47. Birzer, *JRRT's Sanctifying*, xix–xxv.
48. Birzer, *JRRT's Sanctifying*, xix–xx, 133–37.
49. Caldecott, *Power*, 8.
50. Caldecott, *Power*, 8.
51. Caldecott, "Over the Chasm," 21.
52. Birzer, *JRRT's Sanctifying*, 23.
53. Birzer, *JRRT's Sanctifying*, 24.
54. Wood, *Gospel*, ix.
55. Wood, *Gospel*, 4–7.

through its own divine order.[56] Dickerson shows how *Hobbit* and *LOTR* have an "objective morality"[57] by which Tolkien shapes characters that live for the greater good through adversity.[58] The source is a perceptible "spiritual" reality that remains "*unseen*" by the characters,[59] yet is only observable if experienced physically through historical narrative.[60]

My analysis differs from Bernthal, Birzer, Caldecott, Dickerson, and Wood by not interpreting *LOTR* through all of the posthumously published works in Tolkien's "History of Middle-earth" and by focusing on mythological history content extant up to when Tolkien finished writing *LOTR*.[61] This is partly because Tolkien later experimented with alterations to his sub-creativity that distract from interpreting *LOTR* as written and also because it seems improper that the meaning of what was established as a fixed text in 1955 should be reinterpreted by post-*LOTR* writings, especially those which do not have to do with *LOTR* proper and the analogical world of Faërie he argued for with increased intensity the rest of his life. Also, I have not dealt with the films' imaginative impact versus the book. My focus is on *LOTR*'s effects on readers' imaginations by virtue of the mythic meaning through the power of the text based on Tolkien's creativity alone. The films affect the imagination differently because they image *LOTR* in a completely different format and thus fail

56. Wood, *Gospel*, 9, 84, 121.

57. Dickerson, *Hobbit Journey*, 127.

58. Dickerson, *Hobbit Journey*, 131–47.

59. Dickerson, *Hobbit Journey*, 182–83.

60. See Dickerson, *Hobbit Journey*, 187–202.

61. *LOTR* was published in three volumes, from 1954–1955, in the United Kingdom: *The Fellowship of the Ring* (July 29, 1954), *The Two Towers* (November 11, 1954), *The Return of the King* (October 20, 1955) (Anderson, Note on the Text, xi). Tolkien likely completed edits in the summer of 1955 (Scull and Hammond, *JRRT Companion*, 545). The material I use from the posthumously published "History of Middle-earth" (published by Christopher Tolkien in Tolkien, *Unfinished Tales*, and twelve additional volumes since his father's death) precedes this date. Tolkien material apart from the history of Middle-earth dated after 1955 is used to amplify meanings implicit in pre-1955 writings. Notably, this project does not trace the evolving intricacies of the drafts of the "History of *LOTR*" (volumes 6–9 in the "History of Middle-earth") to interpret the meaning of *LOTR*. Examining the countless ideas Tolkien considered but never brought to final form would serve as a distraction. For example, the original Black Rider who appears in *LOTR* shown sniffing for Frodo was initially conceived as Gandalf sniffing for a hobbit named Bingo (Tolkien, *Shadow*, 47–48). It was first conceived that Treebeard, not Saruman, was the enemy who held Gandalf captive—in Fangorn Forest, not Orthanc (363). Though interesting in themselves, such details do not contribute to the plain understanding of the *LOTR* upheld throughout this book.

to capture the essence of divine involvement implicit in the lives of its characters like the narrative text.[62]

I address the fundamental problem Tolkien wished to restore through my use of participation and analogy in relation to the imaginative activity of the reader. Individual imaginations are vessels through which God brings humanity to comprehend meaning anew.[63] When readers awaken to the participatory realism of *LOTR*, they experience a personal aesthetic reaction. It rings true to particular life experience but is contingent on what Tolkien has shown them through the particular lens of *LOTR*, which then becomes an experience every reader shares in non-identical ways. I am interested in showing how *LOTR* triggers many individual experiences that can all be true without imposing one right answer. I argue that God has created each person in God's image (as an *image-bearer*) and that divine involvement is still perceptible within the world. As we learn to read the world throughout the course of our individual historical narratives, we are always affected by people, things, and ideas apart from ourselves. Therefore, there always exists the capability for new awakenings, especially in relation to the presence of God.

As my argument unfolds and myth is articulated as experience that affects personal narratives of life through storytelling, I discuss how *LOTR* compels belief as an *extra-mental* secondary reality readers encounter imaginatively. In other words, it adheres with a pre-existing, independent literary plane completely out of mind prior to a reader's encounter with it.[64] The kind of imaginative reception and response the reader gives to *LOTR* may be explained by whether s/he identifies with what Charles Taylor calls a *buffered* or *porous* self.[65] A buffered person claims to have an inner life that is distinct from the outer, and is resistant, if not impervious, to the spiritual realm or outside influence of the divine, while a porous person is not. I argue that myth affects readers in an "osmotic,"[66] and therefore porous, way. When readers are affected by stories, especially those that awaken sensibilities about the possibility of divine transcendence in the Primary World,[67] this suggests that buffered

62. Shippey, "Another Road," 251–54.

63. Milbank, "Apologetics," 35.

64. See *OED*, s.v. "extra-, prefix; extra-mental."

65. Taylor, *Secular*, 35–42.

66. Kilby, "Mythic," 122.

67. See Noble, "How Stories Unsettle," for a perspective on how stories can produce a sense of disenchantment from secular cultures, introduce alternative ways for envisioning the world, and allow us to engage in helpful dialogue with others.

selves have limitations. The buffer has been shown to be penetrable due to the mythical effects a reader experiences through analogical participation with a text.

Humanity creatively participates in the Primary World in multiple senses, each of which is interpreted as participation *in* God. One sense involves human identity as shaped through what I term "cosmo-*logos*," the Primary World in which God is actively involved. Image-bearers are creative because God gifted humanity with creativity. Therefore, human beings are *connaturally* creative; that is, creativity is a "congenital, innate," and "natural"[68] characteristic humanity shares with each other, from God. In this sense, existence is a form of participation in the God who creates and sustains it, and human life always participates in this way. Throughout the book, I consider such a personal affinity to the divine in an analogical way.

An analogy is a comparison between two different things in order to draw attention to the existing relation between them.[69] Analogies also allow for relations to be made between created beings and God.[70] In each sense, the analogical relation is only upheld when each being sustains its independence from the other; thus, each maintains its own unique being without collapsing into the other. I draw on Hans Boersma, Simon Oliver, T. F. Torrance, Alister McGrath, Erich Przywara, and Luigi Giussani to articulate how to read the existing analogical relation between God's infinite self and the finite world God created. Although from a range of traditions, each contributes language and imagination that enable me to build this analogical understanding.

Boersma, Oliver, Torrance, and McGrath fit in the wide-ranging Protestant tradition; Przywara and Giussani, the Roman Catholic. Each contributes to how one can imagine God through general revelation in the pre-secular Christian way, which was once common in the Western world.[71] Boersma, Oliver, and Torrance offer ways for seeing and interpreting God's presence in the cosmos based on this once-common way of understanding. Torrance argued that reading the intelligibility of the visible world enables humanity to comprehend divine intellect and creativity as its source; thus can it become knowledgeable of God analogically.[72]

68. *OED Online*, s.v. "connatural."

69. Oliver, *Creation*, 68.

70. Betz, Translator's Introduction, 40.

71. See p. 79n40.

72. Torrance, *Reality*, 70–71.

Based on creation and revelation through Jesus Christ, I adopt Torrance's use of how humanity can encounter God within an "open-space of transcendence," where the divine discloses itself and God's communicability transcends the limitations of time and space.[73] Przywara, Giussani, and McGrath provide additional language for describing this analogically within present experience. Drawing from these theologians, I develop an approach suggesting the inter-complementarity of their language can help us comprehend the infinite God (transcendence) within the physical world (immanence). As a result, meaning is given to how humanity may interpret God's mediatory presence to finite beings based on the analogous relation the creature and Creator share.

Human literary sub-creativity is contiguous with the first cosmo-*logos* sense of participation in God, but in accord with meaning related to its own imaginative plane. The acts of building a Secondary World and venturing inside through reading exercise alternatively individuated components. The writer participates in God while sub-creating what I identify throughout as "mytho-*logos*"—a new literary construction through which poetic meaning is made and mediated to others. Readers participate in this sub-creation imaginatively. In each sense of participation, both the maker's and reader's gift of creativity is engaged while continuing to participate in the creativity of God. Whether making or reading, each imagination experiences mytho-*logos* in a personal way. Therefore, connatural creativity from person-to-person becomes a new avenue through which meaning about the divine may mediate. We will now begin to explore how the mythic meaning of *LOTR* can affect readers in a participatory way that may lead them to a formative encounter with God.

73. Torrance, *Reality*, 188.

Chapter 1

Sub-Creativity and Ontological Experience

Introduction

FOR LITERARY BELIEF TO translate into an encounter with God, something about the meaning of the Secondary World must trigger this effect. Readers also need to be open to the possibility that God exists. But this is not necessarily assumed by the Western Primary World outlook on which I am focused. Therefore, since I am examining Tolkien's Primary World outlook analogically, we need to become acquainted with the world *LOTR* parallels.

Tolkien lived in an industrial age cynical about God, one that had become progressively "characterized by the combination of modern science, a global capitalist economy, and the political power of the nation-state."[1] Tolkien held a view of the world common to how most pre-1500 AD Western societies imagined it.[2] It was a pre-industrial age that primarily believed in divine revelation, where people perceived their roles in life as "demanded by" and situated within a vast cosmic order.[3] Because

1. Curry, *Defending*, 12. Birzer discusses how Tolkien's world confronts this in *JRRT's Sanctifying*, 109–26.

2. Charles Taylor marks the year 1500, so I am using this rough number (see *Secular*, 1–89).

3. Taylor, *Language Animal*, 73–74.

I am discussing how readers may be transformed through the story, any effect on a reader's character happens as s/he witnesses transformation in characters in the story. Responses to such affects stem from the nature of the literary world constructed and the reader's participation in it. This chapter focuses on the pre-1500 Primary World outlook and how sub-creativity mediates *mythos* from artist to audience through Tolkien's use of this framework. It introduces vocabulary used throughout the rest of the book—poetics, ontology, *logos*, transcendence, cosmos, *poesis*—to sustain my argument about why transformative effects in readers from *LOTR* bear relevance to their Primary World experience.

Anticipating Tolkien's World

When Tolkien spoke at Blackfriars Oxford in October 1966, he was expected to address the subject of poetry, but he read a fairy-story instead. In his introductory remarks, Tolkien said, "It contains elements that are relevant to the consideration of Poetry, with a capital P. . . . Its primary purpose is itself."[4] It was an assertion about the proper posture for imaginative receptivity: Let the words artfully speak for themselves without interference[5] because poetry should be relayed without the domineering voice of the writer distracting from the story itself.[6] Instead, stories should poetically liberate from real-life presumptions so that the vision the storyteller casts is allowed to "transform [the receiver's] own experience, whatever that experience" is.[7]

Tolkien's view is supported by a once-held view that "*poetry* often covered all imaginative writing" and spoke truth into history while participating in the divine.[8] Maritain argued poetry provides sustenance to the human condition: "Poetry is spiritual nourishment. But it does not satiate, it only makes many more hungry, and that is its grandeur."[9] It is "*art*, the activity of . . . working reason."[10] Spiritual and reason suggest poetry is a means for initiating ontological experience.

4. Tolkien in Scull and Hammond, *JRRT Companion*, 945.
5. Tolkien, "Draft," 89.
6. Tolkien in Scull and Hammond, *JRRT Companion*, 945.
7. Smith, "Tolkien's Catholic," 2.
8. Lewis, *English*, 318.
9. Maritain, *Creative*, 173.
10. Maritain, "Concerning," 37.

This gives a basis for understanding poetry as more than merely an artistic exercise for self-gratification. It is purposefully produced to be meaningfully experienced by others. Both meaning-making and experiencing meaning anew involve *poetics*, the "sphere" of "human activity" in which people make meaning through mind, spirit, and sense in uniquely formative ways through participation in their societal and cultural contexts.[11] Various characterizations of poetics could be interpreted from this, but since we are dealing specifically with literary sub-creativity, I propose a definition moving forward: Poetics are independent creations true in and of themselves, purposefully designed to enhance effectively the lives of those who experience them. Poetic effects are most powerful when experienced holistically. This highlights the significance of personal experience, which cannot be easily measured. It also requires some manner of imagination and creativity, each of which is necessary for nourishment and integral to ontological experience.

Historically, ontology referred to the Western pre-1500 human "outlook on . . . [or] understanding of reality,"[12] which recognized the world as mysterious and acknowledged a greater reality in which beings participated.[13] People envisioned themselves as part of an "ordered totality" within the cosmos.[14] They assumed the cosmos was wholly other than humanity and full of pre-existing meaning that powerfully shaped imaginations.[15] Its mere existence evidenced teleological purposefulness set into motion by some greater cause.[16] Common to this ancient understanding was also "the *physis* of organic being, the *ethos* of personal conduct and social structures, the *nomos* of normative custom and law, and the *logos*, the rational foundation that normatively rules all aspects of the cosmic development."[17] As the intelligible lens of reality, the *logos* communicated the "ontotheological synthesis" between the finite within the cosmos and its emanating transcendent antecedent.[18] *Logos* preserved the notion that

11. Dyrness, *Poetic Theology*, 11, 38.

12. Boersma, *Heavenly*, 10, 20, 22. In each instance, Boersma means more than this. Its fuller context is presented in chapter 2.

13. Boersma, *Heavenly*, 22–24.

14. Dupré, *Passage*, 17–18.

15. Taylor, *Secular*, 33–34.

16. Oliver, *Creation*, 63; Dupré, *Passage*, 22.

17. Dupré, *Passage*, 17.

18. Dupré, *Passage*, 18.

a "divine Mind" permeated the created world,[19] what the Stoics called the "creative reason" of God's creativity within the world.[20]

This ontological understanding perceived divine transcendent reality "around humans (Nature), among humans, [and] within humans," which ultimately influenced how humanity sub-created secondary realities.[21] In other words, transcendence was woven into everything, enhancing the opportunity for ontological encounters anywhere, through anything, including art. In this, divine transcendence can be described as nearness or presence through creation and human creativity. Another understanding of transcendence is how it "may be encountered or experienced, even if only to a limited extent, within the ordinary world. This way of thinking . . . postulates a frontier beyond which human knowledge cannot penetrate, so that there is always a 'beyond' that remains elusive."[22] This directs the imagination to transcendence as essentially other than the mundane.[23] A frontier conveys that transcendence is presently experienced from an unseen source beyond a horizon. Both nearness and distance shape how one can interpret transcendent experience.

Ontological encounters can be viewed as opportunities for a person's being to be affected by objective being(s). Intelligent minds can observe a relation between them because each being shares in an existence that participates in a greater reality. However, ontological encounters in the cosmic order differ from sub-created worlds as discussed throughout this book.

All such encounters happen in historical time and space. Unlike Primary World encounters that are of *this* cosmos, sub-creation is otherworldly, and its effects derive from *that* world's reality. Because human language necessarily "arises out of experience,"[24] and because experience establishes the "parameters" of personal sub-creation,[25] the writer's language provides the substance of meaningful *mythos* others encounter. *Poesis* means "making,"[26] which implies ongoing activity. Artists

19. Barfield, *History*, 117.

20. Bernthal, *Sacramental Vision*, 86.

21. Yandell, "Pattern," 376.

22. McGrath, *Open Secret*, 25–26.

23. McGrath, *Open Secret*, 25.

24. Wood, *Gospel*, 33.

25. Pearce, *Man and Myth*, 12.

26. Dyrness, *Poetic Theology*, 38. There are different spellings of *poesis*, and I use the author's throughout.

participate in *poesis* purposefully, and poets are especially "interested in grasping real being" from their whole selves,[27] making a concerted effort to communicate personal experience vividly.[28] The final assembly of their words intends to capture this accurately. In this way, poets establish a *telos* within, and particular to, their *mythos*.

From the descriptions of *logos* already given, a general understanding of it may be adopted: *Logos* is a creative medium through which meaning is made and interpreted. Since *logos* presents a way for interpreting meaning from reality as well as making meaning, an analogical affinity exists for two different settings for participation: the created cosmos and poetics. On one side of the analogy, what will hereafter be called "cosmo-*logos*," is reading Primary World reality in relation to the divine in ways that still communicate to personal being. "We could say that the world, this reality into which we collide unleashes a word, an invitation, a meaning as if upon impact. The world is like a word, a 'logos' which sends you further, calls you on to another, beyond itself," said Giussani.[29] Whether or not there is a human artist, *logos* is always happening within the cosmos, with a mind behind it bringing substantive meaning that can affect us. Transcendence remains ever-present within cosmo-*logos* as the essence of the divine shapes people through its own *poesis* and prompts individual formation.

The analogical relation is established when the poet uses *logos* through personal *poesis* to sub-create poetic *mythos*, which makes such ontological encounters possible. Part of this involves what Maritain called making by "*affective connaturality*" through "poetic knowledge."[30] The connaturality noted in the Introduction, spoke of the congenital, innate sensibilities all humanity shares from God. Maritain described connaturality as the creative intellectual, spiritual, and intuitive proclivities that progressively move poets to bring their arts into new, unified, completed forms.[31] Thus, connaturality and poetic knowledge are inseparable as the poet awakens to what is being made, which becomes a new "thing in being" in itself.[32] As the poet grasps for being, s/he attempts to "bring together the perception of the person with the deep

27. Farrer, "Poetic Truth," 33.
28. Caldecott, "Over the Chasm," 21.
29. Giussani, *Religious Sense*, 103.
30. Maritain, "Concerning," 64.
31. Maritain, *Creative*, 85–86; "Concerning," 64–65.
32. Maritain, "Concerning," 51.

meaning of things made."[33] The poet observes and absorbs knowledge of other beings, comprehends the meanings of their effects, and produces something "fresh and new"[34] through a concentrated effort that achieves a work with a "mysterious operative spiritual virtue" capable of affecting others.[35] Hereafter, this *thing in being* will be called "mytho-*logos*,"[36] human *logos* that expresses new meaning subjective to the interworkings of its own *mythos*.[37] When mytho-*logos* becomes new art offered to the world, it is capable of sharing meaning that may mediate to the innate creativity of others in a mysterious way.

This resonates with Tolkien's conviction of the mythical impact of poetics and why it should be preserved. When "dissected" by analytical reasoning, art's effects diminish.[38] If experienced without mining the story as if a "quarry of fact" for data and research,[39] the poet's mytho-*logos* transcends the work and produces a potentially formative effect analogous to cosmo-*logos*. In each instance, "*poiēsis* bears a transcendent charge, an ontological weight of bringing something into being, of genesis. The poetic action brings into existence something new, and in that action it also brings about a knowledge of something new."[40] When poetics become affective, *poesis* becomes instrumental to "'making something' of ourselves."[41] Thus, if poetics transcend into being via mytho-*logos*, they create an ontological encounter analogous to how one may be directed *further on* through a meaningful impact akin to Giussani's notion of *logos* in the Primary World. *Ad extra*[42] poetics become a formative "lower medium," directing attention to a "higher" or "richer" frontier,[43] of the greater reality transcending meaning throughout the cosmos. This meaning analogically "becomes" in personal being

33. Dyrness, *Poetic Theology*, 131.

34. Dyrness, "Subjectivity," 99.

35. Maritain, "Concerning," 40.

36. Mytho-*logos* distinguishes human poetics from being confused with the cosmo-*logos* of divine involvement.

37. See Maritain, "Concerning," 45.

38. Tolkien, "Beowulf," 15.

39. "Beowulf," 5–7.

40. Ward, *Politics*, 201.

41. Dyrness, *Poetic Theology*, 38.

42. Maritain, "Concerning," 47, 67.

43. Lewis, "Transposition," 99–103.

something of "what it signifies" objectively.[44] The person subsequently "digests, transforms, [and] transubstantiates" it.[45] Art carries inherent ontological allusions[46] and becomes a "form of intellectual life in which the generativity of the world we encounter and experience is allowed to work in ways that are free from many of the requirements of routine instrumental thinking."[47] Poetics are *meant* to be formative and bring spiritual nourishment by awakening the imagination.

Establishing Tolkien's Mytho-*Logos*

Through his own version of Middle-earth in *LOTR*, Tolkien hoped to re-establish the analogical relation between sub-creation and reality.[48] He based this on a premise he believed was fundamental to humankind since the beginning of creation, namely that the imagination, intellect, language, and storytelling are inextricably linked.[49] Storytelling began the moment human minds started using language to give meanings to things. Tolkien started making meaning through language once he could write,[50] which stemmed from his own "congenital" linguistic predilections.[51] After receiving feedback from readers, Tolkien reflected on how the generativity of *LOTR* affected them:

> Most people that have enjoyed [*LOTR*] have been affected primarily by it as an exciting story; and that is how it was written. Though one does not, of course, escape from the question "what

44. Lewis, "Transposition," 98.

45. Lewis, "Transposition," 103.

46. Williams, *Grace*, 142.

47. Williams, *Grace*, 140–41.

48. *Middle-earth* comes from Old (*Middangeard*) and Middle (*middle-erde* or *erthe*) English, has been used in other works by many other writers, and was once understood to be the cosmic space between heaven and hell or a "region" among regions amidst the land "between the seas" (*Letters*, 220, 239; Gilliver et al., *Ring of Words*, 162–64). While often using real-world prompts, such as places, geography, and astronomy to inform his imagination (see Rateliff, *Mr. Baggins*, 17–21), Tolkien used them to derive his own region of Middle-earth. So, in one sense, the theater of Middle-earth is the Primary World with an old "historical period . . . a little glorified by the enchantment of distance in time" (*Letters*, 239; see Garth, *Worlds*, for actual settings Tolkien enchanted and incorporated into his world). In another sense, these are borrowed things assimilated into a new Secondary World (which Fonstad cartographically lays out in *Atlas*).

49. OFS, 40.

50. *Letters*, 143.

51. Tolkien, "Vice," 220n6.

> is it about?" by that back door. That would be like answering an aesthetic question by talking of a point of technique. I suppose that if one makes a good choice in what is "good narrative" (or "good theatre") at a given point, it will also be found to be the case that the event described will be the most "significant."[52]

The audience was affected in unspecified ways, yet these effects were not measurable through some methodical *technique*. *Exciting story*, *about*, and *narrative* all point to the *significance* of *LOTR* as initiating something more, something whole-felt and reasonable. It is as if the readers' encounters with Tolkien's world validated meaning in accord with their experience, as if the literary plane has an inner consistency that echoes something true about reality.

Tolkien's query *What is it about?* ponders how *LOTR* leaves readers with noticeable sensations that are difficult to describe. This is analogous to real-life experience that cannot always be put into words. Tolkien's fictional world, though different than actuality, mediates some likeness about reality. Through *LOTR*, the audience participates in its lifelikeness, not because experiencing the story precisely matches reality, but because of an ontological kinship that all tales can mediate to free beings. Through stories readers intuit "human systems of meaning" providing "the capacity to see things in terms of other things," thus allowing readers "to connect and to see one event or phenomenon through the lens of another."[53] A person experiences meaning in literary narrative through participatory reading. Instead of a dialectical exchange between artist and audience, there is a consequential diffusion of meaning from mytho-*logos* that concomitantly comes to mean something to the reader. Thus, "knowing is always a form of participation in the active intelligible life of an object, reproducing itself in the life of the subject."[54]

LOTR engages personal participation on an ontological level that happens best when readers encounter Tolkien's world—not by being told what it is about, but by discovering its meaning for themselves. This allows for varieties of meaning not intended to rival actual experience, but to affirm, complement, and enhance it, and subsequently lead to discussions with others about the nature of the story and its impact. This can lead to "postlections," i.e., revisiting the story all over again.[55]

52. *Letters*, 212.

53. Williams, Series Introduction, v.

54. Williams, *Grace*, 30.

55. "Draft," 89–90.

Each encounter with the text allows for mytho-*logos* to produce meaning effectively in new and unforeseen ways.

C. S. Lewis stated that literature caused him to "transcend" himself to a place of inner recognition that registered no other way.[56] Such in-the-moment experience proves difficult to define because meaning surpasses verbiage. Once art has affected its audience it is no longer the material of the artwork, but its effectual nourishment to the person that is of interest. Tolkien's statement about the most significant effects of *LOTR* indicates that there is more to its aesthetic impact than any one thing, suggesting that it owes more to *LOTR*'s *entirety* than parcels of it. Therefore, we should see how Tolkien discerned meaning in the cosmo-*logos* as a basis for discerning the wholeness of *LOTR*.

Poesis is participation in God's "creative agency,"[57] and Tolkien articulated how the divine in the cosmo-*logos* impacted his imagination and spurred his creativity in the poem "Mythopoeia":

> Trees are not "trees," until so named and seen—
> and never were so named, till those had been
> who speech's involuted breath unfurled,
> faint echo and dim picture of the world, . . .
> by deep monition movements that were kin
> to life and death of trees, of beasts, of stars:
> free captives undermining shadowy bars,
> digging the foreknown from experience
> and panning the vein of spirit out of sense.
> Great powers they slowly brought out of themselves[.][58]

The first four lines allude to naming what is already in existence while art via language activates meaning from the cosmos. A poet's naming induces the imagination to see as the world gradually becomes comprehendible. Tolkien maintained that he could only "dimly apprehend"[59] the transcendent through creation. *Poesis*, then, is theologically grounded, "not a ground in oneself, nor paradoxically is the subject absolutely determined, for one's speech is by participation, one's naming and acting is a share in God who in his infinite act is the source of all being and

56. Lewis, *Experiment*, 141.
57. Candler, "Tolkien," 11.
58. Tolkien, "Mythopoeia," 86.
59. "Mythopoeia," 85.

hence meaning."[60] Whether naming the cosmos or making poetics, in each case "language, like being, . . . arrives analogically."[61] Meaning arrives to us through our readings of the world, regardless of whether it is the Primary World or poetics. Similar to how we encounter meaning in the world, poetics enables participation using the "intercommunication between the inner being of things and the inner being of [humanity]."[62] Consequently, what poets image "is not so much a matter of 'looking past' the images to the reality which they signify or indicate, as 'looking through' the images to that reality."[63] The transcendent reality Tolkien dimly perceived evoked his use of the word *monition*.

Monition, defined as "instruction, direction, prompting,"[64] elucidates Tolkien's vantage point of understanding personal being as integral to the whole reality of the cosmos, including the visually unseen. The integrity and harmoniousness of cosmic reality communicates an active presence of otherness in which Tolkien felt ontologically situated. *Digging the foreknown from experience* stems from Tolkien's belief that poets produce meaning through the *great powers* of language. The cosmos compels a response that "abashes and exalts the mind,"[65] and as poets *pan the vein of spirit out of sense*, they become conscious of meaning already in being.

"Mythopoeia" expresses a view Tolkien shared with Owen Barfield, that language participates in making meaning that is non-abstract once we become cognizant of it.[66] In the earliest stages of language, meaning

60. Di Fuccia, *Owen Barfield*, 250–51.

61. Di Fuccia, *Owen Barfield*, 251.

62. Maritain, *Creative*, 3.

63. McIntyre, *Faith*, 11.

64. *OED Online*, s.v. "monition."

65. Lewis, "Imagination," 48.

66. Duriez, *Oxford*, 74–75. Barfield sporadically attended Inklings meetings started by Tolkien and C. S. Lewis (Duriez, *Tolkien and C. S. Lewis*, 75, 127; Scull and Hammond, *JRRT Companion*, 73) and was an influential contributor to the literary rationale of the group, particularly relating to language. For more on the Inklings, see p. 106n42. Lewis recounted to Barfield something Tolkien said, that Barfield's "conception of . . . ancient semantic unity had modified his whole outlook" (Lewis, *Collected Letters*, 3:1509), and Verlyn Flieger expounded upon this as the basis for Tolkien's sub-creativity (*Splintered*, 33–48). Tolkien referenced this in relation to a phrase he wrote in *Hobbit* (*Letters*, 22). Ancient semantic unity "holds that myth, language, and humanity's perception of the world are interlocked and inseparable" (Flieger, *Splintered*, 37) since the "evolution of human consciousness" first began (Barfield, *Poetic Diction*, 30). Flieger insists, "Barfield's theory . . . is the primary influence on Tolkien's mythos" (Flieger, *Splintered*, xxi). That this modified his *whole* outlook is debatable. It is impossible to pin the rest of Tolkien's life and works to one idea. While Barfield introduced the idea

was concrete, whereas "these primary 'meanings' were *given*, as it were, by [the cosmos]."[67]

This is significant for Tolkien because it not only indicates what poetics involves—a person's being interacting with the cosmos—but what poetics *preserves*. For once poetry "has entered . . . deeply . . . into our being we no longer concern ourselves with its *diction*. At this stage the diction has served its end and may be forgotten."[68] Essentially, Tolkien agreed that meaning is the end result of poetry.[69] Meaning transcends words to affect the reader's or hearer's experience.

However, such affectivity is fleeting. "The poetic mood," wrote Barfield, "is kindled by the passage from one plane of consciousness to another. It lives during that moment of transition and then dies."[70] Kindled is a valuable metaphor. Although in a moment's time the poetry's affectivity fades, kindling suggests something new. This relays a

that language participates in the development of human consciousness (Duriez, *JRRT*, 146), Tolkien had already been meaning-making through language since childhood (*Letters*, 143; John Garth discusses this thoroughly in *Tolkien*, before any encounter with Barfield), and Tolkien was thirty-six years old when Barfield published his theory in *Poetic Diction* (1928). Additionally, Barfield's philosophy of language was anthropocentric and places meaning in the hands of humanity, not God (though the divine was integral to Barfield's thought). For Barfield, it is within humanity's province to bring itself into "oneness with God and nature" (Duriez, *Oxford*, 206), or, as Barfield believed, "a kind of progress towards increasing immanence of the divine in the human" (Kuhl, "Owen Barfield," 10). For Barfield, "original participation" leads to eventual "final participation" of human consciousness in "at-one-ment with the principle of creation" (Carpenter, *Inklings*, 36n), which collapses his philosophy into an immanent unity that directly contradicts Christian unity with a transcendent God. Barfield's philosophy never sustained the analogical relationship that distinguishes and maintains the creature-Creator relationship and, therefore, had no "ontological origin" in God's transcendence in-and-beyond the world simultaneously (Di Fuccia, *Owen Barfield*, 205). In the Christian narrative, human comprehension and intelligence began immediately in Eden and common, meaningful language was scrambled at Babel, whereas in Barfield's view, human consciousness has evolved from the "dawn" of humanity (Zaleski and Zaleski, *Fellowship*, 120). Tolkien's mythopoesis was a theocentric means of worship, and the meaning he made through the two primary languages from which he derived Middle-earth were *elf*-centric, not anthropocentric, having been initiated in The One God of Middle-earth. Being theocentric and based in congenital linguistic predilections, Tolkien's world was contrived through an "ontological semantic unity" (Lauro, "Beyond," 314–20) analogous to his personal ontological outlook.

67. Barfield, *Poetic Diction*, 102.

68. Barfield, *Poetic Diction*, 52.

69. As is stated by Barfield in his essay "Poetic Diction," 51. C. S. Lewis told Barfield Tolkien appreciated this essay and read it more than once (Lewis, *Collected Letters*, 2:817).

70. Barfield, *Poetic Diction*, 52.

conscious sense of *awakening*, which directly impacts character transformation. If something affects readers—kindling, greater awareness, or awakening—change has begun. Herein lay the possibilities of transformation for the reader. Such effects are apparent in Tolkien's narratives involving hobbits and were introduced to readers of *Hobbit* through its main character, Bilbo Baggins.

Awakening to Tolkien's World Through Bilbo Baggins

Within a month of *Hobbit*'s release, Tolkien's publisher determined "a large public will be clamouring . . . to hear more from you about Hobbits!"[71] This proved true when *Hobbit*'s immediate success "turned out to be everything that could be desired" by a publisher.[72] After its release, a review of *Hobbit* branded it as "a new star" in the "constellation" of literature for all ages, predicting people would read it over and over.[73] Soon thereafter, Tolkien received an anonymous postcard with only a Latin phrase that contextually "almost always means 'by doing [whatever it is we're doing] we attain glory,'" implying Tolkien had done so via hobbits.[74] Considering what glory Tolkien's sub-creativity achieved through Bilbo's character will affirm how the poetics of *Hobbit* can initiate ontological encounters for readers. The following details provide a basis for understanding Bilbo's world and set up the following discussion:

1. Bilbo is a hobbit; an invented, mythical human creature.[75]
2. The characters in the story perceive their world as one through which meaning is directly derived and thus concrete.
3. *Hobbit* is written in plain language for any reader to understand, thus its meaning arrives without need for philosophical abstraction.

71. Stanley Unwin in Carpenter, *JRRT: Biography*, 186.

72. Rayner Unwin, "Tolkien," 202.

73. Lewis, "Professor," 20.

74. Michael Drout, personal correspondence, April 4, 2018. The bracketed insertion is Drout's, who translates the phrase: "By means of hobbits to the stars!" The phrase was "*sic hobbitur ad astra*," adapted from *The Aeneid*, which may have been referring to Lewis's review (*Letters*, 24, 435n17.1).

75. The *OED* attributes *hobbit* to Tolkien, but the word was in existence before Tolkien made hobbits a unique people group of his own (see Gilliver et al., *Ring of Words*, 142–52).

4. This cosmos includes wizards, dwarves, dragons, and elves, other mythical creatures Tolkien adapted into his mytho-*logos*.

Gandalf the wizard instigated Bilbo's awakening by interrupting the quiet comforts of his life and inviting several dwarves to Bilbo's home without the hobbit's consent. Although Bilbo had become angry and inconvenienced in the preceding text, the following shows the hobbit becoming stirred by the dwarves' singing, an encounter that will later prove transformative:

> As they sang the hobbit felt the love of beautiful things made by hands and by cunning and by magic moving through him, a fierce and jealous love, the desire of the hearts of dwarves. Then something Tookish woke up inside him, and he wished to go and see the great mountains, and hear the pine-trees and the waterfalls, and explore the caves, and wear a sword instead of a walking-stick. He looked out of the window. The stars were out in a dark sky above the trees. He thought of the jewels of the dwarves shining in dark caverns. Suddenly in the wood beyond The Water a flame leapt up—probably somebody lighting a wood-fire—and he thought of plundering dragons settling on his quiet Hill and kindling it all to flames. He shuddered; and very quickly he was plain Mr. Baggins of Bag-End, Under-Hill, again.[76]

Bilbo's Tookishness was innate to his character, just "wait[ing] for a chance to come out."[77] Other beings of the universe have something to do with drawing Bilbo's attention from his own subjectivity to look out the window with a fierce longing, and poetics are instrumental in this. Prior to *Hobbit*'s release, Tolkien acknowledged it had "drawn" from the "mythology and assumed 'history'" of a Secondary World backdrop known only to his closest relations.[78] He later claimed Bilbo "intruded" into the world of his mythological history.[79] Yet, the passage illustrates that the *cosmos* intrudes *on Bilbo*. The mytho-*logos*—inclusive of so much more than Bilbo himself, such as dwarves, nature, music, dragons: just a few participations in the whole cosmos—prompted Bilbo to intuit meaning that stirred his latent being. When this was subdued by the thought of a dragon bringing ruin, it seemed more natural to him to snuff the kindling

76. Tolkien, *Hobbit*, 18–19.

77. *Hobbit*, 5.

78. *Letters*, 21. And to some at his publishing company.

79. *Letters*, 22, 24. Or "strayed," recalled Christopher Tolkien in "*Silmarillion* by JRRT," 5.

out. Yet, the reader witnesses that Bilbo's consciousness was momentarily drawn outside of himself and his comforts.

Readers experience this with Bilbo because of the way poetics induce a generativity of the world we encounter and experience. As Bilbo experiences poetics in the song, readers experience the effects of Tolkien's mytho-*logos*. Generativity shares the same root with the word *progenitive*, a power Tolkien believed inherent in literature that "works from mind to mind."[80] Like George MacDonald, Tolkien affirmed fairy-stories make it so that "mind may *approach* mind,"[81] and readers can experience awakening similar to, but not exactly as, Bilbo does. A recluse such as Bilbo would neither encounter nor experience anything outside his sheltered homeland on his own.[82] Stimulation was needed to generate action, and Gandalf arrived for such a purpose.

However, "appreciating poetry involves a 'felt change of consciousness,'" an "appreciation [that] takes place at the actual moment of change."[83] Yet, Bilbo did not transform immediately at the beginning of the story. Remember Williams's system of meaning: seeing things in terms of other things; looking *through*, said McIntyre. Personal growth requires more than awakening primordial latencies. *Participation* is necessary for transformation to occur, and the imagination is a necessary component of this process.

"Art [is] the operative link between Imagination and the final result, Sub-creation," Tolkien said.[84] Art (poetic meaning) actively links Bilbo's imagination to the greater reality of his cosmos through the dwarves' creativity. It had the progenitive effect that complemented Gandalf's and the dwarves' arrival in the narrative and caused Bilbo to sense a calling to experience the world in a new way through action. By identifying this in Bilbo, such an awakening becomes a possibility for readers as well, which initiates the possibility for transformation.

Recall that Tolkien's mytho-*logos* parallels an ontological outlook and understanding of reality as a cosmos-*logos* preserved and upheld

80. OFS, 82nE.

81. MacDonald, "Fantastic," 8 (emphasis mine). For MacDonald's positive influence on Tolkien, see OFS, 44, 75; *Letters*, 178. For Tolkien's negative reactions to MacDonald, see *Letters*, 351; "Genesis," 85–87. For other discussions of MacDonald's influence on Tolkien, see Anderson, Commentary, 21–22; Bergmann, "Roots," 5–14.

82. *The Shire* had not yet been named as the region hobbits lived as in *LOTR* (Rateliff, *Mr. Baggins*, 16.).

83. Barfield, *Poetic Diction*, 52.

84. OFS, 59.

by a unified order. In *Hobbit*, Bilbo neither fully appreciated nor understood what had happened to him because of his personal ignorance about the greater reality of his cosmos. Recognizing formative change only happens through participation. Bilbo's was sparked when his imagination was captured in an impactful way amidst actual circumstances in time and space that would draw him further on and out into the world. MacDonald wrote, "The best thing you can do for your fellow, next to rousing his conscience, is—not to give him things to think about, but to wake things up that are in him; or . . . make him think things for himself."[85] This was displayed later in *Hobbit* after Bilbo had come into a fuller state of being.

Having passed through many adventures, Bilbo and the dwarves arrived at their intended destination: a dragon's lair. The narrator describes the impact of the moment when Bilbo first saw the treasure: "To say that Bilbo's breath was taken away is no description at all. There are no words left to express his staggerment, since Men changed the language that they learned of Elves in the days when all the world was wonderful."[86] Rateliff noted that the nonconventional word *staggerment* implies that "Bilbo cannot put what he feels at the moment into words. Quite literally, words fail him, falling short of the reality of the experience."[87] Douglas Anderson asserted, "Bilbo's breath was actually taken away, in a literal sense, not a metaphoric one."[88] Both Rateliff and Anderson alluded to the effect of the "odd mythological way of referring to linguistic philosophy" that Tolkien associated with Barfield here.[89] Each assessment is correct, yet neither identifies the fullness of the statement: As with the dwarves' singing, pre-existent meaning in the cosmos intruded *on Bilbo*, instead of the other way around. Tolkien captured this himself through the narrator, which raises three noteworthy points.

First, Lewis claimed Tolkien's whole outlook had been shaped by Barfield's philosophy.[90] Continuing this, Lewis also reported Tolkien

85. MacDonald, "Fantastic," 9.

86. *Hobbit*, 234.

87. Rateliff, *Return*, 535.

88. Anderson, Introduction and notes, 227n1.

89. *Letters*, 22.

90. See p. 24–25n66. To this point, it is more accurate to say that "Barfield's ideas challenged [Tolkien's] preconceptions and forced him to rethink the grounds upon which he based his ideas," thus making them "not . . . Barfieldian, but even more Tolkienesque" (Rateliff, *Return*, 545).

saying, "It is one of those things, that when you've once seen it there are all sorts of things you can never say again."[91] Bilbo's reaction to the treasure indicates that the only expression that could concretely capture the meaning he felt lay embedded in the past. The remarkable point of the passage is not the *words* but that the *meaning* is inexpressible. The narrator notes diction has been left behind while its meaning remains. Despite Bilbo's inability to articulate it, the reader is introduced to a "self-consistent picture" that there is an "impression of depth" about Bilbo's cosmos,[92] "an awareness that gives [Tolkien's] mythological world the texture of reality" weighted with its own history.[93] The statement, meaningful in and of itself, enters the reader's consciousness as evidence that its meaning is not lost.

The lastingness of this depth raises the second remarkable point: the elves, (from when all the world was wonderful), certain beings, from a certain historically old setting. Soon after its publication, Lewis's review of *Hobbit* in *The Times* noted its "characters can pause and say: 'It smells like elves'" because Tolkien had "a nose for an elf."[94] *Hobbit* implies the presence of the old in the now. Elves and the world to which they belong impart how *Hobbit* links to Tolkien's *poesis* of *LOTR*.

From its earliest stages, Tolkien's mythopoeic motivations were driven by religious inspiration.[95] There had always been a sense of Christian mission driving his discovery of meaning through language and art,[96] and this was instilled in the mythological history of the elves he began sub-creating during the First World War. But this happened in a particular way.

Elves hail from Primary World medieval, Victorian, and Edwardian times influenced by the Celtic cultural history of Britain and Ireland where elves (primarily called *fairies*) were believed to be either actual or mythical beings in the cosmic order.[97] Unlike in Tolkien's day, many

91. Lewis, *Collected Letters*, 3:1509.

92. "Beowulf," 27.

93. Garth, *Tolkien*, 60. Regardless of what Tolkien knew about the details behind the statement, it is the impression of depth that is important since it initiates the ontological experience.

94. Lewis, "Professor," 20.

95. Garth, *Tolkien*, 106.

96. Garth, *Tolkien*, 107.

97. Eden, "Elves," 150; Fimi, *Tolkien*, 40; Jacobs, *Narnian*, 15–16.

then considered them an historical reality.[98] "Fairy Faith" believed elves mysteriously inhabited the world yet could disappear; they either co-inhabited Middle-earth with humanity, had a world of their own, or wandered homelessly about in physical or spiritual form; and they could be ageless immortals with strange powers over matter.[99] In such times, cultures experienced nearness and connection to the cosmic order where living off the land was their lifeblood and people might have seen "nymphs in the fountains and dryads in the wood. . . . There was in a sense a *real* (not metaphorical) connection between them and the countryside."[100] This outlook blended humanity and elves into a shared cosmos, each having their own roles.

In *Hobbit*, elves are real as part of the mytho-*logos* in two senses. First, they are encountered throughout Bilbo's adventures as common beings one might meet when traveling from place to place.[101] Second, they are grounded in historical reality.[102] The following *Hobbit* passage links present-day elves Bilbo meets on his journey to the larger history of which readers become increasingly aware. These Wood-elves "differed from the High Elves of the West, and were more dangerous and less wise. For most of them . . . were descended from the ancient tribes that never went to Faerie in the West."[103] As with other aspects of Tolkien's mythological history, this is another instance that "peeped" into *Hobbit*.[104] Notably the setting of Faerie lies westward as distinct from the common space of the world to which Bilbo is accustomed, but in each sense elves are integral in the cosmic order.

Real belief in elves gave rise to the fairy-story tradition in which *Hobbit* is situated. Tolkien discussed this tradition in his Andrew Lang lecture-turned-essay "On Fairy-stories" (OFS), about one-and-a-half years after *Hobbit* was published.[105] OFS argues against the miniscule

98. Eden, "Elves," 150.

99. Evans-Wentz, *Fairy Faith*, xi, 99–100, 117, 134, 182, 211, 307.

100. Tolkien in Lewis, *Collected Letters*, 1:909.

101. As when they visit Elrond's house (*Hobbit*, 51–60) or encounter the wood-elves (153–204).

102. As when Elrond is noted as having an air of timelessness (*Hobbit*, 57) and gives weapons of noble heritage from ancient wars as gifts to Gandalf (Glamdring) and Thorin (Orcrist) (58).

103. *Hobbit*, 182. High Elves had already been mentioned earlier in the story (58).

104. *Letters*, 26.

105. Lecture given at St. Andrews in 1939; essay first published in *Essays Presented to Charles Williams* in 1947 (Flieger and Anderson, "History of 'OFS,'" 126, 131).

depictions of elves in post-medieval poetics.[106] Instead of residents of a "Perilous Realm" who were mysterious, strange, fearsome, beautiful, and awe-inspiring,[107] their stature was diminished over time into juvenile "Tinkerbellism."[108] In the early stages of his mythopoesis, long before *Hobbit*, Tolkien's elves appeared diminutive.[109] In OFS, the meaning of elves crystallized as Tolkien fortified his conception of the setting of *Faërie*.[110] Alan Jacobs described Faërie as "an alternate Britain—Britain seen in a distorting mirror, a mirror one can pass through" that is "exciting and, at the same time, terrifying."[111] Another version of Faërie presents it as a completely distinct cosmos that "sometimes overlaps with Britain."[112] Fairy-story tradition adopted such once-held beliefs about elves to derive newly sub-created worlds of Faërie.

In OFS, Tolkien's primary focus is Faërie's setting, the "realm or state in which [elves] have their being."[113] Contrary to having Primary World reality, elves are "made by man in his own image and likeness; but freed from those limitations which he feels most to press upon him. . . . Their will is directly effective for the achievement of their imagination and desire."[114] Thus, through elves Tolkien exercised his desire to sub-create freely and bring his Secondary World into being.[115] To look upon Faërie, then, is to observe a demonstration of human creativity that appeals to the imagination by way of the beauty and wonder portrayed there,[116] with elves as a natural part of that landscape.[117] In OFS, Tolkien argued for a recovery of elves according to the medieval tradition where

106. OFS, 29.

107. OFS, 32.

108. Olsen, *Exploring*, 151.

109. See Garth, *Tolkien*, 217. This changed somewhat by the time of *Hobbit* but is still partially evident in the story (Gilliver et al., *Ring of Words*, 125).

110. *Faërie* was the spelling Tolkien used in OFS, but he and others spelled it differently in various texts (e.g., Faerie, Faery). I will use Faërie. Any quotations about this place are as written.

111. Jacobs, *Narnian*, 15.

112. Jacobs, *Narnian*, 16.

113. OFS, 32.

114. Tolkien, "Manuscript," 257–58; see Carpenter, *JRRT: Biography*, 101.

115. Elves fulfill two purposes for Tolkien. Within his world they illustrate subcreativity. They are also the conduits of Tolkien's sub-creativity as the speakers of his invented languages whose history upholds the backdrop of his mythology.

116. OFS, 27; "Manuscript," 256.

117. See Duriez, "Sub-Creation," 143.

their "imaginative value" was strongest,[118] but he believed other makers of Faërie had tarnished and weakened their imaginative power.[119] Part of re-instilling this power had to do with the Christian mission of Tolkien's sub-creativity, and central to this was restoring the analogical relation between cosmo- and mytho-*logos*.

How Poetic Awakening Can Lead to Transformation

Tolkien was simultaneously developing OFS while writing *LOTR*. Yet, in real-time, Tolkien had not yet officially grafted hobbits into its fuller backdrop, so Bilbo did not technically belong. *Hobbit* adventure would eventually become a legend fusing itself into a pre-existing history Tolkien was developing,[120] and Tolkien would later claim Bilbo "got dragged [in] against my original will."[121] He had not yet realized, however, how *Hobbit* had already begun bringing his "myth-woven and elf-patterned" mythological history into focus.[122] Even though elves are not prevalent in *Hobbit*, their Faërie is—to Bilbo and those who journey with him. As Bilbo is drawn further out to experience the greater reality of his world, so are readers. All that literally happens to Bilbo, readers understand via diction: The effectual meanings they experience with Bilbo remain with them analogically. When Bilbo is transformed through narrative experience, readers are able to see what happened and how. As observed immediately after his staggerment,

> Bilbo had heard tell and sing of Dragon-hoards before, but the splendour, the lust, the glory of such treasure had never yet come home to him. His heart was filled and pierced with enchantment and with the desire of Dwarves; and he gazed motionless, almost forgetting the frightful guardian, at the gold beyond price and count.[123]

118. Lewis, *Discarded*, 122.

119. OFS, 42.

120. *Letters*, 145.

121. *Letters*, 38.

122. "Mythopoeia," 87. Christopher Tolkien stated what the consequences of *Hobbit* would be for Tolkien's mythopoesis of *LOTR*: "*Hobbit* was *drawn into* Middle-earth—and transformed it; but as it stood in 1937 it was not a part of it. Its significance for Middle-earth lies in what it would do, not in what it was" (Foreword in *Shadow*, 7).

123. *Hobbit*, 234.

This ushers in the third noteworthy point.[124] Bilbo's experience with the greater meaning of his cosmos enabled a different reaction. Whereas before dragons caused him to shy away in fear, he had changed; although fear remained very real, Bilbo stood to face it. He had attained a fuller sense of being through participation in the greater reality of the cosmos.

Through Bilbo, Tolkien demonstrated transformation through kindling based on a personal "poetic fire" he hoped to instill analogously in readers.[125] Before the First World War, long before he encountered Barfield or imagined hobbits, Tolkien shared this fire with a group of friends who formed the Tea Club and Barrovian Society (TCBS).[126] "The group was spiritual in character, 'an influence on the state of being,' and as such it transcended mortality; it was 'as permanently inseparable as Thor and his hammer,'" wrote TCBSian Geoffrey Smith.[127] Although Smith perished in the war, the spirit of the fire remained with Tolkien. He wrote the following to Smith before his death:

> The TCBS had been granted some spark of fire—certainly as a body if not singly—that was *destined to kindle a new light*, or, what is the same thing, *rekindle an old light* in the world; that the TCBS was destined to testify for God and Truth in a more direct way even than by laying down its several lives in this war.[128]

The world "was becoming increasingly disillusioned by its own vision of reality,"[129] one that had become accustomed to separating God from truth by creating its own bases of truth. But this old light has not disappeared. It is misinterpreted, reinterpreted, or deprived of meaning by those who disregard its viability and always remains ever-present to kindle anew.

This was analogically displayed through Bilbo. Even though Tolkien initially maintained that Bilbo "had no necessary connexion," Bilbo's story "naturally became attracted towards this dominant construction";[130] old aesthetic meaning was still present. "In my mind," Tolkien admitted, "[this] caus[ed] the tale to become larger and more heroic as it

124. The final of the three points introduced on pp. 29–30.

125. Garth, *Tolkien*, 180.

126. Garth, *Tolkien*, 6; *Letters*, 10.

127. Garth, *Tolkien*, 180. TCBSian is Garth's word.

128. *Letters*, 10 (emphasis mine).

129. GoodKnight, "Enlargement," 9.

130. *Letters*, 346.

proceeded."[131] Mytho-*logos* enlarged Tolkien's art and Bilbo's character simultaneously. Readers encounter Bilbo's adventures with him. Through analogical participation they experience his growing awareness of his world. If they allow encounters through the text to affect their lives, their own transformation is possible. Since there was a cry for more stories about hobbits and the world to which they belonged, this provided Tolkien an opportunity to undertake *LOTR* with a thoroughgoing intensity to meet readers' desires in a more penetrating way than *Hobbit*.

Nourishment Through Generativity

The responses Tolkien received about *Hobbit* gave him a keen sense that Bilbo's story revealed something that could lead to spiritual edification on a deeper level in *LOTR*. For instance, nearly a decade before *LOTR*'s publication, Tolkien asked his son, "Do you think [*LOTR*] will come off, and reach the thirsty?"[132] Likewise, after *LOTR* arrived in bookstores, Tolkien claimed that it merely "awaited [the] proofs" put forth in OFS, for which "a starving audience" had been waiting,[133] though well-aware it could only do so much.[134] Tolkien's observations insinuate that readers who consume *LOTR* could be nourished.

A few examples give evidence of how *LOTR* touches upon spiritual needs. Tolkien's friend Clyde Kilby, a Protestant, proposed that Middle-earth induces readers not only to desire but to "*require* . . . more" than the "atomized" reality presented to them through pure reason and science.[135] Thomas Smith, a Catholic, noted *LOTR* "mediated divine presence in the world" to him,[136] what Spirito described as "a depth that lives behind the form or below the surface" of what is seen.[137] An Oxford businessman read *LOTR* when in need of "restoration."[138] Another man wrote Tolkien, describing himself as an "'unbeliever, or at best a man of

131. *Letters*, 346.

132. *Letters*, 98.

133. *Letters*, 209.

134. "Those that like this kind of thing at all, like it very much, and cannot get anything like enough of it, or at sufficiently great length to appease hunger" (*Letters*, 121–22).

135. Kilby, "Meaning," 71 (emphasis mine).

136. Smith, "Tolkien's Catholic," 17.

137. Spirito, "Influence," 202.

138. Kilby, "Meaning," 80.

belatedly and dimly dawning religious feeling . . . but you,' he said, 'create a world in which some sort of faith seems to be everywhere without a visible source, like light from an invisible lamp.'"[139] These sensibilities are akin to what revived hopes of opponents to twentieth-century communist regimes in Europe in need of an actual transcendent reality amidst their shattered surroundings.[140] Although banned by the Soviet Union during such times, this did not keep "poorly translated, photocopied [Tolkien] works [from circulating] throughout the Russian underground."[141] Tolkien's world has the capability of affecting personal being amidst, and regardless of, belief system.

Dyrness articulated that aesthetics involves the "formation and reception" of a work of art, which "necessarily involves experience."[142] This occupies both artist and audience, and *poesis* is instrumental to the formation of both. Dyrness adopted a fuller definition: Aesthetics involves "all those things employing a medium in such a way that its perceptible form and 'felt' qualities become essential to what is appreciable and meaningful."[143] Such qualities are indicative of what the sub-creator's *poesis* produces and how s/he achieves it.

LOTR activates ontological responses for so many readers and is worth investigating. As a system of its own meaning, if characters exhibit formation through openness to the meaning of the greater reality of their world, then perhaps readers can analogically know similar transformation in the Primary World, even if they do not have a cosmo-*logos* lens. *LOTR* gives readers its own cosmic lens through mytho-*logos* and is thus able to affect readers "as mind meets mind in and through the medium of word and world,"[144] using the progenitive effects of narrative. Tolkien noted,

> "Aesthetic" is always impossible to catch in a net of words. Nobody believes me when I say that my long book is an attempt to create a world in which a form of language agreeable to my personal aesthetic might seem real. But it is true. An enquirer (among many) asked what the [*LOTR*] was all about, and whether it was an "allegory." And I said it was an effort to create a

139. *Letters*, 413.

140. See Birzer, *JRRT's Sanctifying*, 118–19.

141. Birzer, *JRRT's Sanctifying*, 118–19.

142. Dyrness, "Subjectivity," 92.

143. Dyrness, *Poetic Theology*, 11. This definition is Frank Burch Brown's.

144. Torrance, *Reality*, 188.

> situation in which a common greeting would be *elen síla lúmenn' omentielmo*, and that the phase long antedated the book.[145]

The elvish greeting means "a star shines on the hour of our meeting."[146] Frodo Baggins, Bilbo's cousin and heir,[147] spoke these words when he first encountered elves in *LOTR*. They denote meaning grounded in historical veracity and the cosmic order.[148] The poetic knowledge Tolkien's *poesis* acquired while writing *LOTR* deepened its impression of depth that projects an aesthetic mytho-*logos* with which readers wanted connaturality.

Nourishment from Tolkien's mytho-*logos* is contingent on the whole Faërie setting to which it belongs. He similarly compared Faërie to aesthetic experience: "[It] cannot be caught in a net of words; for it is one of its qualities to be indescribable, though not imperceptible. It has many ingredients, but analysis will not necessarily discover the secret of the whole."[149] Since this Faërie aesthetic is a sub-created Secondary World readers encounter imaginatively, we must account for how to describe this experience through the symbols and characters of the words being read. If we are truly unable to describe the mysteriousness of its essence, there must at least be something to say about what is happening if we are affected. Therefore, it is helpful to use a word that makes sense of many things subjectively experienced without confining these effects to that experience: *myth*, the medium Tolkien employed.

Because "myth has its own polysemy,"[150] it allows for many possible meanings to come from the same source that mediate elements of truth to various people in different ways. Myth must be allowed to maintain its sense of wholeness, remaining "alive at once and in all its parts" without reducing its entirety by "vivisection."[151] This maintains the Aristotelian notion of myth's relation to poetics where "poetry . . . does not copy particulars of Nature; it disengages and represents her general characteristics."[152] Sub-creators bring new things into being via intelligence that nature does not independently have. Poetics offer

145. *Letters*, 264–65.

146. Tolkien, *LOTR*, 79. See Carpenter's endnote in *Letters*, 447n205.2.

147. *LOTR*, 23.

148. Both of which are enriched with deeper meaning through the remainder of the Three is Company chapter in *LOTR* (78–83).

149. OFS, 32.

150. Taylor, *Language Animal*, 72.

151. "Beowulf," 15.

152. Lewis, *English*, 319.

alternative ways of seeing through which "poetic myth shows us what would necessarily or probably or possibly happen in all situations of a certain kind. If you like, it reveals the universal."[153] Poetics introduce different lenses through human creativity to other beings of like intelligence. Inquirers about the affectivity of *LOTR* are clued into how one can experience its poetic myth through Tolkien's metaphor: *tapestry*.[154] Each thing encountered in the narrative is one "*thread*" in "the history of [a] *picture* defined by many threads."[155] *Hobbit* and *LOTR* are historical pictures set against the backdrop of a larger tapestry, and as readers journey through each narrative with its characters, they experience Middle-earth's depth and breadth as its own distinct "imaginative space."[156] *LOTR* is prominent because of the continued effects it has on Tolkien's audience. If his mytho-*logos* awakens being through reading, this must reconcile with something real in the Primary World.

Affective Resonance

Over a quarter century after *LOTR*'s publication, Tolkien reflected on the outcome of the story:

> The book was written . . . as an experiment in the arts of long narrative, and of inducing "Secondary Belief." It was written slowly and with great care for detail, [and] finally emerged as a Frameless Picture: a searchlight, as it were, on a brief episode in History, and on a small part of our Middle-earth, surrounded by the glimmer of limitless extensions in time and space.[157]

What emerged presented *more* than *LOTR*, identified as only one story drawn from a context of countless others. Tolkien's suggestion that *LOTR* is an historical event within *our* Middle-earth confirmed that readers should perceive sub-creation as "an objectively real world" akin to reality, though on a literary plane.[158] It is not as identical to the characters themselves but as sub-creation "at a different stage of the imagination."[159]

153. Lewis, *English*, 319.
154. OFS, 40n.
155. OFS, 40n.
156. Shippey, "Interview," 17.
157. *Letters*, 412.
158. *Letters*, 239.
159. Tolkien, Interview with Gueroult.

Secondary Belief is the natural assent given to the story's verisimilitude because the writer "induces"[160] it through its "inner consistency of reality."[161] Narrative art presents an historical setting capable of demonstrating how characters participate in mytho-*logos*. If well-illustrated, Secondary Belief allows the reader to acknowledge an ontological encounter through the text, which can analogically induce an awakening within the reader and, through the affective connaturality of the story, be formative to the reader's life through an ontological response.

As Tolkien continued his reflection, he observed that *LOTR* also met some deeper personal need: "Very well: that may explain to some extent why it 'feels' like history; why it was accepted for publication; and why it has proved readable for a large number of very different kinds of people. But it does not fully explain what has actually happened."[162] This need was more profound than Secondary Belief. He then stated,

> Looking back on the wholly unexpected things that have followed its publication—beginning at once with the appearance of vol. 1 [*The Fellowship of the Ring*]—I feel as if an ever darkening sky over our present world had been suddenly pierced, the clouds rolled back, and an almost forgotten sunlight had poured down again. As if indeed the horns of Hope had been heard again, as Pippin heard them suddenly at the absolute *nadir* of the fortunes of the West. *But How?* and *Why?*[163]

In ancient times in the Western world, nadir indicated the lowest point in a spirits-filled cosmos that lay opposite the highest.[164] This scene references Pippin as he witnessed Gandalf facing his greatest foe yet. It seemed as though Gandalf and all the good he was fighting for might be crushed beneath the weight of evil. The horns signify the forthcoming aid Gandalf and Pippin so desperately needed: a gracious intrusion of hope at a time that seemed a hopeless end.[165] For readers to experience an absolute nadir implies something had reached them in desperate need of nourishment. Tolkien asked how this was possible, but he had already answered his question: The clouds moved away, and the sunlight poured down. Sunlight resonates with the old light in the

160. OFS, 59n.

161. OFS, 59.

162. *Letters*, 412–13.

163. *Letters*, 412–13. Pippin's experience happened in *The Return of the King*.

164. Barfield, *History*, 145.

165. See *LOTR*, 811, 832.

world the TCBS wished to rekindle. That the clouds just needed rolling back demonstrated that the light was already there. Tolkien's mytho-*logos* had effectively pierced the darkness. Chapter 2 begins to answer the *how* by exploring the way Tolkien read the cosmo-*logos*, participated in its meaning, and shaped *LOTR* through his creativity.

Chapter 2

Analogical Participation in Creation and Sub-Creation

Introduction

CHAPTER 1 DISCUSSED HOW *Hobbit* showed Bilbo being awakened and drawn into participation in a way that would ultimately transform him. This was deepened through the mythic quality of *LOTR*. *Hobbit* and *LOTR* came into the hands of the public with distinct differences. Although *Hobbit* shows Tolkien's mythological backdrop peeping through, *LOTR* references it six hundred times.[1] Each work contributes to the way in which Tolkien's mytho-*logos* provides aesthetic touch-points analogous to cosmic threads amidst a vast tapestry. Whether or not *LOTR* causes readers to "require more" than what is physically visible,[2] it registers something akin to religious experience. But moving through a personal narrative of life differs from literary narrative, especially an actual nadir where one feels hopelessly paralyzed. My argument maintains that Tolkien sub-created a Secondary World true to itself and analogous to a cosmo-*logos* view open to transcendence. If the narrative potentially influences readers to a "transcendental

1. Kilby, *Tolkien*, 45.
2. Kilby, *Tolkien*, 50.

horizon" regardless of belief system,[3] understanding Tolkien's Primary World outlook and its shaping of *LOTR* is integral to how and why it produces the effects it has on readers.

Analogy of Being

The answer to Tolkien's *But How?* near the end of chapter 1 lies in his description of Middle-earth as an objectively real literary world experienced at a different stage of the imagination. That Tolkien identified the "stuff"[4] of his mytho-*logos* as fundamentally concerned with restoring the analogical relation between sub-creation and Primary Reality gives focus to the kind of Primary World to which *LOTR* is related.

First, recall that art is poetic meaning that operatively links imagination with sub-creation. The storyteller's role produces meaning that should always be considered as secondary to, not a substitute for, or idealistic representation of, reality. Yet sub-creation makes new meaning from reality. There are, however, limitations to how literary narrative affects finite being: "Art . . . is content to create a new secondary world in the mind, [not] actualize desire."[5] This is critical to Tolkien's belief that art maintain its proper relationship to reality: not to replace it or create an escapist alternate reality, but to derive meaning from the pure light of God through the "refracted light" of humanity.[6] "To experience *directly* a Secondary World: the potion is too strong, and you give to it Primary Belief."[7] This is delusory[8] and encapsulated the post-Enlightenment problem for many who acknowledged that art "replaced religion" instead of remaining mediatory.[9] While aesthetics involves personal experience, the Secondary World issues its own meaning in a derivative way, establishing its relation to the Primary, though "not [as] any kind of new religion or vision" of reality.[10]

3. Ward, "Narrative," 455.
4. *Letters*, 145.
5. *Letters*, 87.
6. "Mythopoeia," 87.
7. OFS, 63.
8. OFS, 63.
9. Dyrness, "Subjectivity," 92.
10. *Letters*, 283.

Tolkien considered that proper Primary Belief is interpreted according to the interpenetration of two mediums. The Roman Catholic *Catechism* alludes to both: "Truth in words, the rational expression of the knowledge of created and uncreated reality, is necessary to man, who is endowed with intellect."[11] Tolkien viewed Primary Reality as this whole blended cosmos of created and uncreated reality. Humanity has the capability of imaginatively expressing something of its meaning through language. Primary Reality refers to God's speaking the world into being, which reveals God's transcendent truth, goodness, and beauty.[12] As each is perceived in "*derived* existence," attention is directed from creation as existing "*for its own sake*" to the greater reality from which it originated[13]—"God's perfect unity and oneness," what Augustine called the *divine simplicity*.[14] These pre-existing uncreated presuppositions bespeak transcendence emanating throughout the cosmos.

Visible creation is the "stuff" of the Primary World[15]—humanity, nature, and all life-forms in the cosmos created "as given" by God.[16] From the medieval outlook Tolkien adopted, "to understand all reality other than God in terms of 'creation' is to see it as dependent on God for its origin, for its continued existence, and for its good governance."[17] As God's "Primary Art,"[18] it can be perceived by "looking *in*" to the cosmos and intuiting something of God.[19] Duriez described this as Tolkien's "imaginative intuitionism,"[20] which is altogether different from *exacting* truth via the imagination.[21] C. S. Lewis articulated this view as based on assumptions that aligned with Tolkien's—truth becomes known as imagination (the "organ of meaning") and reason (the "organ of truth") coalesce "[undeniably into] a view [that] indirectly implies a kind of truth

11. Catholic Church, *Catechism*, 599.

12. Boersma, *Heavenly*, 52. These metaphysical *transcendentals* are customarily grouped as three: truth, goodness, and beauty (Przywara, *Analogia*, 126; Catholic Church, *Catechism*, 17). Sometimes unity replaces beauty (Koterski, *Introduction*, 114, 119).

13. Boersma, *Heavenly*, 52.

14. Oliver, *Creation*, 45.

15. OFS, 52, 60–61; *Letters*, 144.

16. Spirito, "Influence," 206.

17. Koterski, *Introduction*, 61.

18. OFS, 78.

19. Lewis, "Imagination," 59.

20. Duriez, *JRRT Handbook*, 187.

21. Duriez, "Sub-Creation," 148.

or rightness in the imagination itself."[22] Contrary to post-Enlightenment espousals that humanity can determine the meaning of existence in one "unified theory,"[23] reason attempts to meet a basic human "need to understand existence, that is, the need for an adequate, total explanation of existence."[24] The answer to this stems from outside the self and the material world.[25] For the truth to have meaning requires an imagination that affirms it as reasonable; otherwise, there is no reasonable way to understand meaning.[26] Since reading *logos*-centrically is a way of interpreting reality, translating the *logos* provides a way for making onto-theological conclusions in imaginatively reasonable ways.

Tolkien understood purpose and design as recognized by a Christian image-bearing mind.[27] All that exists has being in a hierarchical way within a "Great Chain of Being":[28] "stones . . . have only being; vegetables, being and life; animals, being, life and sense; man, being, life, sense and reason."[29] For Tolkien, non-living beings at the bottom of this hierarchy have value because they exist; they would be meaningless if there were no purpose to their existence. "One of their functions is to be contemplated by us" because they are purposeful.[30] The natural world exists and functions as God created it, but in such non-living things—oceans, mountains, stones, weather—exact patterns are difficult to determine. They exude pattern, and are circumstantially different, but are discernible to the eye. Take frost on glass, for instance: "The patterns on a given window are practically unpredictable, though one believes that if one knew *all* the circumstances, it would not be so."[31] These reveal that God's creativity is ever *more* than humanity can fathom.

Tolkien delineated this hierarchical chain to living beings (creatures and plants) other than humanity. Animate creatures (without reason and imagination) fashion patterns of their own (e.g., spiders' webs

22. Lewis, "Bluspels," 157–58. See Duriez, "Sub-Creation," 148.
23. Duriez, "Sub-Creation," 138.
24. Giussani, *Religious Sense*, 116.
25. Giussani, *Religious Sense*, 116.
26. Ward, "Good Serves," 66.
27. See "Mythopoeia."
28. Taylor, *Secular*, 129.
29. Lewis, "Imagination," 50.
30. *Letters*, 399.
31. *Letters*, 269n3.

and the habitations of fowls).[32] Such creatures have a mind to do so because this lies in the nature of their being, like the caterpillar whose being participates in God's creativity and transforms into a butterfly according to its nature.

More intriguing are mindless living beings, particularly flowers and trees. Tolkien stated that a plant "presents shape and organization: a 'pattern' recognizable (with variation) in its kin and offspring; and that is deeply interesting, because these things are 'other' and we did not make them, and they seem to proceed from a fountain of invention incalculably richer than our own."[33] What design could be derived by perceiving the mind behind the flower indicates "far more graceful . . . pattern[s] than any hen-and-chickens development" could.[34] Botany particularly affected Tolkien because it "rouse[s] in me visions of kinship and descent through great ages, and also thoughts of the mystery of pattern/design as a thing other than its individual embodiment, and recognizable."[35] To recognize patterns as other than personal being itself further indicates that meaning does not begin or end within the cosmos but in a mind behind it.

Thus, the observable cosmos exists for the intelligibility of humanity to, in a sense, *look into* God: "It is an answer, not a question."[36] "Mythopoeia's" designation of the poetic relationship between creation and Creator asserts creation is already present when humanity is introduced to the world, already adorned with the pre-existing givens of its cosmic tapestry. Uncreated reality is God behind it all,[37] whose mind originated, issued, and still directs every design in the cosmos created *ex nihilo*.[38] God is "The Pattern" from which created reality universally stems.[39] God's transcendence mysteriously permeates through it in both the seemingly wild forces and consistent patterns of nature or instinctual behaviors of animals: A minuscule foretaste of how humanity may understand aspects of the eternal Creator, each offering a means to register the observable and potentially mimic some likeness of such creativity to impact other

32. *Letters*, 107.
33. *Letters*, 399.
34. *Letters*, 403.
35. *Letters*, 402.
36. Lewis, "Imagination," 48.
37. OFS, 77–78.
38. See "Mythopoeia," 85, 86.
39. *Letters*, 121.

imaginations in an effectual way.[40] This assumes a doctrine of creation clearly distinguishing finite creation from infinite God. Tolkien differentiated God's "infinite" uncreated reality as "parallel" to the finite plane of time and space.[41] And though creation evidences transcendence, it is not God. This perception of God's transcendence within immanence is otherwise called *analogy of being.*

The Fourth Lateran Council stated, "One cannot note any similarity between creator and creature, however great, without being compelled to observe an ever greater dissimilarity between them."[42] As mentioned, ontology is an outlook or understanding that acknowledges participation in a greater reality. Analogy of being is the creaturely acknowledgement of participation in God's "essence in-and-beyond existence."[43] Rather than pure intellectualization or independent feeling, analogy of being assumes an imaginatively intuitive personal "posture," which maintains a "decisive," rather than theoretical, outlook on life.[44] As always more than humanity can fathom, God is the ever-present "point of reference"[45] that humanity identifies through participatory living. Each moment is sacred because all ontological encounters happen within the *sacramental* greater reality of God's spatiotemporal transcendence.[46] It also serves as a "frame of reference, not a body of doctrine."[47] Since all creation in existence bears *likeness* in God (having God's *ex nihilo* origination), yet is wholly *dissimilar* (because no finite being exactly images the infinite essence that sustains it), the essence of all creation participates analogously in the essence of God who gives existence.

Since Tolkien's mythopoesis presupposed God's pre-existence, every being is contingent to God's necessary being first. God *IS* before subcreator *was*. Since "analogy is a way of relating . . . to a single common focus,"[48] *LOTR* would need to bring focus to a cosmo-*logos* lens of both the created and uncreated aspects of Primary Reality. But every analogy

40. "Mythopoeia," 86.

41. *Letters*, 99.

42. Betz, Translator's Introduction, 72–73.

43. Przywara, *Analogia*, 131.

44. McAleer, "All Valid Law."

45. Boersma, *Heavenly*, 24.

46. Boersma, *Heavenly*, 24, 71.

47. A. S. P. Woodhouse in Duriez, "Sub-Creation," 135.

48. Oliver, *Creation*, 68.

made about Primary Reality, though sacramental, is "not identical";[49] partly because the finite cannot mirror the infinite, and also because poetics produce something new not made by God. Tolkien viewed storytelling as sacramental,[50] and through his own poetic knowledge, *LOTR* was made. The better we can understand Tolkien's posture and his reading of the *logos*-centric cosmos, the clearer the answer to *But Why?* regarding the nourishment of *LOTR*.

But How?—Imagination

"Mythopoeia" projects imagery of an artist amidst the cosmos "lighted, warmed, and resonant with music."[51] Tolkien aspired to be "a mover, a doer, [and] achiever of great things" if not "a beginner at the very least of large things."[52] This required being available through personal responsibility so that his *poesis* would participate in God's, along with the humility required of those "instruments" God has "chosen."[53] Integral to Tolkien's instrumentality was his belief that he belonged in the cosmic orchestra adhering to "man's *embeddedness* in the physical creation, and his creaturely *vocation* and creaturely *end* within that creation."[54] Humanity is the only creation that bears God's image. Therefore, vocational participation must adhere with one's sense of purpose and end in God. Dorothy Sayers observed the *Genesis* account's mention of one specific commonality humanity shares with God: creativity.[55] Thus, creativity is connatural to every image-bearer. Tolkien thought similarly. He perceived humanity as capable of intelligibly receiving insights through divine creativity and thereby charged with stewarding individual creativity to be an influencer in the world, thus affirming both humanity's vocation and end.[56]

When humanity participates in God through creativity, it lives in "cooperation with" God, "and the action and contemplation that

49. Boersma, *Heavenly*, 70.
50. Duriez, *Tolkien and C. S. Lewis*, 54.
51. C. S. Lewis in Jacobs, "Fantasy," 4.
52. *Letters*, 9.
53. *Letters*, 413.
54. Wolterstorff, *Art*, 68–69.
55. Sayers, *Mind*, 22.
56. "Mythopoeia," 87.

accompan[y] it are both a gift and . . . divinely-mandated."[57] Tolkien's lens for reading the cosmos-*logos* was trinitarian.[58] Catholics believe the Trinity "not [as] three principles of creation but one principle."[59] Protestants also affirm this view. As Poythress articulated, "The original trinitarian reality within God is analogically expressed when God created the world. His acts of creation conform to his character."[60] God spoke and the Son provided the original substantive Word or *Logos* from which all creation was made and given meaning.[61] The Spirit, the life-giving "breath" who makes the power and meaning of *logos* translatable,[62] directs humanity's attention to "the spiritual reality" the cosmos signifies.[63] When creation came into being, all three were (and are) God, and all three were (and are) involved: the ontological unity-in-difference of the cosmos.[64] Yet one must be careful about how to contemplate this. Torrance warned,

> The inadequacy of our formulation of the Trinity of God is an essential element in its truth and precision, that is, in constituting *not a picturing model* with some kind of point to point correspondence between it and God, but *a disclosure model* through which God's self-revelation impresses itself upon us, while discriminating itself from the creaturely representations necessarily employed by the model.[65]

This model provides the ontological basis for discerning the *telos* of the *logos*-centric meaning of reality, which allows the finite mind to comprehend meaning analogically. If disclosed this way, the world can still be interpreted this way. Yet "although analogies are *possible* because of creation, the justification of their *actual* use lies not in their intrinsic capacity to represent God but only in their 'divine authorization.'"[66] Having freely authorized creation *ex nihilo*, God remains the source and sustaining essence of all existence. Therefore, creation does not have a mind of its

57. Wolf, *Building*, 286.

58. *Letters*, 146. And Tolkien sub-created from this basis.

59. Catholic Church, *Catechism*, 68.

60. Poythress, *Chance*, 58.

61. Poythress, *Chance*, 58–59.

62. Poythress, *Chance*, 58–59; Poythress, *Redeeming*, 24–26.

63. Oliver, *Creation*, 103.

64. *Unity-in-difference* is borrowed terminology from López, "Growing Human," 212. I use it here differently, but I cite it in context in chapter 5.

65. Torrance, *Reality*, 162.

66. McGrath, *Order of Things*, 16–17.

own. Rather, it "presuppose[s]" God and an "analogous relation" to God, thus making analogy of being "understood [as] theologically *derivative*, rather than theologically *autonomous*."[67] Analogy of being maintains that God is always in-and-beyond, never "static," preserves God's "absolute distinction" from creation, and "posits a created capacity on the part of the analogy to model God" through creativity.[68]

For Tolkien, *sub*-creators can only endeavor to make from their own creativity because the handiwork of God's creativity preceded them; the nature of their being compels them to do likewise.[69] Poets are able to shed light upon truth in myriad unique and colorful ways, but this will always be done imperfectly: any pure light that sub-creativity emits stems from just one divine source.[70] Therefore, for Tolkien "if sanctity inhabits his work or as a pervading light illumines it then it does not come from him but through him."[71] This presumes the finite "derivative mode" of the sub-creator's role is analogical.[72] Although sub-creation can only go so far, it was an undertaking Tolkien took seriously because of the purposes it could serve.

Tolkien's notion that artistic participation can mediate God's truth allows for the attention of an audience to be directed beyond the work to God as the reference point. But as a parallel it should conform to its own distinct patterning. "A language carries a particular way of seeing the world,"[73] and meaning is projected through how the narrative patterns it. My concern lies in the meaning made through *poesis* and how participation authenticates sub-creation in a way that awakens being to the greater reality of God. Milbank aptly stated how "art . . . can take us beyond what we are capable of understanding intellectually and give us a form of direct access to particulars" in God through an ontological encounter,[74] that which art mediates but the divine orchestrates. This elevates Tolkien's fundamental concern: For art and sub-creation to bear the relation Tolkien believed existed, *how* this relation was made is contingent upon how close sub-creation brings about an inner consistency

67. McGrath, *Theory*, 111.

68. McGrath, *Theory*, 111.

69. See "Mythopoeia," 86, 87, 90.

70. "Mythopoeia," 87.

71. *Letters*, 413.

72. OFS, 66.

73. Duriez, "JRRT for the Ages," 332.

74. Milbank, *Chesterton*, 164.

of its own that triggers an ontological response to particulars of Primary Reality. "Every sub-creator," wrote Tolkien,

> wishes in some measure to be a real maker, or hopes that he is drawing on reality: hopes that the peculiar quality of this secondary world (if not all the details) are derived from Reality, or are flowing into it. If he indeed achieves a quality that can fairly be described by the dictionary definition: "inner consistency of reality," it is difficult to conceive how this can be, if the work does not in some way partake of reality.[75]

Drawing on, *deriving from*, and *partaking of reality*—each depends on receiving something "other" to generate a personal response. Even more, it emphasizes the creature-Creator distinction: Humanity only makes from material already in being *ex nihilo*.[76] New things are made from existing things. For example, eggs, water, and flour can be made into a cake; boards, nails, and glue into a chair, each by human design. In one sense, this making is restricted by the material: The cake ingredients cannot be made into a drum just as a chair cannot be fashioned into a tomato. But the imagination is capable of deriving new ways of shaping material: Bakers modify ingredients to make different pastries; carpenters design different furniture. In both cases, people imaginatively develop their own patterns to make something new. The end results are products of human creativity, intuitively derived to be appreciated by others.

Since the hierarchy of beings can induce one to contemplate the mind behind it, so should an image-bearer's creativity. But poets cannot orally speak cakes and chairs into existence. Although makers model God, their finite designs are *ab initio* (from the beginning) instead of out of nothing.[77] In each instance, although material is involved, creativity does not deal solely with materiality. Some manner of artisanship is needed to craft materials into new forms, and intellection is necessary for a work to be usable. The poet's material is language, thus making the ontological kinship in the creature-Creator analogy more acute: As God created from nothing and spoke *poesis* through the substance of Christ the *Logos*, poets make *ab initio* from *logos* to declare meaning in their

75. OFS, 77.

76. Oliver, *Creation*, 47. This follows with the Thomist sense, that making is analogous to creating (55).

77. *Ab initio* is adopted from Tolkien (*Letters*, 144).

own original way. As such, sub-creators model God by echoing back to the mind behind creation poetics with new meanings.[78]

Echoes are reverberations of sound between two objects. One without the other makes echoing impossible. In "Mythopoeia," Tolkien's first use of the word relates to the way the cosmos impacts the poet.[79] Human language only captures a "faint echo" of meaning in comparison,[80] but this effort alone reverberates back personalized original meaning from the poet's creativity. As "Mythopoeia" builds, the poet's echo intensifies. The sub-creator

> sees no stars who does not see them first
> of living silver made that sudden burst
> to flame like flowers beneath an ancient song,
> whose very echo after-music long
> has since pursued.[81]

Notice first that the ancient song comes from the infinite, nameless beyond. Ever after, creation is an echo longing to return to its source. The intelligent being can recognize that this song "unleashes an invitation."[82] The sub-creator accepts and boldly resonates back to God, not in mere words but in secondary mytho-*logos* with its own implicit meaning. Tolkien envisioned standing before a cosmic empty page or blank canvas and perceived "only a void."[83] Contrary to void meaning barren and destitute, Tolkien's use anticipated an open space of limitless creative opportunity grounded in creation. Where the ancient song pre-exists spatiotemporal reality, the poet produces a poetic echo confined within history through which ontological encounters are possible.

The poet becomes conscious of meaning already present in the world. It is just a matter of being awakened to it. What is awakened in the poet is also capable *through* the poet. Maritain defined creativity as "the power of engendering,"[84] implying it is progenitive. Since language initiates a generativity of its own, poetics are capable of begetting new meaning for those affected: The power engendered through mytho-*logos*

78. "Mythopoeia," 86–87.
79. "Mythopoeia," 85.
80. "Mythopoeia," 86.
81. "Mythopoeia," 87.
82. To recall Giussani, *Religious Sense*, 103.
83. "Mythopoeia," 87.
84. Maritain, *Creative*, 40.

initiates an effect deeper than words, from more than reason alone. The "intellect . . . strives to engender," stated Maritain, but

> it is anxious to produce, not only the inner word, the concept, which remains inside us, but a work at once material and spiritual, like ourselves, and into which something of our soul overflows. Through a natural super-abundance the intellect tends to express and utter *outward*, it tends to sing, to manifest itself in a work.[85]

Poetics produce original reverberations resounding within the Primary World, which produce residual effects.

Chapter 1 discussed how imaginative storytelling allows mind to approach mind, rouses consciences of readers, and challenges them to think for themselves. In OFS, Tolkien deliberately articulated how human imaginations should discern between Primary and Secondary Worlds and observed the following older definition of imagination: "The human mind is capable of forming mental images of things not actually present."[86] This is the *OED* definition of the word *fantasy* which makes it synonymous with *imagination*.[87] Tolkien rejected what imagination had come to mean. On one hand, it set aside fantasy for *fancy*, which he referred to as "a reduced and depreciatory form of . . . Fantasy."[88] The *OED* designates the modern use of fancy as "being used to express aptitude for the invention of illustrative or decorative imagery."[89] Although it had not always been interpreted this way,[90] Tolkien thought this definition weak. Aptitude is only potential and does not designate grounding in concrete meaning. Decorating only attempts to tinker with that which is already present rather than transform it into something original. Meanwhile, by casting off fantasy for a new version, imagination is elevated to a "higher [power] than mere image-making."[91] This is to inhibit and misuse the imagination in literary creativity.[92] The newer definition described

85. Maritain, *Creative*, 40.

86. OFS, 59. See Flieger and Anderson, "Editors' Commentary," 110–11.

87. *OED*, s.v. "fantasy/phantasy." Tom Shippey stated, "The road to Middle-earth lies between the lines of the *OED*" ("Creation," 298). Early in his career Tolkien worked for the *OED* (see Gilliver et al., *Ring of Words*).

88. OFS, 59.

89. *OED*, s.v. "fancy."

90. Carol Blessing, personal correspondence, January 22, 2019.

91. OFS, 59.

92. OFS, 59.

imagination as "the power of giving to ideal creations the inner consistency of reality."[93] The problematic word is *ideal*: "The imitative arts aim neither at copying the appearances of nature, nor at depicting the 'ideal,' but at making an object beautiful by manifesting a *form* with the help of sensible signs."[94] Instead of forcing sub-creation towards an idealistic end, meaning accrues through poetic knowledge over time into its own unique otherness. Active *poesis*—participating in God's creative agency, as if performing an individual part in an orchestra while using one's gift of creativity in cooperation with God—happens through the process of "*becoming*" into something new that manifests itself.[95]

The beginning of this chapter mentioned how art is secondary, not a form of delusion or substitute for reality and religious experience. It acknowledged creativity as free, which analogically corresponds with God's free act of creating. Tolkien argued that imaginations should be allowed to participate freely. The goal of ideal creations implies certain predetermined goals, pre-existing imagery for which the sub-creator pointedly aims. Creative invention must freely *become* as it follows the logic of its own meaning as it is made, not without reason but without being forced to conform to what naturalistic science claims as real with no consideration for a creature-Creator relation.[96] Analogy of being addresses Tolkien's concern about the relation between art/sub-creation and Primary Reality because it encourages freedom in the agency of God's gift, "liberat[ed] from the channels the creator is known to have used already,' [which] is the fundamental function of 'sub-creation,' a tribute to the infinity of His potential variety."[97] Sub-creation should impact the imagination according to its own unique laws (as long as they are non-contradictory).[98] This presents an ontologically formative means for allowing readers to participate freely without the "purposed domination of the author."[99]

Poesis is supposed to produce meaning in new and unforeseen ways once the Secondary World has been made real in its own plane. This understanding is helpfully exemplified in Tolkien's short story *Leaf by*

93. OFS, 59; *OED*, s.v. "fancy."
94. Maritain, *Art*.
95. Maritain in Milbank, *Chesterton*, 19.
96. OFS, 60.
97. *Letters*, 188.
98. *Letters*, 194.
99. *LOTR*, xvii.

Niggle (*Leaf*), which illustrates how ontological encounters through sub-creation can direct readers to God.[100]

Mediated Sub-Creation: *Leaf by Niggle*

Leaf was written at a time when Tolkien "was anxious about [his] own internal Tree, [*LOTR*]," having found himself "*dead stuck*" while writing it.[101] He was at a crossroads with "the knowledge that it would be finished in great detail or not at all, and the fear (near certainty) that it would be 'not at all.'"[102] The heart of *Leaf* underscores Tolkien's hope to mend the problematic relationship between art/sub-creation and Primary Reality if he could finish *LOTR*.

It is a story meant to portray "how [sub-creation] might come to be taken up into Creation in some plane."[103] "In a myth [a storyteller] puts what he does not yet know and [could] not come to know in any other way,"[104] and *Leaf* is a mythical[105] story addressing this dilemma, which Tolkien may not have been able to express otherwise. Chapter 1 mentioned that *poesis* activates meaning from the cosmos through language. *Leaf* expresses how *poesis* injects meaning into the cosmos in a new way that illustrates the impact of *LOTR*.

Leaf centers on Niggle, an artist preoccupied with painting. His specialty was leaves, one of which became his main focus and grew into a tree so large he eventually needed a ladder to continue working on

100. Tolkien, *Leaf*, 87–112.

101. *Letters*, 321. "[*LOTR*] was beginning to unroll itself and to unfold prospects of labour and exploration in yet unknown country as daunting to me as to the hobbits. At about that time we had reached Bree and I had then no more notion than they had of what had become of Gandalf or who Strider was; and I had begun to despair of surviving to find out" (Tolkien, *Reader*, 2). Although Tolkien cited various dates, *Leaf* was written during a time he was also converting OFS into an essay. Its exact composition dates are unclear because Tolkien was inconsistent with his recollections. In his introductory note to *Leaf*, he stated 1938–1939 (*Reader*, 2); in March 1945, he said "more than two years ago," indicating as late as 1943, if not earlier (*Letters*, 113); in September 1962, he thought he probably wrote it prior to World War II (*Letters*, 320); Scull and Hammond allocate it "around April 1942" due to a postcard Tolkien had sent to someone in April 1943. Though unnamed, it is presumed that what he "wrote this time last year" refers to *Leaf* (*JRRT Companion*, 495).

102. *Letters*, 257.

103. *Letters*, 195.

104. Lewis, *Collected Letters*, 3:789–90.

105. *Letters*, 320.

it.[106] But there were three main challenges to completing it. The first stemmed from life's daily distractions—errands, visitors, anything that would break his concentration from painting. Secondly, Niggle was too detail-oriented. His imagination multiplied the tree's span through countless new branches and leaves, not to mention adding the surrounding forest and mountains in the background.[107] Such details and distractions only contributed to Niggle's frustrations. The daily interruptions coincided with stress about the rapidly proliferating Tree.[108] The painting became a sub-created Secondary World in itself, an ever-growing landscape that was increasingly difficult to complete. These two challenges only heightened Niggle's anxiety because he believed he was running out of time; death was near.

The third challenge facing Niggle was others' perceptions of the painting. Although *he* saw his painting as valuable, meaningful work, nobody else validated it. Two visitors confirm this: his neighbor, Parish, and the Inspector. When Parish visited, he initially did not bother to look at Niggle's painting because of his apathy toward it.[109] He thought it nonsense.[110] When Parish actually did look at Niggle's art, all he saw was what interested him most: materials to be used for fixing his leaky roof. Practicality was supreme; art was useless.[111]

When the Inspector arrived, he saw Niggle's art as materials unlawfully utilized that should have gone to fix Parish's house.[112] Society expected law-abiding citizens. The law was for putting materials to use, not for appreciation.[113] These constant interruptions by uncaring people increased the haunting sense Niggle would never complete his painting to the fullness of his imagination before he died.[114] Worse yet, it confirmed the "sinking feeling in his heart" of not being able to capture something significant about the mountains.[115]

106. *Leaf*, 87–88.

107. Mention of the forest and mountains is significant: the forest to the writing of *LOTR*; the mountains because of what they come to mean at the end of *Leaf*.

108. Capitalized as Tolkien does.

109. *Leaf*, 91.

110. *Leaf*, 91, 109.

111. *Leaf*, 93.

112. *Leaf*, 95.

113. This comes into greater focus at the end of the story (*Leaf*, 110–12).

114. *Leaf*, 93–94, 96.

115. *Leaf*, 93.

Death led Niggle into a purgatorial state of existence[116] referred to as a journey,[117] which had three stages. In the first, Niggle was sent to a work-hospital meant to condition, teach, and transform him before he could move into the second.[118] Near the end of his time there, Niggle overheard Voices discussing his life.[119] They observed that, though often well-intended, he had measured his painting's meaning selfishly and in accordance with human approval,[120] not God's. While he genuinely devoted himself to his work, he measured it much like society did. Although it was aesthetically pleasing to him, his efforts were geared toward art for its "own sake" without truly realizing its worth: It had a greater purpose.[121] Significantly, for the first time in stage one, Niggle's art was mentioned *by the Voices*. Niggle had not considered his painting at all. His focus had been on improving deficiencies that had hindered him in life. Stage one had freed Niggle from his poor attitude and the possessiveness his painting once had over him. The Voices thought this significant and, while considering Niggle's condition, conceded that a transformation had occurred. Notably, when the Voices addressed him, Parish's well-being was the pressing matter on Niggle's mind, not his painting. Stage one in the journey had become a time of repentance and learning contentment that allowed him to move on.[122]

Stage two began after Niggle was sent to a land seemingly familiar yet not immediately identifiable. While riding his bicycle through it, he came to an abrupt halt. He recognized

> his Tree, finished. If you could say that of a Tree that was alive, its leaves opening, its branches growing and bending in the wind that Niggle had so often felt or guessed, and had so often failed to catch. He gazed at the Tree, and slowly he lifted his arms and opened them wide. "It's a gift!" he said. He was referring to his art, and also to the result; but he was using the word quite literally.[123]

116. *Letters*, 195.
117. *Leaf*, 87, 96.
118. *Leaf*, 97.
119. *Leaf*, 99–102.
120. *Leaf*, 99.
121. *Leaf*, 100.
122. *Leaf*, 97–98, 101.
123. *Leaf*, 103–4.

Niggle had been wrong; his Tree *was* finished, only instead of being part of a painting, the Tree was now an independent, living organism. From what he painted to what he only imagined, the essence of the Tree and the rest of the landscape lay before him.[124] His sub-creation had been given life in an actual living plane. But this is not what Niggle meant by declaring it "literally" a gift. He was referring to "his art" *and* "the result," which ostensibly mean the same thing. Mention of both signifies a distinction. The result will be discussed in a moment. At present, his art referenced the Tree he painted in life. Purgatory had, to this point, given him the realization that his artistic participation in life displayed something of greater worth than he had imagined. Where the Forest had been art for art's sake, "mere surroundings" in life,[125] they had become a world of actual experience through which he could now venture. Niggle also took notice of the Mountains in the distance,[126] which in life had been only painted "glimpses"[127] or imagined visions not fully completed.[128] Meanwhile, Parish still had a role in the story, and when he joined Niggle, he would add to the meaning of Niggle's gift.

Parish arrived after having been sent by one of the Voices.[129] Upon his arrival, they were on friendly terms before a noticeable shift in outlooks: As Niggle worked the land to fulfill the more practical needs of its design, Parish began absorbing his surroundings aesthetically. Each character exhibited the art's reverse effect after death than when they were alive. Parish now appreciated the landscape and Niggle's Tree in particular, and over time became healed of the limp that had befallen him in life as he increased his role in cultivating the land.[130]

All this time, the Mountains heightened Niggle's curiosity:[131] "They did not seem to belong to the picture, or only as a link to something else, a glimpse through the trees of something different, a further stage: another picture"[132]—stage three. Before, the Mountains only seemed to

124. *Leaf*, 104, 107.
125. *Leaf*, 105.
126. *Leaf*, 104.
127. *Leaf*, 88.
128. *Leaf*, 93. Niggle's reference here speaks of a singular Mountain.
129. *Leaf*, 107.
130. *Leaf*, 106–7.
131. *Leaf*, 104–5, 107–10.
132. *Leaf*, 105.

be drawing closer.[133] Over time, they came to be the focus of Niggle's attention so that his main desire was to go there.[134] The day came when Niggle and Parish travelled to the edge of the landscape, and a guide approached from the direction of the Mountains who could lead them beyond.[135] Niggle knew it was time for him to leave, but Parish wanted to stay.[136] Before Niggle departed, Parish and the guide conversed:

> *Parish*: "Could you tell me the name of this country?"
>
> *Guide*: "Don't you know? It is Niggle's Country. It is Niggle's Picture, or most of it: a little of it is now Parish's Garden."
>
> *Parish*: "Niggle's Picture! Did *you* think of all this, Niggle? I never knew you were so clever. Why didn't you tell me?"
>
> *Guide*: "He tried to tell you long ago, but you would not look. He had only got canvas and paint in those days, and you wanted to mend your roof with them. . . ."
>
> *Parish*: "But it did not look like this then, not *real*."
>
> *Guide*: "No, it was only a glimpse then, but you might have caught the glimpse, if you [tried]."[137]

What Parish failed to recognize in life was now realized in full. Actual participation in the world caused him to see not only the art Niggle labored over in life but also "the result." Its effect transformed him through participation in it. Before Parish arrived, Niggle realized "the Tree was finished, though not finished *with*."[138] What was *not* finished was the continued capacity of the result: how the art was still capable of bringing about an ontological encounter for those who appreciate it as it is. This is indicative not only of the Tree in particular but of the whole canvas. Observers looking at the Tree should be affected by the painting's entirety. The Tree Niggle sub-created while alive not only was *here* as it was in life but *still is* actively capable of producing meaning for those who experience it for themselves. But something from the presented dialogue cannot be disregarded.

133. *Leaf*, 105.
134. *Leaf*, 107.
135. *Leaf*, 108.
136. *Leaf*, 108. Parish remained to wait for his wife.
137. *Leaf*, 108–9.
138. *Leaf*, 105 (emphasis mine).

The guide mentioned that part of Niggle's Country now included Parish's Garden, yet Parish completely ignored the reference by exclaiming, "Niggle's Picture!" Parish recognized Niggle's painting was not nonsense[139] and its effect on him was so great he wanted to remain there. However, the guide's point is important. Yes, Parish realized the Tree and appreciated Niggle's Country, but Parish's Garden also came about through his own participation. Something new was generated, not only by appreciating the Tree as it was but also the world to which it belonged. Since Niggle's sub-creation had been given life, the fact that Parish's Garden existed indicates that Niggle's art awakened a latent aspect of Parish's being. This second stage experience brought about something new and recognizable to each character, applicable in different ways.

Although Parish would remain, Niggle was ready for stage three. The guide's arrival anticipated what Niggle had come to understand: He had to let go of his art and leave it behind. This is the final account of Niggle in the story: He began his

> walk ever further and further towards the Mountains. . . . Beyond that [who knows] what became of him. Even little Niggle in his old home could glimpse the Mountains far away, and they got into the borders of his picture; but what they are really like, and what lies beyond them, only those can say who have climbed them.[140]

These allusions to the Mountains signify an association with transcendence through the word *beyond*. The Mountains themselves do not matter as much as the mystery on the other side. *Leaf* ends by returning to the two Voices reflecting on Niggle's art. One of the Voices declared, "It is proving very useful indeed. . . . For many it is the best introduction to the Mountains."[141] The perpetual nature of Niggle's art—the result of the Tree—is not *finished with*. The Voice's selection of the word "useful" in this context is relevant. It is associated with the significance of the continuous draw of Niggle's art, which will be revisited momentarily. The allure of the Mountains needs explaining first. Tolkien clarified their significance further by returning the narrative to the real world in the story.

139. See *Leaf*, 91, 109. This mirrors what happened to Niggle in stage two. Each character's view of the painting changed.

140. *Leaf*, 109–10.

141. And it is implied that Parish eventually made it beyond the Mountains (*Leaf*, 112).

After Niggle's and Parish's deaths, members of his society—Tompkins and Atkins—discussed Niggle and his painting. The attitudes of Parish and the Inspector were shared by Tompkins. He contemptuously believed Niggle was a mindless, useless member of the community.[142] Any painting worth doing should be utilized for the progress or benefit of society, not to be wasted on outdated gobbledygook imaginings.[143] Tompkins complained Niggle was "always fiddling with leaves and flowers. I asked him why, once. He said he thought they were pretty! Can you believe it? He said *pretty*! 'What, digestive and genital organs of plants?' I said to him; and he had nothing to answer."[144] Niggle was a fool; beauty was trivial. He had insulted Niggle's affection for creation by nominalizing it into his own definition: Plants are strictly scientific organisms. What Niggle saw as beauty transcending creation, Tompkins distorted into a twisted sexualization of the word *pretty*.[145]

Atkins was not so sure. After Niggle's painting had gone to patch Parish's roof, he told Tompkins he had discovered a piece of it in the countryside, "a mountain-peak and a spray of leaves. I can't get it out of my mind."[146] Tompkins sharply responded, "Out of your what?"[147] Niggle's art awakened Atkins's imagination. Tompkins did not have one. What Atkins found captivated him, and he had the mountain fragment displayed in a museum to commemorate Niggle and his art.[148]

Recall what Niggle observed about the Mountains: They did not seem to belong to the picture but were merely a glimpse, a *link*, to that which is beyond. His painting presents a threefold purpose for Tolkien: through Niggle, sub-creation is not useless and wasted; through Parish, transformation happens via participation; through Atkins, sub-creation can direct observers to frontiers beyond the scope of human meaning. Central to each is how sub-creation invites participation in connatural creativity between people as poetic meaning transcends the painting, suggestive of meaning beyond what is imaged. These occurrences would not have happened if Niggle's painting had never existed.

142. *Leaf*, 110.
143. *Leaf*, 110.
144. *Leaf*, 111.
145. Clive Tolley made a similar observation in "Tolkien's 'Essay,'" 47.
146. *Leaf*, 111.
147. *Leaf*, 111.
148. *Leaf*, 112.

This circles back to the Voice's choice of "useful" at the end of the story. The Mountains signify what the finite cannot know about the infinite God beyond them. Niggle and his observers see only glimpses. Yet the Mountains serve as an alluring link within the painting/country through which transcendent meaning draws attention to mystery beyond. This resonates with how mountains have often illustrated an analogical way of encountering God.[149] They "epitomize how God and people relate to each other, both in history and in the eschaton."[150] They instill a sense of *awe*, "an allusiveness to transcendent meaning," possibly "to sense a meaning infinitely greater than ourselves."[151] Through Niggle's Tree and Country, Tolkien demonstrated how sub-creation might prove useful to drawing the attention of willing observers and participants to God's infinite beauty through art.

But How?—Secondary Belief

Leaf illustrates how sub-creation initiates ontological encounters. That sinking feeling Niggle once had about not fully capturing the Mountains need not have been because their placement in the painting directed attention to what was most significant for both maker and appreciator. The painting's meaning preserved them, but the Tree standing foremost in the painting initiated this effect. Recall that Tolkien noted how readers were aware of being "surrounded by the glimmer of limitless extensions in time and space" through *LOTR*.[152] As the Mountains in Niggle's painting beckoned *Leaf* characters, Tolkien's *LOTR* Tree beckons readers to sense something beyond the narrative implied in its mytho-*logos*, which relates to meaning embedded in language.

By profession Tolkien was a philologist, a person who studies the transformative meanings of language through history, culture, and literature.[153] Shippey stated philologists believe in "the reality of history" because of "the philologists' awareness of the shaping of present by past."[154] Language still makes formative meaning from old historical realities.

149. McGrath, *Open Secret*, 60–61.

150. Ryken et al., "Mountain," 574.

151. Spirito, "Influence," 204.

152. *Letters*, 412.

153. Gilliver et al., *Ring of Words*, 45–48.

154. Shippey, *Road*, 29.

Tolkien confirmed this to be true for him: "I like history, and am moved by it, but its finest moments for me are those in which it throws light on words and names!"[155] Unearthing the meaning of old words presently illuminates truths about realities long past. Each statement emphasizes the effects of language and history relevant to Tolkien: Looking back on history allows philology to inform how current circumstances came about, and present-day language offers clues for uncovering old meanings to be presently effective. Each illuminates the imagination with new meaning, which lays at the heart of Tolkien's mythopoesis: "In practical terms . . . he could show a pupil not just what the words meant, but *why* the author had chosen that particular form of expression and how it fitted into his scheme of imagery."[156] Consequently, pupils could experience "capital-P Poetry" based on Tolkien's ability to understand it contextually and solidify its meaning for them.[157]

In this we are reminded of what was discussed about the integrity of poetic myth and the keen sense of personal meaning it brings. Experiencing myth can only happen spatiotemporally and thus requires history. "History often resembles 'Myth,'" asserted Tolkien, "because they are both ultimately of the same stuff."[158] That which transcends into present experience is the "mythical or total (unanalysable) effect."[159] So when Tolkien stated that while writing *LOTR* "the story grew [and] it put down roots (into the past),"[160] he was claiming that narrative affirms history as relevant. This returns the discussion to Secondary Belief in the historical episode depicted in *LOTR*.

Historical narrative presents an ontological setting within which characters participate. To make a strong argument for this, Tolkien rejected the idea of Secondary Belief as a "willing suspension of disbelief."[161] Proper mytho-*logos* "commands or induces"[162] an effectual

155. *Letters*, 264.

156. Carpenter, *JRRT: Biography*, 138. Tolkien's "unique blend of philological erudition and poetic imagination . . . distinguished [him] from other scholars" (Bliss, Preface, v).

157. Thus Tolkien's tedious emphasis on properly teaching such texts (see Lee and Solopova, *Keys*, 6–7).

158. OFS, 47.

159. OFS, 48.

160. *LOTR*, xvi.

161. OFS, 52. This is a rejection of the phrase by Samuel Taylor Coleridge (see Flieger and Anderson, "Editors' Commentary," 107n50).

162. OFS, 59n.

suspension of disbelief without the intellect needing to activate the will, thus making it automatic or "involuntary."[163] Secondary Belief is successfully progenitive when imagination and reason coalesce and transcend from the Secondary World by manner of its own truth or rightness, thus becoming a bridge into sub-creation. The one who crosses over should find inner consistency "with the laws of that world. You therefore believe it, while you are, as it were, inside. The moment disbelief arises, the spell is broken: . . . Art, has failed."[164] If Secondary Belief is sustained, art (poetic meaning) sustains its operative linkage between the imagination and sub-creation, and the story analogically sustains literary truth on its own plane.

If Secondary Belief remains dichotomous to reality, the reader's suspension on the bridge between Primary and Secondary Worlds offers a keen vantage point: clarity in the Primary World because of the Secondary. After Tolkien's son Christopher expressed how *LOTR* affected him, the elder responded:

> It just shows the difference between life and literature: for anyone who found himself actually on the stairs of Kirith Ungol would wish to exchange it for almost any other place in the world, save Mordor itself. But if [literature] teaches us anything at all, it is this: that we have in us an eternal element, free from care and fear, which can survey the things that in "life" we call evil with serenity (that is not without appreciating their quality, but without any disturbance of our spiritual equilibrium). Not in the same way, but in some such way, we shall all doubtless survey our own story when we know it (and a great deal more of the Whole Story).[165]

In *LOTR*, Mordor is hell on Middle-earth. Cirith Ungol overlooks an entryway into it.[166] When readers reach the stairs of Cirith Ungol with Frodo's companion Sam, they encounter it differently than he does, though they know the gravity of the moment by journeying there with him. Readers do not have the exact same realistic experience as Sam, but they participate with him analogically. They survey his particular hellish circumstances without having dislocation from their everyday circumstances, but in a way meaning may applicably resonate with

163. Flieger and Anderson, Introduction, 12.

164. OFS, 52.

165. *Letters*, 106–7. At this point, Tolkien was still writing *LOTR*.

166. Spelled *Cirith* in *LOTR*.

actual hellish circumstances in their own lives. In communicating the difference between literature and life, Tolkien conveyed that edification transcends literature. But Secondary Belief in Middle-earth offers something more profound: an analogically sub-created cosmos derived through its own original mythic-ness.

Tolkien insisted that myth affects "as a whole, accepted unanalysed."[167] Kilby described myth as "a cosmic pattern which permeates man by some osmotic design."[168] Myth mediates into experience and impacts us as we are and as we grow and understand our personal narratives of life. So, if history resembles myth in story as in reality, myth mediates through history similarly in each world. Therefore, "if the story has literary 'truth' on the second plane," stated Tolkien, "a sudden glimpse of Truth" may be analogically verified in reality: "This is indeed how things really do work in the Great World for which our nature is made."[169] It thereby reaffirms how literature can bring clarity about the Whole Story in which a reader's threads of personal experience belong.

Therefore, mythical stories purposefully engage readers to encounter the writer of reality.[170] C. S. Lewis asserted, "What flows into you from the myth is not truth but reality (truth is always *about* something, but reality is that *about which* truth is), and, therefore, every myth becomes the father of innumerable truths on the abstract level."[171] The abstract level is that which humanity cannot know exactly about God because humanity cannot know the infinite exactly. However, myth issues concreteness into experience; hence, it is not abstract.[172] Something about God's abstractness may be known by virtue of myth's operations. In this way the uncreated interpenetrates created reality through ontological encounters that prove history and myth provide a direct avenue through which the divine becomes relatable. "It is only while receiving the myth as a story that you experience the [universal] principle concretely."[173]

167. "Beowulf," 15.

168. Kilby, "Mythic," 122.

169. *Letters*, 100.

170. See OFS, 78.

171. Lewis, "Myth," 66. Lewis addressed mythology generally before explaining this as perfectly true in Christianity.

172. Lewis, "Myth," 66.

173. Lewis, "Myth," 66.

The lastingness of stories—their "permanent value"—is evidence that their transcending effects remain,[174] glimpses of truth about uncreated reality throughout the cosmos. These effects provide "nourishment and are not cut off wholly from the sap of life: for the beauty of the story while not necessarily a guarantee of its truth is a concomitant of it, and a *fidelis* is meant to draw nourishment from the beauty as well as the truth."[175] Simon Oliver affirmed this quality is not escapism but a mode of perceiving and receiving something real. As was common belief in ancient times, "a myth was a story that conveyed truth, albeit in a form that was figurative, imaginative and therefore more accessible."[176] Tolkien was restoring this in his own way in *LOTR* through its own analogical cosmos projecting its own transcendent aura unique to the tapestry to which it belongs.

When sub-creation induces Secondary Belief, readers assent to their surroundings effortlessly because of what the poet's creativity engenders. It begets an ontological response triggered by its interworkings. The poet drawing on, deriving from, and partaking of reality produces a medium through which the greater reality of God seems more accessible. Thus does myth present a "truthful discourse,"[177] causing people to consider whether there is a greater significance about how things really do work in the Primary World. If there is a transcending effect through Secondary Belief, attention should be directed to that which is awakened in the reader's reality. Everything that is secondary must necessarily be determined from the knowledge of that which preceded it.[178] The discussion now turns to how Tolkien's ontological outlook produced mythic meaning through *LOTR* that analogically awakens finite being to participation in God.

Ontological Botany

Poetics do not create transcendence, but they can acknowledge it by making something new that directs attention to it. *Leaf* provides a helpful link to understanding the analogical relationship between *LOTR* and Primary

174. *Letters*, 109.
175. *Letters*, 109.
176. Oliver, *Creation*, 33.
177. Milbank, "Tolkien," 188.
178. Lewis, "First," 280.

Reality. Tolkien admitted his anxieties over his own Tree, *LOTR*, compared to Niggle's.[179] And as he was writing *Leaf*, he was preparing his lecture OFS into an essay for publication, adding new material to the original lecture. He introduced a seventeenth-century term—*effoliation*—in relation to fairy-stories.[180] In the *OED*, effoliate means "to open into leaf."[181] "Who can design a new leaf?" Tolkien speculated, before subsequently discussing the unlimited scope of the sub-creative story patterns humanity has, can, and will employ in the "Tree of Tales" for all time.[182] Reminiscent here is how sub-creators echo God's infinite variety through creativity. *LOTR* is analogically patterned after Tolkien's own Tree of Tales.

As a philologist who deliberated over "every word" of *LOTR*,[183] he used effolia*tion* intentionally. According to *The Treasury of Botany*,[184] effoliation means "*removal* of leaves."[185] This implies relinquishing control of sub-creation, allowing it to become detached, and offering it up while imitating the most profound sacrifice of the Christian faith. Tolkien's contextual use follows:

> The Christian has still to work, with mind as well as body, to suffer, hope, and die; but he may now perceive that all his bents and faculties have a purpose, which can be redeemed. So great is the bounty with which he has been treated that he may . . . actually assist in the effoliation and multiple enrichment of creation.[186]

Removed leaves die, decompose, and nourish the earth, fertilizing soil that produces new life. This metaphorically suggests God might "take up sub-creation into creation": If sub-creators relinquish control of their creative labors yet worshipfully pour themselves into their work, God might use it as an instrument of grace to enrich those affected. When consumed by the reader or hearer, the meaning of the story by effoliation breaks down

179. See *Letters*, 257, 321. Tolkien referred to *Leaf* as "part apologia" of his own writing struggles (*Letters*, 113).

180. This was probably in 1943, when Tolkien added *eucatastrophe* to the essay and correlated fairy-stories with the gospel in the New Testament, which seems not to have been part of the 1939 lecture (see Flieger and Anderson, "History of 'OFS,'" 130, 135).

181. *OED*, s.v. "effoliate."

182. OFS, 66.

183. *Letters*, 42.

184. To which the *OED* references this word (s.v. *effoliation*).

185. Lindley and Moore, *Treasury*, 441 (emphasis mine).

186. OFS, 78–79.

and is absorbed into "one's personal compost-heap" for nourishment.[187] An air of Niggle is apparent in Tolkien's description. Only after death did he learn to relinquish possession of his art and recognize sub-creativity's redemptive nature and enrichment of creation.[188]

Tolkien created a word with meaning that associates the transcending effects of poetics to an enriching ontological encounter with the divine: *eucatastrophe*.[189] Eucatastrophe is the impact of a "sudden joyous 'turn,'" which "is a sudden and miraculous grace: never to be counted on to recur."[190] Eucatastrophe is an ontological touch-point in time and space with concrete truth about reality, "giving a fleeting glimpse of Joy, Joy beyond the walls of the world."[191] These walls coincide with Niggle's Mountains. In Niggle's painting, the mountains are unapproachable features in the distance.[192] But as the poetic meaning of *Leaf* makes clear, the reader's imagination is directed to God. Thus is the reader's attention mythically directed to the infinite answer to every unfulfilled longing through myth.

The best fairy-stories should echo God's creativity to provide a clear pathway by which God may mediate grace "leading to insight into and contact with [the] reality"[193] of God's self. The Christian gospel declares that the story of Christ satisfies the "fulfillment of Creation" marred by the Fall of humanity, and sub-creation is supposed to bring readers into contact with it.[194] If achieved, such mediation may look forward to both the paradisiacal hope of salvation, the yet-untold story for those in life who long for redemption, and the original creation embedded in humanity's edenic prelapsarian primordial state: "We all long for it, and we are constantly glimpsing it: our whole nature at its best and least corrupted, its gentlest and most humane, is still soaked with the sense of 'exile.'"[195] After the Fall of humanity, the longing has remained unsatisfied, where humanity's "whole nature feels chained in

187. Tolkien in Carpenter, *JRRT: Biography*, 131.

188. Although Niggle died first and hoped second.

189. Tolkien "coined the word" (*Letters*, 100). The *OED Online* references its origin to Tolkien (s.v. "eucatastrophe").

190. OFS, 75.

191. OFS, 75.

192. See *Letters*, 110–11.

193. Duriez, "Sub-Creation," 139.

194. OFS, 78.

195. *Letters*, 110.

material cause and effect, the chain of death."[196] Fairy-stories continue to whet this desire,[197] and they provide glimpses of what people can always look forward to with hope in God.

Analogy of being acknowledges "God [is] the creative primordial ground of all being."[198] Since God created and sustains all being, humanity may recognize "its primordial contact with God's agency."[199] In this, God draws all things to divine beauty,[200] and the deeper meaning of eucatastrophe signifies impactful concrete moments meant to satisfy present longings and needs in God.

Eucatastrophe comes from outside the walls of this world in real time, which echoes analogy of being in-and-beyond the cosmos. Eucatastrophe stems from the essence of Tolkien's "Eucharistic" outlook on reality.[201] In Christian thinking, Jesus Christ's coming blended created and uncreated reality through his historical participation in creation, incarnation, and resurrection as God made Primary Reality sensible and interpretable through the lens of Christ as *the Logos*:[202]

> In Jesus a new principle of divine life had entered the human race and the natural world by which mankind is raised to a higher order. Christ is the head of this restored humanity, the firstborn of the new creation. . . . Hence the Absolute and the Finite, the Eternal and the Temporal, God and the World were no longer conceived as two exclusive and opposed orders of being standing over against one another in mutual isolation. The two orders interpenetrated one another, and even the lower world of matter and sense was capable of becoming the vehicle and channel of the divine life.[203]

This reconstitutes a sacramental imagination according to a divine mind from beyond made personal. Christ is the Word of the Trinity through whom creation was spoken into existence,[204] and his historical participation restores humanity to God while also reaffirming God's

196. *Letters*, 100.
197. OFS, 34.
198. Przywara, *Analogia*, 292.
199. Williams, *Grace*, 25.
200. Maritain, *Art*.
201. Grant, "Tolkien," 165, 177–82.
202. Boersma, *Heavenly*, 22.
203. Dawson, *Progress*, 124.
204. Poythress, *In the Beginning*, 45.

creation as good. "A sacramental ontology insists that not only does the created world point to God as its source . . . but that it also subsists or participates in God" through Christ.[205] He is the "sacramental link" for how early Christian ontology read uncreated reality through created reality: the incarnate *Logos* of creation coming to redeem and bridge the Old Testament by virtue of the New.[206]

Tolkien not only associated human creativity as analogous to God's creativity, but also his own method—*logos* through language as the essential source and substance that issues creative meaning.[207] The Christ-*Logos* issues a sacramental ontology for "both the *structure* of creation and a *process*, our active encounter with creation by which we relate to reality" from the entirety of our image-bearing selves.[208] Not only does the Christ-*Logos* affirm "participation—sharing in God's primordial creativity,"[209] but it also provides a lens through which humanity may interpret life and purpose in God. Christ's activity via creation, incarnation, and resurrection disclose how humanity is to participate in the cosmos: the glory of the infinite Creator born into the world, sacrificing his life unto God for the sake of fallen humanity, whose resurrection offers hope for the restoration of all creation because his historical participation has redeemed it. Therefore, "the material order and the historical progress of time may be valued, but they find their significance precisely because they are part of a larger tapestry: they point *beyond* themselves and participate in the eternal Word of God."[210] Christ modelled perfect participation in God, the "Author of Reality"[211] who transcends time and space through the greatest story written.

Tolkien's mytho-*logos* induces a sacramental sensibility in *LOTR* without allegorizing Christ incarnate in the story, what Tolkien acknowledged to be "an *infinitely* greater thing than anything I would dare

205. Boersma, *Heavenly*, 24.

206. Boersma, *Heavenly*, 38–39.

207. The relevance of *logos* to Tolkien has been discussed by Flieger (*Splintered*, 38–39), Bernthal (*Sacramental Vision*, 81–103), and Sebanc ("JRRT: Lover"). *Logos* can be linked to Tolkien's devotion of John's gospel association of *logos* to Christ (Carpenter, *Inklings*, 51–52; see also Bernthal, *Sacramental Vision*, 82–90).

208. Godzieba, "Catholic," 17.

209. Oliver, *Creation*, 47.

210. Boersma, *Heavenly*, 50.

211. *Letters*, 101.

to write."[212] Remember that myth allows for abstractions to be made concrete through experience. Tolkien explained how this is shown in the first chapter of John's gospel where the Word of creation is Christ: one can pick up the English translation and comprehend the infinite abstraction made concrete in Jesus because English has traditionally been "a language that could move easily in abstract concepts."[213] That is, so long as these concepts are not restricted to the words on the page. Once the diction is spoken, it is the meaning that remains not the "writing down, flattening, Bible-in-basic-English attitude" that collapses meaning into immanent confinements.[214] Language is meant to "enlarge" being,[215] and the Christ-*Logos* lens incorporates and transforms the whole outlook of existence in his character.

> The peak revelational intensities of Creation, Incarnation, and Resurrection give the believer a glimpse at the divine poetic imagination, God's "otherwise." The sacramental imagination is founded upon and is our response to these peak revelational intensities. The Incarnation especially functions as the benchmark for our own imaginative "thinking otherwise."[216]

This gives humanity a way to read all creation through a "mythopathic" lens,[217] creation echoing the ancient song of the divine mind who freely sang it into existence through Christ. The poet echoes creativity back through mythopoesis, however faintly. If successful, sub-creation issues "a far-off gleam or echo of *evangelium* in the real world,"[218] which returns the discussion to the meaning of eucatastrophe.

Fairy-stories parallel spatiotemporal reality as secondary planes with their own cosmoses. As readers track with characters, they encounter the reality of the characters in narrative parallel to their life experience. Sub-creative eucatastrophes depend on context just as lived experiences happen contextually moment-by-moment. In fairy-stories, eucatastrophe "is not an easy thing to do; it depends on the whole story which is the

212. *Letters*, 237.

213. Tolkien in Curtis, "Remembering," 429.

214. *Letters*, 310–11.

215. *Letters*, 311.

216. Godzieba, "Catholic," 23.

217. Lewis, "Myth," 66; Carpenter, *Inklings*, 45. Tolkien helped bring Lewis to this realization.

218. OFS, 77.

setting of the turn, and yet it reflects a glory backwards"[219]—old meaning brought into consciousness. But as in life, moments of eucatastrophe come and go: "We get a piercing glimpse of joy, and heart's desire, that for a moment passes outside the frame."[220] Evidence of this was apparent at the end of chapter 1. *LOTR* had pierced the darkness and through the limitless extensions in time and space "[rent] . . . the very web of story [to let] a gleam come through."[221] Eucatastrophe penetrated time and space as Pippin and Gandalf heard the horns, just as it would if one were rescued from Cirith Ungol at utmost need. Even though *LOTR* is a fairy-story, it is affective because it echoes how the Author of Reality intruded into time and space through the salvific story of Christ and continues to presently do so. Tolkien, like Niggle, came to this sudden realization of eucatastrophe while riding his bike.

> I remember saying aloud with absolute conviction: "But of course! Of course that's how things really do work." But I could not reproduce any argument that had led to this, though the sensation was the same as having been convinced by *reason* (if without reasoning). And I have since thought that one of the reasons why one can't recapture the wonderful argument or secret when one wakes up is simply because there was not one: but there was (often maybe) a direct appreciation by the mind (sc. reason) but without the chain of argument we know in our time-serial life.[222]

Tolkien realized that eucatastrophe was the "highest function" of fairy-stories[223] because it echoes God's flawless model of disclosure through the revelatory nature of Christ's forming and redeeming of creation. Eucatastrophes indicate the most meaningful moments within narrative by providing needful encounters through moments of grace in time and space. And though by definition they technically refer to the *peak* moments of grace that come about by divine intervention, any moment may seem eucatastrophic depending upon the person or situation. Readers can empathize with these moments in stories not only because of what they know through the narrative. If they are affected personally, the story may become applicable to real life when the transcending effect of

219. OFS, 76.
220. OFS, 76.
221. OFS, 76.
222. *Letters*, 101.
223. OFS, 75.

eucatastrophic meaning remains with the reader. The story has provided an analogy through the secondary plane that brings clarity into the primary, not because it was intellectualized but because it exemplifies some manner of how things really do work in the Primary World. But a fairy-story is still merely sub-creation, not Primary Reality.

This chapter discussed how sub-creation imitates God's creativity, but analogy of being distinguishes the creature-Creator relationship: There is an absolute difference because each similarity between creature and Creator implies the ever-greater dissimilarity between the finite and infinite. Creativity is the sub-creator's image-bearing gift. Chapter 3 discusses visualizing *LOTR* based upon what Tolkien hoped to project into imaginations to induce Secondary Belief. If *LOTR* pierces the darkness and reaches readers as with Pippin, it is important to delineate the kind of world we are viewing through Tolkien's *elvish* sacramental lens.

Chapter 3

Historical Planes of Meaningful Experience

Introduction

Tolkien said, "The theatre of my tale is this earth, the one in which we now live, but the historical period is imaginary."[1] By saying so, he reemphasized Middle-earth as objectively real at a different stage of the imagination. *We* and *our* imply sharing both the cosmic space between heaven and earth and *LOTR* as we read. But there is a difference between imaginary and unseen. Faërie is upheld by imagery constituted by the writer; "unseen worlds (as Heaven or Hell)" are traditional actualities neither invented by humanity nor experienced in life.[2] Since imagining a literary world happens in actual time, readers experience it as they visualize what they read as if watching a theatrical production.

LOTR is what Tolkien portrayed as "Faërian Drama."[3] When looking at the stage, we may be affected by what we see in Tolkien's Faërie. From the outside looking in, "the real desire" for readers should not be "to enter these lands as a natural denizen (as a knight, say, armed with a sword and courage adequate to this world) but to see them in

1. *Letters*, 183.
2. *Letters*, 239.
3. OFS, 63.

action and being as we see our objective world—with the mind free from the limited body."[4] Dramatic narrative projected into the imagination is experienced analogically to the personal history that presents the dynamic for two worlds in action. The language revealing the drama allows readers to be affected in the Primary World as they envision the Secondary imaginatively playing out. Readers experience Faërian Drama "contiguous"[5] with their narratives of life. This chapter discusses the kind of theatrical stage the reader looks upon while experiencing *LOTR* and why it may be personally impactful.

Understanding Smith's Experience

Tolkien described *LOTR* as a Frameless Picture, which compares to a stage play that seems to be ongoing when it begins and continues long past its end.[6] Sub-creation should feel like this, and Tolkien produced a theater of Middle-earth according to his "nose for elves." Chapter 1 introduced how the medieval understanding of elves was replaced by silly diminutive creatures only children believe in. Tolkien sub-creatively restored them to their mysterious medieval stature, where "they are greatly dreaded, and called 'the good people' not because they *are* good but in order to propitiate them."[7] Although elves were often presumed dangerous and instilled fear,[8] they could also inspire wonder by their beauty in ways present-day minds cannot appreciate without the same collective imagination.[9] But unlike the actual fairy faith in which many Celtic cultures believed, Tolkien was emphatic that Faërian Drama "is *not* religious," nor is Faërie "Heaven or Paradise. Certainly its inhabitants, Elves, are not Angels or emissaries of God (direct)."[10] Therefore, whatever religiousness is perceptible in Faërie, it is not synonymous

4. "Manuscript," 294.

5. Tolkien, "Essay," 115.

6. See Pask, *Fairy Way*, 135. Pask speaks to C. S. Lewis's point that Tolkien's world impresses its own "diuturnity" (Lewis, "Gods Return," 34).

7. Lewis, *Collected Letters*, 3:514. Tolkien referenced this letter dated October 9, 1954, in "Genesis," 85–86. *Propitiate* means "to render propitious or favourably inclined; to appease, conciliate" (*OED*, s.v. "propitiate"), and this is the context to which Tolkien alludes (Tom Shippey, personal correspondence, May 5, 2018).

8. OFS, 27, 32.

9. Lewis, *Discarded*, 129–32.

10. "Essay," 143–44.

with ours. The Christian mission of Tolkien and the TCBS meant to rekindle the old light, and Tolkien would fuse religious mission into the aura of his elf-patterned mythology. The "religious mission [of elves], then, can be seen as a metaphor for the enlightening impact of fairy-stories" on readers.[11] Tolkien displayed what this should look like by writing a fairy-story about it: *Smith of Wootton Major* (*SWM*).[12]

Significantly, *SWM* shows elves as credible, having "'real' existence, . . . in their own right and independent of human imagination and invention"[13] in a cosmos contiguous to a Primary World cosmos within the story. Tolkien took what was once believed as a natural view of elves and incorporated them into an independent cosmos, interacting with the human town of Wootton Major. As the story demonstrates, Faërie affectively impacts its main character Smith and illustrates how readers can be similarly impacted by *LOTR*.

A birds-eye view of *SWM* illustrates how Faërie can affect human experience:

1. It can gracefully enlarge being and bless others by means of grace;[14]
2. It offers a much-needed "glimpse" or "awaking"[15] to human imaginations in a world becoming increasingly closed-minded;[16]
3. Although humanity does not truly belong inside Faërie, encounters with it may prove purposeful;[17]
4. It should be passed on to others who need it.[18]

Two significant aspects of Faërie's value to humanity are illustrated through two scenes between Smith and his son Ned. Midway through *SWM*, Smith returns home after a visit to Faërie with an enchanted glowing flower. Its light casts Smith's shadow upon the wall, and Ned,

11. Garth, *Tolkien*, 113; see also 107, 112.

12. *SWM* is the fairy-story relevant to capital-P Poetry mentioned in chapter 1.

13. "Essay," 111.

14. Tolkien, *SWM*, 16–20.

15. *SWM*, 32.

16. This is captured primarily with Nokes's character (*SWM*, 7–15, 46–55), but the rest of Wootton Major had also generally become callous ("Essay," 129).

17. *SWM*, 33.

18. *SWM*, 38. These are only a few takeaways, and there are various ways of interpreting *SWM*. Others have been made by Flieger and Shippey, "Allegory versus Bounce"; Kocher, *Master*, 195–204; Long, "Two Views."

until then mute, speaks for the first time: "You look like a giant, Dad."[19] Years later, after Smith's final visit to Faërie, Ned reminds his father: "Do you remember the day when you came back with the Flower? And I said that you looked like a giant by your shadow. The shadow was the truth."[20] Smith's shadow emphasized how great he had become after embracing Faërie throughout his life.

Tolkien thought science and philosophy had rejected and deprived the imagination of traditional biblical stories, myths, legends, and fairy-stories.[21] These once-formative stories became "half-forgotten and less than half-understood stories," now unbelievable and relegated to the "lumber-room" of adult imaginations where things are left to be forgotten.[22] Smith never disbelieved Faërie from youth to old age, but for most residents in Wootton Major, such stories and traditions had fallen out of repute and belonged in the nursery.[23] However, Faërie had not disappeared because the common attitude toward it had shifted. It was still effective to those who permitted its existence. Smith's time in Faërie evidenced how instrumental it was not only in transforming him but in having an impact on his wider community. After Ned affirmed the greatness of Smith's character, a renewed vigor had Smith devote himself to the family business for the sake of the townsfolk and to nurture and mentor his son.[24]

As with the "missionary" role of elves in the earliest stages of Tolkien's mythopoesis,[25] *SWM* shows how human contact with Faërie maintains the same "beneficent"[26] role of elves to humanity.[27] It depicts how elves "had come to cure."[28] Their objective was the "enlightenment and vivification" of "practical and plain normal men and workers" (not know-it-all intellectuals) to be awakened to the greater reality of their roles in

19. *SWM*, 29.

20. *SWM*, 46.

21. OFS, 45, 67, 70, 81ND.

22. Tolkien, "Sir Gawain," 87. See *Letters*, 109.

23. "Essay," 129.

24. *SWM*, 45.

25. Garth, *Tolkien*, 112.

26. "Essay," 115, 130, 136.

27. "Essay," 126, 133, 140.

28. "Essay," 137. Tolkien was speaking only of Alf, the only elf (and King of Faërie) who came to Wootton Major. I am also referring to the Queen of Faërie who, though she never entered Wootton Major, shared in Smith's formation after he encountered her in Faërie.

the world.[29] As fairy-stories are wont to do, *SWM* sub-creatively shows how propitiating elves has positive real-world effects. The reader can see how elves fulfill their mission to Wootton Major as the story affirms the enlightening impact Faërie should have on those who experience it. The reader sees it is an actual place "'within' the tale" yet wholly distinct from Wootton Major's human history where Faërie can be experienced and "enjoyed without dislocation of . . . normal human life."[30] In other words, Faërie's historical cosmos impacts Wootton Major's in ways that neither delude nor detract from everyday existence.

As Smith visited Faërie throughout his lifetime, so can readers visit Middle-earth through *LOTR*; as Smith was a foreigner absorbing Faërie's pre-existing otherworldliness as it was revealed to him, so are readers observers of *LOTR*'s Faërian Drama unfolding; and as Smith journeyed through a particular realm of Faërie, readers journey similarly through *LOTR*. *LOTR* is contiguous to readers' narratives of life as they read, and as the eyes of hobbits are opened to their cosmos, so are readers' imaginations opened to Tolkien's Faërie. We now turn to the personal dynamic of this.

Patterning Tolkien's Sub-Creativity

Chapter 2 introduced how the inner consistency of stories induces Secondary Belief as poetic meaning operatively links imagination and sub-creation. But imagination belongs to each individual reader. The challenge lies in meaningfully linking imagination and sub-creation so there is not only Secondary Belief, but also the possibility for ontological encounters through the text to be translatable to the reader's reality. A starting point for making sense of the meaning of *LOTR* is identifying how Tolkien's personal creativity derived it.

Tolkien articulated his creative ambitions as such: "I have something that I deeply desire to *make*, and which it is the (largely frustrated) bent of my nature to make. Without any vanity or exaggerated notion of the universal importance of this, . . . I tend to be imprisoned in my own taste, so much as to be burdened with my own small but peculiar 'message.'"[31] Tolkien's humility was supported by a deep monition

29. "Essay," 141. This know-it-all mentality is exemplified in Nokes.

30. "Essay," 115.

31. *Letters*, 126–27.

compelled by God: "I would not presume to think that I was offering to God a perfect thing, since that is beyond human power; but I would not presume to offer Him anything less perfect than I could make it."[32] In this, Tolkien echoes what he said about the TCBS decades before—to testify for God, which aligns with his sense of being God's instrument while deliberating over each word of *LOTR*.

Stewarding creativity and displaying imaginative imagery for the benefit of others is active worship.[33] Thus, we may view Tolkien the sub-creator as having what Kuyper called "a sharper eye" than the non-artist.[34] The artist "sees what you do not see. . . . What he sees he captures in his soul. From his soul he incarnates that impression in his imagination. From that imagination he brings it to the canvas,"[35] which fortifies my argument about the subjectivity of Tolkien's meaning-making. God commissions artists to worship creatively. Thus, "human art . . . has the calling to ennoble nature and along with it, human existence on earth" by artists in their own particular ways.[36] Tolkien said Christ "admires more than does any man the gifts He Himself has bestowed,"[37] and although he acknowledged a foremost audience of one, his ambition was to ennoble all others who would give him audience.

Chapter 1 established the basis for ontological encounters via analogy—*logos* presents a way for interpreting reality as well as making meaning through *poesis*, thus designating the cosmos and poetics as different settings for participation. To continue with cosmo-*logos*, Maritain described God as the "First Poet," the infinite originator of created reality whose "purely *formative* and *forming*" creativity still upholds it.[38] God's transcendence "is enigmatically signified in a diffused, dispersed, or parcelled-out manner, by works which are deficient likenesses of and created participations in [God's Essence]."[39] This presents a medium for *general revelation* whereby God is plainly knowable within the created

32. Tolkien, Letter to Joan O. Falconer.

33. Kuyper, *Wisdom*, 162.

34. Kuyper, *Wisdom*, 164.

35. Kuyper, *Wisdom*, 164. Although specifically referring to a painter, Kuyper's broader point addresses creativity in general.

36. Kuyper, *Wisdom*, 156.

37. *Letters*, 128.

38. Maritain, *Creative*, 81.

39. Maritain, *Creative*, 81.

order and capable of recognition by image-bearers.[40] God is the source of every good, and general revelation allows humanity to experience it through *common grace*, which acknowledges "God's restraint of the full effects of the Fall, preservation and maintenance of the created order, and distribution of talents to" humanity.[41] This affirms a sacramental view of God involved in the cosmic space where humanity resides. But here I want to build upon God's *poesis* as still happening historically to sharpen the lens through which the mythopathic imagination sees otherwise. Tolkien declared eucatastrophe as the way things really work. We need to understand what this means, not just take his word for it.

The basis for cosmo-*logos* that participates in God as "Author" and "Poet" is rooted in God's ontic nature. *Ontic* implies actual grounding in God's real, *factual* presence in the cosmos.[42] Through the sacramental lens, God is "seen" *through* creation apart from "any understanding of nature possessing this capacity intrinsically and autonomously"; thus is the "link between nature and the divine" upheld.[43] This reads the First Poet's "creation [as] always participating in God . . . at every moment,"[44] proclaiming spatiotemporal nearness or with-ness. God readily shapes the formative and is forming from the purity of the divine simplicity, which allows for human growth and transformation moment-by-moment. Thus, creation already "owes its being . . . to God's gift of created existence,"[45] which is not to confuse finite creation with God (there is always the greater dissimilarity) but to understand that creation always allows for God's transcendence within immanence. Instead of being read as two separate spheres, nature and grace remain conjoined because "nature is always already graced."[46] This view takes Plato's theory of forms and,

40. See Oden, "Without Excuse," 55–68. Oden lays out the basis for God's general revelation made plain to all humanity as affirmed from the first centuries of the early Christian church—"pre-Protestant, pre-European, premedieval" and "prior to its divisions" (56)—and "reconfirmed by Luther, Calvin, Wesley, and North American evangelical revivalism" (68). Based on Romans 1:18–22, creation evidenced a divine mind through its catholicity long before the Reformation and scientific naturalism: From the earliest days of the Church, "everything in creation has the capacity to refract the glory of the Creator" (60).

41. Bacote, Introduction, 26.

42. See *OED Online*, s.v. "ontic."

43. McGrath, *Open Secret*, 189.

44. Oliver, "Nouvelle."

45. Oliver, "Nouvelle."

46. Oliver, "Nouvelle."

instead of them being eternal emanations having coincided *as* eternally divine to be shaped into creation, places their origination in the eternal Trinity who created them *ex nihilo*.[47]

Since *poesis* means "making," it is a recurring activity in time, which presents innumerable opportunities to encounter God (in-and-beyond, never static) in life. Transformation happens through participation. Non-human beings participate in the goodness and essence of God according to the nature designed for them, as when the caterpillar transforms into a butterfly or an acorn an oak. Each exercises God's creativity by design. Chesterton speculated,

> It is possible that God says every morning, "Do it again" to the sun; and every evening, "Do it again" to the moon. It may not be automatic necessity that makes all daisies alike; it may be that God makes every daisy separately, but has never got tired of making them. It may be that He has the eternal appetite of infancy; for we have sinned and grown old, and our Father is younger than we. The repetition in Nature may not be a mere recurrence; it may be a theatrical ENCORE. Heaven may ENCORE the bird who laid an egg.[48]

The trinitarian disclosure model is displayed here. Since creation is *ex nihilo*, the Trinity maintains analogical continuity in the present: God the Father "expressing [his] character in his plan" (Do it again decrees from God's eternal appetite), God the Son expressing it creatively through his *Logos* substance (actively upholding sun, moon, daisy; bird and egg), and God the Spirit declaring the power of divine presence (continued daily encores that make God's transcendence translatable).[49] This is the infinite "tri-unity" of God in action.[50] From what Chesterton knew about God, creation, and scripture,[51] he provided a way to imagine what no living human has actually witnessed alongside God in the heavens and how humanity still witnesses the First Poet's commonly graced general revelation. He gave meaning to God's goodness and creativity in a new, mythical way.[52]

47. Boersma, *Heavenly*, 33–34, 38–39.

48. Chesterton, *Orthodoxy*, 60.

49. Adapted from the "God's Work of Creation" diagram of "Analogy for Creativity," Figure 5.2 in Poythress, *Chance*, 61.

50. Candler, "Tolkien," 38.

51. And Catholic Church tradition.

52. This does not mean that others have not expressed something similar. But if so,

The world signifies purpose and order in God, and by speaking imagery to God's handiwork, Chesterton's encores declare *more* than strict science and material for material's sake in a personalized way.[53] Sub-creation is an encore but different in kind. It is not about daisies and birds but world-making in a distinct humanly way. Tolkien's Secondary World is a creative tribute to God according to its own virtuousness, which can awaken readers to the greater reality of the divine through its own originality.

Purposeful *Poesis* Through History

When asked about the purpose of life, Tolkien replied, "to increase according to our capacity our knowledge of God by all the means we have."[54] If God spoke creation into existence, it has meaning and purpose. Each needs discovering, and intelligent minds are equipped to do so. "While as living creatures we are (in part) within and part of [the Universe]," wrote Tolkien, "our ideas of God and ways of expressing them will be largely derived from contemplating the world about us."[55] Two significant points emerge here. First, there is more to humanity than can be seen by the naked eye. Second, ideas about God do not cause humans to know God exactly due to limits in their understanding. Although intuition is capable of discerning God's encores, the catastrophe of humanity's fall has left it "dim and cracked"[56] so that God seems only to be glimpsed through the "chinks of the universe about us."[57] A Christian view of history places humanity's fall after creation *ex nihilo*. Tolkien referenced this as an historical reality throughout his lifetime[58] to explain how to interpret the sense of longing that makes life feel exilic.[59]

---

this strengthens any argument for human affective connaturality through imagination. It also emphasizes two things: similar expressions have been uttered meaningfully from different people with diverse personal histories (thus making the meanings they make unique in themselves), and those who may never encounter Chesterton's writings in their lifetimes can be influenced by someone else imagining similarly to Chesterton.

53. See Chesterton, *Orthodoxy*, 58–60.

54. *Letters*, 400.

55. *Letters*, 400.

56. *Letters*, 194.

57. *Letters*, 101.

58. See *Letters*, 48–54, 88, 98, 110, 147, 243, 285–86; OFS, 42, 65, 73, 79.

59. *Letters*, 110.

For humans, encores happen differently. Sinful nature rejected the image-bearing gift of God's essence as its source of being so that humanity's posture shifted from God-orientation to self-orientation. Christ necessarily came and unified "the harmonious and divine structure of the *cosmos*,"[60] thus making Christian transformation possible by his life, but not without hindrance. Unlike the rest of the created order of beings, people may reject God. Whether one responds to God's call or not, it is significant that God's *poesis* is ever available, and God's purely formative and forming power is an option for transforming individuals into the perfecting image of Christ. Trinitarian disclosure models how to translate God's *poesis* for humanity: Submission to God through Christ transforms human participation in the power of the Spirit.[61] The gospel narratives tell the only perfect sacramental story. Through God the Poet, "the Art is . . . in the story itself rather than in the telling; for the Author of the story was not the evangelists."[62] Thus, it is the meaning of the gospel that mythically transcends and transforms us.[63] The fullness of all poetic meaning resides in the story of God: "beautiful, and moving: 'mythical' in . . . perfect, self-contained significance; . . . the greatest and most complete conceivable eucatastrophe."[64] The permanent value of this story is sustained by its infinite permanence and "pre-eminently" verifies reality's inner consistency.[65] Here, as in the *logos*-centricity of creation, *logos* is always happening—the redemption story incorporating the creation story, where each is capable of affecting being: From beyond the walls of the world, human transformation is possible within its walls.

Many may find eucatastrophe's *consolation* in time acceptable.[66] The gospel consoles, and all good fairy-stories should do similarly. But others may meet this with unconvinced circumspection, scorn, or outright rejection because that is not what *they* experience. Tolkien insisted that eucatastrophe is only possible if *dyscatastrophe*—"sorrow

60. Luc Ferry in Keller, *Every Good*, 205.

61. Derived from "Christ's work as God and man on earth" and "our work as human beings on earth" diagrams in Figure 5.2, "Analogy for Creativity" in Poythress, *Chance*, 61.

62. OFS, 78n.

63. Which is how C. S. Lewis, through Tolkien, returned to the Christian faith (McGrath, *C. S. Lewis*, 149–51).

64. OFS, 78.

65. OFS, 78.

66. OFS, 75.

and failure"[67] and all else stemming from the Fall—exists. But this does not have to be a person's finality. Human *poesis* happens spatio-temporally, and so does God's. In this manner many experience the necessary eucatastrophes which bring personal encores through spiritual awakenings. "Direct experience . . . alone goes really to the heart. The burnt hand teaches most about fire," Tolkien said.[68] This applies to eucatastrophe's intrusiveness and how it can alter personal trajectories of lives damaged by the catastrophe of the Fall. The road to transformation lies in historical participation and other aspects of history that also enhance the analogical effects of *LOTR*.

Tolkien was speaking both of history and of the present when he told his son Michael, "At any minute it is what we are and are doing, not what we plan to be and do that counts."[69] In other words, people often prepare for an unforeseeable future that may never come. Stewarding *now* matters most, but personal life can seem purposeless in a chaotic world. When dyscatastrophe unhinges our lives, the hardest thing to do is to gather our wits and persevere.

The historical plane situates humanity between two poles—the pre-Fall beginning and now. The future is only ever anticipated. Eucatastrophic encounters happen historically, but they always foreshadow salvific hope-fulfilled outside history. Yet, to live farsightedly is to detach from the present. Personal being must deal with daily suffering and evil which, Christian or not, is a certainty whether we like it or not.[70]

Literature helps us *survey our own story when we know it*, which suggests that knowledge does not always impact us immediately; comprehension happens over time. Literature also presents *a great deal more of the Whole Story*, the *eternal element* part of our nature. But in order for secondary reality not to be deemed escapist, it should consist of identifiable troubles and challenges. Dyscatastrophe must be present because evil repeatedly rears itself. It is one of the inevitable patterns of history in a fallen world of which Tolkien observed three challenges.

First, the world had changed more rapidly in his lifetime than in any other generation before.[71] Second, humanity forgets too easily; every generation is so fleeting it hardly remembers its own history to

67. OFS, 75.

68. *Letters*, 76.

69. *Letters*, 46.

70. See "Mythopoeia," 88.

71. He saw generations in spans of seventy years (Tolkien, Interview with Gueroult).

have learned from previous mistakes.[72] This is particularly problematic in the transiency of the Western mind's collective historical consciousness. Third, and not attributed to the Fall, is this: when considering the complexity and differences of every individual, the problem is magnified. Tolkien found this intriguing: "I always feel, even when you walk into a room you really feel you ought to know the history," said Tolkien, "not of the room, but of the people. We walk in with all this tremendous history behind us."[73] Every person's own imagination, coupled with individual history, exponentially increases the challenges for evaluating the scope of history on a large scale, let alone an individual one. These observations all fit beneath the following overarching themes.

First, humans are historical beings. Experience happens historically, which is unavoidable. Second, since reading is participatory, humans simultaneously experience parallel narratives historically. Third, because history is everchanging and humanity generationally forgets, evil's tenacity is an inevitable recurrence. The dynamic of human fallenness and evil's continuity throughout time shaped one way Tolkien viewed history, as nothing "but a 'long defeat'" because of the endless "weight of human iniquity."[74] These are all facts about human narratives of life, and each is unique depending on a person's historical context.

Tolkien's reading of history was through the lens of *sub specie aeternitatis*—"from the aspect of eternity."[75] In this, he perceived he was surrounded by "cosmic conflict" between good and evil.[76] Christianity translates God's infinite interactivity in time, and Christ sacralizes how history may be interpreted because of God's transcendence despite the prevalence of evil. One need not believe God exists to recognize evil. Nor does one need to believe in God to be affected by the religious sensibilities of Tolkien's mytho-*logos*. They need only let *LOTR*'s narrative context draw them further into experiencing its mythic meaning in the parameters of its sub-created plane. Situational contexts only "become intelligible" within the narratives to which they belong.[77] Applicability may be taken from them similar to other narratives from which we receive meaning, whether

72. Specifically, every thirty years. *Letters*, 75–76.

73. Tolkien, Interview with Gueroult.

74. *Letters*, 80.

75. *Letters*, 76; Candler, "Tolkien," 38.

76. Sayer, "Recollections," 8.

77. MacIntyre, *After Virtue*, 210.

actually historical or feigned. If feigned well enough, *LOTR* might be able to affect the trajectory of a person's living narrative.

Impactful Feigned History

Ancient Greek thought deemed *feigned history* truthful according to its own plane as a "whole story . . . 'grounded in solid truth.'"[78] Even though not actual history, it still imaginatively "exhibited [truth]."[79] When the late medieval period overlapped the Renaissance,

> the man who, in his "feigned history," improved on Nature and painted what might be or ought to be, did not feel that he was retreating from reality into a merely subjective refuge; he was reascending from a world which he had a right to call "foolish" and asserting his divine origin.[80]

Creative invention was welcome, and even if poetics were fictive, audiences understood they were not being lied to, nor did they confuse it with actual events.[81] Tolkien believed this still to be an inherent gift from God, the essence of which has remained undeteriorated over time.[82] If sub-creation improves nature amidst inadequate Primary World counter-narratives, it can direct attention to God in more meaningful ways than matter-of-fact platitudes.

In the Foreword to the second edition of *LOTR*, Tolkien wrote that he favored "history, true or feigned, with its varied applicability to the thought and experience of readers," and that applicability "resides in the freedom of the reader."[83] He was speaking in terms of narrative mediation. Whether reality (true history) or sub-creation (feigned history), both are experienced as narratives. I will not be discussing the variant ways of interpreting true history, but Tolkien held that there

78. Macrobius in Lewis's *Discarded*, 65.

79. Macrobius in Lewis's *Discarded*, 65.

80. Lewis, *English*, 321.

81. Lewis, *English*, 318–19.

82. See "Mythopoeia," 87.

83. *LOTR*, xvii. In the decade after *LOTR*'s first edition, Tolkien received countless inquiries about allegorical meanings, which caused Tolkien to believe he had made the initial Foreword too personalized (see Tolkien, "Appendix," 26). The second Foreword rejects allegorical associations to real-world likenesses and encourages readers simply to enjoy it as a story.

was a proper manner for reading *LOTR*'s history. Its foundation lies in the writer's arrangement.

Early in *LOTR*, two characters deliberate their imminent dilemma. The following exchange happens before the reader is brought into a greater realization about the role the characters will play:

> *Mentee*: "I wish [this] need not have happened in my time."
>
> *Mentor*: "So do I, and so do all who live to see such times. But that is not for them to decide. All we have to decide is what to do with the time that is given us."[84]

This conversation is not unlike how two individuals might discuss troubling events in their lifetime. The mentee despairs, and the mentor validates life's harsh reality. It exemplifies how narrative can make truth sensible and personable to readers.[85] Yet plucked from the story, it is merely conventional wisdom. Removing characters and context make the dialogue's use indistinguishable from Tolkien's world. To remove this and any other aspect of *LOTR* for uses apart from the story makes them "nonentities, as shape is a nonentity apart from the body whose shape it is."[86] Although the lines stem from Tolkien's sub-creation, the operative link to the imagination—the poetic meaning—is missing. In this case, that which is applicable cannot be identified from its context and the greater implications of the story.

The mentee/mentor dialogue can be universally applied because it typifies basic human experience. Yet with Tolkien's deep devotion to God, unique compulsion to make, and desire to awaken readers, he was speaking beyond generalities. Alasdair MacIntyre stated, "both purposes and speech-acts require contexts" to be properly understood.[87] Tolkien had both purpose and intent, especially regarding his use of mytho-*logos*, as his note about applicability in *LOTR*'s second edition demonstrates. If *LOTR* is to be appropriated, its context should be properly understood because "if you get the story wrong, your response will be wrong."[88]

When Tolkien spoke figuratively of the spiritual hunger and thirst of readers, this correlated with what would be supplied through *LOTR*'s

84. *LOTR*, 50.

85. See *Letters*, 194.

86. Lewis, *Experiment*, 84.

87. MacIntyre, *After Virtue*, 210.

88. Keller, *Every Good*, 156. Keller references MacIntyre here.

mytho-*logos*. If awakening initiates transformation, then applicability is relevant. Chapter 1 discussed how the most significant lessons are tied to the story's aesthetic nature, evidencing an ontological kinship. Tolkien equated applicability to significance,[89] the effects of which mythically mediate into personal experience. Since this is supposed to happen analogically through the text, it should parallel how reality may be experienced. As Giussani described,

> In Greek "up" is expressed with the word *ana*. This is the value of *analogy*: the structure of the "impact" of the human being with reality awakens within the individual a voice which draws him towards a meaning which is further on, further up—*ana*. Analogy: this word sums up the dynamic structure of the human being's "impact" with reality.[90]

Noteworthy are the already familiar words awakening, reality, and meaning; each suggests applicability via *impact* within the cosmo-*logos*. Analogy is experienced by looking *up* and *outside* of the self as if being *drawn toward meaning*. To perceive the fullest and most accurate impact, historical context is important for proper orientation in the world. History reveals the spatiotemporal contingencies significant to understanding a person's development, but this is difficult to pinpoint in a given moment. Narrative brings clarity. If apprehended analogically, the moving quality of the text as a whole can awaken readers in their own narratives of life. When reality becomes difficult to translate, an inner consistent text can mediate meaning in "clear cut" ways.[91]

C. S. Lewis stated, "Every art is itself and not some other art. Every general principle we reach must, therefore, have a peculiar mode of application."[92] When the literary artist orders *logos* through *poesis*, poetic knowledge uses life experience to develop it into a "spirit" and "feel" of its own, something new that has "come to life."[93] When complete, it is no longer in an active state of making. It shifts from participatory *poesis* into past tense *logos*, "something *said*," and *poiema*, "something *made*."[94]

89. *Letters*, 297–98.

90. Giussani, *Religious Sense*, 109.

91. *Letters*, 78, 242.

92. Lewis, *Experiment*, 28.

93. Lewis, *Experiment*, 81–82.

94. Lewis, *Experiment*, 82 (emphasis mine).

This leaves an end-product that may be "good for us here and now."[95] The artist's creativity has engendered something new into which s/he has poured his/her soul and exhibited an intellectual continuity that manifestly mediates meaning to others.

To see *LOTR* as *poiema* acknowledges that Tolkien's *poesis* purposefully ordered *logos* into forms that may be used by God's *poesis*. This, in turn, shapes readers who might be transformed through the glimpses of truth, goodness, and beauty revealed in the text. If so, the poetic meaning from *poiema* bridges this into the reader's imagination. There may be greater implications or applications if *LOTR* is allowed to be experienced and appreciated as feigned, to let its mytho-*logos* as *poiema* speak truth in and of itself.

Adding the contextual details to the mentee/mentor dialogue issues in much more than a general application:

> *Gandalf*: "Last night I told you of Sauron the Great, the Dark Lord. The rumours that you have heard are true: he has indeed arisen again and left his hold in Mirkwood and returned to his ancient fastness in the Dark Tower of Mordor. That name even you hobbits have heard of, like a shadow on the borders of old stories. Always after a defeat and a respite, the Shadow takes another shape and grows again."
>
> *Frodo*: "I wish it need not have happened in my time."
>
> *Gandalf*: "So do I, and so do all who live to see such times. But that is not for them to decide. All we have to decide is what to do with the time that is given us. And already, Frodo, our time is beginning to look black. . . . We shall be hard put to it. We should be very hard put to it."[96]

The context clarifies that general harsh realities of life are not the subject. Something greater is at stake. There is a notable difference between each character's perspectives about their plight in the story. Frodo is reasonably selfish; difficult times call for desperate measures that he would rather observe from a distance, if at all. Although Gandalf affirms Frodo's concern, he also recognizes that time is a gift to be purposefully used. Through his empathy for Frodo, Gandalf sees the moment as a meaningful opportunity, however grim, and accepts it as such, regardless of the

95. Lewis, *Experiment*, 134.

96. *LOTR*, 50.

circumstances.[97] Unlike the plain mentoring dialogue, the reader understands that the stakes are higher than conventional wisdom espouses. The details indicate a larger context. Even though Frodo is troubled by his circumstances, the reader can see that he is not disoriented at all; bemoaning his predicament does not equate to losing his grip on life. The narrative immediately shows that Gandalf has a handle on the gravity of the situation due to his knowledge. Although he does not know everything, he knows enough to advise next steps.

Although a fragment of the larger narrative, adding the details reveals how a greater context leads to a different way for translating what is applicable. When Tolkien spoke of applicability to the freedom, thought, and experience of readers, he implied a certain posture toward *poiema* that allows it to be absorbed as-is. The difference lies in coming to the text as we are to encounter the world as it is, not translating Middle-earth based on what we bring and eisegeting from *LOTR* what is not there. This will become clearer over the next sections.

Upon the Threshold: Letting Meaning Be Free

When Tolkien awakened Bilbo and the reader to the prospect of a larger, elf-patterned, greater reality, it was akin to what he observed through the *Beowulf* poet. The poet presented "an indication of the precise point at which an imagination, pondering old and new, was kindled, [where] new Scripture and old tradition touched and ignited."[98] Tolkien's essay on *Beowulf* argued for the significance of appreciating it holistically as poetic art.[99] As such, Tolkien observed the poet's attempt to capture the tension between newfound Christianity and northern myth. The poet found himself postured between heaven-directed and pagan earthbound texts while artfully capturing his vantage point in history: "a learned man writing of old times, who looking back on the heroism and sorrow feels in them something permanent and something symbolical."[100] This precision point is like a moment of suspended

97. More on this in chapter 8.

98. "Beowulf," 26.

99. While also arguing the monster's essentiality and centrality to the poem ("Beowulf," 19, 22–23, 25; Bliss, Preface, 4).

100. "Beowulf," 26.

"imaginative apprehension."[101] It is a concrete moment, "a fusion . . . *at a given point* of contact between old and new, a product of thought and deep emotion."[102] Through *Beowulf*, Tolkien was awakened to a literary realm subsistent unto itself—a sub-created "extra-mental existence"[103] induced by poetic power. The *OED* defines *extra-mental* as "beyond the mind; independent of mental apprehension."[104] If the threshold of Middle-earth can be apprehended similarly by readers of *LOTR*, ontological encounters through Tolkien's mytho-*logos* might mediate more than just an "exciting story."[105] Unlike the stage play metaphor where the audience looks up and watches drama unfold at a distance, a threshold situates readers on the brink of the Secondary World itself.

Thresholds *in* life experience differ from how literature may be applicable *to* life experience. In reality, a threshold is a thoroughfare between one place and another. In a home, for example, the room a person exits becomes part of past experience. The next room is potential future experience. If s/he stops on the threshold, the present moment is the brink for surveying both: With one foot in each room, s/he is in two places simultaneously.

The analogy is more difficult to apply to life in action. Time never stops, and nobody can truly have one foot in the past and one in the future because moment-by-moment experience is the only historical reality a person physically experiences at once. Present time is a starting point that only allows history to be in our past. The future is never a guarantee. Therefore, a threshold experience offers a mental picture for how readers participate in both Primary and Secondary Worlds at once, with the ability to survey both concurrently. There are two kinds of poetics at work here. Reality presents the plane where creation participates in God's *poesis*. The Secondary World presents the writer's analogically. Whereas God's *poesis* is ever-presently working, the poet's becomes finalized *poiema* left to history.[106] The human artist leaves behind works that

101. "Beowulf," 20.

102. "Beowulf," 20.

103. "Genesis," 86. I have added the hyphen to make it consistent with its usage later in the book.

104. *OED*, s.v. "extra-, prefix; extra-mental."

105. *Letters*, 212, 267, 297.

106. A. E. Cherryman wrote in *Truth*, August 6, 1954, that in publishing the first *LOTR* volume Tolkien had "added something, not only to the world's literature, but to its history" (Carpenter in *Letters*, 444n149.4).

are both historically permanent and symbolic, ever-available thresholds for imaginative apprehension for future encounters.

Finalized poetics shift the act of producing sub-creation (Niggle while he lived) to the sub-creation produced (Niggle's "result" after death). Within history it maintains its own inherent pre-existing meaning prior to all future encounters, which makes what was said through *poesis* matter as *poiema*. "A word which simply 'was' and didn't 'mean' would not be a word,"[107] and the same is true of mytho-*logos*. When readers experience *LOTR* for the first time, it is a new encounter with a seemingly old world that for many readers has become a product of thought and deep emotion because of its poetic meaning. It impacts life experience similar to Giussani's description of cosmic reality analogically impacting and drawing a person's attention beyond the self amidst the "ontological space" of God's *poesis*.[108] Tolkien's mytho-*logos* produced its own feigned ontological space. How this is presented accentuates *LOTR*'s mythic effects and will help us understand how God's *poesis* might use "the result" of Tolkien's sub-creativity to direct readers to God's self in concrete ways.

Owen Barfield stated, "Mythology is the ghost of concrete meaning. Connections between discrete phenomena, connections which are now apprehended as metaphor, were once perceived as immediate realities."[109] If mythical meaning was *once* perceived, and if myth *was* a story conveying truth,[110] these suggest that concrete truth is no longer communicated this way. However, the "older" sense of "metaphor suggests *participation* between different agencies,"[111] and Tolkien's world presents something *still* alive at once in all its parts. Tolkien evidenced this when Bilbo's spirit awakened in his hobbit hole. The reader experiences a fuller sense of this through the dialogue between Gandalf and Frodo in the same hobbit hole years later in *LOTR*. Though each hobbit only dimly apprehends it, its intrigue still actively exists.[112]

Continuing Barfield's statement, "the poet strives, by his own efforts, to see [these once perceived immediate realities], and to make others see

107. Lewis, *Experiment*, 28.

108. Willard, "Language, Being."

109. Barfield, *Poetic Diction*, 92.

110. Oliver, *Creation*, 33 (emphasis mine).

111. Williams, *Grace*, 29.

112. Echoing that, though the poet only sees a dim picture of the world, it is still perceptible.

them, again."[113] To some extent, Tolkien said he set *LOTR* in "our Middle-earth" at a different stage of imagination to establish an immediately old sense of such realities. But this is feigned, and Tolkien believed original meaning at the roots of human history were irrecoverable.[114] Therefore, he was not presenting mythological ghosts of concrete meaning in Primary Reality but analogy to it. "These tales are 'new,'" Tolkien said. "They are not directly derived from other myths and legends."[115]

This brings the discussion back to impact and applicability. *LOTR* stems from Tolkien's mytho-*logos* whose poetic meaning bridges readers' imaginations into his world. If reality and sub-creation are surveyed from this threshold in a state of spiritual equilibrium, readers may freely experience each world from a neutral position, which allows for the *telos* of the literary world to speak for itself.

If *poiema* is good for here and now as new art according to its own subjectivity, what Tolkien intended as applicable history stems from his desire "to *make*," and the true operative link is the poetic meaning of the work, from the work, not what the reader makes it mean. Making and taking are different things. Applicability is associated with takeaways. The *logos* of *poiema* is something said and made (past tense), and this makes it peculiarly applicable according to

> two different kinds of order. On the one hand, the events (the mere plot) have their chronological and causal order, that which they would have in real life. On the other, all the scenes or other divisions of the work must be related to each other according to principles of design. . . . *Our feelings and imaginations must be led through.*[116]

By virtue of analogy, it is the otherness of mytho-*logos* that draws one towards the further meaning of the *telos* of the *poiema* that has not changed even though the art may be read at different moments in history. In reality, God's *poesis* makes history translatable by making Christ the lens for reading "significance and order."[117] In this, there is always the possibility that eucatastrophe transforms us as participatory ontology leads our feelings

113. Barfield, *Poetic Diction*, 92.

114. *Letters*, 268.

115. *Letters*, 147. This is not to say that Tolkien did not use "borrowings" from extant stories, poems, languages, history, geography, and mythologies to be variously incorporated in Middle-earth (see Kilby, "Tolkien as Scholar," 9–11).

116. Lewis, *Experiment*, 83 (emphasis mine).

117. Dawson, "History," 268.

and imaginations through the "mysterious and unpredictable" challenges of life.[118] Since a feigned history's order and structure are a permanent *poiema* from history, it remains an unchanged medium that may bring clarity amidst unpredictability. Because myth and history are ultimately of the same stuff, the order by which readers are led through any variant of feigned history gives different outlooks, which may work to the "enlargement of our being,"[119] that is, the awakening of our being *to* reality due to analogical participation in *poiema*. Something has been made applicable because of the orderly way the mytho-*logos* affects us.

Therefore, it is noteworthy that Tolkien contentiously argued for applicability through history as opposed to allegory since, (1) *LOTR* is not allegory because, (2) it was intentionally not written as one. Yet this "allegory issue" haunted Tolkien from the time of its publication.[120] In a 1964 interview with Tolkien, Denys Gueroult asked about certain trees in *LOTR*, wondering if they symbolized meaning in Tolkien's personal life. Tolkien responded emphatically: "They're not symbols to me at all. I don't work in symbols at all. Other people find that they are symbolic. . . . I'm entirely historically minded."[121] Gueroult asked other leading questions to which Tolkien made similar replies:[122]

> *Gueroult*: "Why did you choose . . .?"
>
> *Tolkien*: "I didn't."
>
> *Gueroult*: "Did you intend . . .?"
>
> *Tolkien*: "I didn't . . ."
>
> *Gueroult*: "Did you evolve a system . . .?"
>
> *Tolkien*: "No. I didn't . . ."[123]

Each dismissal signifies a dichotomy in Tolkien's imagination. Gueroult was attempting to translate meaning about *LOTR* based on certain assumptions and interpretations about Tolkien's creativity, but Tolkien confidently answered with a different rationale.

118. Dawson, "History," 269.

119. Lewis, *Experiment*, 137.

120. Murray, "Tribute," 174.

121. Tolkien, Interview with Gueroult; *Letters*, 239.

122. These are given in brief to illustrate the common way readers tried to get at the "facts" about Tolkien's world and the "psyche" behind his writing.

123. Tolkien, Interview with Gueroult.

After *LOTR*'s publication, Tolkien repeatedly rejected eisegesis by readership.[124] When asked if the five wizards represent the human senses or if Orcs represented communists, Tolkien found this preposterous.[125] He unreservedly rejected that the former dwarf habitation in *LOTR* (Moria) has to do with the patriarch Abraham (in Moriah), stating "my mind does not work that way."[126] He also repeatedly declined providing biographical information, insisting it had nothing to do with how *LOTR* should be read, nor with how it was written.[127] Psychoanalysis diminishes Tolkien's mytho-*logos*. When personal experience is assumed or misinterpreted, the reader can be inhibited from fully experiencing the poetic power of *LOTR* as-is.[128] This helps clarify one of Tolkien's most notorious statements:

> [*LOTR*] is of course a fundamentally religious and Catholic work; unconsciously so at first, but consciously in the revision. That is why I have not put in, or have cut out, practically all references to anything like "religion," to cults or practices, in the imaginary world. For the religious element is absorbed into the story and the symbolism.[129]

Tolkien admitted the Catholicity of *LOTR* because it lay at the core of his being. Others have verified this by reading *LOTR* through this lens.[130] But this merely affirms Tolkien's belief that all sub-creators have "only . . . our humanity to work with. It's the only clay we've got."[131] The one "building a story has to build it out of some of the things he himself knows. . . . That would be the material out of which he constructs."[132] One writes from "where [his] imagination comes from,"[133] Tolkien be-

124. Not always. He often had positive responses to insightful readers.

125. *Letters*, 262.

126. *Letters*, 383.

127. *Letters*, 257, 288, 414. Resnick, "Interview," 38. "I do not . . . belong *inside* my invented history," Tolkien asserted, "and do not wish to!" (*Letters*, 398).

128. See *Letters*, 288, 414.

129. *Letters*, 172.

130. Such as Robert Murray, the priest to whom Tolkien wrote the Catholic acknowledgement above, which was in a letter later published in *Letters*, 171–73. Other Catholic interpretations of Tolkien and his work are examined in Bernthal, *Sacramental Vision*; Birzer, *JRRT's Sanctifying*; Pearce, *Man and Myth*; Caldecott, *Power*; Kreeft, *Philosophy*; Kerry, *Ring*.

131. Tolkien, Interview with Gueroult.

132. Tolkien, Interview with Gueroult.

133. Resnick, "Interview," 41. He was specifically referring here to the geography of northwestern Europe.

lieved, where "you must consult your roots"[134] and where "inevitably one's own taste, ideas, and beliefs get taken up."[135] The point is not to diminish Catholic influence. It is evident. Naturally "in a story written by a religious man," one will find "a plain indication that religion is not absent but subsumed."[136] Instead, I want to draw attention to the broader context of the remark, which is dichotomous to exact Catholicism. The lower *c* catholicity is more accurate. Tolkien's claim about being entirely historically minded allows us to see how this dichotomy consists of the elvish religiousness in Middle-earth, while also negating presumptions that *LOTR* represents our Primary World. It is not an attempt to allegorize Christianity or anything else.

By stating "consciously in the revision," Tolkien recognized explicit references to his faith were *un*consciously evident in drafts of *LOTR*. These were purposefully removed because Tolkien thought Primary World religiousness should not be explicit in mythmaking after the spread of Christianity.[137] The Arthurian legends fail precisely because of their blatant Christian allusions.[138] Stories should follow the logic fulfilled through writing with no distractions coming from an authorial voice apart from the text.[139] This bothered Tolkien so much that he intentionally removed Christian references in *LOTR* prior to publication.[140] Tolkien argued against allegorical interpretations of *LOTR* because it limits applicability from two different directions.

134. *Letters*, 212.

135. *Letters*, 267.

136. "Essay," 142.

137. Pagan mythologies differ since they incorporate a cosmic outlook prior to Christian influence (*Letters*, 144).

138. *Letters*, 144.

139. They should follow the "logic of the story" (*Letters*, 252, 330), "plot" (252), and "tale" (325).

140. He realized it appeared too Catholic. William Dowie made a similar observation in "Gospel," 284–85. Notably, for readers who see *lembas*—elvish food in *LOTR*—as compared to the Eucharist, in Middle-earth it is a food only the High Elves were allowed to eat, unless there were others who might desperately have need for it. It was originally made by one of the gods from corn first grown in the paradisiacal West and thereafter by elven-women (see "Of Lembas," 403–5). Thus, it does not signify the body and blood of Christ. Meanwhile, in early drafts to Tolkien's "Names," an accompaniment meant for those who would translate *LOTR* into different languages, Tolkien wanted the word *Yule* in *LOTR*'s Appendix D to be translated into a word that had "no recognizable Christian reference" (Hammond and Scull, *"LOTR" Companion*, 726). Notably, before the Christianization of England, "'Yule' [was] celebrated as the winter solstice but [was] given no religious significance" (Rutledge, *Battle*, 7).

First, from the writer, if the logic is fulfilled connaturally through poetic knowledge, *logos* drives *poesis* to produce *poiema*. When discussing Faërie and *LOTR*, Tolkien considered allegory a "narrative strategy"[141] the writer intends to represent, communicate, or prove a point.[142] "I dislike real allegory in which the application is the author's own and is meant to dominate you," Tolkien said.[143] This inhibits not only free creativity through writing, but also its receptivity. Meanwhile, reading allegory into *LOTR* diminishes the impact of the whole because it fails to allow myth to freely impact the reader naturally.

Second, applicability is hindered by allegory when the reader interprets *LOTR as* allegory. Consider the figurative ways Tolkien speculated *LOTR* might potentially meet spiritual needs through the metaphors of hunger and thirst. When he spoke of allegory regarding fairy-stories and Middle-earth, he used language illustrating opposite reactions. He readily admitted, "I dislike allegory whenever I smell it,"[144] that it gave him "an instinctive distaste."[145] Such expressions emphasize nausea, not nourishment. They make sense of why Tolkien expressed his "dislike [for] allegory in all its manifestations," so much as to have "[grown] wary . . . to detect its presence."[146] Analogy emphasizes likeness through difference, thus making the poetic meaning operative from a separate plane. Tolkien's clarification about applicability in the second edition's Foreword was to dissuade readers from wondering whether *LOTR* allegorically represented the evils of World War II or symbolized his personal life. He refuted this by resourcing Middle-earth's historical context, which he explicated from *LOTR* itself.[147] Here is an example of Tolkien illustrating applicability by encouraging his son Christopher while drawing from Middle-earth:

> We are attempting to conquer Sauron with the Ring. And we shall (it seems) succeed. But the penalty is . . . to breed new Saurons, and slowly turn Men and Elves into Orcs. Not that in real life things are as clear cut as in a story, and we started out with a great many Orcs on our side. . . . Well, there you are: a hobbit

141. Abrams, *Glossary*, 6.

142. Abrams, *Glossary*, 5.

143. Tolkien in Scull and Hammond, *JRRT Companion*, 945.

144. Tolkien, Interview with Gueroult.

145. "Genesis," 86.

146. *LOTR*, xvii.

147. See *LOTR*, xvi–ii.

> amongst the Uruk[-]hai. Keep up your hobbitry in heart, and think that all *stories* feel like that when you are *in* them. You are inside a very great story![148]

Although it may seem like Tolkien made allegorical comparisons, he really did not. An analogical breakdown of the meaning of Tolkien's statement follows.

Similarities:

Tolkien's World		*Reality*
Sauron with the Ring	akin to	Hitler with a destructive weapon
New Saurons	akin to	Leaders seeking power and domination
Men and Elves	akin to	Children of God
Orcs/Uruk-hai	akin to	Corrupted beings devoted to evil

Differences:

Reality		*Tolkien's World*
Hitler and destruction	are not	Incarnate demon with a weapon of sorcery
Power-hungry earthly leaders	are not	Dark powers trying to rule Middle-earth
Image-bearers of God	are not	Different races of the Children of Eru[149]
Wicked people	are not	Counterfeit beings deformed by evil gods

Analogical reading discerns the likenesses and differences, and this example shows the dichotomy. Tolkien's world and reality are wholly different, not only because *LOTR* is literary but because neither plane can be accurately translated into the contexts of the other. Yet the similarities vividly enhance reality through an imaginative world issuing its own meaning. Because of what Christopher knew about Middle-earth and because of what readers know of *LOTR*, their own envisioning of reality may be enlarged by it. Had Tolkien made the same statement at another point in history, the analogies drawn would be different. The narrative remains the same for new meaning to be made in those awakened by *LOTR*'s mytho-*logos* whenever it is encountered.

148. *Letters*, 78. The second omission in the text is the editor's.

149. Eru is the God of Tolkien's mythology.

To return to Tolkien's statement to Gueroult about the trees: in reality trees did hold a symbolic meaning for Tolkien, but not in the way Gueroult speculated. From his historically-minded perspective, Tolkien saw the trees in question as they belonged to the mythological history and the religious element absorbed into the story and symbolism of Middle-earth, not Catholicism, paganism, or another religion. Readers should imagine Tolkien's world as its own plane, not make it to mean something else. A helpful way of translating the religious dynamic of *LOTR* is as "a mode of thought" as opposed to allegory, "a mode of expression"[150] attempting to make a point through masked imagery. Tolkien's world came from "transforming into *another* form and symbol"[151] and thus is analogous according to a mode of thought tied to its own plane through an "imagination in search of its own integrity."[152] For Tolkien, "literary credibility" was "pure" when detached from allegorical intent and interpretation, as all fairy-stories should be.[153] All symbols within the imaginary world of *LOTR* are intended referents to the history of Middle-earth alone, so that any Secondary Belief remains secondary. In the next chapter, we will investigate the intricate nature of how Tolkien's sub-creativity utilized language and imagination to affect his readers by exercising their own imaginative power.

150. Lewis, *Allegory*, 48.

151. *Letters*, 85 (emphasis mine).

152. Brewer, "*LOTR*," 254.

153. "Papers," 164.

Chapter 4

Sub-Creation and Meaning

Introduction

TOLKIEN THOUGHT FAIRY-STORIES "OPEN a door on Other Time, and if we pass through, though only for a moment, we stand outside our own time, outside Time itself, maybe."[1] *Door* reinforces the threshold metaphor through which *poiema* may bring new understanding. But instead of the threshold separating two rooms side-by-side, Tolkien posited two worlds: the reality we pass through and Other Time. He also left open the possibility that there is some "mythical or total (unanalysable) effect"[2] that not only allows for this threshold between worlds, but also a way to experience the transcendence of God from *outside Time itself.* He did not say it actually does, just *maybe*, which is contingent on the time and setting of the fairy-story itself, for an "effect produced *now* by these old things in the stories as they are."[3] *Old* references the literature ingredients from "the history of story-making"[4] simmering in the "Pot

1. OFS, 48.
2. OFS, 48.
3. OFS, 48.
4. OFS, 46.

of Soup, the Cauldron of Story."[5] Intentionally added ingredients make each story unique and should be wholly appreciated according to the maker's design as-is.[6] In this chapter, we explore the ways Tolkien's sub-creativity enhanced the "soup" of *LOTR* so that it might be a nourishing experience for those who consume it.

Intentional, Meaningful Narrative

Tolkien insisted poetics are most affective when one reads and appreciates them simply as stories without scrutinizing them as some kind of rare collector's item,[7] which reemphasizes how *poiema* is most impactful: when appreciated alive at once and in all its parts. A tale's patterning is critical to this, especially if it models its own mytho-*logos* after a particular kind of cosmo-*logos*.

Chapter 2 discussed the patterns Tolkien observed in the cosmos, how he intuited and perceived what was already "there." Yet, "there is a part of man which is not 'Nature,' and which therefore is not obliged to study it, and is, in fact, wholly unsatisfied by it."[8] Seeing nature only through a scientific lens is a "cheated" form, "some kind of new religion" devoted to reason alone to the detriment of imagination.[9] Science and nature only tell parts of the story of history and its setting. Sub-creation aspires to satisfy another part of humanity:

> The fine arts, but above all sacred art, . . . "are directed toward expressing in some way the infinite beauty of God in works made by human hands. Their dedication to the increase of God's praise and of his glory is more complete, the more exclusively they are devoted to turning men's minds devoutly toward God."[10]

This resonates with the possibility of God transcending poetics made by humanity, in addition to how the awakening of the imagination can turn human minds to God through the impact of fairy-stories.

Tolkien's Soup of Story and Tree of Tales metaphors account for the myriad patterned efforts of sub-creators' past. But according to Tolkien,

5. OFS, 44.
6. OFS, 40.
7. OFS, 49.
8. OFS, 81ND.
9. OFS, 81ND.
10. Catholic Church, *Catechism*, 601.

each story should be appreciated independently as it is. Kreeft affirmed, "Art is very different from science in that it creates worlds; it creates meaning and beauty and forms and structures and natures, while science discovers them. In science, the world is the standard for our ideas about it. . . . In art . . . the artist's ideas are the standard for the world he creates."[11] In nature, the ideas behind created reality resemble Plato's theory of forms, of which the visible are signs of uncreated reality.[12] Christianity originates these ideas in God as their source, the one who created them out of nothing to signify divine meaning. As they are, one can see God's *logos*-centric *poesis* is still happening.

Human narratives utilize *logos* in order to convey reasonable truth through their own *poesis*. Tolkien's aim was the "elucidation of truth, and the encouragement of good morals in this world, by the ancient device of exemplifying them in unfamiliar embodiments."[13] From personal experience sub-creators make use of what is observed to form into new "secondary patterns."[14] Meaning derived through narrative patterning communicates a new unfamiliar embodiment originated by the poet. When shaping mytho-*logos* according to patterns contextual to an otherworld, the sub-creation produces new history that does not copy the Primary World's.[15] This highlights the significance of right translation because mistranslation leads to misinterpretation of meaning on two fronts.

First, Tolkien hoped *LOTR* would rightly be translated because of how he intentionally crafted it to communicate meaning closely associated with his personal aesthetic.[16] When *LOTR* began being translated into other languages, he produced a guide for translators to follow. First they should note his "On Translation" points in Appendix F,[17] but then

11. Kreeft, *Philosophy*, 43.

12. Kreeft, *Philosophy*, 42.

13. *Letters*, 194.

14. *Letters*, 298.

15. See Garth, *Tolkien*, 62.

16. Allan Turner explains the difficulties in interpreting *LOTR* as Tolkien desired in "Theoretical Model," 1–30. Challenges facing the translator are the historical vantage point from which s/he translates, the inability to know the meaning of the author exactly, duplicating the effects of *LOTR* as a "pseudotranslation" as Tolkien did, and considerations of posthumously published "History of Middle-earth" material, among others. This may have been why the Tolkien Estate would not allow Tolkien's "Names" to be republished in the second edition of Lobdell's, *Tolkien Compass*. My point here is to emphasize the extent to which he desired his personal aesthetic to be upheld, not that this was entirely possible.

17. *LOTR*, 1107–12.

translate *LOTR* from English "*according to their meaning* (as closely as possible)" because Tolkien had already "translated" *LOTR* into English via meanings of his own personal language-making.[18] He also created new names "which are not 'meaningless'"[19] but were grounded in the "essential *Englishness*" he hoped would be preserved.[20] So the narrative readers encounter in English lies embedded not only in its own feigned world history, but also its "feigned linguistic history."[21]

The second front returns us to Tolkien's problem with allegory. When Rayner Unwin[22] suggested that *LOTR* was an allegorical "struggle between darkness and light," Tolkien objected.[23] To him, it was "just a particular phase of history, one example of its pattern,"[24] but one with a unique context unto itself in its own secondary plane. The Primary World continues spatiotemporally according to multiple patterns. The struggle between good and evil is only one of them. Each world contains its own particular details that make it different from another. Recall that *LOTR* is merely a "brief episode." *Episode* is another way of saying *phase*, a narrative belonging to the larger backdrop of history itself. When Frodo mentioned "a star shines on the hour of our meeting" in elvish, Tolkien indicated he created a situation for this to be said and that this "phase" had "long antedated the book." There are three ways to interpret this: (1) the elvish language Frodo uttered belongs to an historical period when its use was common; (2) the meaning of Frodo's response about the star is an ontological encounter in a cosmology where sub-creation and image-bearers participate in a greater reality, acknowledging there is more to time and space than the present;[25]

18. "Names," 155.

19. "Names," 156.

20. Scull and Hammond, *JRRT Companion*, 647.

21. "Names," 156.

22. Rayner was the son of Tolkien's publisher, Stanley.

23. Carpenter's note in *Letters*, 119–20.

24. *Letters*, 121.

25. This is neither an over-statement nor reading into what Frodo said. His statement is not a figure of speech but a phrase stated to High Elves in their own language. The fact that it has been translated into English signifies that the fullness of its meaning is not fully known. Its translation allows the reader to understand something nearer to its true meaning rather than not at all. In addition, its utterance came at a critical juncture in the story. In the medieval cosmos an "encounter" with High Elves "is not accidental" (Lewis, *Discarded*, 130). Thus, in *LOTR* it signifies some mysterious purpose in a greater reality at a time when eucatastrophe is desperately needed (for context, see *LOTR*, 73–83).

and (3) the meaning established in the past transcends into the present. Each reading allows history to be experienced presently in a new way but not as the actual events themselves, which raises a noteworthy point about history and its influence on the imagination.

Tolkien asserted that once an historical event happens it "[becomes] an intellectual, and it live[s] on . . . in memory. It live[s] on only in time, but not present time."[26] Past events remain permanent unchanged historical fixtures that "never had an existence unless . . . it still has that same existence" as it happened in the past.[27] There actually is a

> "true story," the real Past. If you really had a look back at the Past as it was, then everything would be there to see, if you had eyes for it, or time to observe it in. And the most difficult thing to see would be, as it always is "at present," the pattern, the significance, yes, the moral of it all.[28]

The challenge this raises for us is that we can only ever experience real history in our imaginations. Narrative episodes give us windows through which to see, and although they never give us the big picture, each glimpse makes a bigger picture perceptible.

Each narrative has its own details and patterning, and though these may be imitated in various ways, they are never repeated in time and space exactly the same way. In *Hobbit* and *LOTR*, Tolkien was looking back through the elf-patterned mythological history, a "permanent element" of "imaginative energy throughout his life."[29] Through narration and the characters' eyes, readers observe phases of this history when Bilbo is in the dragon's lair and Frodo meets Gildor and the elves. Through Frodo in particular, there is a weight of historical reality that resounds presently as readers experience the viability of its authenticity. *LOTR* reinforces this cohesive historicity as the narrative unfolds. Therefore, what Rayner assumed as allegorical was according to his own lens of reality. Tolkien refuted this from his vantage point through the mytho-*logos* of Middle-earth. Tolkien continued to encounter interpretations similar to this in part because people read Primary World experience into *LOTR*, but also because *LOTR* compels literary belief so powerfully that some may not

26. Tolkien, Interview with Gueroult. Tolkien had a specific historical event in Middle-earth in mind when he said this, but it aligns and applies here.

27. Tolkien, Interview with Gueroult. The ellipsis captures Tolkien's pause in the conversation.

28. "Papers," 230.

29. C. Tolkien, "*Silmarillion* by JRRT," 5.

imagine it distinctly from the real world. These are the effects of being transported into Other Time, which we will now explore.

Transport to Secondary Belief

Diana Wynne Jones discussed how *LOTR* feels like a movement in a symphonic composition.[30] As the hobbits discover their cosmos, it expands the reader's perception of time and space within the story.[31] Present moments are "mere instants" between ancient history and uncertain future.[32] As readers experience the narrative's events, we see "that ordinary people can get forced to make history" because "history [forces] itself" upon them indiscriminately.[33] We might describe everyday life experience similarly: Sometimes life feels like being caught up in something larger, but time forces itself upon us, ready or not. Consequently, moment-to-moment experience may suffocate and disorient us beneath the gravity of real time, making us feel very small and insignificant in the world. *LOTR* draws readers up and out of Primary World intensities and insecurities into an imaginative space set in Other Time

> intended to have literary effect, and not [be] real history. That the device adopted, that of giving its setting an historical air or feeling, and (an illusion of?) three dimensions, is successful, seems shown by the fact that several correspondents have treated it in the same way—according to their different points of interest or knowledge: i.e., as if it were a report of "real" times and places.[34]

Tolkien clarified these intended effects to someone who had interpreted *LOTR* as Christian theology rather than analogically, causing the correspondent to raise issues about heresy.[35] But Tolkien saw sub-creation as a celebration of and tribute to God's potential variety. "I wanted people simply to get inside the story and take it, *in a sense*, of actual history," Tolkien insisted.[36] This included its own sense of theol-

30. Jones, "Shape," 87–107.

31. Jones, "Shape," 92–93.

32. Jones, "Shape," 95.

33. Jones, "Shape," 105–6.

34. *Letters*, 188.

35. *Letters*, 188. See Carpenter's preview of the letter's context (187–88). Tolkien apparently never mailed this response (196).

36. Tolkien, Interview with Gueroult (emphasis mine, but Tolkien emphasizes the entire phrase in the interview).

ogy. Yet this individual had taken the feigned account and read it as if it were to be given Primary Belief.[37]

With *LOTR* in hand, readers experience a *different* religious sensibility.[38] If there is applicability, something of its meaning is validated as true. Since the imagination is an organ of meaning capable of comprehending concrete truths about reality, and if poetic meaning is the operative link between imagination and sub-creation, there must be a way to explain how such meaning arrives. Therefore, a mode for traveling into Other Time should be identified.

Chapter 3 ended by mentioning Tolkien's desire for pure literary credibility. Therefore, it is critical that narratives communicate believability without deterring from the plausibility of the mytho-*logos*. The manner in which narrative transmits meaning through its action is integral to compelling literary belief through what is happening within the story, and this is contingent upon the inner consistency of the otherworld. Tellers of fairy-stories "make their own worlds, with their own laws."[39] Because Middle-earth maintains its own inner consistency, its historical plane differs from both reality and other stories, though there will be various notable analogies. Since Tolkien aimed to make *LOTR* an exciting story, this aligns with his description of the feel of Other Time as a sensation akin to pleasurable activities in which time seems to pass quickly. The theater, books we cannot put down, and enjoying meaningful companionship are among them, the latter of which, Tolkien claimed,

37. *Letters*, 188.This echoes Tolkien's point in chapter 2: His mythological history was not meant to be a new religion or vision. Markus Altena Davidsen researched groups who have adopted personal religious practices based on "Tolkien spirituality" via his mythological history and the religious impetus derived through his creativity ("Spiritual Milieu," 185–204). They make *LOTR* a "frame narrative" of actual history (188). Davidsen observed there was an initial "wave" of Tolkien spirituality following *LOTR*'s second edition in 1965, and another after the Peter Jackson films, which Davidsen designates into three "Tolkien religionist" groups: "Middle-earth Pagans, Middle-earth Christians and Legendarium Reconstructionists [who] combine Tolkien material with other alternative religious beliefs and practices, each in a different way" (190–200). Near the turn of the century, young adults in Russia established an "occultist ideology" inspired by Tolkien in place of "the communism of their youth" (Birzer, "Christian Gifts").

38. R. J. Reilly described it as "romantically religious" because "both heartening and frightening—heartening because it offers solace for the world's ills of evil and death, frightening because in order to offer this solace it must stress the existence of these ills, and the inevitability of them" (*Romantic Religion*, 194).

39. "Papers," 169.

seemed best experienced in taverns, "for nowhere does time 'fly' so fast compared with daily experience" like it does while enjoying drinks and conversation with those you find most endearing.[40] Participation in such activities links personal being to a belief that such meaningful experiences make it seem as if real-time is somehow altered or "other." Tolkien translated this into mythical experience by using a literary vehicle of transport into Other Time, but not before rejecting two specifically improper literary devices: time machines and dreams.

Time machines are "preposterous and incredible" in stories.[41] "They pretend to be probable" but really are not because people never actually use such machines to move to other places in history or future.[42] Time- and space-travel machines in stories do not parallel how readers experience reality; therefore, such vehicles kill "literary credibility."[43] "Real fairy-stories don't pretend to produce impossible mechanical effects by

40. "Essay," 114.

41. OFS, 34.

42. "Papers," 164. In the mid-1940s, still years from completing *LOTR*, Tolkien scribed the "The Notion Club Papers" (*Sauron*, 145–327). Their genesis was an agreement Tolkien had with C. S. Lewis. Tolkien would write a time-travel story and Lewis a space-travel story (*Letters*, 105, 118; C. Tolkien, Introduction to "Papers," 145). "Papers" present a setting similar to the Inklings meetings started by Tolkien and Lewis who, along with other regular attendees, met weekly to read, criticize literary writings (including their own), and debate. They record the minutes of fictional meetings like these. While some biographical information and personal attributes are evident in the characters, Christopher Tolkien's introductory comments affirm what a read-through of "Papers" clarifies: The characters are not exact caricatures of Inklings members (C. Tolkien, Introduction to "Papers," 150–52). Rather, the writings evidence Tolkien's knack for borrowing from life experience and making new meaning through an original format.

Part of Tolkien's and Lewis's travel-story discussion involved the idea of "true dreams," and in Lewis's story one of the characters had the "tendency to dream real things" (C. Tolkien, Introduction to "Papers," 153n1). Whereas Lewis completed his space-travel trilogy by 1945, Tolkien never finished his story. "Papers" were written somewhere between 1944 and 1946, a time when he was still writing *LOTR* and had not yet published the OFS essay that would appear in *Essays Presented to Charles Williams* in 1947.

The main theme of "Papers" explores time-travel through dreams and memories because of language, but they serve a different purpose here. Although the format is conversational narrative, the movement of the discussion articulates Tolkien's argument for literary credibility and Secondary Belief in ways discussed thus far. After much deliberation amongst the characters about time-traveling through dream and memory, the presence of an ancient "Elvish Drama" (193) or Faërian Drama set in Other Time is brought into present-day consciousness for Notion Club members to experience imaginatively for themselves.

43. "Papers," 163–76; C. Tolkien, Introduction to "Papers," 146.

bogus machines."[44] Tolkien was concerned that literary credibility should be encountered as "waking fiction" through a pre-existent, not-yet experienced "external" spatiotemporal place "that is not yet in the mind"[45] and impacts a person's "waking life" (while a person is awake).[46]

Chapter 3 noted how Tolkien apprehended *Beowulf* as a sub-created extra-mental existence beyond and independent of the mind. Such apprehension anticipates meaning from something external to the self. The writer presents this "literary parallel" where "literary invention" can "*see* two places at once."[47] After the "sharper eye" of the sub-creator makes *poiema*, the opportunity for others to imagine this becomes possible; not exactly as the writer does, but in some such way through the text. Time machines present difficulties in maintaining an actual literary parallel. Life is narrative. A parallel journey is required, and a journey understood and experienced as an actual or figurative trip through time involves historical experience without gaps in time. Time-travel like this is inimical to literary credibility because inconceivable in reality; so are dreams. The reason why is discoverable when learning about the type of fairy-story *LOTR* is.

When readers arrive at the threshold of Middle-earth in *LOTR*, they are confronted with a fantastic otherworld of "arresting strangeness" through mytho-*logos*.[48] Something both other and strange implies that its meaning is derived in a way unfamiliar to those participating in it and that it does not originate with the reader.[49] Since the imagination is a shared aspect of human existence, there is some applicability from stories to life, but since it is not identically shared, applicability will not be exactly the same. Rather, *LOTR* analogically allows an "accommodating [of] applicability that can be sustained by the text."[50] *Poiema* evidences what one imagination shares with others, and Tolkien's produced *fantasy*.

Chapter 2 indicated that fantasy can be understood as synonymous with imagination. In reality, people are always using their imaginations,

44. "Papers," 170.

45. "Papers," 175. The context of what is being explained in "Papers" is speculative, but Tolkien is describing from his own experience.

46. "Papers," 184–86, 198, 238; C. Tolkien, Introduction to "Papers," 286n38. Tolkien also used "waking time" (185) and "waking hours" (201) synonymously.

47. "Papers," 176.

48. OFS, 60.

49. Echoing "unfamiliar embodiments" above.

50. Bernthal, *Sacramental Vision*, 30.

forming mental images of things not actually present in physical form; not absentmindedly, but without actually stopping to think and ponder the minutiae of everything. Human thoughts and imagination are active in waking time-serial life where ontological encounters happen.[51] But their use is restricted in the present to past memories or future envisioning, which is how people participate in daily life on the threshold of present time.

Literature, on the other hand, is static and always encountered presently while reading the text. When Tolkien apprehended *Beowulf* extra-mentally, he was immediately observing and encountering an external world of fantasy.[52] Tolkien's notion of dreams helps, (1) clarify the simultaneity of analogical two-world participation, even though, (2) he rejected them as feasible vehicles as stories.[53]

Fantasy is artful, and it is the sub-creator's role to take readers there imaginatively.[54] While dreams may be used within fantasy, Tolkien disagreed that dreams should be the mode of transport to explain how we arrive in Other Time and the strangeness of the marvels encountered there.[55] Although one can argue that dreaming is experiencing two worlds simultaneously, dreaming does not make anything consciously or intentionally intellectual. Tolkien confirmed a relation between dreams and fantasy because each result in forming mental images of things not actually physically present, but other problems with dreams-as-vehicles are as follows. Like time machines, a writer may use them "to explain the apparent occurrence of its marvels," but these are lazy quick-fix solutions for explaining the strangeness of Other Time that base it on "illusion."[56] Dreams do not explain the actual journey and, therefore, do not move the reader from here-to-there in the way a credible literary narrative requires. While experiencing a dream, the sleeping person is not conscious of Primary Reality as s/he would otherwise be in waking life: "If a waking

51. How Tolkien realized the truth of eucatastrophe's meaning to reality (see *Letters*, 101).

52. Shippey, "Feeling," 14.

53. Tolkien's argument was not against dream stories such as *Alice in Wonderland* where "the 'dream' element" is integral and "inherent in the action and transitions" of the story's operations (OFS, 79nA). He was speaking of fantasy as Faërie, which *Alice in Wonderland* is not (36).

54. OFS, 60.

55. OFS, 35, 60n.

56. OFS, 35.

writer tells you that his tale is only a thing imagined in his sleep, he cheats deliberately the primal desire."[57]

Tolkien aspired to awaken through sub-creation "the realization, independent of the conceiving mind, of imagined wonder."[58] Restoring the analogical relation between sub-creation and Primary Reality concerns awakening in consciousness, which is not possible for unconscious sleepers. Consciousness is required to comprehend ontological encounters, which amount to nothing if they were only dreamed. Dreams nevertheless provide a helpful metaphor for participating in two worlds simultaneously.

In one sense, when minds "move," it is as if thoughts jump from one to another.[59] Therefore, venturing into Other Time bears an association with traveling.[60] But dreams are insufficient because of the sleeper's physical state of being. Since sleeping is unconsciousness, dreams just happen. Plus, critics often associate fantasy with dreams as well as with "mental disorders, . . . delusion and hallucination," which Tolkien thought was both foolishly and unkindly erroneous.[61] If fantasy is imagination, it is, in fact, a logical activity.[62] Whether sub-creatively or imagining things not physically present, people do it all the time, every day.

Because of the literary credibility fairy-stories require, "arriving" in Other Time ought to align more with how we experience life. In reality, dreams require no creativity and, therefore, no art.[63] But dreams capture a sense of how the imagination freely moves (figuratively "jumps") effortlessly into Other Time where time seems to "fly." Whatever marvels there are upon arrival should naturally cohere with its inner consistency. The best way of integrating marvels natural to a Secondary World without dislocation from daily life is narrative.[64]

Life is ongoing activity from birth to now. People are always moving through time in space, and even though they may not be physically traveling from Point A to B, time is the medium for growth—physical, spiritual,

57. OFS, 35.

58. OFS, 35.

59. "Papers," 178.

60. "Papers," 178–79.

61. OFS, 60. Because people regularly experience dreams in life while maintaining their sanity.

62. OFS, 60n.

63. OFS, 60.

64. "Essay," 114.

and otherwise. Narrative functions as an historical medium through which meaning is derived and presents the setting for participation in reality and poetics analogically. MacIntyre stated, "The notion of a history is as fundamental a notion as the notion of an action. Each requires the other."[65] Thus, history and action are inseparable from our advancement through life. What qualifies as fundamental to the "characterization of human actions" is that "narrative history"[66] should be read serially and contextually because each determines the intelligibility of each course of action.[67] This echoes how Tolkien perceived humanity passing through history. It is also the way readers experience *poiema*, which is based on the meaningful language that engages them.

Affective Philology[68]

Tolkien used the aesthetic impact of philology to bridge his creativity to readers in a way that could affect them personally because of an *ontological semantic unity*[69] embedded analogically in the cosmos. Where I noted Tolkien believed *he* had congenital linguistic predilections, he actually thought all people have their "own personal linguistic potential."[70] Everyone has the "ready-made clothes" of a "cradle-tongue," a birth-given propensity for making and expressing meaning uniquely personal.[71] This differs from the language that ultimately becomes the dominant means of expression and communication of the cultures in which people are born.[72] The Fall of humanity created an ontological rift between creature and Creator, hindering the unity humanity shared with each other in articulating pure meaning in the presence of God.[73] The "curse"[74] placed on humanity

65. MacIntyre, *After Virtue*, 214.

66. MacIntyre, *After Virtue*, 208.

67. MacIntyre, *After Virtue*, 209.

68. To study Tolkien as a philologist and the technicalities that come with this is beyond the scope of the book. My concern is with the lasting effects *LOTR*'s meaning can have on readers. Technical aspects of Tolkien and philology are discussed in Shippey, *Road*; *JRRT:Author*; Gilliver et al., *Ring of Words*.

69. See p. 25n66.

70. Tolkien, "Welsh," 190.

71. "Welsh," 190; "Vice," 220n6; Tolkien, Interview with Gueroult.

72. "Welsh," 190; "Papers," 201.

73. Zaleski and Zaleski, *Fellowship*, 120.

74. *Letters*, 65.

at the Tower of Babel initiated further disunity between humans as language was scrambled from one into many; thus were common meanings and understandings between peoples frustrated.[75] For *LOTR* to bridge the ontological divide, Tolkien would need to speak meaningfully to the congenital sensibilities of readers on a level *deeper* than words.

Long before Tolkien wrote *LOTR*, he learned through "thought and experience" that language, myth, and history "were not divergent interests—opposite poles of science and romance—but integrally related."[76] Philology can be like searching for "the key to 'spiritual life.'"[77] Although Tolkien knew or had some working knowledge of ten to fifteen languages other than English (Old, Middle, and contemporary),[78] he invented his own. Two in particular lay at the foundations of his elf-centered sub-creativity.[79] They were the invented "linguistic aesthetic"[80] that breathed the life of story into his mythological history. "It was an inevitable, though conditionable, evolvement of the birth-given. It has been always with me: the sensibility to linguistic pattern which affects me emotionally like colour or music," he said.[81] Seeing colors and hearing music trigger affective, moving sensibilities: an outside source prompting an inner response. Tolkien's response to language coincides with how he believed meaning could be formative.

When speaking of his desire to *make* Tolkien associated this with an imprisonment to his own tastes, burden, and message, and claimed the "need [for] *food* of particular kinds."[82] Language provided such sustenance. Tolkien found words not only visually stimulating[83] but audibly striking.[84] Just as gratifying was the "poetic context" of a word, where it

75. See "Welsh," 194; Zaleski and Zaleski, *Fellowship*, 120.

76. *Letters*, 144.

77. Shippey, *Road*, 13–19.

78. Scull and Hammond discuss more than twenty languages Tolkien utilized throughout his lifetime, some expertly, others not. He probably knew between ten to fifteen well (*JRRT Companion*, 461–75).

79. *Quenya* and *Sindarin*, both elvish languages (*Letters*, 176, 380–81).

80. *Letters*, 220, 231.

81. *Letters*, 212. Edmund Weiner examined this as Tolkien's "phonaesthetic" in-depth in "Tolkien Aesthetics."

82. *Letters*, 126.

83. Even as a child, Tolkien "was *excited* by the Welsh names on coal-trucks, by the 'surface glitter' of Greek, by the strange forms of . . . Gothic words" (Carpenter, *JRRT: Biography*, 136).

84. "*Plenilune* and *argent* . . . are beautiful words *before* they are understood—I wish

was "clothed" in its own unique "phonetic incarnation" through which its aesthetic meaning was issued.[85]

Incarnation happens when a word, written or uttered, comes into existence to signify meaning of its own, from thought into the world. "Without symbols you have no languages; . . . language begins only with incarnation and not before it."[86] Whatever the context, these are the relational components: "sound: sense; symbol: meaning."[87] The maker articulates sound into sense, whose symbol exudes new meaning. When applied to literary works, the scope of narrative incarnation becomes more than words in a meaningful context. Otherwise, "spoken forms would simply be mere audible forms."[88] *Poesis* makes use of the corpus of language ingredients for the making of incarnate *worlds* in their own living, poetic contexts. Just as when Frodo spoke elvish to Gildor, each "linguistic situation in [*LOTR*] would receive meaning and significance according to . . . situation, and to the nature of the story."[89] This also applied to Tolkien's writing of *LOTR* in deriving meaningful characters,[90] circumstantial events,[91] and poetic expressions uttered by characters.[92] Applicability becomes suitable for readers when stories have "relevance to the 'human situation'" that "*exemplify* general principles" innate to humanity, which make their keenest impact when relayed and identified through historical situations.[93]

Tolkien wanted to evoke in readers something akin to what he experienced through his favorite poems. In Tolkien's translation of *Beowulf*, Christopher Tolkien pointed to his father's "vivid personal evocation of a long-vanished world—as it was perceived by the author" to illuminate

---

I could have the pleasure of meeting them for the first time again!—and how is one to know them till one does meet them? And surely the first meeting should be in a living context, and not in a dictionary, like dried flowers in a hortus siccus!" (*Letters*, 310).

85. *Letters*, 309–11. In this letter, Tolkien addresses this in detail, using examples of words from *Bombadil*, 27, 36.

86. "Papers," 203.

87. "Papers," 225.

88. *Letters*, 383.

89. *Letters*, 383.

90. As with the historical character Eärendil (*Letters*, 385).

91. As when Frodo was saved by grace on Mount Doom (*Letters*, 233–35, 252–53, 325–27).

92. *Letters*, 396.

93. *Letters*, 233–35.

both the "meaning and intention of that poet."[94] Tolkien was compelled both to honor his most admired works and to bring them to life again, and proper translation was key. "A translator must first try to discover as precisely as he can what his original means, and may be led by ever closer attention to understand it better for [the art's] own sake."[95] The best translation is "valuable, not so much for the version it produces, as for the understanding of the original which it *awakes*."[96] This was not merely personal, but something to be shared[97] because finding keys to spiritual life might awaken more lives than the philologist's.

LOTR is based on Tolkien's personal linguistic aesthetic, but readers experience this aesthetic through narrative mytho-*logos* written in English, not elvish.[98] Earlier in life, Tolkien realized that language must be used to engender meaning and a medium through which it can develop. Over time he learned how "language construction will *breed* a mythology" of its own inherent meaning through a "natural human mythopoeia."[99]

Recall that a language carries a particular way of seeing the world. People articulate and communicate meaning from personal standpoints, primarily expressed through cultural language already in existence. Language-making is different because it is not pre-existent and is developed through the artist's personalized predilection.[100] Since myth and history have an intrinsic relationship to each other and language, we must consider how myth can be a medium that mediates meaning because when dealing with myth's osmotic design, we are not dealing with tangibles. It comes by way of some otherness apart from the self, so if an original language-bred mythology issues its own particular way of seeing, then poetic knowledge acquired through *poesis* is something said through mytho-*logos* based on someone else's own mode of thought:

> Just as the construction of a mythology expresses at first one's taste, and later conditions one's imagination, and becomes inescapable, so with . . . language. I can conceive, even sketch, other

94. C. Tolkien, Preface to *Beowulf*, ix.

95. Tolkien, *Sir Gawain*, 7.

96. Tolkien, "Translating Beowulf," 53 (emphasis mine).

97. Thus, reinforcing why Tolkien wanted *LOTR* translated as closely as possible to *his* meaning and according to guidelines he proffered.

98. With the exception of some dialogue, poems, and songs in elvish and other invented languages.

99. "Vice," 210–11.

100. Tolkien deemed language-making art ("Vice," 198).

> radically different forms, but always insensibly and inevitably now come back to this one, which must therefore be or have become peculiarly mine.[101]

A personal, peculiar, conditioned, and inescapable language that breeds mythology is subject to the "different vision of life" to which the sub-creator's language gives meaning.[102] The manner by which verisimilitude is crafted in a Secondary World is due to the "underlying thought" of its mytho-*logos*.[103] Tolkien's world issued the effects of real history so that it feels like *vera historia*[104]—a true story set within a large historical tapestry not physically present. This is fantasy, where distinctly imaginative "new form is made."[105]

Occasionally, Tolkien suggested his endeavor was more effortless than sub-creative: "I had the sense of recording what was already 'there.'"[106] This allowed him to maintain, "I have long ceased to *invent* . . . I wait till I seem to know what really happened. Or till it writes itself."[107] Tolkien "had been inside language,"[108] having developed meaningful word-senses conditioned through original thought patterns. "I used what I knew," he said of his own "linguistic wisdom."[109] This brought him to the cusp of constructing a feigned history of Other Time, full of countless opportunities to make anew.

Unlike God creating *ex nihilo*, Tolkien was clear that human *logos*-centric meaning could only be "made not created"[110] because human meaning is only sub-creation. To begin with, language-making always has pre-existing substance. When woven into its own poetic relationships with word-meanings, incarnated into literary mode, and published, its meaning is not confined to letters and words but transcends the narrative into the lives of readers.

As Tolkien constructed the mytho-*logos* of Middle-earth, he described it as taking "abstract" sensibilities of personalized language-making and

101. "Vice," 212–13.
102. Tolkien in Garth's *Tolkien*, 230.
103. *Letters*, 33, 283, 379.
104. *Letters*, 33, 365.
105. OFS, 42.
106. *Letters*, 145.
107. *Letters*, 230.
108. From Tolkien's obituary; its writer remains anonymous ("Professor JRRT," 12).
109. Tolkien, Interview with Gueroult.
110. "Vice," 204.

"making them more conscious,"[111] thus more concrete. It moved from mere words into a fuller composition patterned in its own way, thus bringing about its own meaning[112] through language according to its own conventions.[113] But this needs to be translatable for others: "Though you give your words meanings, they have not had a real experience of the world in which to acquire the normal richness of human words."[114] The natural progression of engendering art moves from abstract sensibility into symbolism that issues meaning, thus moving art from undisclosed personalization into a medium where others may verify it as artistic.[115] He insisted *LOTR* was an "essay" of his language-making aesthetic rendered meaningful through the story.[116] In other words, *LOTR* was a formal attempt to employ his cradle-tongue to impact readers on a level deeper than their dominant first-learned language.

From his capabilities for uncovering the "mental archaeology" of history and language, Tolkien could revive old poetics by re-presenting something of their meaning.[117] He would produce similar new and original effects through *LOTR*, a world agreeable to his linguistic predilections. The personalized ordering and the intentional way the language is used allowed him definitively to claim ownership of the meaning made through it. The reader experiences this when Frodo meets Gildor in the woods and speaks what Tolkien referred to as "Elven-Latin," a "dead" language issuing meaning in the present.[118] That Frodo's utterance to Gildor came from a different phase of history emphasizes this, yet the reader and Frodo access it anew. It takes old meaning and makes it a "living language."[119] Through this unique lens, the meaning of an invented language may be translated into a living one, and according to its own rules:

> You have not to grope after the dazzling brilliance of invention of the free adjective, to which all human language has not yet fully attained. You may say *green sun* or *dead life* and set the imagination leaping. Language has both strengthened imagination and

111. "Vice," 218.
112. "Vice," 218.
113. "Vice," 219.
114. "Vice," 219.
115. "A solitary art is no art," Tolkien said (*Letters*, 122).
116. *Letters*, 220.
117. Steiner, "Oxford's," 187.
118. *Letters*, 176; "Papers," 241.
119. "Vice," 218.

> been freed by it. Who shall say whether the free adjective has created images bizarre and beautiful, or the adjective been freed by strange and beautiful pictures in the mind?[120]

Tolkien's zeal stemmed from taking these newly derived kinships of word-sense and introducing unknown and untold meanings into human consciousness.[121]

This presents two ways to see how creativity generates ontological encounters through meaning-making to awaken personal being in new ways. The first relates to how the cosmos was originally articulated poetically in chapter 1. Before a sub-creator called the sun green, green was declared of grass in the Primary World first; the sun white or yellow.[122] Each describes the free creativity of God recognized by and made conscious to the human imagination. Human creativity works analogically but is unbound by these daily patterns in nature. Though humanity's imagination is imaged after God's,[123] it is not nature, nor wholly satisfied by it. If green sun or dead life originated from a personalized aesthetic, the sub-creative world will always only be an analogical otherworld, which is another way creativity generates ontological encounters through meaning-making. Its derivations work according to the laws of its incarnated poetic context in ways connatural minds can grasp.

Literature initiates mind-to-mind progenitivity from its individuated poetic context using the familiarities of language to recall the reader's personal imagery to mind. For instance, when silver is written in a story, readers have their own conceptions of it. When a person describes a car as silver, the receiver may envisage the gleam of aluminum foil used to wrap a sandwich in the sunlight of the kitchen window. Someone who regularly uses unvarnished kitchen utensils for daily meals may imagine dullness. Whatever the case, each recognizes silver's familiarity and images, "a peculiar personal embodiment in his imagination."[124] Though individual perceptions of it differ based on personal experience, plain meaning of silver is still shared. Something similar would be true of bread, trees, or stones.[125] The point is threefold. First, at least some of

120. "Vice," 219.

121. "Vice," 218.

122. See OFS, 41.

123. See MacDonald, "Imagination."

124. OFS, 82nE.

125. See "Papers," 200; OFS, 82nE.

the plain meaning moves from mind to mind; second, the sub-creator initiated the meaning-making; and third, any awakening in the receiver happens from the context of the story.

Since fantasy is new form, the meaning originates in the story. Its progenitivity is triggered when communicable meaning is "at once more universal" but also "poignantly particular,"[126] something both-and, something other and external that affects another person's inner being. To apply the threshold metaphor, Middle-earth is a subsistent world of extra-mental existence envisaged through *LOTR*, and the reader is brought to the threshold whereupon s/he may be awakened to its mytho-*logos*. But every reader comes to the threshold from a different room.[127] Societies shape the social contexts of these rooms, and individuality poses a greater challenge because each image-bearer is unique. But while reading *LOTR*, each stands on the brink of the same room. The next chapter discusses the significance of why Tolkien's *logos* matters as a "same room" *poiema* for each reader.

126. OFS, 82nE.

127. Joseph Coleson, personal correspondence, May 24, 2018.

Chapter 5

Allocating Religious Sense Through Ontic Grounding

Introduction

CHAPTER 4 CONCLUDED BY asserting the progenitive power of fantasy produces a *more universal* and *poignantly particular* experience. Simultaneously, the poetic meaning shared between those who experience fantasy also becomes uniquely personalized. *LOTR* appeals to readers in concrete ways regardless of who they are because of what it mythically mediates through language: meaning generated by the underlying thought communicated through narrative from the author, yet not limited to the imagery these words symbolize, which stirs innate sensibilities via encounter through the text.

"Myth points, for each reader, to the realm he lives in most," wrote C. S. Lewis.[1] Indeed, "the value of the myth is that it takes all the things we know and restores to them the rich significance which has been hidden by 'the veil of familiarity.'"[2] Instead of defining myth, Lewis described how it initiates ontological encounters through subcreation. Tolkien stated, "The whole point of literature" is that "it *is* the

1. Lewis, "Gods Return," 33.
2. Lewis, "Dethronement," 14.

real world; while you're inside,"[3] which is significant to determining that to which *LOTR* can analogically awaken readers.

Chapter 2 discussed Tolkien's fundamental concern: the analogical relation between art/sub-creation and Primary Reality needed to be restored. The Primary Reality of *LOTR* is analogical to the "old" participatory ontology Tolkien lived, and he intended for it to issue a *sense* of actual history effectively in a multidimensional setting like it. *LOTR* provides a lens for "seeing things as we are (or were) meant to see them" apart from the veil of familiarity impeding cosmic reality.[4] It challenges contemporary ideological and scientific societal constructs inhibiting the imagination from experiencing transcendent involvement. Analogy is a way of relating to a single common focus, and what we are meant to see inside *LOTR* focuses readers on "its own full world of mythic meaning."[5]

I am arguing that we can best recognize God's interactivity in the world through a cosmo-*logos* lens where God's transcendence throughout the world is a given. For those who believe in a higher power, this may be easy; for those who do not or are not open to the possibility, it will pose a challenge. For Christians, Christ is vital to revelation. The means of grace and revelation of the church, creation, and scriptures also assure Christians about the truth of a life with God, but this is still largely mysterious. Thus, they must live by faith, trusting that God somehow osmotically permeates their being moment by moment in Christ by the Spirit. Every potential future moment is uncharted, so mysteries in the present and future are not unique to Christian experience. This is universal to all humanity, though each experience is particular to each person. Individuals must still act without knowing whether they are exactly right, and even if they are, there is no guarantee what will happen next—misfortune, success, or something else. Bad things may happen to good people, and vice versa. Either way, narratives of life carry on and can lead to character transformation if God still authors the greater narrative.

This chapter discusses how, if religious sensibility is perceptible in a feigned mythological history authored by Tolkien, it is merely an echo of that to which image-bearing readers are meant to be awakened to about the Author of Reality. I do this by exploring how Tolkien's *logos* draws

3. Resnick, "Interview," 41.

4. OFS, 67.

5. Kilby, "Tolkien as Scholar," 11.

readers into *LOTR* in a way that coheres with what Luigi Giussani called the *religious sense* and answers Tolkien's question, *But Why?*

A Means of Discerning More Through Tolkien's *Logos*

Tolkien's regard for literary credibility coincided with his demand for a true inner consistency of reality within a Secondary World of Other Time. The beginning of chapter 3 suggested that answers to questions in the Primary World might be derived via participation in a Secondary World narrative. But if a gap existed between sub-creative art and Primary Reality as Tolkien supposed, there was need to bridge this gap so that the sense of an existing relation to the divine could be analogically perceptible through Secondary Belief.

When Tolkien declared *LOTR* "is about God, and His sole right to divine honour" he referenced the divine mind behind Middle-earth.[6] The God of Middle-earth is Eru,[7] and although his name is never mentioned in *LOTR*, the narrative is weighted with transcendent sensibility.[8] *LOTR* as *poiema* was meant to illustrate a divine mind active through mytho-*logos*, which is contingent on what Tolkien meant by this divine mind.

Eru, also called Ilúvatar,[9] was described as "The One"[10] and "The One Only."[11] As "supreme . . . Creator; outside, transcendent,"[12] Tolkien considered Eru beyond the cosmos of Middle-earth. Yet he also regarded Eru as "that one ever-present Person who is never absent and never

6. *Letters*, 243. He also indicated that *LOTR* sustains other underlying themes—the Fall (147), grace (172), the war of good against evil (197), motives of characters and domination over others (199), death and immortality (246, 262, 284), and achievements of specially graced and gifted individuals (365). These are secondary matters to the primary creator of Middle-earth. Readers might describe any of these as most significant, among other things. *LOTR* is about all of these in some way.

7. Meaning, "He that is Alone" (Tolkien, *Silmarillion*, 329).

8. This parallels the "old" light introduced in chapter 1, because the germ of Tolkien's mythology began long before hobbits entered the picture. Thus, before there were hobbits, there was Eru.

9. Eru's original name in Tolkien, *Lost Tales*, where it meant "Lord of All" (264) and later also "Father of All" (*Silmarillion*, 337).

10. *Letters*, 155, 204, 235, 253n, 284–85, 287, 345; *Silmarillion*, 15, 329.

11. Tolkien, Interview with Gueroult.

12. Tolkien, Interview with Gueroult.

named."[13] Furthermore, Eru drove the logic as "the Writer of the Story (by which I do not mean myself),"[14] as if the God of Middle-earth had interwoven himself into *LOTR*, though he is not a formal character in it.[15] Of course, Tolkien was the actual writer as "transcendent Sub-creator,"[16] but his specific exposition of Eru's role insinuates analogy of being within the narrative of *LOTR*. Analogy of being is the creaturely acknowledgement for participating in God's essence in-and-beyond existence. Tolkien was not assuming the place of the transcendent God. Neither could he, as a finite being, sub-create infinite transcendence. Therefore, whatever transcendent sensibilities a reader may perceive come from what is communicated through the mytho-*logos*. Some brief introductory points give us a view into Tolkien's creativity as *LOTR* was being written.

The "Ainulindalë," or "Music of the Ainur," records Tolkien's creation myth.[17] It begins by introducing the divine Mind: "There was Eru" who spoke the cosmos into existence.[18] One word from Eru set the creation myth into motion—"*Eä*!"[19] meaning "It is" and "Let it be."[20] The reader of *LOTR* cannot see Eru or know that the world was spoken into being by his will. Yet, these are significant notions Tolkien infused into his poetic mode of thought. Eru is part of the onto-theological synthesis and rational foundation that normatively rules all aspects of the cosmic development of *LOTR*. But this is sub-creative, and "all invention that occurs in [sub-creation] must remain analogous, in some way, to the Primary World in order to be comprehensible" as an independent secondary plane.[21] Since character transformation happens through participatory ontology within *LOTR*, it is important to register how this can happen analogically for readers in the Primary World.

Chapter 2's exploration of *Leaf by Niggle* illustrated how sub-creation can be transformative, emphasizing how one can be drawn to God "beyond." But this did not account for the *in-and* harmony analogy

13. *Letters*, 253. Tolkien borrowed this line from an unnamed critic who observed this in *LOTR*.

14. *Letters*, 253.

15. Although "the One" is referenced in Appendix III (*LOTR*, 1013).

16. *Letters*, 232.

17. Posthumously published by Christopher Tolkien in *Silmarillion* (15–22).

18. *Silmarillion*, 15.

19. *Silmarillion*, 20.

20. *Silmarillion*, 325.

21. Wolf, *Building*, 37.

of being requires. Although one may intuit God as beyond, experience in the Primary World demands concreteness. Analogy of being takes a decisive posture, acknowledging God as the reference point beyond, but this must be complemented by sensible *presence*—here and now. If God's presence can somehow be apprehended through a certain way of reading the *logos*, this may aid us in appreciating what Tolkien meant by Eru being ever-present in *LOTR*.

God's Pattern: Ontological "I" and the Presence of God

We have seen how Tolkien perceived God as the Author of Reality. He also believed God was still the active "Writer" of the narrative we find ourselves in.[22] Readers of narratives do not actually see their authors because their eyes are on the text and because the author usually is not in the same room. Yet readers know an author exists. If this can be known about literary authors, the same is true about the Author of Reality if the meaning of cosmo-*logos* is restored.

Returning to the old meaning of *logos* provides clues for intuiting the divine writing of the cosmic text: as a whole onto-theologically synthesized "'true' order, not just in the sense that a description of the cosmos in its terms would be 'true' in the normal sense; but in the deeper sense that this is the right order; this order follows a plan which it itself dictates."[23] The *normal* sense Charles Taylor refers to here is akin to how general revelation displays harmony in the order of things. The *deeper* sense aligns with the notion that the essence of the divine mind permeates and preserves creation. Comprehending meaning through that which is visible is thus integral to reading the greater reality of the invisible divine beyond. Secularized scientific naturalism claims "no one can say with certainty why the universe popped out of the void."[24] This presumes that God does not author reality, removing a transcendent determinant and rendering the cosmos as deprived of teleological origination; it just happened.[25] But the earlier reading of *logos*—the true, deeper, right order—allows for meaningfully more and can lend

22. *Letters*, 252.
23. Taylor, *Language Animal*, 73.
24. Willard quoting from Time-Life's *Cosmos* (1989) in "Language, Being."
25. See Willard, "Language, Being."

to a sense of natural relation with a divine Writer. Those who read *logos* this way can claim the following realizations in first person:

1. The fact of my existence evidences I belong within the narrative because the divine mind has written me in;
2. Reading a rightness in the order of things set in motion according to a plan suggests there is a moral to my existence because I am part of this plan;
3. That I can read this as I participate implies that the writer is still active because the narrative is happening as I read it;
4. My continued existence means that the writer is still mindful of me and is continuing my role in the story.

Each observation asserts personal and purposeful significance in God's *poesis*. None declares finite beings as central to the story; the narrative continues according to the design of the greater reality in which everything participates. God's *poesis* is the ever-available purely formative and forming power prolonging the narrative.

By "looking *in*"[26] to discern something of the greater reality of God as a means of finding answers given to us, humanity cannot observe the *telos* of the narrative exactly, but can be assured that there is one. Tolkien's own reading registered this. Chapter 3 discussed his responses to the question, "What is the purpose of life?" Before answering, he made an inquiry of his own: "What does the question really mean?"[27] His answer was synonymous with an "ontic grounding of meaning";[28] that is, to know God, the source and meaning of Primary Reality.[29] Such a reading sees the divine as a living component—fact, not phenomenon—of reality.[30] If the Writer is factually involved, the narrative is stating something true about the Writer, allowing for us to comprehend things about God concretely. As originator of meaning, God holds the answers to every "human curiosity" pertaining to purposes and morals, patterns and designs,[31] the "reasons and motives" of which "can only refer to . . . a Mind [that] can

26. Lewis, "Imagination," 59.
27. *Letters*, 399.
28. Taylor, *Secular*, 303.
29. See *Letters*, 399–400.
30. See the discussion of the ontic nature of God on p. 79.
31. *Letters*, 399–400.

have purposes in any way or degree akin to human purposes."[32] Therefore, people can only truly and properly know who they are and why they exist as they remain ontically grounded in God and recognize God as their beginning and end because God's essence and *poesis* sustains existence. Although this describes an ontic reading of the divine, one does not need to read Primary Reality identically to understand there is more than can be seen with the naked eye.

Tolkien's reading of the cosmos is like the older, traditional reading of reality, where it was a given that humanity was embedded within "a 'meaningful' order" situated within the "ontic logos."[33] Christianity enhanced this reading through its "ancient confidence" about God's continued involvement in the world,[34] seen through the "profound integration of logos and being, which it discerned in a transcendent way in the living and active God, and in a creaturely and contingent way in created reality—'being' . . . understood . . . as including movement, creative activity in God and becoming or motion in the creature."[35] Implicit within the layers of Primary Reality, one would read the "*truth of being*" or "intrinsic rationality of reality"—the *logic* of the story—as the ontic *logos* was concomitantly making, shaping, and transforming.[36]

Ontic grounding in God implies grounding in the Christ-*Logos* because they are "infinite and equal."[37] Through God's creativity "reality is a multi-layered unity" in which the hierarchy of beings "find their lodging and their guarantee. He is the source of connection, the one whose creative act holds in one the worldviews of science, aesthetics, ethics[,] and religion, as expressions of his reason, joy, will, and presence."[38] Such an "interlocking" of the "character of . . . creation" is manifested in and through Christ,[39] whose incarnation substantiated and verified God's presence when he stepped into history from outside time, participated

32. *Letters*, 399.

33. Taylor, *Sources*, 161.

34. Duriez, *C. S. Lewis*, 136.

35. Torrance, *Reality*, 7.

36. Torrance, *Reality*, 7. "The Word, the *Logos*, combines two notions, one Greek, one Hebrew. For the Greek the *logos* was the rational ordering principle of the universe. For the Hebrew the word of the Lord was God's activity in the world. (In Hebrew *ddbar* means both word and deed; Hebrew is a language based on verbs, on action)" (Polkinghorne, *One World*, 116).

37. *Letters*, 99.

38. Polkinghorne, *One World*, 116.

39. Polkinghorne, *One World*, 116.

within creation, and reconciled it. The Christ-*Logos* is the *logic* of God's narrative. By interlocking reality in himself, the Christ-*Logos* communicates the means through which one may know the true, deeper, and right order of things in God. Christ bridged the gap between finite and infinite planes by making the cosmos sensible, challenging the "old static sense" of perceiving God at a great distance by conceptualizing God as near.[40]

Such unity was necessary to confidently perceive oneself participating in a narrative of life concretely coinciding with actual divine presence without losing the sense that this also extends from infinity outside of time and space. Thus, God's "eternity . . . doesn't abolish time, but gathers it into [God's] instant. This we can only have access to by participating in God's life."[41] C. S. Lewis helpfully captured this viewpoint through Boethius: "Strictly speaking, [God] never *fore*sees; He simply sees. Your 'future' is only an area, and only for us a special area, of His infinite Now. He sees (not remembers) your yesterday's acts because yesterday is still 'there' for Him; he sees (not foresees) your tomorrow's acts because He is already in tomorrow."[42] Finite being is only ever on the threshold of now with no guarantee of a future. God is the only one who takes the Whole Story into account outside the measure of time. Within creation, *logos* decrees everywhere that God's presence is discernible. Christ incarnate personalized transcendence by making God with us. Ontically grounded readers participate with confidence that this is still a given, not ancient, even though the full details of the Whole Story are unknowable. Because God omni-laterally knows past, present, and future, by participating in the good of God, people can be secure that whatever happens is not apart from God's "instant." They feel secure as they steward their roles, but there is no guaranteeing that life will always be safe or free of harm. Living life is driven by a state of being not so much concerned with whether or not death is at hand, but whether purposeful participation transcends the "shadowy bars"[43] imprisoning the fallen world while meaningfully living for God. God's infinite intentions for personal roles in the story are not fully known to us.

Tolkien read the cosmo-*logos* similarly. His creativity was motivated by participation in God's life and in a way that it might transcend the shadowy bars of time and space once his role in God's narrative ended. While

40. Torrance, *Reality*, 7.

41. Taylor, *Secular*, 57.

42. Lewis, *Discarded*, 89.

43. "Mythopoeia," 86.

deliberating the problematic relation between sub-creation and Primary Reality, Tolkien claimed that one of his main poetic concerns in Middle-earth was mortality.[44] In relaying what he meant, Tolkien blended Primary and Secondary World language and notably disassociated creativity from pertinent everyday physical needs. Mortality, in particular,

> affects art and the creative (or as I should say, sub-creative) desire which seems to have no biological function, and to be apart from the satisfactions of plain ordinary biological life, with which, in our world, it is indeed usually at strife. This desire is at once wedded to a passionate love of the real primary world, and hence filled with the sense of mortality, and yet unsatisfied by it.[45]

Tolkien was anxious that he might not leave behind relevant, enduring art that might direct others to God beyond the Mountains.[46] Affective art surpasses physicality where no biological function can hinder it. Any lasting effects from it are timeless. In the Primary World, all things perish because of the Fall of humanity, but sub-creation can survive the ages if its meaning sustains progenitive effects powerful enough to keep it moving through imaginations from generation to generation. By completing this art through *LOTR*, Tolkien could leave God a result that might transcend mortality, testify to God and truth, and nourish those who encounter it.[47] *LOTR* displays Tolkien's "clumsy loom,"[48] which analogically parallels the tapestry of Primary Reality to an infinitely lesser extent. But in each case, creativity stems from an originator. God holds the key to the meaning of Primary Reality. "I hold the key" to the meaning of *LOTR*,[49] Tolkien said, because it came from his particular "leaf-mould of the mind."[50] So this is not a matter for uncovering exact meaning or finding the key but arriving at how readers might best "decide . . . what to do with the time that is given to"[51] them now through participation in God in their own narratives of life. This is perceptible through *LOTR*'s mytho-*logos*, but there needs to be a way

44. *Letters*, 145. Mortality is one of three concerns listed, the other two being fallenness and the machine, each of which contributes to mortality in Middle-earth.

45. *Letters*, 145.

46. *Letters*, 321.

47. Like Niggle's art and its result.

48. "Mythopoeia," 88.

49. Resnick, "Interview," 38.

50. Carpenter, *JRRT: Biography*, 131.

51. Gandalf to Frodo in *LOTR*, 50.

this generates a recognizable affinity to experiencing *logos* in the actual cosmos, which is ultimately mysterious and not easily defined.

The Mystery of Narrative Space

The essence of "The Pattern" of God's infinite interactivity resides in the divine alone, but God reveals divine mysteriousness through the Whole Story as the *logos* decrees itself.[52] No creature can know the exactness of God's complexity and completeness and must rest in the knowledge that creation originates in God's divine simplicity from which the transcendentals stem. Comparatively, a person's reading of the *logos* derives dim and cracked notions of God's cosmic interactivity, thereby making mystery a given to participatory life in God. Tolkien described this poetically:

> Great processes march on, as Time unrolls
> from dark beginnings to uncertain goals;
> and as on page o'erwritten without clue,
> with script and limning packed of various hue.[53]

Although Tolkien knew there was no perfect finite interpretation of the workings of God within the world, his *sub specie aeternitatis* outlook anticipated God's irremovable presence, not anciently, but concurrently with confidence in the meaning of the gospel story.[54] He described some of his Christian perceptions of God as variously parallel to finite time

52. This considers the beginning, middle, end, and afterlife, which Christians have a general understanding about through biblical revelation and the church. They believe they will go to heaven, but the afterlife is not yet experienced. Such revelation neither illustrates nor gives instruction about how to act in every instance. Though scripture and the church teach how to live in God, even the faithful who live uprightly have limited foresight about what will actually happen. Only God knows the exact plan communicated through the *logos* and can see beyond the threshold of now. Deciding what direction is right or wrong is largely debatable and not within the scope of this book to tackle. I am arguing that something must still be done, and that the next step is best discerned when one participates in God. If nature is always already graced, whatever happens next is included in God's instant. People cannot know what God already knows unless they pass the threshold, and even then only finitely. Whether or not Christ-*Logos* is the lens for reading the narrative, a general *logos* view of transcendence maintains people have a role, and that as long as they exist, there is a rightness to their continued existence that has purpose in the divine mind, even if the consequences seem unfavorable now.

53. "Mythopoeia," 85.

54. OFS, 77–79.

and space through guardian angels, the Blessed Sacrament, and prayer.[55] All hinged on how God's transcendence actively mediated through history's finite manifestations. They also exhibited means through which God was concretely experienced. Though each draws from the Christian tradition, Tolkien's theology of mediation may differ from other theologies. But Christianity traditionally espouses some form of God-mediation within history that emphasizes relationships between God and people through their living narratives. God's story and the gospel story impact humanity spatiotemporally, and if transformation occurs as God's truth transcends these stories, the same *mythos* affects beings, each in uniquely personal ways. Neither story is experienced as physical presence but intuitively via the imagination.

LOTR is not a sacrament, religious Christian symbol, or doctrine of Christianity. It is *mythos* experienced historically. Christianity lies within actual history; *LOTR* is feigned. The effects of each permeate from the osmotic design of a maker. The impact can be explained mythically, not in the sense that myth equals lies but as a way to explain how and why *mythos* affects us. So, if *LOTR* elucidates truth according to its own plane and awakens readers to something to which they assent as true of Primary Reality through the text, "art has been verified" in personal being if the divine mediates something true about God's relationship to us.[56]

Tolkien claimed his world was not sub-created according to any "general, particular, or topical, moral, religious, or political" slant.[57] Such associations and interpretations are uncontrollable once a work enters the public sphere, and when certain lenses are assumed as the *only* lenses through which to read stories, they distract from letting mytho-*logos* speak for itself.[58] Tolkien intended for *LOTR* to embody its own divine sensibility parallel to a cosmo-*logos* outlook. The challenge lay in convincing readers that the feigned historical continuity of his *logos* is not directly concerned with Primary World matters. This included himself. Even "I do not . . . belong *inside* my invented history," Tolkien

55. *Letters*, 66, 99 (angels); 53–54, 99, 338–39 (Sacrament); 66, 252 (prayer).

56. OFS, 78.

57. *Letters*, 220. See *LOTR*, xvii.

58. Such lenses cannot be subtracted as if they were never part of a reader's life. They are certainly part of their ontological makeup. But it is important that they are recognized and disarmed to keep them from hindering the poetic meaning mediating through the story.

said[59] because "confusing . . . real personal matters with the . . . Tale is a serious mistake."[60] Allegorical reading and writing "assigns symbolic significance [of Primary World matters] to textual details" represented within the Secondary, which can erroneously blur *LOTR*'s *mythos* with real-world matters.[61] Thus, Tolkien's attempt to encourage a neutral lens for reading *LOTR* in the second edition's Foreword.

To free readers from tempting assumptions and automatic presumptions, he exhorted them to just enjoy it: "The prime motive was the desire of a tale-teller to try his hand at a really long story that would hold the attention of readers, amuse them, delight them, and at times maybe excite them or deeply move them."[62] That *LOTR* needed to be exciting was a recurring point Tolkien made to correspondents,[63] and this was how many experienced it.[64] Great tales withstand the ages because they continue to give pleasure and spur disagreement or debate. As such, they not only work progenitively from writer to reader, but reader to reader, thus perpetuating further "postlections"[65] solely based on the art's inherent affectivity. To emphasize this is how he hoped it would be read, Tolkien was insistent that his aim in writing *LOTR* was to produce "a *work of narrative art*" to be embraced and appreciated "with only the book itself as [the] source."[66] This is another way of claiming *LOTR* "is not 'about' anything but itself" to detract inquirers from fishing for hidden meanings about it.[67] *LOTR* is based on its own ontological semantic unity, so its meaning is its own.

The language-making Tolkien based his world upon issued "a particular *how* of thought"[68] woven into his *poesis*. "Language-building" is not "code-making" but an artistic endeavor to "find a relationship [between] sound plus sense, that [personally] satisfies . . . when made

59. *Letters*, 398. "The story is not about [me] at all," Tolkien said (239, 288).

60. "Appendix," 26.

61. Plummer, *Forty Questions*, 87.

62. *LOTR*, xvi.

63. *Letters*, 212, 232–33, 267.

64. *Letters*, 212.

65. See p. 22. The root word *lection* implies that readers would repeatedly choose to read the same story.

66. *Letters*, 414.

67. *Letters*, 220.

68. Sapir, *Language*, 180.

durable" and gratifies its maker.[69] The literary pleasure readers experience stems from the linguistic pleasure in Tolkien first.[70] Thus it is neither the reader nor solely the text issuing meaning, but that this pleasurable "meaning . . . is a construction of intelligent thought. Texts can convey meaning, but texts cannot construct meaning"; this "lies in the purview of the author."[71] The underlying thought here is twofold. First, language issues what would otherwise never have been revealed unless the sub-creator did so. Second, narrative gives readers a new way to imagine, "*making present*" what was previously "absent" to the mind's eye.[72] Each point integrates previously unknown meaning(s) now revealed through contextual narrative to other personal narratives of life.

To compare *LOTR* analogically to the Primary World, language is needed to lend credence to the way Tolkien fortified the existing relation to Primary Reality through poetic meaning. The cosmos is the space of God's ordered *logos*, which is not limited to lingual utterances or symbols on paper. The divine mind permeates throughout, but its patterning is not strictly defined because it resides in infinite divine meaning unbound by definition. Yet this is the only space humanity experiences transcendence alongside inanimate and animate beings. Tolkien appreciated these through his "wonder and delight in the [natural] earth" and love for everything God freely created.[73] Beauty, wonder, and love evidence meaning. That they are stirred within a person suggests awakening. Through a *logos*-centric reading, each can perpetuate a sense of relation and free participation with a sense of belonging.

Giussani provided useful language describing personal belonging in a *logos*-centric reading of the cosmos. It requires a collision between people and "other" meaning so intriguing it is as if another "voice" draws them into deeper meaning.[74] This *logos* encounter is the "*gift*" of God's "being," a "presence that imposes itself"[75] as the "'objective side' of the religious experience [that] requires perceiving the concrete analogy

69. "Papers," 240.

70. Tolkien referenced this pleasure throughout his life. See "Vice" (entire essay); "Welsh" (189–94); Interview with Gueroult (in two places); *Letters*, 172, 213–14, 374n, 380.

71. Plummer, *Forty Questions*, 130.

72. Ward, "Narrative," 440.

73. Resnick, "Interview," 41.

74. Giussani, *Religious Sense*, 103, 109.

75. Giussani, *Religious Sense*, 101.

of being through transcendental determinations."[76] In other words, God is "not some abstract entity,"[77] but the essence of Primary Reality who transcends the concrete gifts of the cosmos to draw humanity to the divine self. Since analogy of being sees God decisively as the pre-existing cause (essence) for everything in creation (existence), through the "ontic residue"[78] of the cosmos, humanity can recognize meaning apart from itself that it did not create. *Residue* evidences a precursor, and *gift* implies a giver. Therefore, created being is contingent upon a "self-existent" being "ontically prior to itself."[79] The only one ontically prior to created existence is God who created out of nothing.

Each meaningful encounter with any thread in the tapestry is a *sign*: "a reality which refers me to something else. The sign is a reality whose meaning is another reality, something I am able to experience, which acquires its meaning by leading to another reality" beyond.[80] Through time and space, the gift of God is always "a mystery, always present and ever greater, that speaks to man in infinitely different ways."[81] If one allows for this transcendent link to the divine, s/he can more keenly intuit a participatory ontology where "*I do not make myself*, I am not making myself. I do not give myself being, or the reality which I am. I am 'given' . . . from something else, more than me."[82] So not only is humanity given personhood, and not only is everything other than me gifted into existence, but these all follow from the divine gifting of God's being first. This is implicit in reading the *logos*. Signs signify a greater reality from which their existence derives throughout history. Divine encounters are possible because God still weaves the tapestry. If the cosmos is ontically grounded in a greater reality, every awakening encounter suggests God's presence: It is like "bumping into a sign, an objective reality that moves the person toward his *telos*."[83] "Through the sign . . . the presence of the transcendent *touches* the flesh."[84]

76. López, "Growing Human," 216.
77. Giussani, *Religious Sense*, 101.
78. Willard, "Language, Being."
79. Willard, "Language, Being."
80. Giussani, *Religious Sense*, 111.
81. López, "Growing Human," 218.
82. Giussani, *Religious Sense*, 105.
83. Giussani in López, "Growing Human," 219.
84. Giussani in López, "Growing Human," 219.

When the cosmos is read as always already graced in God, divine presence is detectable through the givens of creation: God transcendently here, not elsewhere. This is central to Giussani's concept of *religious sense*, the "capacity to enter in relation with God, (that) characteristic feature of our nature, which disposes the soul to aspire toward God."[85] If nature and grace are unified and not divided into separate spheres, creation remains firmly graced within the ontic *logos*, maintaining "the ontological unity-in-difference between God and the world."[86] To read God's transcendence as the rational foundation who still rules all cosmic development is to read not only something said (*poiema*) through all God has made but also what God is still saying (*poesis*). God is not creation, nor does creation exist apart from God.[87] Yet God is "*transsignified*" through this cosmic reading—the divine's greater reality evidenced through creation itself.[88]

Tolkien's imaginative intuitionism recognized this transignification "beneath the ancient song" of God through which he sub-created his own mytho-*logos*. In "Mythopoeia," Tolkien resolutely accepts God as the ontic foundation of the cosmos whose essence issues forth more meaning within the world than humanity can imaginably ever assign to it.[89] Imaginative intuition anticipates meaning already *here*, and Tolkien was reading God's transcendence as linked through the cosmo-*logos* tapestry. Such a reading views natural theology as a "pathway"[90] and "bridge"[91] to understanding God's in-and-beyond presence within the cosmos. Just as nature and grace remain conjoined through Christ, imaginative intuitionism unifies mind and spirit, unlike an intellectual endeavor that attempts to reify the infinite exactly. By deriving a Secondary World according to imaginative intuition, Tolkien was "re-stating and restoring an imaginative tradition . . . by natural intuition [which] the reader knows to be in some sense true."[92]

85. Giussani in López, "Growing Human," 215. Specifically, "the pertinence of Christian faith to human experience" (214). López uses parentheses for "(that)" instead of brackets.

86. López, "Growing Human," 212.

87. See McGrath, *Open Secret*, 189.

88. McGrath, *Heresy*, 19.

89. McGrath, *Order of Things*, 62. McGrath called "Mythopoeia" Tolkien's "natural theology of the imagination" (62, 96).

90. McGrath, *Order of Things*, 96.

91. MacQuarrie, "Natural Theology," 405.

92. Duriez, *JRRT Handbook*, 187.

The trinitarian disclosure model from chapter 2 provided a way to understand the "constitutive relation . . . to the living personal God" that mysteriously permeates the Whole Story.[93] It is important to re-emphasize this is not a *picturing* model, but an acknowledgement of trinitarian authorization and involvement. Although it is impossible for the finite to replicate the infinite trinitarian being sub-creatively or to imagine with a trinitarian mind, this disclosure model allows for adherents to comprehend an analogous relation to God's continued transcendence within immanence through natural theology from a Christian ontological standpoint.

In this chapter we have seen how Tolkien's participatory ontology perceived God as ever-present, instead of belonging solely to ancient history—not in a way that solves God, but preserves divine mystery within the cosmos. It is a lens that reads the cosmo-*logos* from inside the Whole Story. In this Story, humanity can experience an ontological space harmonized through analogy of being in an "open-space of transcendence" where "the divine self-communication transcends the self-communication of the creature and lifts it above and beyond itself, making it open to others, and open to the world."[94] In this space, one can find firmer unity, grounding, and clarity about the religious sense. *LOTR*'s mytho-*logos* is meant to parallel this kind of cosmos to direct readers to the God of Primary Reality. However, there is no guarantee that readers will interpret themselves as experiencing an awakening to God through the story. When there are hindrances or deficiencies to *logos*-centric reading, challenges arise. If God is not given ontic prioritization, the shadowy bars obstructing the reader's view will affect how s/he reads the Primary World. The next chapter discusses these possible obstructions.

93. Torrance, *Reality*, 196.

94. Torrance, *Reality*, 188.

Chapter 6

Cosmic Imaginaries that Transcend Secularity

Introduction

Chapter 5 answered Tolkien's question *But How?* by arguing that he sub-created an imaginative space parallel to his reading of a *logos*-centric cosmos. Secondary Belief within *LOTR* can generate effects akin to an experience where readers can intuit a religious sensibility they discern in some sense to be true. But the end of chapter 5 also mentioned possible hindrances to the existing relation image-bearers have to God and how they interpret the religious sense. Tolkien hinted at these in his recognition of spiritual malnourishment and dark clouds veiling light in the world. This chapter draws on another Tolkien metaphor to address how narrative may penetrate a prison-feel of existence imposed by such hindrances.

The end of chapter 4 noted that readers come to the threshold of Middle-earth from different rooms. The variety of societal and individual distinctions makes it impossible to qualify the differences of these rooms. According to Charles Taylor, however, there is a common feature of the vast majority of those inhabiting Western countries since roughly 1500.[1] An "ontic doubt about meaning" has grown and

1. Taylor, *Secular*, 26, 28, 374.

dislodged humanity from confidently reading cosmo-*logos* in the centuries since.[2] The shift has been from one perceived as grounded in the transcendent to an age that often deems a divine mind as doubtful or impossible to fathom. Then, participation in a greater reality had been primarily a given. Since, "human identity" has gradually shifted to a "new historical formation [and re-creation]" of itself.[3]

This new identity has obstructed how to read the cosmos. "We need . . . to clean our windows" to set our minds free, argued Tolkien.[4] "Why should a man be scorned if, finding himself in prison, he tries to get out and go home?" he asked.[5] In my interpretation for contemporary understandings of this concept, the secularists are the jailers, and their philosophies grime up the windows and fortify the prison walls.[6] Ontic doubt is stirred within these walls. *LOTR* offers a means for *recovery*, "re-gaining . . . a clear view"[7] about Primary Reality. Through fantasy Tolkien proposed an analogical alternative to immanence-only claims about reality. Fantasy induces imagery in the mind, and the imaginative effects moving from mind to mind become shared experience. Therefore, what the "language *communicates*" through narrative is "a sharing of that to which the language refers and which it seeks to light up."[8] *LOTR* illuminates and shares an otherworld upheld by its own ancient confidence, and one that can affect readers through its characters' confidence. Each person analogically participates in the "same room" of the world while reading, and Charles Taylor helpfully articulates the sensibilities of the ontological space by which many Western readers have been affected. Although he cannot account for the specifics of each individual, he provides a helpful framework-aura of North Atlantic time and space.

But before we explore this, it is useful to draw attention to why *LOTR* has been so inviting to readers. It is mythic, and since myth personalizes

2. Taylor, *Secular*, 303.

3. Taylor, *Secular*, 560.

4. OFS, 67.

5. OFS, 69.

6. Tolkien did not say *secularist*, but he considered contemporary natural scientists and philosophers as creators of the prison-feel that inhibits the imagination from being free to imagine otherwise based on their own claims about reality (see OFS, 70, 81nD, 83nG). He also thought increased "philosophical and theological suspicion" about God's transcendent involvement diminished how Western cultures read the divine in the cosmos and appreciate Faërie ("Manuscript," 256).

7. OFS, 67.

8. MacQuarrie, *Principles*, 128.

a story's meaning, *LOTR* can mysteriously awaken personal latent sensibilities through imaginative intuition. Consequently, something of the old historical identity can be recognized through the story *now*, despite any distortions a secular age propagates. I submit that if *LOTR*'s mytho-*logos* awakens readers to the potential of an actual cosmo-*logos*, this answers Tolkien's *But Why?* We will first begin to examine why Tolkien's narrative draws readers in before shedding light on the prison-feel of secularity.

Absorbed into Living Narrative

In chapter 1, Kilby (the Christian) and the unbeliever alluded to how *LOTR* can broaden Primary World experience. Kilby asserted Tolkien's world can prompt readers to require more of reality than science and intellectualization. For the unbeliever, *LOTR* illumined a world pervaded by religious sensibility that seemed different from the reality to which he was accustomed. Each account implies an ontological discontinuity for such readers: Secondary Belief garnered through *LOTR* instills the sense that there may be a fuller meaning to personal experience. In other words, certain beliefs readers customarily assume to be true about the Primary World may be jostled by Tolkien's mytho-*logos*. When its progenitive effects move through the medium of word and world, it is possible that *LOTR* portrays something readers can know in some sense to be true. I am not suggesting that *LOTR* is a true Primary World story, but that something about its mytho-*logos* can trigger ontological responses about something that is actually true.

Tolkien's ontic reading of God's presence in the cosmos caused him to sub-create *LOTR*'s mytho-*logos* so that it might mediate a similar sensibility. Each coheres with the old sense of the ontic *logos* where transcendence ubiquitously threaded the cosmos and was predominantly axiomatic.[9] There used to be no doubt or question about an *a priori* human-divine affinity.[10] The mythic meaning in *LOTR* is capable of triggering ontological responses that can re-establish concrete awareness about an existing relation with God by awakening the religious sense based on the progenitive power of Tolkien's mytho-*logos*.

9. Taylor, *Secular*, 3–4.

10. In both the ancient Greek (M. B. Foster in McGrath, *Nature*, 139) and medieval (Yandell, "Pattern," 376) senses.

When conveying meaning constructed through intelligent thought, a general consensus is that communication relays purposefully intended meaning. Tolkien intended his mytho-*logos* to relay a sense of religiousness "consonant with" his own reading of Primary Reality.[11] Although the essence of Christianity is "detectable within" it, *LOTR* "is pure drama, the shape of the story being the burden of its message."[12] Recall that Tolkien was burdened by a *peculiar* message and was making something original according to *its own* religious sensibility. When incarnated into an original narrative that also borrows ingredients from other tales throughout history, these familiar elements become contextually different. Thereby "all three things: independent invention, inheritance [from the ancestry of storytelling], and diffusion [of various story elements incorporated into a new story], have evidently played their part in producing the intricate web of Story."[13] All these elements take on new meaning when shaped into independent sub-creation.

Drama's form consists of events linearly interlaced together, and its felt impact is designed to be experienced holistically from beginning to end. *LOTR* depicts a literary drama, but not through ocular theatrics. Only after our feelings and imaginations are led through does one experience the whole.[14] While moving through the narrative, its shape bears the burden of the story's meaning. If meaning awakens readers through the story, this happens apart from the reader's control, and the narrative is the source.[15]

To use hearing music as an analogy, when pianists read sheet music, they read the notes as arranged. When they begin to play, listeners are not actually hearing half note, quarter note, and rest symbols, but the whole of the melody as composed. The pianist plays the entire piece to its final note for the fullest effect: "A Chopin étude is inviolate; it moves altogether in the world of piano tone. . . . Chopin plays with the language of the piano as though no other language existed (the medium

11. *Letters*, 355.

12. Cavaliero, *Charles Williams*, 173.

13. OFS, 40–41.

14. This is true of personal narratives, too: we come to a fuller realization of our part in the narrative only after it is lived.

15. Of course, the reader controls whether or not to keep reading, but by continuing on, what happens within the narrative is driven by sub-creative assembly. What a story triggers within any particular reader is unique to himself or herself, but these are generated by the story.

'disappears')."[16] Chopin's technical mastery of piano and musical composition is absorbed by the listener without a second thought or consideration for the technicalities of sheet music. When the composition is played, it becomes alive at once in all its parts, and the lasting effect of the music remains with hearers. Listening triggers an ontological response while experiencing a pleasurable melody.

A similar effect happens with stories when sub-creators command their craft through mytho-*logos*.[17] As language leads readers through, "the material 'disappears' precisely because there is nothing in the artist's conception to indicate that any other material exists. For the time being, he, and we with him, move in the artistic medium as a fish moves in the water, oblivious of the existence of an alien atmosphere."[18] This is the essence of Secondary Belief. Mytho-*logos* is the "water" maintaining the inner consistency through which the reader moves. Readers believe it while inside without a second thought. This is paramount because as water is life for the fish without its recognizing the need for it, mytho-*logos* is the story's life. As it is experienced, the language disappears while mediating the story's meaning.

As a whole finished work, *poiema* transsignifies meaning from its sub-creator. Here, we may revisit Giussani's use of *sign* to broaden the lens for reading *LOTR*. In framing religious experience, signs are ways to encounter God. Signs "refer to the dual unity of gift and logos that characterizes finite beings"[19] in God. Giussani avoided "symbol" because when symbols acquire particular meanings in time and space, they often become "culturally determined" and "historically conditioned" by what they once meant at various points throughout history.[20] Thus, they "have no claim to universality or ontological depth" now because there is no guarantee they can now be affirmed concretely in exactly, or even a similar, way.[21]

16. Sapir, *Language*, 183n4.

17. Tolkien admired *Beowulf* as "a composition, not a tune" (Tolkien in Kilby, "Meaning," 74), and spoke of his whole *legendarium* as a "composition" of its own (*Letters*, 143), implying there is that much more to *LOTR* than the story itself, although *LOTR* certainly is a composition of its own (*Letters*, 297).

18. Sapir, *Language*, 182–83.

19. López, "Growing Human," 218.

20. López, "Growing Human," 218.

21. López, "Growing Human," 218.

Symbols have a tendency to impose certain meanings that inhibit the sign from freely impacting being in its independent context.[22]

However, if the cosmos is allowed to be seen as a divinely upheld open-space of transcendence, we can consider it a sign in its entirety: an ontological space where each human is an individual sign among many through which the presence of the transcendent can touch the flesh in a personal way. With God as Writer of the Story, all signs are threads within a whole tapestry still being woven because the narrative is still being written. Although narrative serves as a helpful illustration, analogy of being reminds us that God's "writing," though having some similarity to finite sub-creation, will have an ever greater dissimilarity from a human author's. Tolkien modelled his mytho-*logos* after this, and if we can describe what being inside *LOTR* feels like, we will then have a better grasp on how an ever-present transcendent sensibility might be perceptible in *LOTR*.

Narrative demonstrates to readers how characters participate in mytho-*logos*. *LOTR* is a fairy-story whose mytho-*logos* shares meaning in a way that is plainly and specifically orchestrated. Tolkien emphasized this by applying the following not only to the logic of *LOTR* but to all tales:

> The tale should tell . . . a story, of related events, . . . especially as they are arranged in sequence from the chosen beginning to the chosen end. I say "chosen," meaning "by the inventor," because the beginning and end of a story is to it like the edges of the canvas or an added frame to a picture, say a landscape. It concentrates the teller's attention, and yours, on one small part of the country. But there are of course no real limits: under the earth, and in the sky above, and in the remote and faintly glimpsed distances, and in the unrevealed regions on either side, there are things that influence the very shape and colour of the part that is pictured. Without them it would be quite different, and they are really necessary to understanding what is seen.[23]

A story gives a carefully constructed, concentrated snapshot of Secondary World history set against a larger backdrop.[24] Significantly, Tolkien

22. López, "Growing Human," 218.

23. "Draft," 92–93.

24. This is *frame narrative*, or "story within a story" (Flieger, "Frame Narrative," 216–18). See p. 105n37 about how many readers have given Primary Belief to *LOTR* as an actual frame narrative of world history.

expounded on the relevance of details: the story is meaningfully ordered (arranged sequence), purposefully and particularly placed (chosen beginning-to-end), and intentionally crafted to illustrate one small part of that world. But readers are capable of fathoming more. Fairy-stories say "once upon a time" and "they lived happily ever after" to acknowledge belonging to the limitless art of storytelling, while also recognizing they do not declare the end-all, be-all as many "modern realistic" storytellers claim to.[25] When the landscape of a small part of the country is framed, there is much more that is not. The painting or snapshot is indicative of a vaster "visionary scene" and "casement of the Outer World."[26] The frame is an addition, and one that necessarily focuses both reader and storyteller on the essential details therein. This makes the Outer World that much more important because these unseen, unrevealed regions outside share a relation to the glimpses within the frame. Such limitless extensions in time and space are evidenced within *LOTR* and influence its shape and color.

Notably, Tolkien called *LOTR* a Frame*less* Picture.[27] Not an endless story, but one that illuminates only the part of the world that is shown as if by a searchlight.[28] Instead of beginning with *once upon a time*,[29] "we might say that when we open to the first page of *LOTR* we enter into an *always already* involved world—complete and complicated."[30] Nor does *LOTR* conclude with *happily after ever* or *The End*.[31] Although Tolkien utilized neither fairy-story normality in *LOTR*, it does have a beginning and end, but its frame is obscured because of the greater tapestry. The story is strewn with signs, a visionary scene set within the greater intricate web of story to which it belongs.[32] Its casement shows an intentionally written historical episode, tied to various things unrecorded in its prose. Without these glimpses, the narrative would be different. *LOTR* is effectual because they are there. Therefore, both the

25. OFS, 83–84nH.

26. OFS, 83nH.

27. Emphasis mine.

28. Illuminating over 1,137 pages, including the index, but not maps.

29. See *LOTR*, 1.

30. Lauro, "Beyond," 187.

31. See *LOTR*, 1008.

32. Evidenced by its own constellations (such as Menelvagor, Swordsman of the Sky [*LOTR*, 80]), deep history of Treebeard and the Ents (452–64), songs and cries to Elbereth the unseen (78, 229, 231, 712, 894, 1005), and remnants of what once was a much larger "garden of Gondor" in the land of Ithilien (636), as a few examples.

sum of the threads (between beginning and end) as well as each individual thread (details as arranged) should be observed holistically with consideration of an Outer World: "For with the picture in the tapestry a new element has come in: the picture is greater than, and not explained by, the sum of the component threads."[33] They prompt readers to imagine more than the story alone.

Implicit in these metaphors is Tolkien's assumption that they generate mental images of things not physically present without the reader consciously pausing to stop, think of a tapestry, then think of a picture, then think of how a picture fits into a greater tapestry, and then connect this to story. Similar to Secondary Belief, if the illustrations given are sound enough, there is no problem with the reader visualizing the imagery. The connection is made through a common understanding, and the images enhance the capability for effectively communicating meaning.[34] The reader can know that Tolkien has described storytelling, not textiles hanging on castle walls. Thus, the imagery allows readers to see storytelling and *LOTR* through metaphorical lenses that show the reader what Tolkien was trying to illustrate through *LOTR*.

Mytho-*logos* communicates meaning with language as the modus operandi to direct imaginations about what to envision. Narrative focuses readers on a particular landscape as "can be seen through a telescope."[35] What is captured through the lens, though from a distance is "limited," it is "clear and coloured; flattened and remote," with vivid details of whatever part of the country the lens focuses on: "threadlike waters really falling; wind ruffling the small green leaves and blowing up the feathers of birds on the branches."[36] The lens makes "seeing [different] from [merely] imagining."[37] To pause here, Tolkien was not separating seeing from imagination, but articulating a more intensive level of mind-to-mind progenitivity—"*seeing* . . . not subject to optical laws"[38] and seeing as if illuminated by a "light," but not physical light.[39] The inventor sees first and

33. OFS, 40n.

34. Even if the imagery is not automatically perceptible, at least some sense of what is being described is translatable upon second thought.

35. "Papers," 172.

36. "Papers," 172.

37. "Papers," 172.

38. "Papers," 198n.

39. "Papers," 198.

thus enables others to see similarly.[40] When "living shapes . . . move from mind to mind," mytho-*logos* illuminates other minds.[41]

The telescope is another way of understanding narrative as a vehicle of transport in waking life and enhances the crispness of the view Tolkien was eliciting in *LOTR*. In chapter 4, the focus was literary credibility inside Other Time, its main emphasis being the temporal sensation of traveling through a literary world without physically being there. Where that dealt with movement through *time* within parallel narrative, the telescope evokes the sensibility of *spatial* movement, or traveling *to*. Customarily telescopes are used to span great distances to see something barely visible from a present location. In the moment the telescopic lens is used, it is as if viewers travel from "here" to "there,"[42] seeing close-up that which is "moving and real."[43] For readers participating in *LOTR*, the moment one enters the already involved narrative, it is as if they are transported into the details that induce the sensibility that it is part of a larger complete and complicated composition. Telescoping into Other Time can bolster the sense of being freed from a Primary World prison sensation.

If *LOTR* displays a vast world beyond the text that induces Secondary Belief, how the narrative was constructed matters. If feigned history instills perceptible transcendent sensibility, it suggests an analogical relation about Primary Reality.[44] Tolkien "says something" through the mytho-*logos* of *LOTR* that compares to what the cosmo-*logos* "says." This does not necessarily correlate with how narratives of life can often feel, especially when disoriented amidst worldly fallenness and adverse emotions. Recall Tolkien's encouragement to Christopher, "all *stories* feel like that when you are *in* them." Stories can be windows, doorways, or lenses that help us see a greater story and bigger picture beyond imminent intensities.[45]

History and myth are the same stuff integrated into each narrative of life. People experience narrative by serially living from birth to the present, and they experience narrative worlds revealed from beginning to end. Myth is experienced as people participate in the spatiotemporal substance of each narrative space. Recall how myth has been discussed

40. "Papers," 169.

41. "Mythopoeia," 87. See Flieger, *Splintered*, 43.

42. Which essentially creates the effect that *there* is *here*.

43. "Papers," 172.

44. Though readers may not be conscious of it.

45. See Lewis, *Experiment*, 138.

thus far: It permeates by some osmotic design and affects us when accepted and appreciated at once and in all its parts. Myth can only permeate and be wholly alive in time and space. Therefore, it is experientially interlaced into the fabric of existence.

Narrative mediates myth as an "integrative form of thought."[46] This is like the meaning of Tolkien's *mythos*—the underlying mode and how of thought—that allows us to see that myth, *logos*, and history are inseparable since they share the same makeup. A mythopathic Primary Reality reading of the cosmos sees divinity as factual experience, where "narrative and myth attribute *significances*"[47] or "meanings"[48] about the greater reality people can know as they participate in life. Narrative and myth display a "modelling [of] events by infusing them with meaning and linking them by analogy," whereby people are able to concretely experience the divine as they participate in the Writer's narrative.[49] Such participation exemplifies looking out and up to the greater reality through which *ens creatum*—being created—transformation is possible.[50] This is intermingled with the true, deeper, right order of the cosmos. Tolkien modelled this through his own creativity. His mytho-*logos* bound his own linguistic predilections through *poesis* "capable of establishing" the "full world of mythic meaning"[51] presented in *LOTR*, which speaks to the religious sense in an axiomatic way. But secularity presents challenges to deter confidence about it.

Self as Central: Downward and Inward

After reading *LOTR*, "we know at once that it has done things to us," said Lewis. "We are not quite the same men."[52] Kilby's and the unbeliever's observations indicated as much, yet noted how being inside *LOTR* created a disparateness about Primary World experience. After backing away from the telescopic view of Middle-earth through *LOTR*, they indicated how *LOTR* stirs a desire for an ontically-based objective

46. Taylor, *Language Animal*, 72.
47. Taylor, *Language Animal*, 76.
48. Taylor, *Language Animal*, 147.
49. Taylor, *Language Animal*, 76.
50. Taylor, *Secular*, 96–97.
51. Kilby, "Tolkien as Scholar," 11.
52. Lewis, "Dethronement," 15.

reality as described at the end of chapter 5. Giussani suggested why present-day reality might seem like this:

> There is an irreligiosity in our time that begins, without anyone noticing it, with a detachment between God as source and meaning of life (origin and meaning "of life," and hence relevant to the things that happen, to the events that we undergo) and God as a fact constructed by thought, as a fact of thought, understood according to the needs of man's thought. This results in a separation of the meaning of life from experience. The denial of God, up to the denial of its extremely reasonable and evident consequence that "God is all in all," implies a detachment of and a distance between the sense of life and human experience. This is the case because the meaning of life is God.[53]

If the divine mind has been removed as the ontic foundation of the cosmos and relegated to a made-up idea to cling to when needed, this is a reversion to the old reading of reality. The onto-theological bond is imaginatively de-synthesized when God is no longer the primary cause, Writer, and transcendent participant within the cosmos. Thus, meaning is interpreted as mediating differently and the true order of cosmo-*logos* is replaced because the cosmos does not transsignify a mind whose intrinsic rationality rules cosmic development.

Tolkien's metaphors of the darkening sky, spiritual malnourishment, and prisonlike feel are reminiscent of what Charles Taylor called the *immanent frame* of Western society, which "constitutes" reality as confined to the observable natural order without any possible transcendent involvement.[54] This was the apparent consequence of *secularization*, the theoretical disappearance of religiousness as humanity became freed from sacred restraints because of naturalistic science and the age of reason.[55] Instead of arguing that God or the possibility of the transcendent has disappeared, Taylor asserted that over the centuries "the background to all our thinking" has shifted.[56]

LOTR offers a background that challenges this thinking by telescoping readers into Tolkien's own *cosmic imaginary*, which stems from what Taylor more broadly called *social imaginaries*: the common, nontheoretical ways many societies share an outlook and actively practice a

53. Giussani in López, "Growing Human," 215n12.

54. Taylor, *Secular*, 542.

55. Casanova, "Secular." See Taylor, *Secular*, 779n1.

56. Taylor, *Secular*, 780n17. See also *Secular*, 15–16.

way of life.[57] Cosmic imaginary is another term for the pre-1500 cosmos grounded in ontic *logos*.[58] If meaning in God or a divine mind is severed from being the source of cosmic development, people will be more challenged to find themselves grounded in reality than they might have prior to 1500. Even if they do, this cannot be in exactly the same way as it once was since their current setting and background differs. The experiences to which Kilby, the unbeliever, and Giussani alluded are the after-effects of the new formation and re-creation of human identity that supplanted the cosmo-*logos* lens. They express a view "as though the creation of a thick emotional boundary between us and the cosmos were now lived as a loss"[59]—not that it has completely disappeared, but that many live as though it has. Taylor outlined three stages of secularization that occurred gradually from 1500 to present day:

1. Religiousness moved into the private realm, taking a "retreat" from "public spaces" (Secular 1);[60]
2. Religious "belief and practice" decreased in common everyday life (Secular 2);[61]
3. A "change in the conditions of belief" happened,[62] "a move from a society where belief in God is unchallenged and indeed, unproblematic, to one in which it is understood to be one option among others, and frequently not the easiest to embrace" (Secular 3).[63]

I want to focus on how the movement from ontic grounding in a greater reality into a theoretical reading of reality affects how people experience Secular 3. Formerly, they participated *in* an orderly cosmos of transcendence. Secularization altered the lens so that common discourse resolves to "talk *about*" the world instead of seeing a "complementary relation" between creation and the divine.[64]

57. Taylor, *Secular*, 171–72.
58. See Taylor, *Secular*, 322–51.
59. Taylor, *Secular*, 38.
60. Taylor, *Secular*, 423; Warner et al., Editors' Introduction, 8.
61. Taylor, *Secular*, 423; Warner et al., Editors' Introduction, 8.
62. Taylor, *Secular*, 423; Warner et al., Editors' Introduction, 9.
63. Taylor, *Secular*, 3; Warner et al., Editors' Introduction, 9.
64. Taylor, *Language Animal*, 74.

A mythopathic reading of Primary Reality designates a meaningfully ordered cosmos. But if reality becomes predominantly oriented according to theory, critical challenges arise regarding the surety of ontic *logos*. "The highest product of analytic thought, and its governing construct, is the formal *theory*, an integrative device that is much more than a symbolic invention: it is a system of thought and argument that predicts and explains. Successful theories often convey power."[65] Theoretical science is a human means for ascribing the inter-workings of material reality. Instead of deriving meaning mythically, theories move to formalize systematic regimentations of facts according to disciplinary specificities strictly bound to the observable order.[66]

Taylor's three phases are not theories but observations about how the historical momentum of human thought progressively superseded the cosmo-*logos* reading of reality. Whereas the cosmic imaginary involved participation of whole being in the divine, theory became "an externalization of thought"[67] apart from the intrinsic rationality upheld in the *logos*. As religiousness was "supposedly" subtracted as a given from natural human inclinations,[68] participating in God was subtracted as a common ontological outlook. The human imagination was freed from these sacred restraints. Primary Reality was divided: Created reality was dislodged from being grounded in uncreated reality, cosmos and creation became nature and universe, and the natural order was determined by immanent meanings independent from a Creator.[69] Naturalism relies on human-made presuppositions to develop "impersonal" strictures, their "task" being to examine reality according to these "laws" independently.[70] Thus, the natural world "eclipsed" transcendence so that all meaning and significance were derived from within the immanent frame.[71]

Instead of looking further on, further up to a greater reality, naturalism created the prison barricade. Strict science castigates those believing in God, rejects the divine, and deems it as un-rational, putting an "embargo on the transcendent, without offering any scientific justification for

65. Merlin Donald in Taylor, *Language Animal*, 75.
66. Donald in Taylor, *Language Animal*, 75–76.
67. Taylor, *Language Animal*, 75.
68. Casanova, "Secular."
69. Smith, *How (Not) to Be*, 34–35.
70. Poythress, *Redeeming*, 261.
71. Smith, *How (Not) to Be*, 22–23, 26.

doing so."[72] Answers to questions once satisfied by the cosmic imaginary tethered through "vertical" onto-theological interactivity should be found solely within the "horizontal" realm.[73] This downward turn away from God also prompted an inward turn of the personal "I." Naturalism shifted participation in God to an *exclusive humanism* where individualism determines "meaning and significance" without acknowledging God.[74] Of this, Taylor observed four consequential anthropocentric shifts:

1. Sense of purpose moved from God-orientation to self-orientation. Human flourishing became the self's foremost good, not God's.[75]
2. Grace disappeared; reason and self-discipline reigned. The world became humanly conceptual; human intellect had no need for God.[76]
3. The mystery of God and God's interworking in the world was removed.[77]
4. God no longer transformed; instead, humanity transformed itself.[78]

These downward and inward turns depict the ontological space of Secular 3, so that "the immanent [frame has become] more than a theory"[79] to Western society, which masquerades its own givens and facts about actuality.

Taylor called this new individualism the making of the *buffered self*.[80] Unlike how the ontic *logos* embedded participants in the cosmic order, secularization attempted to alter this reading to "the abandonment of one's self to nothing but the force of one's reactions, instincts, fancies, and opinions."[81] Such desertion allows for countless possibilities that exacerbate how individuals find personal orientation. Having intellectually staved off God, buffered selves also escape from the "state of

72. McGrath, *Nature*, 130.
73. Taylor, *Secular*, 556.
74. Smith, *How (Not) to Be*, 141.
75. Taylor, *Secular*, 222.
76. Taylor, *Secular*, 222–23.
77. Taylor, *Secular*, 223–24.
78. Taylor, *Secular*, 224–25.
79. Taylor, *Secular*, 780n17.
80. See Taylor, *Secular*, 27, 37–42.
81. Giussani, *Religious Awareness*, 10.

captivity" of primitive religious inhibitions.[82] Of course, each individual in Western Europe and North America is not defined or confined to the restraints of buffering. Thus, it is beneficial that Taylor aspired to capture the *feel* of Secular 3 so that there might be a better understanding for this ontological space.[83] A few more features that contribute to this sensibility will be discussed before returning to how Tolkien engaged common perceptions about Secular 3 through his creativity.

Within the immanent frame, *immanentization* promotes new imaginings of meanings "enclosed within the material universe and natural world,"[84] threatening the religious sense of everyone. Humanism and science are placed atop the whole tableau as absolute certainties. The consequences of remaking via buffering scrambled social imaginaries with various immanence-only readings. Therein, a vague, disorderly aura fills it with innumerable *cross-pressures*—tantalizing amounts of "spiritual options" with an allure of transcendence yet grounded in the world of self, nature, and ideas.[85] The consequences of exclusive humanism promote the *nova effect*, the "spawning [of] an ever-widening variety of moral/spiritual options, across the span of the thinkable and perhaps even beyond."[86] In scientific naturalism, all other bases for truth dissolve.[87] Nature, it is said, became the only source and means for determining reality based strictly on deductible observation.[88] Yet this is contradicted by other propounded "truths" that cannot be measured scientifically.

Three *isms* describe this quandary: "[Relativism] robbed us of any transcendent standard against which we can measure our thoughts, our words, and our deeds; [existentialism] has emptied our lives of any higher meaning, purpose, or direction."[89] Relativism claims no absolute authority, and as existentialists, individuals determine their own way. MacIntyre added a third ism: *emotivism*, the "doctrine that all evaluative judgments and more specifically all moral judgments are *nothing but* expressions of preference, expressions of attitude or feeling, inso-

82. Taylor, *Secular*, 301.
83. See Smith, *How (Not) to Be*, 60–61.
84. Smith, *How (Not) to Be*, 48.
85. Smith, *How (Not) to Be*, 140.
86. Taylor, *Secular*, 299.
87. See McGrath, *Nature*, 126.
88. McGrath, *Nature*, 126.
89. Markos, *On the Shoulders*, 10.

far as they are moral or evaluative in character."[90] Even if emotivism is a doctrine by which one attempts to live, it can only be theoretical at best, and even then is always historically conditioned to the individual's circumstances.[91] It is as if people sever themselves from the past altogether. Emotivism rather depends solely on each person's particular evaluations of the present moment.[92] Nonetheless, some form of ambiguous authority exists as each individual justifies one thing over the next with a wave of the hand at whatever grounds of authority acts as their momentary moral basis—the law, God, or whatever seems proper. This ostensibly amounts to rational justifications for personal standards of morality that do not have roots.[93] "For what emotivism asserts is in central part that there are and can be *no* valid rational justification for any claims that objective and impersonal moral standards exist and hence that there are no such standards."[94] Attached to all of this is a common assumption that this is the way everyone, everywhere, for all time, has also conceived the world.[95] It is as if common sense is inescapably derived by navigating through an "ethical wilderness"[96] where infinite potential aligns more with aimlessness than rootedness.

None of these isms agrees with the others. Instead of giving a clear impression about an inner consistency while moving through life, when innumerable individuals determine reality according to their own whims, the ontological space becomes murky and confusing. Human-made meanings over the past five hundred years have affected how variant ideologies and theories created instability and uncertainty about how we navigate through life because the background for our thinking now and in recent history is not ontically grounded. It is as if it has disappeared almost without notice. Secularists declare reality in certain, yet not agreeable, terms—and not without fracturing wholeness, like a "cacophony" of ideas "replacing meaning,"[97] what Tolkien called the

90. MacIntyre, *After Virtue*, 11–12.
91. MacIntyre, *After Virtue*, 12–22.
92. MacIntyre, *After Virtue*, 13.
93. MacIntyre, *After Virtue*, 19.
94. MacIntyre, *After Virtue*, 19.
95. See MacIntyre, *After Virtue*, 19.
96. Bellah, "Christian Faithfulness," 78.
97. Taylor, *Secular*, 552.

"noise and confusion" of his time.[98] It is "the essential malady of" societal and "self-made misery."[99]

One of the givens of the immanent frame is that ontic doubt is a fact of existence. Since divinity is called into question, transcendent sensibility is uncertain at best and should be contended by or defined according to human rationalization. Naturalism and individualism rule and supposedly set the self free. But amidst such claims, there is still a need for some manner of *fullness*. In short, fullness is what all people want: complete fulfillment in life[100] rooted in a *telos* "to which we orient ourselves morally or spiritually."[101] But there is a difference in how secular imaginaries perceive this in comparison to the cosmic.

Immanent frame rules maintain that individual fulfillment must be pursued within a rote, naturalistic, closed system. The various isms and epistemic starting points for intellectual knowledge fracture meaning into countless strands of *belief* where "we say we have moments of transcendent experience"[102] but have difficulty finding ontological footing due to the multitude of specific individualistically determined meanings. Taylor called these *closed world structures* (CWSs). CWSs are "ways of restricting our grasp of things which are not recognized as such,"[103] and in a way that "our contemporary experience" is bent towards immanentization.[104] In other words, we do not often initially comprehend CWSs because our actual experience does not cohere with these rationalizations. As grounded in the mind, a CWS is "an intellectualization" that often gives "an underlying picture which is only partly consciously entertained, but which controls the way people think, argue, infer, [and] make sense of things."[105] Thus, a CWS is like a theory that sounds smart and exudes a sense of power but contrives an intellectualization that merely makes a close-minded claim about reality that may not actually amount to anything realistic at all. Yet, when human-made construals are assumed as facts about the world, the burden of proof is upon old or primitive views to meet the demands of new frames of thought, and

98. Resnick, "Interview," 42.

99. OFS, 72.

100. Taylor in Warner et al., Editors' Introduction, 12n19.

101. Taylor, *Secular*, 6.

102. Taylor in Warner et al., Editors' Introduction, 11.

103. Taylor, *Secular*, 551.

104. Smith, *How (Not) to Be*, 140.

105. Taylor, *Secular*, 557.

according to CWS rules. As God was gradually removed as a given of the cosmos, ontic *logos* self-identification gradually became replaced by such newly formed buffered claims of identity.

However, fullness in a secular age maintains a desire for interconnectivity "to a more-than-immanent transformation perspective."[106] So in a way, this acknowledges a desire, if not need, for more beyond the buffer, possibly even without recognizing it. But this cannot be God (because of science); or, if one believes in God, the backdrop of the immanent frame designates belief in God as doubtful, superstitious, or childish. Consequently, secularization "not only makes *un*belief possible; it also *changes belief*."[107] These rules maintain what beliefs are acceptable or not on a conditional basis.[108] Thus, the backdrop of the immanent frame has become more than a theory.

All of this does not seem much different than fantasy where the human mind is capable of forming mental images of things not actually present. The imaginative shift was really a switch of lenses. That the secular lens commonly replaces the cosmic does not mean that the latter cannot be revisited, nor that divinity has gone elsewhere. Secularization has merely created social imaginaries for seeing at different stages of the imagination. Tolkien engaged imaginations with a counternarrative to the social imaginaries of his day to stoke the fires of the old light and kindle the religious sense presently. To comprehend more fully, we must reconcile how this old sense may be fueled through a fresh new lens.

Engaging Individualistic Lenses

Buffer implies a type of protective barrier that might ward off or lessen a blow from an exterior threat. Therefore, buffer*ing* is not synonymous with invincibility. It compares to the insulated walls of a house on a frigid night. The insulation keeps out the coldest air but is never 100 percent effective.

Significantly, buffering makes it *seem* as though the self is impervious to any figurative "cold air" by elevating the individual to the center of the universe. However, individualization presented more of a mixed bag. "Power, reason, invulnerability, [and] a decisive distancing from

106. Taylor, *Secular*, 530.

107. Smith, *How (Not) to Be*, xi.

108. Smith, *How (Not) to Be*, 18.

age-old fears" cannot completely be severed from; "we all still have [it in] some sense, not only from history, and not only from the as yet unenlightened masses, but also because they resonated somehow in our own childhood."[109] Yet, this created the posture for an "enormous condescension of posterity"[110] where "we no longer belong to this world; we have transcended it."[111] Because the buffered self escapes this age-old state of captivity, it assumes a mentality that its invulnerability is virtuous.[112] Regardless of these beliefs, if some manner of fullness is desirable, some measure of vulnerability exists. Moreover, external influences still can make their way in. The imagination is a gateway for meaning to awaken innate sensibilities in ways that sidestep restrictions imposed by the immanent frame.

Every human outlook necessarily involves the imagination. When dealing with social imaginaries, this not only includes how cultures envision reality, but also how one participates in the life of that culture. Buffered sensibilities likely imagine reality now upheld by the recreated narratives of their social imaginaries, a shift that did not happen overnight, but as a gradual transition from the old reading that shifted self-identification away from the ontic *logos*. *Subtraction stories* are "earlier" and once "certain" stories now seen as "confining horizons, illusions, or limitations of knowledge" that "human beings [have] lost, sloughed off, or liberated themselves from."[113] Being freed from these sensibilities emboldened the invulnerability of Secular 3. The question becomes whether such people actually escape from the old sense of self and whether they are truly invulnerable. It also becomes a matter of discussing from what the buffered self is freed from.

Taylor portrayed the old sense of self as osmotic. The *porous self* was integrally bound within an ontological space, a living reality in a spirit(s)-filled cosmos where the self is penetrable, susceptible, and vulnerable—not weak—to the spiritual realm.[114] Creation was everywhere "charged" with affective "causal power" where the things outside the self could "impose meanings" inherent in themselves and thereby "bring about

109. Taylor, *Secular*, 301.

110. Edward Thompson in Taylor, *Secular*, 301.

111. Taylor, *Secular*, 301.

112. Taylor, *Secular*, 300.

113. Taylor, *Secular*, 22.

114. Taylor, *Secular*, 36.

physical outcomes proportionate to their meanings."[115] From the outside working in, these "exogenously inducing"[116] meanings impressed a heavy, seemingly unrestricted influence over humankind.[117] Yet, they were all inseparable from understanding the cosmos as having both providential intent and interactivity, that the orderly interworkings on display were contingent upon a Creator.[118] With divinity perceived as "micro-functioning [through] society," society's response naturally based reality on and interpreted reality through the divine as its foundational principle.[119] This was lived "*experience*, not . . . 'theory,' or 'belief.'"[120] So instead of talking about the reality in which people lived with a sense of separation, they participated in an inter-penetrably active "living religion" reality.[121]

Thus, porousness was a fact of existence, which allowed and accepted that there would be experiential tension in life even amidst the presence of transcendent reality. Embedded in this reality was the understanding that God was the greatest good, and that it was "inconceivable" that goodness could be associated with anything other than divinity,[122] though evil ranged throughout the world at odds with it. To ignore this tension would be to disregard the ethos in which such societies were transformed. Un-Christianized cultures viewed tension in opposites—order and chaos, structure and anti-structure—perceived as needed to maintain equilibrium.[123] "The aim is frequently . . . to bring them to some kind of synergy; to make the structure less self-enclosed, and at the same time to allow it to draw on the energy of anti-structure in order to renew itself."[124] Another form of this equilibrium is evidenced through a hierarchical complementarity; regardless of a person's role in the vertical order of society, each person was crucial to the whole—highest to lowest, and vice versa.[125] Within this "Great Chain of Being" everyone participated in

115. Taylor, *Secular*, 35.
116. Taylor, *Secular*, 34.
117. See Taylor, *Secular*, 33–39.
118. Taylor, *Secular*, 25.
119. Taylor, *Secular*, 43.
120. Taylor, *Secular*, 39.
121. Taylor, *Secular*, 147.
122. Taylor, *Secular*, 544.
123. See Taylor, *Secular*, 46–51.
124. Taylor, *Secular*, 53.
125. Taylor, *Secular*, 123, 392.

the "complex unity" that "*precedes*," and is "not created by the . . . action of its members. . . . It is grounded in the order of things itself."[126]

> Something rather different happens within an understanding of the cosmos as a hierarchy of forms. There it is obvious that the human observer is on a certain level, and while he is aware that there are levels which are higher, and has some idea of their nature, it is also accepted that his grasp of them will be imperfect. In this sense, seeing the whole tableau, in which all parts and levels are equally intelligible, because identically placed in relation to the thinker, is obviously impossible. The view of the whole is from a certain position within it, and it essentially reflects that placing.[127]

Fundamentally, society accepted the impossibility of knowing and comprehending everything, and it was acceptable that there were mysterious unknowns layered within this reality.[128] Experiencing good and evil in a spiritually active cosmos was manifest. Christianity made sense of this tension by claiming that faith in God was necessary for both the individual and society to flourish and transform.[129] In that setting, present purposes were clearer due to the cosmic imaginary being interwoven with God's mysterious transcendence. An ontological grounding through Christian *logos* brought about a "transformed disposition of the knower" because of the new thought patterns it presented for "discernment of deeper levels of reality than unaided human reason or sight permit."[130]

Tolkien viewed Primary Reality as presenting a similar porous environment that was not theorized about or believed in but *experienced*. Telescoping into narrative surpasses theory because reading is active experience, not speculation or belief. If readers attain Secondary Belief, mytho-*logos* generates an ontological response that circumvents buffered invulnerabilities. Tolkien's mytho-*logos* does this through two relevant mediums that can affect human sensibilities: fairy-story and myth. Each appeal to the porous side of human nature Tolkien believed still exists.

The problem with fairy-stories today is that they are usually interpreted as either childish or akin to what the buffered self only deems

126. Taylor, *Secular*, 392 (emphasis mine).

127. Taylor, *Secular*, 232.

128. Taylor, *Secular*, 232.

129. Taylor, *Secular*, 43–44.

130. McGrath, *Heresy*, 19.

nostalgic due to immanentization.[131] In recent history fairy-stories have become disqualified as being acceptable among adults.[132] They have either been discarded to the "lumber-room" of their imaginations to be forgotten or dismissed merely as nursery tales.[133] Either way, fairy-stories still exist in the history of storytelling, but in neither case is the issue about believing whether or not they are real. Tolkien contended that while fairy-stories resonate with exilic longings caused by the Fall, they touch on latent aspects of personal being by appealing to the need for fullness on moral grounds. Children show poignant awareness of this when they read fairy-stories, but in a secular imaginary this fades with age and maturity. Children are more receptive to the moral directives fairy-stories present as givens than are adults. Tolkien claimed that while "Is it true?" is a question rightly raised by children, "far more often they have asked me: 'Was he good? Was he wicked?' . . . They were more concerned to get the Right side and the Wrong side clear. For that is a question equally important in History and in Faërie."[134] In other words, if a child asks *Is it true?* the question is based upon the need for clarity about its meaning to discern its moral for applicability's sake.[135] The fictional substance provides moral orientation that is not always clear-cut in the child's growing awareness of the world. The fairy-story thus functions as a vehicle for satiating desire for knowledge. Tolkien explained how via his own testimony:

> I had no special "wish to believe." I wanted to *know*. Belief depended on the way in which stories were presented to me, by older people, or by the authors, or on the inherent tone and quality of the tale. But at no time can I remember that the enjoyment of a story was dependent on belief that such things could happen, or had happened, in "real life." Fairy-stories were plainly not primarily concerned with possibility, but with desirability. If they awakened *desire*, satisfying it while often whetting it unbearably, they succeeded.[136]

131. Taylor, "Buffered."

132. Duriez, "Fairy Story," 21.

133. OFS, 51.

134. OFS, 53n.

135. OFS, 53. This elevates the significance of understanding the meaning rightly. We ought to get the story right to discern whether its meaning is applicable.

136. OFS, 54–55 (*know*, emphasis mine; *desire*, emphasis Tolkien's).

As with Bilbo, awakening implies pre-existing dormancy, and formative encounters involve embracing awakening. A fairy-story's meaning has the capacity to draw one "further on, further up" because it enhances how to discern right or wrong when presented with moral dilemmas in life. Asking about the moral is akin to seeking the point of the story. If it is true that fairy-stories are equally important in History as Faërie, then something about an ontological encounter through Faërie has applicability to actual experience in some way as a mediatory "vehicle of Mystery."[137]

A vehicle like *LOTR* is experienced in a Primary World setting instilled with its own mysteriousness. "The unfathomable Mystery" is the uncreated God in which creation participates, who is "the object of the religious sense," said Giussani.[138] "Therefore, it is understandable that man ponders this in such a way that he has a thousand thoughts about it."[139] But this does not guarantee that one recognizes God as Mystery, nor the "human fact" of Christ.[140] Individual consciousness is roused through the wonder of first encounters with otherness in the cosmos. After awakening to the original wonder of the world in childhood, this fades over time and disappears: "Everyone lives without the wonder of this first encounter, as if it were something obvious; and so they enjoy nature less, they enjoy time less and space, they enjoy reality less."[141] Humanity needs the wonder of encounter to be reawakened and restored, not as an end unto itself, but so that the encounter may point to the true object of the religious sense. The cosmic imaginary exuded "the transcendent character of reality,"[142] and the gospel can reinvigorate wonder and orient people to the origin and object of religious sensibility. But this is difficult in a fallen world because secularization subtracted grounding in transcendence and shifted the self's ontic placement.

Tolkien perceived ontic *dis*placement in his social imaginary. The need for clean windows and breaking down prison walls implies something is still beyond them: "The world outside has not become less real because the prisoner cannot see it."[143] Tolkien's critique was that

137. OFS, 44.

138. Giussani, "Religious Sense and Faith," 3.

139. Giussani, "Religious Sense and Faith," 3.

140. Giussani, "Religious Sense and Faith," 3.

141. Giussani, "Religious Sense and Faith," 4.

142. Taylor in Warner et al., Editors' Introduction, 11.

143. OFS, 69.

prisoners should break out, if possible. If unable, it is hardly unreasonable that they should try to imagine life beyond the walls.[144] The secularists' CWSs confine reality within their own boundaries with barred filthy windows. Tolkien confronted the bewildering claims of such "philosophical puzzlement."[145] The prisoners have ontic doubt about what they have been told is true about reality and *LOTR* offers a pre-secular lens to see otherwise.

As vehicles of mystery, fairy-stories can bridge the gap between secularity and estrangement from the religious sense. Grownups claim fairy-stories deny reality by escaping to Neverland, and Tolkien agreed their purpose should not be to produce "Peter Pans."[146] But fairy-stories preserve "innocence and wonder"[147] that can touch innate sensibilities by way of analogy to recover a clear view purposefully. "I do not say 'seeing things as they are' and involve myself with the philosophers," Tolkien said, "though I might venture to say 'seeing things as we are (or were) meant to see them'—as things apart from ourselves."[148]

Taylor asserted that there are "no analogies in our present understanding" to describe the cosmic imaginary where all of the meaning was "already there."[149] The backdrops of our social imaginaries are much different, and there is not the ontic confidence there once was. But an analogy can be experienced via poetic meaning, linking a reader's imagination to a sub-created cosmic imaginary apart from ourselves. Even though we cannot experience exactly the pre-secular cosmic imaginary in its old sense, readers can experience the meaningful order of *LOTR*'s mytho-*logos* by virtue of its mythic operations. It is analogical participation inside real sub-creation at a different stage of the imagination that can awaken human nature to the old light still present through the reader's own porousness.

When Tolkien analogically modelled his creativity after God's, he was participating in creativity as the medieval Christian poets did. To them, as the Christ-*Logos* revealed God's involvement within the cosmos, human *logos* was believed also to "express timeless truth" that could remain as an historical record about the eternal God they apprehended

144. OFS, 69.

145. Taylor, *Secular*, 30.

146. OFS, 58.

147. OFS, 58.

148. OFS, 67.

149. Taylor, *Secular*, 33.

presently.[150] This was only accessible by participating in God's life. Thus, the poet believed he was writing under God, unto God, and in a way that "authorship [belonged to] God."[151] Although a finite dim picture, this was a mimetic means for seeing literature as both "mediator" and "conjoiner of the two realities,"[152] thus affirming Tolkien's hope that sub-creation could be "taken up into Creation in some plane."[153] It also addressed the fundamental problem between sub-creation and Primary Reality while presenting the possibility for readers to "stand outside their own time" and also "outside Time itself, maybe."[154] The next chapter explores how Tolkien sub-creatively did this.

150. Jeffrey, "Tolkien," 68.
151. Jeffrey, "Tolkien," 68.
152. Jeffrey, "Tolkien," 68.
153. *Letters*, 195.
154. OFS, 48.

Chapter 7

Enchantment Awakens Personal Creativity

Introduction

The prison walls with filthy windows described in chapter 6 figuratively depict imaginative obstructions, which is further obscured by the "philosophers" who issue lenses that blur an ontic reading of transcendent reality. But although devaluation of God's active involvement inhibits the old reading of the Primary Reality *LOTR* parallels, when a reader is awakened or nourished through mytho-*logos*, something desirable that may also be true about the Primary World permeates the story, suggesting possible defects to buffered self-insulation.

That so many have been drawn to *LOTR* suggests at the very least that Tolkien excited and pleased readers, but something more penetrable is happening if a story deeply moves them. When *poiema* triggers a response where one is "surprised by the satisfaction of wants we were not aware of till they were satisfied," perhaps after "looking back on the whole . . . we shall feel that we have been led through a pattern or arrangement of activities which our nature cried out for, . . . good for us here and now."[1]

1. Lewis, *Experiment*, 134.

LOTR was an unintended consequence of *Hobbit*'s popularity. Because *Hobbit* touched readers, they demanded more of the world Tolkien had shown them only glimpses. *LOTR* was his response, intended to fulfill such demands. This chapter focuses on Tolkien's creativity and how it displayed the larger tapestry of Middle-earth through *LOTR* in a way that involves the reader's own creativity. Those readers awakened through Secondary Belief through the secondary patterns within the narrative's arrangement may better ascertain what is best here and now as they consider their own historical narratives. Through this exploration, we will come to a better understanding for how *LOTR* conveys ontic grounding through mytho-*logos*. If it causes readers to desire something similar to which Primary Belief can be given, its effects can be formative to their narratives of life and satisfy something their image-bearing natures cry out for.

The Best Kind of Window

Tolkien believed stories can affect readers unaware of or uninterested in a Christian reading of reality,[2] yet even the slightest hints of allegory are too manipulative. In such instances, "one-to-one correspondences" where "one thing equal[s] another" blocks "the free play of the imagination"[3] to the detriment of Secondary Belief. Thus, when Tolkien spoke of the need for clean windows, he insinuated they allow observers to give "fresh attention" to what is transsignified through what is seen without interference.[4] Fantasies are new windows displaying worlds according to their own laws. When peering through, "the things seen clearly," whether stationary or active, should appear as "freed from the drab blur of triteness or familiarity."[5] Science and philosophy grounded in a God-less cosmos impede how people imagine otherwise. By inhibiting primordial latencies, they "legally and mentally" categorize reality by means of their own "appropriation."[6] Fantasy should surpass these constraints, and Faërie

2. Mills, "One Truth," 20. Other writers Mills listed who shared this perspective were Flannery O'Connor, T. S. Eliot, Evelyn Waugh, Dorothy Sayers, C. S. Lewis, and Graham Greene.

3. Wood, *Gospel*, 5.

4. OFS, 67.

5. OFS, 67.

6. OFS, 67.

> represents at its weakest a breaking out (at least in mind) from the iron ring of the familiar, still more from the adamantine ring of belief that it is known, possessed, controlled, and so (ultimately) all that is worth being considered—a constant awareness of a world beyond these rings. More strongly it represents love: that is, a love and respect for all things, "inanimate" and "animate," an unpossessive love of them as "other." This "love" will produce both ruth and delight.[7]

Tolkien's vision for experiencing fantasy communicates this expectation: Sub-creation should transform how one envisions life in the real world, which may serve to penetrate ironclad, close-ended belief systems in the immanent frame. *Breaking out in mind* can effectively challenge these conditions of belief appropriated by those who disregard the cosmo-*logos*. Therefore, fantasy should awaken the viewer's sense of "perceiving [the] likeness and unlikeness"[8] of everything other in the Primary World in a new way; that is, restore a cosmic sense of analogical participation in the order of things apart from the confinements of secularity's *rings*. If it does, poetic meaning (Art) operatively links Imagination to Sub-creation.[9] Tolkien's capitalizations of *art*, *imagination*, and *sub-creation* emphasize their transsignification of deeper meaning than the words themselves.

We have discussed aspects of medievalism's influence on Tolkien's notion of sub-creativity.[10] In medieval illuminated manuscripts, capitalization was meant to "exhort the reader to pay attention."[11] Illustrations, colors, and other ornate details in such manuscripts were a means for communicating how to interpret meaning with more than merely the text.[12] In OFS, Tolkien just used words. Although he was not writing an illuminated manuscript,[13] he capitalized art, imagination, and sub-

7. "Essay," 144.

8. OFS, 67.

9. Introduced on p. 28.

10. Aspects of the medieval reading of reality clarify how we can comprehend Tolkien's reading of the cosmo-*logos*. One need not become medieval to understand; rather, such notions can still teach and transform us (Snyder, *Making*, 39). If so, old ways of reading reality shed light on how things may be seen happening now.

11. Milbank, *Chesterton*, 67.

12. University of Nottingham, "Introduction to Medieval Books."

13. Although in *Hobbit* and *LOTR*, he provided maps, runes, and illustrations to deepen the reader's impression of Middle-earth's inner consistency.

creation, insinuating that these terms were intended to grab the reader's attention and emphasize deeper meaning.[14]

Similar capitalization was used in communicating Tolkien's fundamental concern, the "problem with the relation of Art (and Sub-creation) and Primary Reality."[15] His allusion was to a needful restoration for seeing things as we are meant to see them, but his acknowledgement of the iron and adamantine rings of belief stresses the difficulty in doing so since they effect entire social imaginaries. If Tolkien could re-establish the relation in a general sense, it could then have a formational impact on how the relation could be restored in a personally particular sense. Then mytho-*logos* might serve as a conduit of meaning that could jostle readers from unilateral secular conditions of belief. If so, they might better register the awakening of the religious sense through *LOTR*. We now explore this possibility.

Circumvention Through Connatural Creativity

How one might break through iron and adamantine rings is difficult but not unattainable. Chapter 6 explained buffering as that which largely prohibits unwanted things from penetrating these surroundings. Self-centered restlessness that begins to feel like imprisonment suggests a need for meaningful answers to relevant *Life Questions* outside the self.[16] Life Questions help us make sense of "the sort of person one *should* become and the sort of life one *should* lead, concerning what one *should* value and what one *should* prioritize."[17] Such questions imply an inability to answer them without help, especially amidst the various

14. There does not seem to be a philological impetus to Tolkien's capitalizations, although when he did capitalize, he did so purposefully, yet inconsistently throughout his writing (personal correspondences with Jeremy Marshall, June 18, 2018; Edmund Weiner, July 5, 2018).

15. *Letters*, 145n. There was a different audience in this instance than the previous one. OFS was meant for a public audience. This second occasion was in a personal letter written to a publisher without foreseeing that it would be made public over thirty years later. However, the occasion of the letter—trying to have *Silmarillion* published alongside *LOTR* because they were "interdependent and indivisible" (Carpenter in *Letters*, 143)—stresses the significance of their capitalization based on the fact that both works were intended to restore this relation.

16. Gregory, *Unintended*, 74.

17. Gregory, *Unintended*, 74.

cross-pressures of secularity. Personal buffers are compacted by other buffers in secular social imaginaries that reinforce the ontological space within the immanent frame. Therein, existential instability may be found at every turn, hinting that transcendence might be possible *if* God exists. Likewise, Christianity *could* be true, but not without "seem[ing] implausible, unimaginable, even reprehensible."[18]

Immanentization consists of metaphorical Keep Out signs (various self-absorptions, isms, CWSs) scattered throughout secularly influenced societies that create a "firmer sense of boundary" to inhabitants.[19] Remarkably, they may not be aware of such signs. They are assumed as givens of their landscapes. Present-day secular imaginaries might be able to maintain firmer grounding if limitations to reason and science had not become some kind of new religion that has put an embargo on transcendence. Stories can change one's trajectory in life by introducing various outlooks readers might not have known without experiencing them.

Stories have regenerative power that is neither limited to the writer's original audience nor by a reader's social imaginary. Although unmaking present-day social imaginaries is impossible, new encounters that broaden the imagination and transform lived experience presently are within the realm of the possible. The effects will differ depending on reader and setting, but the story remains the same.[20] Therefore, if readers are deeply moved and nourished, this must have something to do with the story's substance, the "mysterious operative spiritual virtue" unified through mytho-*logos*.[21] Its affective capacity, then, may extend beyond *poiema* within readers after they step away from being inside.

However, a challenge arises for how *LOTR* translates into secular social imaginaries. *LOTR* parallels *Tolkien's* view of cosmic reality, which differs from the social imaginaries of many of his readers, hence

18. Ashford, "Jordan Peterson."

19. Taylor, "Buffered."

20. However, after seeing the *LOTR* films, both the adaptation of the story and the visual imagery may "colonize" the imagination in a way that will affect the pure imagery initiated by the text alone (Bratman, "Tolkien"). Birzer voiced his fears about this before the films' releases (see Birzer, "Christian Gifts"). While the poetic meaning implicit in the text remains, it becomes a matter of what the book impresses upon imaginations versus what the film projects. Notably, anyone willing to adapt text to film indicates that the literary version has a power in itself that makes it worth bringing to the attention of a wider audience through an alternative medium, but cinematic visuals do not mediate identical experience to what the text triggers the reader to visualize independently.

21. Maritain, "Concerning," 40.

the ontological predicament between *LOTR*'s cosmic imaginary and how its meaning is interpreted by a secularly-conditioned imagination. While its mytho-*logos* may be powerful, how it is received depends on the reader's ontological outlook. Tolkien believed the kind of story he was telling could shed light on an alternative way of seeing. With so many rundown, careworn, "imaginatively starved"[22] and "orphaned souls, asphyxiated by the banality of modern life,"[23] why should a prisoner not try to get out and go home?[24] There is no escape from the social imaginaries in which we live, but imaginative windows can instill a sense of truthfulness and rightness to personal being through Secondary Belief that brings relief in stifling cultural atmospheres.

Tolkien believed the imagination could truthfully accomplish this through myth.[25] Mythic stories and legends have a formational impact both because of their intrinsic virtue as constructed,[26] and because illuminating truth served as the basis for why they were originally told.[27] They stand the test of time because their regenerative power throughout history not only proves their substance as personally edifying but also resonates with having a spiritual power.[28] Thus, myths can potentially have a life-altering impact on those who absorb them:

> From the profundity of the emotions and perceptions that begot them, and from the multiplication of them in many minds—and each mind . . . an engine of obscured but unmeasured energy. They are like an explosive: it may slowly yield a steady warmth to living minds, but if suddenly detonated, it might go off with a crash: yes: might produce a disturbance in the real primary world.[29]

The imagination is integral to how such mythic disturbances are meant to affect readers and hearers, whether cruel or delightful. Narrative

22. Helms, *Tolkien's World*, 15.

23. Sebanc, "JRRT: Lover," 88.

24. The previous two footnotes express the feel of secularized ontological space in the twentieth century. This has carried over into the twenty-first century as *LOTR* still speaks to "people today [who] are spiritually underdeveloped [and] famished" (Jerry Root in Siewers, "Tolkien's Cosmic-Christian," 139).

25. *Letters*, 189n.

26. "Papers," 228.

27. *Letters*, 189n.

28. "Papers," 228.

29. "Papers," 228.

myths contain both dyscatastrophic and eucatastrophic elements that impact individual narratives presently, but from a different plane. For Tolkien, these are best understood in the context of meaningful order grounded in ontic *logos*. Rather than reprimanding those who believed differently than he, Tolkien used creativity to provide these experiences so that they might produce mythic effects that resound with readers' personal lives by virtue of their own creativity and imagination.

Keep Out signs are human-made and meant to deter from certain ways of thinking, but there are ways to bypass them because the imagination can see at different stages. Since reading is voluntary, literature progenitively passes on new meaning regardless of social imaginary. The mere hunger for fantastic stories enhances the capacity for mediation through buffers in unexpected ways despite any safeguards raised.[30] Therefore, instead of eradicating transcendent sensibility, buffering really only enhances the existential ambiguity that inhibits a sense of grounding in ontic *logos*.

The Christian view of creativity discussed in chapter 2 provided a lens for re-establishing the sense that God's transcendence remains here with us. It discussed the connatural gift of creativity people share with God and each other. Regardless of time and space, humanity's embeddedness in the cosmo-*logos* still stems from its metaphysical existence in God, and its creaturely vocation and end within creation remain upheld by the essence of God. Furthermore, creativity is gifted to all humanity, not just the vocational artist, affirming that although sub-creativity produces *poesis* that brings poetics into being, *poesis* is also making something of ourselves when we participate in the greater reality of God's ever-present *poesis*. But this is difficult to comprehend unless we experience an awakening and exercise the unique creativity in our personal narratives of life according to God's vocation for us.

Hobbit exhibits Bilbo discovering his own *telos* through his own narrative. Although readers may have been intrigued by particular details of the narrative, all are contextually drawn from the feigned cosmic imaginary into which *Hobbit* was being grafted. The further Bilbo is drawn into his cosmos, the more readers experience the substantive effects of Tolkien's mytho-*logos*. Readers wanted more of this because of the nourishing effects they experienced while journeying with Bilbo. *LOTR* was Tolkien's response to satiate their desire.

30. See Jacobs, "Fantasy," 5.

Addressing His Audience

Recall Tolkien's advice to his son: "At any minute it is what we are and are doing, not what we plan to be and do that counts." He assumed personal character now is essential to how one is prepared to take the next best step in answering Life Questions. Tolkien portrayed this through Bilbo from beginning to end in *Hobbit*. Bilbo's responses to one thing after another as the narrative unfolds are made without having any definitive answers about what to do other than to act upon what he knows based on what is required of him. Ennoblement happens over time, not in an instant. Readers witness this transformation as it happens, and Gandalf acknowledges this at the end of the story: "My dear Bilbo! Something is the matter with you! You are not the hobbit that you were."[31] The many things troubling Bilbo at the beginning of the story hardly mattered in the end.[32] He had transformed without loss of identity after being receptive to the greater reality of his cosmos.[33]

Feigned mythological history can have lasting effects on readers in search of their own orientation and grounding in the Primary World. Every story brought to bear upon the present has a contextual pre-existence through the storyteller for a particular purpose, to a particular audience.[34] But everyone's "soil of [life] experience" is inevitably "extremely complex" and historically based in a particular period of time and place.[35] Readers of *Hobbit* were hungry and thirsty for more stories like *Hobbit* because of its poetic effects. Therefore, however Tolkien would develop a follow-up story needed to nourish readers' needs presently. He evaluated such needs in light of the ontic displacement he perceived all around him throughout his life.

31. *Hobbit*, 326.

32. See *Hobbit*, 327–28.

33. Bilbo was perfectly content in his own little world before Gandalf arrived, seemingly with no need for answering Life Questions. But afterwards "he was quite content" in a wholly new way (*Hobbit*, 327).

34. Notably, *Hobbit* originated as a stream of tales he told to his children and eventually started to write down. A rough manuscript passed through a number of hands over the course of a few years without Tolkien expecting it to end up with a publisher. When it did, the manuscript ended abruptly and was incomplete (see Scull and Hammond, *JRRT Companion*, 385–93).

35. *LOTR*, xvii; *Letters*, 76.

In an interview with Henry Resnick in 1966, Tolkien illustrated how sub-creative lenses promote clarity amidst societies infiltrated by the nova effect:

> *Tolkien*: "My view of current affairs is not as depressed as some people's. I should say that I'm a bit frightened that the Greeks hadn't got something in the saying that those whom the gods wish to destroy they first drive mad."
>
> *Resnick*: "Is there a parallel in our modern world?"
>
> *Tolkien*: "It's like the tower of Babel, isn't it? All noise and confusion."
>
> *Resnick*: "Then you think we're either mad or on the brink of it?"
>
> *Tolkien*: "Yes, but I think that a little history cures you . . ."[36]

In answering Resnick's first question, Tolkien observed that many people seemed to have incoherent readings within their social imaginaries.[37] Of Tolkien's three comments, the first two take historical references to apply to his contemporary situation, claiming that proverbs and narratives make useful parallels when their meanings come to bear upon present situations. Since Tolkien equated a story's significance with applicability, his application of each parallel validates their significance to current circumstances. Each instance demonstrates how stories can have a universal impact at any point in history. Tolkien took these stories, old as they are, to communicate meaning orally without presenting all the details.[38]

In the oral tradition, although "casual details [would] not long survive change in everyday habits," they were initially inserted "because they had a story-making value" from the start.[39] Those that lasted have done so because they remain significant to the human condition.[40] "Oral narrators, instinctively or consciously, felt [the] literary 'significance'" of these values.[41] Their intended purpose was to create stories that stand the test

36. Resnick, "Interview," 42.

37. Affirming it as hectic without snobbishly claiming he is right and they are wrong.

38. Granted Tolkien merely referenced these stories without their fuller narratives, but just the mention of them brought certain meaning to Resnick's mind so that he understood Tolkien's point.

39. OFS, 79–80nB.

40. OFS, 80nB.

41. OFS, 49.

of time.[42] Tolkien's dialogue with Resnick demonstrates how their survival can bear significance in new ways based only on scant details or mere mention of a story by name. That anyone still affectively experiences old stories today is by virtue of their literary worth to generations of people; they would not have lasted otherwise.[43] Tolkien's particular purpose through *LOTR* was to offer a story with universal appeal to whatever audience was willing to encounter his mytho-*logos*.

During his lifetime, Tolkien observed how much "harder[,] crueller[,] and more mocking" the world had become.[44] Life experience seems chaotic enough, and this is compounded when considering the problematic challenges to the patterns of history in a fallen world.[45] Historical memory often allows stories such as Babel and *Beowulf* to stand the test of time, but in an age of pluralism, today's artists "do not have the luxury enjoyed" by those of earlier ages where they were "living in a world with common understandings, and common readings of visual things."[46] A world filled with multiple isms makes it difficult to determine shared common meanings about existential concerns let alone shared basic meanings of ideas and things, plus all the different names and definitions given to them. This makes meaning communicated through print significant because the details of narratives are preserved. If readers cannot perform an exegesis of a narrative's contextual history, they at least have the body of the text from which to derive meaning. This then becomes shared experience: from subcreator to reader and between reader and reader. Each shared experience engages the creativity of its participants so that while experiencing the same otherworld they are impacted by the same mytho-*logos*, despite how different their social imaginaries may be.

Chapter 3 discussed feigned history and how its verisimilitude communicates applicable truth according to its own plane. Literary art fails if not feigned well enough.[47] In *LOTR*, Tolkien wanted readers to experience meaningfully his personal Faërian Drama where the "scenes

42. OFS, 80nB.

43. OFS, 48.

44. *Letters*, 340. Partly because he had witnessed two world wars.

45. Summarized here from chapter 4: The world changes more rapidly with each generation; humanity consistently becomes short-sighted and often forgets its past mistakes and heritage; historical experience is unique to each individual and is thus innumerable.

46. Knippers, "Old Story," 69. Although Knippers was a painter discussing a painting, this was in the context of narrative storytelling's impact on the imagination.

47. See *Sir Gawain*, 21.

look real, but are feigned," and "not complete like a 'slice of life.'"[48] Dull "copies of 'real life' . . . teach us nothing" and offer naught worth remembering.[49] That fantasy is new makes it both different and other. It is neither copied nor typical, and it certainly cannot reflect a "slice" of anyone else's experience exactly. This enhances the significance of a literary world's effects through strangeness; when transported to a sub-creation's borders to experience it as if inside, it is the strangeness and imagined wonder that make it worth telling at all.[50]

Tolkien was interested in how affective experience apart from the five senses is feasible through feigned sub-creation. He called *LOTR* a "heroic romance,"[51] and C. S. Lewis described how this should seem with Tolkien's world in mind: "like a flower whose smell reminds you of something you can't quite place. I think the 'something' is the whole quality of life as we actually experience it."[52] A fragrance is always preceded by its source and is noticeably strange when compared to the plain fresh air of everyday breathing. Its lingering scent is unseen evidence of the source's presence.[53] If the *LOTR* is experienced fragrantly, it is as if the sub-created reality of the story has been absorbed into the reader. What Tolkien perceived imaginatively became incarnate upon *LOTR*'s canvas.[54] His paint was mytho-*logos*, and he "wanted a large canvas" indicative of more beyond the frame.[55] The next section ventures into why the imagery given to readers through narrative presents an experience that awakens the sense of grounding one might desire in the Primary World after having been inside Middle-earth.

48. "Papers," 193. *Slice of life* references the naturalistic empirical approach to dramatic storytelling at the turn of the twentieth century where audiences were given dull depictions of reality without definitive meaning. "Slices" were fragmentary scenes meant to display "typical . . . everyday life" before abrupt inconclusive endings leaving audiences guessing or drawing their own conclusions (*OED*, s.v. "slice, slice of life"; Turney, "Notes on Naturalism").

49. Hooper, "Tolkien and Lewis," 196.

50. See OFS, 27, 47, 59–60, 64, 80nB.

51. *Letters*, 210, 346.

52. Lewis in Hooper, "Tolkien and Lewis," 195.

53. Whether the fragrance is still present or not does not matter; the flower is still the source.

54. See *Leaf*, 66–75.

55. *Letters*, 216.

The Capabilities of Enchantment

A fairy-story's mytho-*logos* presents a brief look into another world where "if you read it, you enter . . . with the author as your guide. He may be a [good] guide . . . if he knows something about [it], and has himself caught some glimpses of it which he is trying to put into words."[56] This echoes the artist's attempt to show what s/he sees imaginatively to compel Secondary Belief. The exactness of the sub-creator's vision is never precisely duplicated in another mind, but Tolkien took pains to "guide"[57] readers on a formative journey through Middle-earth in *LOTR* by means of *enchantment*. Tolkien's mytho-*logos* is modelled after Primary World enchantment, the examination of which will allow us to see how Tolkien's sub-created enchantment aligns with it.

Cosmic imaginary enchantment consisted of a spirits-filled cosmos with the divine mind as the highest good and embattled forces of light and darkness active throughout.[58] As spiritual and physical creatures, humans were susceptible to other unseen spiritual powers within a lived reality where they might also encounter visible manifestations of such beings or experience possession.[59] Such was the porous inner consistency of the ontological space of the enchanted cosmos. Since Secondary World enchantment requires a literary text, it cannot reflect the Primary World's as though using a mirror. It needs to be put into form that resonates analogically. This is particularly difficult when considering the infinite difference between Creator and sub-creator, which returns us to *parallels*.

Tolkien perceived the uncreated reality of infinite God as parallel to finite creation through trinitarian disclosure. Christ is the lens that distinguishes the parallels while creating and mediating a unity between them. By incarnating his infinite self in the substance of material creation Christ became the "record of absolute reality . . . in history,"[60] giving humanity a way to see all creation as participating in God's eternal narrative of life. This introduced a new way for reading "the sacramentality of creation—that materiality and history together are the means by which God has chosen" to reveal divine involvement.[61]

56. "Draft," 95–96.
57. *LOTR*, xvi.
58. See Taylor, *Secular*, 30–42.
59. See Taylor, "Buffered."
60. Norwood, "Tolkien's Intention," 18.
61. Godzieba, "Catholic," 16.

Historical creation consists of the spatiotemporal materiality through which humanity experiences "grace" that "necessarily mediates the presence of God that enables our participation in the divine life, on God's initiative."[62] In this, the sacramental imagination reads parallel realities at different stages: The cosmos continues to signify the gift and *logos* of creation redeemed through the Gift and *Logos* of Christ and continues to be an open space where humanity can encounter God *sub specie aeternitatis* with a sacramental imagination.[63] In this space, "the Divine touches our humanity" through materiality and narrative.[64]

Tolkien framed God's enchantment as interactive within this narrative in distinct terms: *miracle* and *magic*.[65] Each is relevant to how one can read God's involvement in the world, but their "close relation . . . obscures their radical difference."[66] "The *miracle* produces real effects, and alters either the past or the future or both. It is effected, as a creative or recreative act, only by God . . . transcendent, outside the World but master of it."[67] *Effected* implies God's ability to accomplish infinite purposes amidst and despite spatiotemporal finiteness according to The Pattern only God knows fully. Miracles are only possible through "a power directly proceeding from God" and can "only be Good . . . in purpose and in effect; it is essentially moral. It cannot be reduced or perverted to any lesser purpose."[68] Thus, miracles happen from God beyond the Mountains, the effects of which are carried out, encountered, and "clothed in the garments of time and place."[69] Humanity can perceive them because of the religious sense and know the deeper

62. Godzieba, "Catholic," 16. Godzieba's argument is also based in scripture and tradition with Christ as the centerpiece of the sacramental imagination. Material and history are not exhaustive. They account for the actual imaginative space humanity utilizes.

63. Aided by scripture and Christian tradition.

64. Howard, "Sacramental Imagination," 24.

65. "Manuscript," 252–53, 267. Although these drafts are not included in the published version of OFS, they show how Tolkien arrived at his specific differentiation between "pure" enchantment and magic as "possessive." Significantly, they contrast his view of Christian reality from his personal creativity.

66. "Manuscript," 252–53.

67. "Manuscript," 253. See *Letters*, 99–100, for Tolkien's comparison between Jesus's healing of Jairus's daughter and a modern-day miracle recounted during Mass. Each case depicts God's/Jesus's miraculousness matter-of-factly, the godhead's right to intrude whenever it wills.

68. "Manuscript," 267.

69. *Letters*, 212.

meaning of them by participating in the divine life.[70] These intrusions are eucatastrophic at their core, and though they may not bring about joy through tears, they always evidence grace, which is meant to direct the trajectory of personal narratives by means of *evangelium* toward their purposed end in God.[71] Such intrusions will not coincide with how regular mundane events ordinarily operate and can be attributed to the intervening "Finger of God."[72] One may experience miracles by moving past the threshold of the present, but there must be something that ontically constitutes this movement forward: God's *magic*—the inherent, given functionality of creation's happening now, *ab initio*.[73]

Creation preceded all subsequent miraculous interventions of God, and God's creativity continues to sustain creation, which may be observed in many "encores" by means of magic within the cosmos. Magic originates in God[74] whose essence is the "efficient cause" from the beginning.[75] In Aristotelian terms, efficient cause "designates" God as "the agent which initiates the change, the maker of the thing made, and the producer of the changing."[76] Thus, God is "the primary source of change or rest."[77] God's wisdom is the *how* of created existence,[78] the fullness of everything "efficiently" brought into being[79]—all *ex nihilo*.

God is *the* (not *a*) "sufficient reason"[80] for the "causality" of creation,[81] the lens through which to read and interpret the origin and final end of the essence of created beings.[82] And God is the ontic ground who makes

70. God may also mediate miracles through finite instruments, but they are always God's doing, whether in response to prayer or through agents testifying for God ("Manuscript," 253) and "absorbed in the will of God" (267).

71. See OFS, 75.

72. *Letters*, 205, 235. Although Tolkien referenced this terminology as demonstrating Eru's involvement in his mytho-*logos*, it metaphorically describes God's involvement in the Primary World.

73. "Manuscript," 253.

74. See "Manuscript," 258.

75. "Manuscript," 254.

76. Brown, *From the Ancient World*, 43. McIntosh adjoins efficient causality to Tolkien through Thomas Aquinas in *Flame Imperishable*, 58.

77. Cohen, "Aristotle's Metaphysics."

78. Barron, "Adventures."

79. Fradd, "Four Causes."

80. Koterski, *Introduction*, 56.

81. Koterski, *Introduction*, 207.

82. This is sufficient reason in its early medieval sense, before Leibniz (Koterski, *Introduction*, 36n57).

sense of the potential *telos* of each being. Since God is infinitely good without a hint of evil, creation is good *per se*—meaning, "in respect of itself"[83]—as a gift from God. "A *per se* cause is a cause on which the effect directly depends with respect to that proper *esse* that it has insofar as it is an effect."[84] If God created the essences of all beings *ex nihilo* and gave them the potentiality of becoming, then God has also determined their *telos* and affirmed their proper trajectory *ab initio* and again through Christ. The initial act of creation in God and redemptive re-creation in Christ affirm and reaffirm each being's essence, "the what it was to be"[85] from God *per se*. In each individual instance, *logos* defines the essence of each being, which also means that the truest meaning of each being's essence must be found in the *logos* from which it originated.[86] If God upholds existence according to the infinite divine essence, all that has life and being remains good in respect of God's goodness itself even though creation has been encumbered since the Fall of humanity.

Therefore, God somehow still effectively accomplishes his purposes in a way that directly depends on his essential good even though finite humanity may not perceive it. For Tolkien, "the result" of what is seen in creation is not God but "an essentially 'magical' operation" of God's "arrangement."[87] Thus, miracles and magic illustrate God's *marvels*, which are "simply the unfamiliar which we cannot at once classify"[88] or "place,"[89] yet they uphold the fact that an enchanted reading of the cosmo-*logos* is ontically grounded in the essential mystery of God.

Naturalism displaced God's ontic creativity via subtraction story. Instead of being harmoniously orchestrated by a divine mind, the cosmos became "a 'universe' that has its own kind of . . . immanent order of natural laws," and creation was renamed "nature."[90] Reverence to God was replaced by Father Time and Mother Nature, and marvels were to be read simply as facts without mystery and wonder, thus disenchanted.

83. Cohen, "Aristotle's Metaphysics."

84. Suárez, "Types."

85. Cohen, "Aristotle's Metaphysics."

86. Cohen, "Aristotle's Metaphysics."

87. "Manuscript," 254.

88. "Manuscript," 252.

89. "Manuscript," 267. In respect to this and the previous footnote, "Christian theology" clarified their "close relation" (252–53).

90. Smith, *How (Not) to Be*, 34–35.

Poesis re-enchants through mytho-*logos*, which does not supplant God's magic but can issue a mode of participation according to its own laws analogical to the enchanted cosmo-*logos*. Personal encounters through mytho-*logos* are integral to the awakening of readers to Primary World reality apart from the text. They adhere with magic in the cosmos that has not been withdrawn beyond the immanent frame. Therefore, if the mythic quality of *LOTR* issues an ontological encounter through reading, it initiates an awakening of the religious sense that God's *poesis* may use to shape a person's character.

Enchanting Machinery

The "essential face" of *LOTR* is "Magical"[91]—mytho-*logos* giving the impression of a cosmic imaginary analogous to a mysterious enchanted reading of Primary Reality. Magicians with an enchanted reading of the world perceived "'scientific' operations" as that magical "power inherent" within the cosmic order, yet they discerned these were not their efficient causes, but their effects.[92] They knew if they arranged things in certain ways they could produce particular results, such as using fire to boil water: the fire under the kettle produces this effect every time.[93] Such operations are "in themselves inevitable" by virtue of the inherent causality placed in creation by God.[94]

When writing narrative, language enchants through the new meaning contrived. Mytho-*logos* cannot work miracles. Those reside in the province of God alone. Magic, however, can be imaged analogically by way of what narrative awakens through imaginative intuition: "Narratives are the primordial ways in which we make sense of the world we live in. They are the basis for an analogy between the creative author and the Creator God."[95] This happens through personal *poesis* as with storytellers' creativity throughout the ages, from the first moment human imaginations began telling stories. The more powerful the story-building elements, the greater chance there is for enchanting readers and producing lasting effects within human imaginations.

91. OFS, 44.
92. "Manuscript," 253–54.
93. "Manuscript," 253.
94. "Manuscript," 253.
95. Ward, "How Literature," 77.

Meaning precedes stories that are told and the reasons they are told,[96] and storytellers are the efficient causes of their stories. The arrangement of *LOTR*'s inner teleology can affect readers now because of how the narrative feels as they experience it. When readers begin imagining otherwise, they may begin living otherwise.[97] Therefore, instead of positing a theory to reify this experience into exacting intellectual terms, it will be helpful to articulate how the shared experience of Tolkien's mytho-*logos* distinctly affects readers' unique narratives of life, which lies in the power of myth.[98]

Myth "offers an integrative form of thought, in which what we define as elements are given meaning in wholes."[99] No thought can be made sense of in isolation but belongs to the context through which such a mentality arrives. If we remember that myth's polysemy speaks to the world we live in most, we understand how myth can be universal and personal simultaneously. In this way, *LOTR*'s *telos* can testify to God and truth, the purposed final cause of humanity, the fullness of Primary Reality's mythic meaning. In the sense that *logos* "in some contexts [means] 'word,' in others 'discourse,' in others 'account,'"[100] whether cosmos-*logos* or mytho-*logos*, it does not matter; both operate similarly in ways that personal being is permeated by some osmotic design in various ways without knowing the design exactly.

As the basis of analogies, human narratives permit readers to participate in feigned history in ways they can empathize and resonate with parallel to personal history. Therefore, instead of being an incomprehensible secondary plane of nonsense, fantasy necessarily "depends on" the "sharp outlines"[101] and "hard recognition that things are so in the world as it appears under the sun."[102] In other words, fantasy requires the essentials of that which is plain to everyday existence, and this requires a lens for seeing reality in visible and invisible ways that are obvious to everyone. For example, someone who sees a flower can also know that the fragrance s/he smells comes from it without calling into question the source of the scent.

96. Ward, "How Literature," 76–77.

97. Godzieba, "Catholic," 20.

98. There are undoubtedly other ways for explaining this.

99. Taylor, *Language Animal*, 72.

100. Taylor, *Language Animal*, 338.

101. OFS, 83nG.

102. OFS, 65.

Lewis's flower metaphor referenced the experience of *LOTR* as a story—what we are visibly meant to see with a clear view under the sun of Middle-earth. It is one of the "tricks" of fantasy to transport readers there: not manipulatively, but through its meaning and mythic effects.[103] Such magic imitates how humanity has given meaning to things throughout history. It gave grass its name and designated its color green, and there is no debate about whether the grass is green.[104] The same is true of blue skies, the color of blood, and the language we now use to describe things as "*light, heavy, grey, yellow, still, swift*."[105] Naming meaning in this way is similar to a scientist who sees God as the sufficient reason for creation's marvels, who names and explains "facts" about the cosmos through imaginative intuitionism by extension of God's creative causality.

Creativity through fantasy frames "facts" according to *sub*-creative laws. Just as those who named meaning in the cosmo-*logos* throughout history, this same human imagination "also conceived of magic that would make heavy things light and able to fly, turn grey lead into yellow gold, and the still rock into a swift water. If it could do the one, it could do the other; it inevitably did both."[106] Tolkien's argument stems from what language images and the power of words to craft new meaning through such imagery. The magic through which water is made to boil by fire is inherent in the material needed to produce this effect, and we know this will be the outcome every time. However, the magic of storytelling is *more* magical: Not only do sub-creators use words that already have their own inherent power, but new meaning is originated through how their words are arranged. Skilled artisans take pre-existing material to apply "a knowledge and feeling for clay, stone[,] and wood which only the art of making can give."[107] They are the efficient causes of their work, shaping the material into bowls, statues, and tables, and one can reasonably see how final causality was achieved through their creativity and the potentiality of their materials. But literary sub-creators have an "enchanter's power."[108] Their material is words arranged through the poetic knowledge that informs the magical operations of mytho-*logos*, putting its word-sense into

103. OFS, 64–65.

104. OFS, 41.

105. OFS, 41.

106. OFS, 41.

107. OFS, 68. This list of material is non-exhaustive.

108. OFS, 41.

a contextualized plane perceivable apart from the five senses. As applied to the laws of the Secondary World, the sub-creator's "desire to wield that power" is derived extra-mentally within that plane.[109] As the sub-creator's imagination "awakes"[110] through *poesis*, his or her capacity to enchant increases. Therefore, "the keener and the clearer is the reason, the better fantasy will it make" if effectively in line with the reason of its own plane.[111] Thus, any marvels that induce Secondary Belief are consequences of the writer's ability to enchant according to that reason.

Recall the power of the adjective—the Secondary World's sun may be green or may illustrate "dead life" according to the narrative's inner consistency in a way readers may find their "imaginations leaping" into Secondary Belief when enchanted. Not physically leaping but "*moving* . . . as the waking mind can be said to *move*" into "seeing" something extra-mentally not yet in mind.[112] Significantly, the magic of the words engenders and reemphasizes that texts convey meaning according to the purview of the author. The sun is green and there is dead life only after the sub-creator has made it so. It would be unreasonable to think this meaning was made by the reader since the Primary World sun is not green, dead means lifeless, and the story initiates this strange imagery.[113] But it is reasonable that the reader can see a green sun after having been inside the Secondary World because "fantasy is a natural human activity" in everyday experience.[114] As surely as the imagination can picture a yellow bike and a dog with four legs not present, it is capable of picturing a green sun as much as comprehending verities explained by science.[115] It is not supposed to rival science from an ontic standpoint but apply reason differently.

As readers move through *poiema*, they are awakened to think things for themselves according to the reason established in the secondary plane. This does not differ much from how imaginations come into new realizations as they move through life. On a daily basis, each person is shaped by experience from past to present. Although they may not

109. OFS, 41.

110. OFS, 41.

111. OFS, 65.

112. "Papers," 175.

113. Although there *is* green in the sun. It prisms the entire color spectrum so that it appears white to the naked eye. See "What Color Is the Sun?"

114. OFS, 65.

115. OFS, 65.

necessarily experience an enchanted social imaginary, they still participate in the *machinery* by which their social imaginary operates.[116] At first glance, *machine* might invoke conceptual imagery of a mechanical device with many parts assembled to make life more resourceful, easy, and economical. Such devices as tractors, computers, and chainsaws have multiple components arranged so the inherent qualities of the materials used amount to some robotic magic we operate with means to an end. Poetic sub-creation is not this kind of machinery.

An older common meaning of *machine* is the "material or immaterial . . . structure" or "fabric" of the world,[117] another way of describing a cosmic imaginary. When scientific naturalism proffered a new lens for reading the cosmos, divine marvels became explained mechanistically.[118] Secondary World machinery operates according to the innerworkings of its own fabric. If such machinery induces Secondary Belief, it can free the imagination from exclusively humanistic and mechanical ontological outlooks.

Tolkien believed the machinery of language is the "backbone" of comprehending meaning.[119] He also referred to machinery in other ways. Language-making presents the opportunity for machinery that is at once "*more consciously and deliberately, and so more keenly*" personalized by the maker, yet may be "admirable and effective" in expressing meaning to others.[120] *LOTR* is the machinery through which Tolkien's mytho-*logos* operates.[121] "Adumbrated in [its] logic"[122] is the meaningful language that bred and developed the immaterial machinery of his mythological history.[123] *LOTR* is the material fabric through which Tolkien's literary

116. Machinery here is not to be confused with technology, industrialization, war, and destruction disenchanting Western Europe in Tolkien's lifetime (see *Letters*, 87–88, 105, 111, 115), but the result of humanity's replacing God's enchantment with a mechanistic way of redefining how creation participates. Likewise with the covenantal institution of marriage: In making divorce acceptable instead of remaining married, Tolkien noted "horror at seeing good machines ruined by misuse," which was true of any "abominable" behavior done contrary to the goodness of how God ordained it (*Letters*, 60–61).

117. *OED*, s.v. "machine."

118. "Manuscript," 252.

119. Tolkien, *Middle English*. The rest of this paragraph describes ways Tolkien associated *machine/machinery* with language and storytelling.

120. "Vice," 212.

121. "Appendix," 26.

122. Basney, "Myth," 193.

123. See Tolkien, *Tolkien in Oxford*.

enchantment is capable of arresting strangeness that compels readers to imagine otherwise. This happens because of what fantasy progenitively shares with readers: an imaginative "realism and immediacy beyond the compass of any human mechanism."[124]

Consequently, *LOTR* gives readers a world on "the verge of communication,"[125] which consists of Primary World language interwoven with personalized mytho-*logos*. But it is common language that awakens each reader's memory to his or her *own* imagery.[126] If *LOTR* narrates about trees, this triggers the memory readers have of trees. But through the otherness of mytho-*logos*, they become "secondary world marvels" of their own.[127]

By first appealing to the reality of these things and subsequently altering them through tricks of de-familiarization, the sub-creator's magic holds the attention of readers and induces Secondary Belief "when we are enchanted" by what is seen inside.[128] Even though the sub-creation's trees may differ from the reader's, there is still a shared meaning of trees that characters and readers recognize.[129] The impact point between two worlds is where readers are stirred through the creativity of another image-bearer who has brought new fantasy into being. Although strange, its meaning is translatable through imaginative intuition that allows one to perceive that the story communicates secondary reality that is true to its plane. When readers step away from this threshold verge of communication, "transformation can occur . . . that does not fade upon reentry into the Primary World but . . . casts new light upon the Primary World. It is, in a sense, a medium of revelation."[130]

124. OFS, 63. Here, mechanism is associated with manipulatively exerting force ("Manuscript," 252–53; *Letters*, 160) and "'scientific' materialism" inconsiderate of God (*Letters*, 110).

125. Garth, *Tolkien*, 62.

126. See OFS, 82nE, where Tolkien describes how fantasies use common everyday language to not only help readers or hearers imagine a Secondary World in the manner the writer wishes them to, but also make use of their own knowledge and memories triggered by the words written. So that, for instance, when certain words are used to describe a river in the landscape of that world, a person imagines the river described while also causing him/her to recall rivers s/he has actually seen. By doing so, Tolkien articulates the universal way language shares meaning while simultaneously appealing to personal experience.

127. Barber, "Structure," 68–69.

128. OFS, 32.

129. See "Papers," 200, where the common words are *bread* and *water*.

130. Johnson, "Tolkien's Mythopoesis," 33.

Tolkien's belief in God as Author of Primary Reality offers an analogical means "to describe the existing relation between the being of God and the being of creation."[131] *Relation* implies interactivity with God divinely authorizing the cosmos without asserting God as creation itself or a physical character within it. *Author* presents one way God might be imagined as involved in the cosmo-*logos* being scribed. Thus, the relational problem between sub-creativity and Primary Reality needs to be bridged by implying an existing relation of divine authorization within *LOTR*. Fantasy cannot communicate this adequately simply by enchanting readers into Secondary Belief about a green sun. It needs to engender the sense of a divine mind actively involved in the mytho-*logos* in a personal way.

Tolkien preferred not to write about hobbits again because his heart was set on the pre-history he would never publish in his lifetime. He was partly to blame. "I'd got Hobbits on my hands, hadn't I?" Tolkien later reflected.[132] But Bilbo's story proved to be the link[133] that would expose the pre-history's yet unrevealed regions in *LOTR*. Although Bilbo's ring provided plot linkage between *Hobbit* and *LOTR*,[134] Tolkien suggested immaterial linkage to *LOTR* inherent in the dialogue between Gandalf and Bilbo at the conclusion of *Hobbit*:[135]

> *Bilbo*: "Then the prophecies of the old songs have turned out to be true, after a fashion!"
>
> *Gandalf*: "Of course! And why should not they prove true? Surely you don't disbelieve the prophecies, because you had a hand in bringing them about yourself? You don't really suppose, do you, that all your adventures and escapes were managed by mere luck, just for

131. Betz, Translator's Introduction, 40.

132. Tolkien, Interview with Gueroult.

133. Scull and Hammond, *JRRT Companion*, 404.

134. In *LOTR*, Tolkien would make Bilbo's ring from *Hobbit* the One Ring made by Sauron, the darkest evil in Middle-earth (xvi). In the original version of *Hobbit* (1937), the magic ring Bilbo found had not been linked to the Necromancer (*LOTR*'s Sauron), and Gollum actually shows Bilbo the way out of the dark tunnels beneath the mountains as they part on rather amicable terms. In 1951, the current version of chapter 5 in *Hobbit* would be published to account for this linkage to *LOTR* (Scull and Hammond, *JRRT Companion*, 396).

135. Which Tolkien alludes to in *Letters*, 365.

> your sole benefit? You are a very fine person, Mr. Baggins, . . . but you are only quite a little fellow in a wide world after all!"[136]

This hints at an "old light" in the narrative and foreshadows the ontic grounding Tolkien would embed into the logic of *LOTR*. Hobbits and wizards are the material machinery of the fabric of Middle-earth, but the dialogue between Bilbo and Gandalf suggests more in the mytho-*logos* than themselves, a discernible immaterial aspect through which readers might be awakened to an existing relation about the Primary World. In the final chapter, we will see how this immaterial relation with the material is instrumental in the machinery of *LOTR*, the effects of which are capable of awakening the reader's religious sense to encounter God.

136. *Hobbit*, 330.

Chapter 8

Reality from Beyond and Meaning Within

Introduction

In chapter 3, C. S. Lewis mentioned how feigned history was a means through which human creativity can assert its divine origin to edify the world while using God's gifts to model divine creativity. Chapter 6 directed us to the notion that Tolkien's sub-creativity could conjoin and mediate truth, the concreteness of which God is the true Author. If so, *LOTR* may be seen as a transient medium through which readers can attribute Primary Belief about reality generated by Secondary Belief. By remaining analogous to the Primary World, the Secondary World becomes comprehensible on its own grounds and can lead readers to recognize significant things about a true, deeper, and right order about Primary Reality otherwise veiled by their social imaginaries.

Tolkien's participatory ontology ushers readers into a narrative that illustrates how "the wheels of the world" work inside the "hobbitocentric" *LOTR*.[1] As Frodo embarks on an "untoward . . . journey,"[2] he does so with ontic grounding in the historical truths of his world. If *LOTR* is a "flower" that testifies to God in some way, we need to identify

1. *Letters*, 237.
2. *Letters*, 240.

the "fragrance" remaining with us after having passed through the story, because this is what affects us in our own personal ways on our untoward journeys of life.

Chapter 6 also discussed mytho-*logos* as the "water" that mediates the life and meaning of the story. From *LOTR*'s first pages, the Prologue immerses readers through the "narrative phenomenon of embedding"[3]—Middle-earth is made "intelligible" based on its "larger and longer history"[4]—one of crisscrossing stories, histories, events, and characters that carry the reader's attention to the end of the second chapter, Shadow of the Past.[5] By this point, Frodo Baggins has decided to flee with the Ring, and the reader witnesses how other narratives have embedded into his own, shaping who he is presently while informing how he might discern the best next step. Like Frodo, each person reaches present experience through the "diachronic embedding"[6] or "unfolding"[7] of living narrative. "'How things came to be,' in the sense of explaining why, or giving causes"[8] allows one to render meaning about life, through life.

As Frodo participated in the greater good, his ennoblement was concurrently subsumed into what Eru, the "Writer," was doing. And although Eru is not presented as an incarnate being in *LOTR*, there is a way of observing causality of a divine mind within the story in a way that parallels how a reader might experience the invisible God of Primary Reality. This is, however, contingent upon the narrative's action, which provides the historical context necessary for properly evaluating and understanding purpose and meaning. Tolkien's world has a "mediatory radiance . . . rendering it both wholly real and yet witnessing to a reality beyond"[9] in a way secular social imaginaries obstruct. "To tell a story is to affirm that there is meaning to life, and that experience is shaped and has an entelechy" according to its own "intentionality and narrative character."[10] Although the reader's experience cannot mirror Frodo's, that which is intuited through mytho-*logos* can mediate formative insights instrumental to the reader's experience. Before returning to Frodo's story,

3. MacIntyre, *After Virtue*, 222.
4. MacIntyre, *After Virtue*, 212–13, 222–23.
5. *LOTR*, 1–63.
6. Taylor, *Language Animal*, 300.
7. Taylor, *Language Animal*, 303.
8. Taylor, *Language Animal*, 291.
9. Milbank, *Chesterton*, 25.
10. Milbank, *Chesterton*, 11.

we will first look at how Tolkien saw participatory ontology as furthering character transformation through the narrative of life.

Seed, Soil, and *Praxis*

Tolkien described character development botanically: "A seed [has an] innate vitality and heredity, [a] capacity to grow and develop. A great part of the 'changes' in a man are no doubt unfoldings of the patterns hidden in the seed."[11] The *seed* comprises the essential qualities and capabilities inherent in a person's being from the outset of an image-bearer's creation. *Unfoldings* happen in time, and growth requires cultivation. Thus, each person is also "a gardener, for good or ill. I am impressed by the degree in which the development of 'character' *can* be a product of conscious intention, the will to modify innate tendencies in desired directions," Tolkien said.[12] That character transformation *can* happen consciously insinuates that unknowns will impact personal formation. How people *will to modify* depends on how they are co-authors of their lives amidst the countless things they can and cannot control: Just as people cannot determine when and where to be born, neither can they avoid all peoples, actions, and events that intersect their narratives.[13] Co-author compares to gardener—each relates to the person's role in building character: How one cultivates or writes who s/he becomes shapes the active part s/he plays in the greater narrative happening apart from his or her control.

Gardening and authoring are metaphors for *praxis*. The Aristotelian sense of *praxis* means "acting, doing,"[14] or "being involved in an activity," each of which is part of developing character.[15] *Praxis* "consists" of making use of human freedom for the greater good of humanity and God, the "ultimate end"[16] and true "Good."[17] This happens through the extremely complex soil or substance of lived experience. We are who we are through our personal narratives. Each is enmeshed in an "historical version" of experience where, if all pain and suffering were "visible," the "amazed

11. *Letters*, 240.
12. *Letters*, 240.
13. MacIntyre, *After Virtue*, 209, 213.
14. Ward, *Politics*, 200.
15. Ward, "Narrative," 448.
16. Maritain, *Art*.
17. Ward, *Politics*, 182.

vision of the heavens" would be veiled by a "dense dark vapour."[18] But amidst threatening darkness, we can intuit the invisible from the visible if we conceive that "all things and deeds have a value in themselves, apart from their 'causes' and 'effects.'"[19] God's *poesis* still speaks and prompts the ontic in-and version of God's involvement amidst the darkened haze. However, "no man can estimate what is really happening at the present sub specie aeternitatis. All we do know, and that to a large extent by direct experience, is that evil labours with vast power and perpetual success—in vain: preparing always only the soil for unexpected good to sprout in."[20] In other words, evil exists whether we like it or not, but God sustains cosmo-*logos* where seeds are cultivated to spring life that confronts it.

Fairy-stories should contain threats to existence that may be overcome. "A safe fairy-land is untrue to all worlds"[21] and, therefore, is not escapist. The best fairy-stories deal with "the *aventures* of men in the Perilous Realm or upon its shadowy marches."[22] *Aventures* captures the thrill of an exciting new adventure combined with the inevitability of mystery and danger.[23] In a medieval sense, its root meaning was adjoined to the concept of moving "forward" with full knowledge of doing so with "risk or peril . . . into unknown territory."[24] Analogically experiencing the intensity of the thrills and dangers of Faërie differs from actual experience, but narrative shows how characters navigate *aventur*ous terrain and observe how their seeds develop.

Untoward journeys are impactful because they narrate different formative experiences exemplifying general relevant human situations. They provide "fact[s] of ordinary observation without any need of symbolical explanation"[25] because they bear witness to contextual praxeology. What, why, and how we view other narratives unfolding allows us to ascertain appropriate meanings in the same manner we gain comprehension about our own narratives of life. While readers may identify with certain aspects of a character's journey, every image-bearing seed differs, and each

18. *Letters*, 76.

19. *Letters*, 76.

20. *Letters*, 76. Tolkien's Latin is not italicized.

21. *Letters*, 24.

22. OFS, 32.

23. Flieger and Anderson, "Editors' Commentary," 93.

24. Flieger and Anderson, "Editors' Commentary," 93.

25. *Letters*, 240.

person's soil produces its own unique story. Recall that Faërie is its own cosmos meant to affect the imagination of readers. Tolkien speculated,

> Faery might be said . . . to represent Imagination (without definition because taking in all the definitions of this word): esthetic: exploratory and receptive; and artistic: inventive, dynamic (sub) creative. This compound—of awareness of a limitless world outside our domestic [environment]; a love (in ruth and admiration) for the things in it; and a desire for wonder, marvels, both perceived and conceived.[26]

Sub-creators define the imaginative space of Faërie according to laws that should essentially free the reader's imagination from the drabness of trite familiarity in stagnant social imaginaries. Apprehending this imaginatively should induce some amazed vision of the heavens through a fragrance that inspires readers to think for themselves and see what they were meant to see more clearly. "'Faery' is as necessary for the health and complete functioning of the Human as is sunlight for physical life: sunlight as distinguished from the soil, . . . though it in fact permeates and modifies even that."[27] So we have these analogies: Faërie as sunlight and a social imaginary as the soil of experience. Thus, Faërie should illuminate and affect life experience for the vitality of personal being.

Botanically, life is latent within the seed, but seeds require "minerals, organic matter (living and dead), water, and air" to spring to life.[28] Seeds cannot provide these for themselves. Human seeds have unfolding hidden patterns, equipping them for their image-bearing potential, but how one grows depends on the health of the soil in which one is embedded. While "the ethics and ends of any action" has the potential to transform character, the true fullness of *praxis* only comes when "the securing of the Good is . . . a divine achievement."[29] Gardening and authoring meaningfully name how people cultivate or scribe their character as well as they may, but this may be dulled in social imaginaries not embedded in ontic *logos*.

The soil of secular imaginaries deprives image-bearing seeds of necessary sunlight and nutrients of the cosmo-*logos*, where grounding in God is crucial to development. Image-bearers need the *telos* of the divine mind

26. "Essay," 144.

27. "Essay," 144–45.

28. Lindbo et al., "Know Soil," 6.

29. Ward, *Politics*, 182.

in order for their ethics and ends to move them meaningfully beyond the threshold of the present for the greater good in God. If God is actively writing the narrative in which humanity mysteriously participates to some unknown end, how we achieve our ends are not accomplished solely on our own. After we consider how Tolkien viewed human participation as instrumental to God's mediation through the cosmo-*logos*, we will have a clearer visual for how *LOTR* offers readers an analogous experience that can awaken them to encounter God amidst their own embedded narratives. If Faërie, like sunlight, awakens imaginative intuition to Primary Belief in a divine mind, it can transform how readers translate meaning in the action of their living narratives.

By Means of Instrumentality—Mediation Through Sub-Creation

Tolkien's historical use of *instrument* pertaining to humans was not locked into one specific meaning.[30] Instrumentality broadly referred to God's interactivity to, with, or through humanity in the economy of grace. It evidences God as originator of good according to divine teleological purposes. But instead of dictating how God works with strict and absolute human definitions, Tolkien referred to instruments as ways God mediates purposefulness within the cosmos. Sermons by the Church-ordained are instruments,[31] as are the "life and circumstance[s]" God might use to lead two people into marriage.[32] The "just retribution" of someone bent toward a life of depravity could be seen as an instrument of grace through whom God spares many people serious affliction that otherwise might have resulted.[33] Conversely, God may be seen as extending additional grace to those who make sacrifices and persevere for the divine's greater good after their own strength is spent.[34]

30. The rest of this paragraph describes specific ways Tolkien associated *instrument* to God's relationship with humankind.

31. *Letters*, 75.

32. *Letters*, 51.

33. This was the case with Gollum's demise in *LOTR*. After biting off Frodo's finger with the Ring, Gollum fell to his death, destroying the threat of the Ring with him (*Letters*, 221; *LOTR*, 925). This is the opposite of Christ willingly going to the cross for the sin of humanity.

34. See *Letters*, 326–27, including 327n. Describing Frodo's state of mind at the end of *LOTR*, Tolkien indicated how, even after participating in the good throughout the narrative, finite being is always capable of the inevitable sins of the flesh, regardless

Although merely a handful of instances, each uses a theocentric lens to interpret divine involvement contemporaneous with personal decisions and actions. Participants grounded in the ontic *logos* trust that God is involved and depend on this as the actual basis for the fulfillment they experience because of or regardless of life circumstances. But this is based on "the complexity of any given situation in Time," the "absolute" objective of which decisively "belongs to God" and God's writing of the whole story.[35] Although it is impossible to pinpoint how this works, Tolkien sub-creatively derived a narrative that mediates an analogous mysteriousness through the hard and sharp outlines recognizable under the sun in *LOTR*. This cannot be shown as if given a solitary image; it must be shown or experienced through narrative revelation.

Notably, fantasy works analogously to how reality becomes known to people in their everyday settings: Physical and nonphysical reality is revealed over time, and after they are comprehended, these experiences become stored as memories. Consequently, after looking through a fantasy's lens to see trees in that world, readers image their own past encounters with trees, now fused into the imagery of *poiema*. The same is true for intuiting how fantasy names the nonphysical, similar to a flower's fragrance—wind by blowing leaves, for instance; love through another person's intimacy and reassurance; growth when potentiality becomes actualized in a living creature. Whether physical or not, an impact of meanings occurs. Secondary Worlds generate imagery that weds to personal experience and gives shape to new forms of thought, thereby making present what was, until then, absent.[36]

But the infinite God is impossible to image sub-creatively because of finite being's limitations, let alone that God is foreign to immanentized social imaginaries. The matter arises of how sub-creation could be "flowing into" and "partaking"[37] of infinite reality when the writer has no capacity for reproducing the immaterial essence that created and

---

of one's achievements (328). In Primary World experience, this analogically implies a cosmo-*logos* reading where the glory belongs to God who is to be ultimately credited for achievements attained by those living by faith.

35. *Letters*, 325.

36. This illuminates how myth's polysemy mediates many meanings through one source. When the world is not allowed mysteriousness but must be depicted according to human mechanisms, this becomes "sorting out the world into categories" according to particularities of language whose "definition[s]" become "symbols [to] 'define' the world (rather than vice versa)" (Donald in Taylor, *Language Animal*, 71).

37. See discussion on p. 50.

sustains the fabric of the world. Further, there must be more than "just life" happening if sub-creativity mediates a whole-felt and reasonable sensibility suggestive of more than immanentization. Likewise, an answer must be given for why *LOTR* can "make us feel we have *understood* when we have really been refreshed by contact of quite a different kind with Reality."[38] The implication is that this kind of Reality has been made known to us, not the other way around. So *LOTR* must poetically reflect something akin to actual divine transcendence to show how this kind of "contact" can awaken us to the possibility of this Reality. What follows is how Tolkien's view of Primary Reality was analogically derived into the mytho-*logos* of *LOTR* to awaken this.

The Secondary World only has its prose to communicate its own theocentricity. Tolkien consciously removed allusions to Christian religiousness while revising *LOTR* so as to not distract from *its own* religious element and symbolism. This religiousness was enhanced through Tolkien's sub-creative reliance on interlacing instrumentality into his *poesis* through his conception of Eru.

In chapter 7, God was named as Tolkien's basis of causality for Primary Reality. God's absoluteness belongs to God's self. Therefore, God is the sole "principal cause" to which every good "action is attributed properly and absolutely"[39] from before time, *ex nihilo*. So, if Eru is the Writer whose sole right to divine honor is meant to be displayed in *LOTR*, this makes Eru the principal causality of the life inside the story. By imagining an uncreated reality of Eru at work behind the scenes, Tolkien's *poesis* was able to instill a transcendent sensibility into the mytho-*logos* of *LOTR*. To understand how Tolkien infused this into the narrative, we must consider how instrumentality is shown as originating in his mythology's creation myth—*The Music of the Ainur* (*Music*).

Tolkien expressed his desire to restore the analogical relation between art/sub-creation and Primary Reality in a letter he wrote to Milton Waldman hoping to convince his firm to publish *Silmarillion* in conjunction with *LOTR*. As *LOTR* was being written, it became adjoined to the mythological history in a way *Hobbit* had not originally been. Tolkien's letter maintained that neither work should stand alone.[40] In the latter years of writing *LOTR*, Tolkien worked and reworked *Music* set before

38. Lewis, *Collected Letters*, 2:445.

39. Suárez, "Types."

40. See Carpenter in *Letters*, 143.

the beginning of history.[41] Its unpublished manuscript emphasized its significance with "illuminated capitals,"[42] and Tolkien's letter to Waldman communicated how *Music* was foundational to *LOTR*'s logic.

Most importantly, it established Eru as the divine mind behind Middle-earth. The most relevant takeaways from *Music* for this discussion follow:

1. Eru is portrayed as the ontically prior essence, *the* sufficient reason for creation's coming into existence.[43]
2. After Eru creates the first finite beings (Ainur, the lesser gods) to play music, evil is originated by those who use their instrumentality contrary to Eru's design, thereby eliminating an *ex nihilo* dualism that evil is infinite.[44]
3. The eventual incarnation of life comes from Eru alone,[45] but what he speaks into being is the product of the "sub-creative Fall" of *Music*.[46] Thus, the physical world, *Eä*, is fallen from the beginning of time.
4. The gods "exercise delegated authority in their spheres (of rule and government, *not* creation . . .)" after the physical world appears.[47]

41. This had been extant in its earliest versions since the 1930s, but between 1946 and 1951 Tolkien brought the "Ainulindalë" (*Music*) into the form Christopher Tolkien based the published *Silmarillion* version on (Scull and Hammond, *JRRT Companion*, 29–30).

42. Scull and Hammond, *JRRT Companion*, 30.

43. The One who spoke creation into existence (*Silmarillion*, 15). "As its metaphysic," Tolkien explained, "Creation [is] the act of Will of Eru" (*Letters*, 190n), which is "secret" and "unknowable to all wisdom but One" (*Letters*, 149).

44. Introduced by Melkor, greatest of the Ainur, into the second theme (*Silmarillion*, 16–17).

45. In early drafts of the Ainur's *Music* (before being named "Ainulindalë"), that which "giveth Life and Reality" was named the "Secret Fire" (*Lost Tales*, 50–51, 53). It later also came to be called the "Flame Imperishable" that "kindled" the Ainur to life (*Silmarillion*, 15).

46. *Letters*, 146n. Thus, Eru "guarantee[d] that what they devised and made should be given the reality of Creation" (*Letters*, 195). That is, Eru conferred "reality to [their] conceptions" (*Letters*, 190n). Although "they shared in [the world's] 'making'" through the music, "the realization of it, the gift to it of a created reality [was] of the same grade as their own" (*Letters*, 235n). It is noteworthy that neither the published "Ainulindalë" nor the "Valaquenta" (the other "closely associated" [C. Tolkien, Foreword to *Silmarillion*, viii] accompaniment published in *Silmarillion*) ever uses *create*. Everything is described in terms of making.

47. *Letters*, 146; *Silmarillion*, 18–22.

5. The Children of Eru are elves, humans, and hobbits but are not *sub*-created. Rather, they are mysteriously "propounded," woven into *Music* from the mind of Eru alone before the music ended.[48] Thus, they have their own unique purpose from, and direct relation to, Eru that the gods do not.

This is part of the "supernatural machinery"[49] and immaterial fabric of Tolkien's *poesis*, the imaginative foundations through which Tolkien mediated the impression of a divine mind in *LOTR*.[50] Though much has happened off stage, *Music* is really necessary to understanding what is seen on stage. It provides the ontic residue, the sunlight of Tolkien's Faërie working through the soil in which Tolkien developed his characters. When readers analogically participate in *LOTR*, they participate not only through the text but also through the osmotic design and mode of thought upholding the inner consistency of Tolkien's mytho-*logos*. So that this may be recognized by the reader, this must be relatable to some potential causal interactivity in-and-beyond Primary World experience.

Tolkien described God's activity in the Primary World as happening through unspecified life circumstances, the complexity of which is impossible to untangle and the absolute objective of which belongs to God alone. This maintains that the Writer's involvement remains mysterious to every being other than God, and if God is infinitely good, divine interactivity works this good in ways finite creatures cannot comprehend entirely and despite those who use free will contrarily. To speak of God's infinite causality working consonantly with or alongside instrumental causes returns us again to the word *parallel*.

One way to describe how one experiences this in-and presence of God beyond is "*concursus*," or "running together."[51] That is, those in the ontic *logos* can decisively posture themselves as active participants in the sacramental greater reality of God's presence in-and-beyond the cosmos. Here is where Tolkien's distaste for allegorical interpretations of *LOTR* becomes most lucid. Tolkien perceived that all the characters, ideas, events, and situations would always be found "in solution in the Secondary . . . World," thus enhancing the mythical effect compelling

48. *Silmarillion*, 18. This was woven into the third of three themes.

49. Abrams, *Glossary*, 28, 82.

50. Sub-creation in a literal sense—that which Tolkien's mytho-*logos* portrays as a sub-created world brought into existence by Eru through finite sub-creativity. When Eru spoke it into existence, it was not directly from his conceptually "infinite" mind.

51. Poythress, *Chance*, 57.

literary belief.[52] This especially applied to Eru. C. S. Lewis posited that allegory "belongs" to the *human* imagination, and "it is of the very nature of thought and language to represent what is immaterial in picturable terms."[53] God is immaterial, and Exodus 20 commands that humanity should make no image to represent God. Tolkien's reverence for infinite God negated allegorical Primary-to-Secondary World representation. "The double meaning is not present" for him mythopoeically.[54] Tolkien's *Music* is the prehistory pretext for instrumental causal *concursus* in *LOTR*. Eru is to be imagined as The One God of a sub-created mythology who is analogically transcendent, and it is this logic that accompanies the vistas and glimpses of the mythological history Tolkien superimposed on Eru as Writer of the Story, not the image of the Judeo-Christian God. This sub-created causality is integral to what readers experience as they witness characters being transformed through *LOTR*.

Attaining *Telos* Through Instrumentality

A principal cause either works by its own power alone or mediates through the "sufficient power" for which it has equipped another; thus can other beings participate in the principal cause's power.[55] Since Eru is not incarnate in *LOTR*, Tolkien's sub-creativity needed to impress mythically the immaterial essence of divine causality active within the story. Tolkien's Primary Reality lens allows us to see how this could be analogically arranged through the purpose and morals woven into the cosmic order. His sacramental reading of creation's participation in God emphasized the significance of innumerable other created beings, each having a *telos* of its own. Just as general revelation allows image-bearing intelligent beings to detect that other beings exist for purposes other than mere existence, this is also true for comprehending their own purposes. This echoes Aristotle's "classical theism,"[56] the teleological "moral

52. C. Tolkien in Bailey, *JRRT*.

53. Lewis, *Allegory*, 44. Walter Hooper noted both Lewis's and Tolkien's understandings of allegory stem from this part of Lewis's book (Hooper in Lewis, *Collected Letters*, 3:789n256).

54. C. Tolkien in Bailey, *JRRT*. This thought would extend to "the Incarnation of God" being "*infinitely* greater than anything" Tolkien "would dare to write" (*Letters*, 237).

55. Suárez, "Types."

56. MacIntyre, *After Virtue*, 60.

argument" whose "central functional concept" was sustained through both ancient and medieval Western European cultures before secularization, where "the concept of *man* [was] understood as having an essential nature and an essential purpose or function" in the divine order of things.[57] The theistic mind is "one which knows its place and boundaries in the world."[58] Within these parameters, the moral function of classical theism inclusively understood "man-as-he-happens-to-be" motivating him toward "man-as-he-could-be-if-he-realized-his-essential-nature" which "presupposes" that an essential purpose may be fulfilled through action.[59] *Telos* was wedded to lived experience and credited to people as good when their innate essences caused them to act as they ought.[60] As with seed patterns that remain hidden prior to cultivation, when pursuing one's *telos* the essential pattern of personal character unfolds as essential purpose is mysteriously fulfilled.

In pre-secular "heroic societies,"[61] this was tied to the whole cultural stratum.[62] Thus to exist was deemed good and implied purpose; to participate purposefully in present experience affirmed a moral to existence that was complementarily good for self and society alike.[63] The immanent frame discourages belief in the divine and undercuts firm grounding in the ontic *logos* to the detriment of identities. But classical theism constituted personal identity as one achieved *telos* through participation in the greater narrative.[64] Thus, individuality and societal structure were cosmically linked. Classical theism had no basis for, or notion of, being able to take an objective view of their lived experience as if from the outside looking in.[65] Exclusivity could only be experienced by someone alien to society; likewise, to remove from society would be to erase personal identity.[66] This encapsulates the pertinence of the "narrative structure" of the social

57. MacIntyre, *After Virtue*, 58.

58. Pereira, "Morals," 174.

59. MacIntyre, *After Virtue*, 52.

60. MacIntyre, *After Virtue*, 58–59.

61. MacIntyre, *After Virtue*, 121. "Classical" heroic societies included "Greek, medieval or Renaissance [cultures], where moral thinking and action" were taught via storytelling (121); this included the air of the Anglo-Saxon and Northern myths (122) Tolkien admired.

62. MacIntyre, *After Virtue*, 123.

63. MacIntyre, *After Virtue*, 122.

64. MacIntyre, *After Virtue*, 123–24, 126.

65. MacIntyre, *After Virtue*, 126.

66. MacIntyre, *After Virtue*, 126.

imaginary's soil: To know and understand how to live, one determines what ought to be done within historical contexts.[67]

LOTR depicts a cosmos made up of such societies based on its own narrative structure, theistic under The One.[68] It communicates *telos* brought about through Tolkien's *poesis* in the years spanning *Hobbit*'s and *LOTR*'s publications. During this time, Tolkien incorporated the mythical effects illustrated in *Music* into *concursus* with the Bagginses initiated by Gandalf and complemented by Aragorn, the future King of Gondor. Through these characters, an innate sufficient power is revealed as each demonstrates his willingness to be instrumental in the greater narrative aided by an efficient causality.

Much as the Primary World is rife with evil, so is Middle-earth. But unlike the Primary World where the origins of good and evil may seem ambiguous, because we have *Music*, we can state these facts about Middle-earth: Teleology originates in Eru and ends somewhere within his conceptually infinite theme;[69] and he did not originate evil. Evil was the consequence of the sub-creative Fall. Therefore, we can interpret evils in *LOTR* as contingent upon this sub-created reality *ab initio* (but not *ex nihilo*). We can also interpret that which rivals evil in history as some proof of what Eru foretold before speaking Eä into existence: Evil will not be spatiotemporally unmade, and though it persists, none can divert the mysterious causality of *Eru's* music: "For he that attempteth this shall prove but mine instrument in the devising of things more wonderful, which he himself hath not imagined."[70] While writing *LOTR*, Tolkien's *poesis* linked this through what was already extant in *Hobbit* to fulfill these prophetic words illustratively.

Hobbit's concluding conversation shows Gandalf directing Bilbo's attention to the fact that Bilbo's adventures were not "managed by mere luck, just for [his] sole benefit."[71] *Managed* indicates outcomes

67. MacIntyre, *After Virtue*, 174–76.

68. *Letters*, 220.

69. Only Eru knows what this entails because it does "not proceed from the past" (*Silmarillion*, 18).

70. *Silmarillion*, 17.

71. *Hobbit*, 330. Before publication, Tolkien tinkered with using "contrived" instead of "managed" (Rateliff, *Return*, 692). In another pre-published version, Tolkien considered "managed by you yourself" without mentioning "mere luck" (Rateliff, *Return*, 693). The context of each version communicates the same mentality of each character: Bilbo unassumingly reacting to prophecies having come true; Gandalf affirming the end result happened through Bilbo's participation, but not without outside influence;

orchestrated according to some design that both Gandalf and Bilbo participated in without having complete control.[72] Tolkien's decision to conclude the story this way emphasizes his intentions to imply that the characters accepted the fact of an authority behind such luck.[73]

Luck is integral to causality working through instruments within the narrative and may be observed as a way of linking God's presence in-and-beyond the cosmos working in conjunction with human free will. In Old English, luck came from the word *wyrd*, and as time unfolded, God's purposes were fulfilled through the instrumentality of finite beings without divine interference in human decision-making.[74] By not dominating or diminishing free will, *wyrd* signified the mysterious and "continuous interplay" between divine and human freedom,[75] without collapsing *wyrd* into anthropomorphic meaning.[76] Those who participated in their essential nature could attain their essential teleological ends, but "people can 'change their luck,' and can in a way say 'No' to divine Providence, though of course if they do they have to stand by the consequences of their decision."[77]

Therefore, *mere* before *luck* indicates that Bilbo's success did not happen out of thin air but denotes purposeful activity concurrent with his participation: As Bilbo continued to respond to the demands he was awakened to moment-by-moment, something else was at work that Bilbo would not have known had he not acted. Although one of *Hobbit*'s

---

and Bilbo, never claiming his own glory, replying, "Thank goodness," each time. The final word selection supports an inner consistency that grounds both characters in theistic ontic *logos*.

72. To use "contrived" might have too closely associated Bilbo's success to something of his own devising. While writing OFS, Tolkien used *contrive* in relation to how magicians ordered things to bring about an intended result ("Manuscript," 253), while the sub-creator contrives in order to enchant the reader into Secondary Belief according to mytho-*logos*. Using "managed" underscores how the outcome of Bilbo's story was in the hands of a power other than his own.

73. Olsen's *Exploring* analyzed *Hobbit*'s original 1937 ("Solo Stage") edition and 1951 ("Revision Stage") revised edition (9–15). The latter edition replaced 1937's version of Bilbo's first encounter with Gollum (see p. 180n134). From each stage, *Hobbit* could not have been interpreted as would be possible after *LOTR* ("Assimilation Stage") and *Silmarillion*. Significantly, despite all the ways one can now interpret Tolkien's works in light of posthumously published writings, the conclusion of *Hobbit* prior to *LOTR* still alluded to a divine mind behind Bilbo's adventures (304).

74. Shippey, *Road*, 152.

75. Shippey, *Road*, 152–53.

76. Dubs, "Fortune," 215.

77. Shippey, *Road*, 152.

characters thought Bilbo might be "possessed of good luck,"[78] which in an "old-fashioned, pre-modern" sense was once believed as something "one can own, and perhaps even give away or pass on,"[79] luck rather was *with* Bilbo instead of being either an object of ownership or an ambiguous force controlling him like a puppet.[80] The narrative is interwoven with many fortunate occurrences and ultimately has a happy ending, but not without its share of inconveniences and bad luck, from a spooked pony running away with almost all of Bilbo's and his companions' food, to the death of Thorin their leader.[81] An efficient causality attained final causality via participatory instruments to bring about a final outcome for the greater good coincidental to the acts and wills of other characters and other narratives intersecting their journey. Tolkien linked this existing relation to the narrative structure of *LOTR*.

While preparing *LOTR* for publication, Tolkien developed additional prehistory material to fortify the impression of divine sensibility within his mytho-*logos* with the phenomenon of embedding.[82] In doing so, Tolkien

78. *Hobbit*, 230.

79. Shippey, *JRRT: Author*, 27. Shippey was referring to this instance.

80. Olsen's book discusses how luck gradually becomes a prominent theme throughout the story (*Exploring*, 65–68, 106, 139–41, 158–60, 183–84, 202–5, 222–25, 284–87, 303–4), noting how Bilbo and other characters are instruments interwoven for the good of the whole (67, 160, 304).

81. *Hobbit*, 37, 312.

82. Part of this was the Appendices (*LOTR*, 1009–1112), which Tolkien was still working on in 1955 for the final installment's (*The Return of the King*) publication (Hammond and Scull, "*LOTR*" *Companion*, xxxiv). Others considered here: "Of the Rings of Power and the Third Age" ("Power") in *Silmarillion* (285–304), but not as part of the "Quenta Silmarillion" proper (C. Tolkien, Foreword to *Silmarillion*, viii); "The Quest of Erebor" and the first portion of "The Istari" ("Istari") in *Unfinished Tales* (321–36, 388–92); and "The Annals of Aman" ("Aman") and "The Later *Quenta Silmarillion, Phase 1*" ("LaterQS1") (in Tolkien, *Morgoth's Ring*, 47–138, 141–99).

"Power" bridges the previous ages of the mythological history up to the time of the hobbits at the end of the Third Age and was probably written late in 1948, before *LOTR* was preliminarily finished in 1951 (Scull and Hammond, *JRRT Companion*, 851–52). The first portion of "Istari" was written in 1954 ("Istari," 388), "Aman" around 1951 (Scull and Hammond, *JRRT Companion*, 51) and "LaterQS1" in 1951–1952 ("LaterQS1," 141). I primarily concentrated on the instrumental causality of Gandalf in these works and his historical meaning as recorded at the publication of *LOTR*. In "Power" and "Istari," Gandalf is called by his Elvish name Mithrandir. Wizards are incarnate spiritual beings who in Valinor (the land of the gods beyond the western sea) are known as Maiar. Though not specifically named in "Aman," Gandalf was in Tolkien's mode of thought where the Maiar are mentioned (49, 56, 59, 65–66, 99, 110), and in "LaterQS1," he is referred to as Olórin (147), a name which appeared in *LOTR* drafts in 1944 (Tolkien, *War*, 153).

enhanced Gandalf's stature in the echelon of the supernatural machinery. By extension, Tolkien used Gandalf to portray participation in a sufficient power beyond him that efficiently works through an innate attribute in the seed of his character, and as the narrative deepens, Gandalf's character may be seen as a mediator of divine power at work.

As readers move further into *LOTR*, they become aware of different names for Gandalf. One character recollected how Gandalf once told him, "Olórin I was in my youth in the West that is forgotten," who was also named "Mithrandir among the Elves."[83] Each name suggests more about the wizard's being than the name Gandalf alone. In Olórin, Tolkien extended Gandalf's personal history outside the frame into the deeps of time to the seed of his immaterial self, long before befriending Bilbo.[84] Olórin of the forgotten West makes him more ancient than his careworn appearance, implying there is more to his being than deep wisdom and mysterious power. Mithrandir emphasizes his diuturnal nature because elves are immortals whose memories of him extend back hundreds of years.[85] Mithrandir is first used in a song of lament by the elves.[86] It means "Grey Pilgrim,"[87] which reflects how hobbits and readers know him until his untimely death. *Grey* veils his immaterial nature, and readers are given a glimpse of his teleological devotion when he declares himself "servant of the Secret Fire" immediately before he perishes.[88] At which point *concursus* is coincidental: Gandalf "was handing [himself] over to the Authority that ordained 'the Rules.'"[89] When he returns, Gandalf is first recognized as Mithrandir by Legolas the elf,[90] and his reappearance enhances the mystery of his character and the power he serves.[91] His return

83. Faramir in *LOTR*, 655.

84. In the prehistory, Olórin of the Maiar was created by Eru before the world ("Aman," 66) and was a "faithful" instrument devoted to fulfilling Eru's divine design by both stewarding the world and caring for Eru's Children ("LaterQS1," 147). Olórin was rival to Melkor, initiator of the "sub-creative Fall" ("LaterQS1," 147).

85. Thousands, if they knew him as Olórin in the West.

86. *LOTR*, 350.

87. "Istari," 390.

88. *LOTR*, 322.

89. *Letters*, 202. The inset quotes are not in this exact quote, but Tolkien inset "the Rules" in the previous sentence of the letter.

90. *LOTR*, 483.

91. The story implies Eru "devising something more wonderful" through Gandalf's death. Gandalf's return impresses an enlargement of the narrative by some greater design (*Letters*, 203).

as Gandalf the White (instead of Grey) deepens the mysteriousness of his meaning and purpose in a way that simultaneously enlarges him and other characters' roles in the narrative. Upon his reappearance, Gandalf meets his friends at a time of great distress, and if readers experience a kindling of spirit akin to the characters, this happens by virtue of the mytho-*logos* Tolkien brought to bear on the narrative in a eucatastrophic way: an unlooked-for, yet-untold encounter that satisfies present desire from beyond the walls of the world. As the meaning of Gandalf's nature became embedded through Tolkien's *poesis*, it intensified the immaterial fabric of the mytho-*logos* readers experience. Significantly, this happens as Gandalf faithfully pursues the greater good, the *telos* of which is tied to causality implicit in the text. The progenitivity of this was further enhanced in the way Tolkien derived how to communicate how transcendent presence works within his mytho-*logos*.

In preparing *LOTR*'s appendices, Tolkien noted how Gandalf's "action" led to the Bagginses' roles in the history of the Ring.[92] "Many suppose that all this was in his conscious purpose," Tolkien wrote, but "probably not. [Gandalf] would say he was 'directed,' or that he was 'meant' to take this course, or was 'chosen.'"[93] Being directed and chosen reaffirm external mediation concurrent with the creaturely participation through which Gandalf's discernment is un-buffered by a strictly immanent view of reality. Because of his love for all the free peoples of Middle-earth, Gandalf is shown detecting something significant in the seeds of hobbits—a "dormant" but "strong 'spark' yet unkindled" in Bilbo.[94] In this, Gandalf saw innate vitality and capacity in Bilbo's character and, therefore, "chose" him "as an instrument" to be "educated" in the ontic truths of his world.[95] This was how Tolkien's *poesis* assimilated Bilbo to *LOTR*, with an enhanced desire for elves crucial to their religious sense.

Recall Tolkien's nose for elves in a myth-woven and elf-patterned tapestry. The meaning derived through his personal languages became the spirituality embedded in the underlying mythology of Middle-earth[96]—the living religion into which the Bagginses become absorbed[97] and the cosmic imaginary readers participate in analogically. How

92. "Making," 282–83.

93. "Making," 283.

94. *Letters*, 365. Making this consistent with *Hobbit* as examined in chapter 1.

95. "Making," 283.

96. Duriez, "JRRT for the Ages," 324.

97. Madsen, "Light," 39–40.

Tolkien's mytho-*logos* portrays divine *concursus* in *LOTR* strengthens why it may be applicable to those things about the Primary World that may awaken readers.

For Frodo and his friends, propitiating the elvish heritage they know to be true enhances their roles in the greater tapestry. Tolkien's mytho-*logos* communicates how they encounter the principal causality that brings salvation to Middle-earth through their actions. As *LOTR* begins, the reader's imagination is bridged into this heritage through Gandalf and the Bagginses. Initially, the "prevailing mood" of most hobbits is "distrust of all Elvish lore,"[98] which suggests an indifferent or skeptical posture toward certain truths about their elf-patterned cosmos. Thus, they are little concerned with the greater historical truths of their world. Following Tolkien's assimilation of *Hobbit* to *LOTR*, Gandalf discerns that Bilbo's role in possessing the ring is over.[99] Bilbo's *Hobbit* adventures made him porous to the greater narrative that designates him friend of the elves,[100] and Bilbo departs to live with them. Frodo embodies a similar spark for elves, and he inherits the ring along with Bilbo's estate.[101] As Bilbo's heir, Frodo's narrative becomes embedded into historical "Elvish affairs"[102] by no decision of his own, and what now concerns him is that after having learned the true nature of Bilbo's ring, Gandalf informs Frodo it is the One Ring made by Sauron,[103] who means to enslave Middle-earth. Gandalf, first the rival of Melkor and then Sauron, sits in Frodo's study recounting the truth of his predicament.[104] If Sauron repossesses this Ring, everything good in the world is likely to fall under his dominion of darkness, torture, and fear. This frightening reality looks like bad luck, a "dreadful chance"[105] of which the reader becomes aware as Frodo does. Readers might resonate with such a dreadful chance. But if they have a secular social imaginary, what they decide to do next may differ. Whether

98. *Bombadil*, 9; see *LOTR*, 24, 43–44.

99. This is evident as Gandalf persuades Bilbo to let Frodo inherit it (*LOTR*, 32–34) and in a statement of finality at the Council of Elrond (263).

100. *LOTR*, 7.

101. *LOTR*, 7, 41, 65.

102. *Letters*, 198.

103. The evil incarnate Maia, servant of Melkor ("Aman," 52).

104. Although Frodo and the reader do not know the fuller meaning of these details, they are weighted by a deeper sense of mythological meaning.

105. *LOTR*, 50 (mentioned twice).

the conditions of belief in readers' cultures are open to transcendent reality can influence the reception of the text.

Tolkien's mytho-*logos* shows how Frodo responded after uniquely and purposefully personalizing this chance through divine appointment through the instrumentality of Gandalf who waters the seed of Frodo's character by implicating the same manager who orchestrated Bilbo's adventures. "Behind" Bilbo's finding the Ring, "there was something else at work, beyond any design of the Ring-maker. I can put it no plainer than by saying that Bilbo was *meant* to find the Ring, and *not* by its maker. In which case you also were *meant* to have it."[106] Frodo's plight is unique to him and for a good reason. Readers observe this real-time on the brink of the moment: the *aventures* of life, where mystery and danger combine with perduring truths of history, to be confronted according to the unknown risks of moment-by-moment decision-making, which requires decisive action for the greater good. History and supernatural involvement have made this intelligible.[107] Historical truth references what has actually happened, and in Middle-earth it can also influence how characters can move closer to their *telos* and realize their essential purpose. In so doing, characters' actions can argue for the morality embedded in Middle-earth's cosmic imaginary. Readers have no reason to doubt that everything up to this moment is not true, not even the divine aura affirmed to Frodo. Secondary Belief allows them to accept it as actually true.

A scene near the midpoint of *LOTR* shows the common relevance of living purposefully on moral grounds through another character influential to Frodo's journey: Aragorn. Éomer, a man from Rohan, asks Aragorn, "How shall a man judge what to do in such times?"[108] Aragorn, believes "there are . . . powers at work far stronger" than the material world evidences,[109] and such belief is implicit in his response. "As he ever has judged," Aragorn says, "Good and ill have not changed since yesteryear; nor are they one thing among Elves and Dwarves and another among Men. It is a man's part to discern them, as much in the Golden Wood as in his own house."[110] He stresses that the choice lies in whether

106. *LOTR*, 54–55.

107. By *supernatural* here, I mean Gandalf as an incarnate servant of the gods who alludes to the Writer and Manager.

108. *LOTR*, 427.

109. *LOTR*, 394.

110. *LOTR*, 428.

to serve good or evil but does not specify how to decide. Like Aragorn and other created beings in Middle-earth, humanity is "bound by the limits of . . . discernment"[111] and has to determine whether to pursue good or evil. Neither is ambiguous in *LOTR*. Aragorn affirms each is discernible. Even so, decision-making *now* is difficult. A greater narrative interlaced with countless others complicates how to make decisions about definitive courses of action presently. Although knowing the Writer's story exactly is unattainable, Aragorn's character models as he instructs Éomer. Whatever happens, he "is what he does," which thus shall be judged good so long as he fulfills his role in pursuing his teleological end.[112] As Aragorn and Gandalf faithfully fulfill their roles, so does Frodo because, like them and Bilbo before him, he responded to the innate sense of being awakened and was drawn further on.

Gandalf's affirmation that Frodo's *telos* is tied to the greater historical narrative instills the premonition that he needs to act now, but like Éomer, Frodo expresses frustration before he leaves the Shire: "Why did [the Ring] come to me? Why was I chosen?" Frodo asked.[113] I mentioned that luck is integral to the impression of divine causality working instrumentally throughout *LOTR*. Frodo's question associates *wyrd* with his being meant and chosen to have the Ring. Even though Gandalf encouraged and affirmed Frodo up to this point, Frodo is clearly not comforted. But this displays an example of the continuous interplay between divine and created beings. The chance and luck present in *LOTR* suggest an out-of-frame manager within the narrative who has an instrumental purpose for Frodo concurrent with free will decision-making.[114] Readers without ontic grounding in the cosmo-*logos* may view chance and luck as "impersonal."[115] Chance spoken of as a power of its own is a "substitute for God,"[116] and the same is true of luck. A sacramental view reads this differently: yesterday, today, and tomorrow are simultaneously gathered into the infinity of "God's instant,"[117] and Tolkien's mytho-*logos* analogically associates chance and luck with the mystery of divine involvement.

111. Madsen, "Light," 40.

112. See MacIntyre, *After Virtue*, 122, 125.

113. *LOTR*, 60.

114. See Dubs, "Providence," 137.

115. Poythress, *Chance*, 91–96.

116. Poythress, *Chance*, 96.

117. Initially discussed on p. 125.

I highlight this because it not only sets the stage for the rest of *LOTR* but is similar to such crucial moments in readers' lives: the brink of impasse before regression or action toward formation. Revisiting Tolkien's words underscore this: "At any minute it is what we are and are doing, not what we plan to be and do that counts." If there is no manager, who cares? But if we are part of a greater narrative of a divine Writer whose goodness created us for relationship and purpose, how we steward our narratives of life matters. Tolkien gives readers the impression of divine sensibility in this scene, an extra-mental visual for how characters assent to the givens of their world: tension without ontic doubt.

The choice that confronts Frodo based on what Gandalf has narrated to him is tied to what kind of instrument he will be in the heroic stratum of Middle-earth. Whatever worldly complexities are happening outside Frodo's homeland, Gandalf has gone through the pains of unravelling various historical threads to clarify this precise moment in history for him. Historical veracity amidst his cosmic imaginary brings Frodo to conclude he must keep the Ring from Sauron by taking it from the Shire. The "living tradition"[118] passed down to Frodo as-he-happens-to-be initiates his movement toward realizing-his-essential-nature in the cosmos. As the spark of Frodo's Tookish nature is kindled similarly to Bilbo's, he accepts with certainty what he must do amidst uncertainty: "He did not tell Gandalf, but . . . a great desire to follow Bilbo flamed up in his heart. . . . It was so strong that it overcame his fear."[119] Gandalf has thus awakened in Frodo that which surpasses the "wanhope and distress"[120] that initially chilled Frodo with fear. Even though *LOTR* illustrates this on an epic scale, we are given a valuable picture of decisiveness amidst conflict through mytho-*logos*. It is a plain, everyday dilemma clothed in the garments of heroic romance.

As in Primary World experience, although neither Gandalf nor Frodo have a choice about the time and place in which their narratives are being lived, they demonstrate how to choose the best course of action according to what they know. Their predicament coheres with a mysterious interplay between transcendence in the mytho-*logos* and those living purposefully out of the resourceful seeds of character for which they are

118. MacIntyre, *After Virtue*, 222–23. "Living traditions . . . continue a not-yet-completed narrative [to] confront a future whose determinate and determinable character, so far as it possesses any, derives from the past."

119. *LOTR*, 61.

120. "Istari," 391.

sufficiently equipped. This illustrates how character transformation moves toward realization; only through action can it be actualized.

Readers encounter this soil of the mytho-*logos* on the threshold of *LOTR* where there is always some form of eucatastrophe glimpsed, subtly if not pronounced. Eucatastrophes will differ from reader to reader, as will their interpretations of their own dreadful chances, but when deeply moved by *LOTR*'s enchantment, its mytho-*logos* may awaken readers to a causal presence that awakens willing participants to a sufficient power in the text through which purpose is attained as they move further on in the narrative.

The Living Impact of LOTR

The highest function of fairy-stories is to impact the life of the reader with eucatastrophe. Tolkien accomplished this at *LOTR*'s climactic emotional "peak"[121] when Middle-earth's history is salvifically altered from outside the walls of the world. As Frodo's strength reaches its end, his faithfulness is rewarded by an unexpected grace.[122] When too weak to destroy the Ring himself, his nemesis surprises him, bites off the finger wearing it, and falls into the fires of Mount Doom with it, thus destroying the Ring and saving Middle-earth in a way only the entirety of the narrative makes clear. Analogous to how Christ is the eucatastrophe that redeems those faithful to God in human history,[123] this is the fullest sense of eucatastrophe in *LOTR*. It happens at the height of Gandalf's, Aragorn's, and Frodo's stewarding of their roles. The phenomenon of embedding through interlacement makes sense of "events . . . in flux" according to some "pattern underlying them" to bring order amidst chaos.[124] It is what Tolkien intended in making *LOTR* an exciting story that affects readers mythically.

In a world always already graced, a eucatastrophic quality immerses the whole of existence because God's transcendence is an existential fact: God's magic is ever-present, and divine miracles are always possible amidst all the dyscatastrophes. One who sees Primary Reality through a gospel-centered Eucharistic lens has a transformed view of

121. Tolkien in Hammond and Scull, "*LOTR*" *Companion*, 748.

122. See *Letters*, 234.

123. *Letters*, 101.

124. West, "Interlace," 79.

how to see and think otherwise in moment-to-moment experience through the sacramental imagination. This is why Gandalf's encounter with Frodo in his hobbit hole illustrates something equally, if not more, significant than the climax.

Character formation begins at moments of decision without guarantees about outcomes and can only be realized after looking back on such moments to see who we have become over time. Who we are now matters most, and how we act now shapes who we become. Nobody other than Frodo saves the world by taking a magic ring made by an incarnate spiritual servant of the devil of Middle-earth; that is *his telos*. But he exhibits something common to the human race: perseverance amidst adversity.[125] All readers persevere through personal narratives to discover purpose. As they venture through the mundane world and face the imposition of life's harsh realities, everyday chance-and-luck *aventures* happen, good and bad. A person's own journey to Mount Doom need not equate to saving the world; that may not be their purpose. And if it is, it is an end goal that is unattainable without attending to the present. Fulfilling purpose requires concentration on the threshold of now, which is the only place one can experience fullness. The past is etched in memory, and there is no guarantee of tomorrow.

Recall that extra-mental existences are wholly independent of the perceiver. But this only means they preexist one's experience of them. "Medieval 'realism' . . . assumes the participation of words in the extramental reality they signify,"[126] and although readers do not participate in *LOTR* from medieval times, they analogically participate in its mytho-*logos* as they journey through all that it transsignifies: divine involvement working instrumentally through characters transformed by narrative action. They experience Middle-earth mythically as they imagine it.

Remember also what feigned history is meant to show—an improvement on what might be or ought to be, not by retreating from reality, but by re-ascending from a world which the sub-creator had a right to call foolish by asserting his/her divine origin. Tolkien poetically demonstrated the ennoblement of characters that transcend their perceptible limitations for the betterment of themselves and their world. Readers witness these transformations as they unfold and are shown an analogical form of "self-transcendence" via classical theism where created beings "participate *in*

125. See Tolkien's discussion of Frodo in Interview with Gueroult.

126. Grant, "Tolkien," 164. Grant does not hyphenate *extramental*.

part in a transcendence over [their] environment" because they do not allow themselves to be confined by life circumstances.[127]

When stepping away from *LOTR*, if the story itself induces readers to require more of their social imaginaries after having been inside Middle-earth, something caused by the religious feeling that seems to be everywhere has the capacity to impact readers by more than its peak moments of eucatastrophe. As a "fixed" text[128] engendering "a fixed tradition"[129] that transsignifies a transcendent sensibility analogical to a pre-secular cosmic imaginary, maybe it can direct readers to an always already graced Primary World—still present yet veiled by immanentization.

Tolkien's faith came from a Christian tradition that encourages *concursus* similar to *LOTR*, where the individual participates in God out of free will for the greater good. "Double agency" is the means through which God works instrumentally through human participants: "God acting in the actions of creatures but always in a way that lets them retain their integrity as real beings rather than in a way that overrides or cancels their real being."[130] In so doing, God's activity "does not cancel the creature but lets it be itself," and in this way, "we find both that there is more than ourselves acting and that we are more truly and fully ourselves."[131] This allows a person to recognize that God mysteriously works through personal experience without breaking it down to an exact science.[132] Even when people may erroneously stray, God works through them nonetheless and moves them teleologically further on in

127. Sire, *Universe*, 32.

128. Basney, "Myth," 193. Since 1955, edits have been made to newer editions of *LOTR*, the latest being for the fiftieth anniversary edition in 2004 and reprint edition in 2005 (Hammond and Scull, "*LOTR*" *Companion*, xxxix–xliv, 783). These were mainly due to *LOTR*'s length and printing errors that were primarily typographical, which were encouraged by Christopher Tolkien *so long as they did not alter the meaning of the whole* (xliii). For the anniversary edition, 229 areas for correction were recommended (xlii). In the end, 344 errors were corrected (783–811), with 3 more identified after the 2005 edition went to print (812).

129. C. Tolkien, Foreword to *Silmarillion*, vii.

130. Henderson, "Austin Farrer," 45. This echoes Torrance's comment from chapter 5 about the "profound integration of logos and being discerned in a transcendent way in the living and active God, and in a creaturely and contingent way in created reality—'being' understood as including movement, creative activity in God and becoming or motion in the creature."

131. Henderson, "Austin Farrer," 45.

132. Henderson, "Austin Farrer," 46.

the greater reality God is authoring in a transformative way.[133] Tolkien's Faërie can awaken this possibility through imaginative intuition in readers regardless of social imaginary.

In chapter 2, I discussed Tolkien's belief that humanity receives insights from divine creativity to worshipfully "echo after-music beneath the ancient song" of God through mytho-*logos*. Tolkien also reasoned how this might ennoble its hearers should God use it to reveal concrete truths to a naturalistic world.[134] In "Mythopoeia's" closing lines, sub-creators view their artistic accomplishments from paradise after death, where poets see their own creative inventions freed,[135] being played like music unobstructed from the hindrances of ordinary life. These sub-creators gain fresh perspective about how their works honor God through creativity faithfully exercised—though creative from a fallen state of being, whether or not they stewarded this perfectly in life,[136] they now observe their artistry clearly and continue being creative in the afterlife.[137]

Human creativity presents "a virtually infinite multiformity"[138] of poetic works that have lives of their own in tribute to the infinity of God's potential variety. While sub-creators may not have seen the effects of their creativity while alive, when looking back on the divine's use of it through unfettered lenses, they may see that something like God's truth has been made to reflect from it.[139] This end result is not definitive, but potential: God may "*perchance*"[140] make it reflect reality *about which* the truth is, and even then only a likeness to divine reality. If this happens, "far greater things may colour the mind in dealing with the lesser things of a fairy-story."[141] This is noncommittal language about how God could use sub-creation: Greater things may perchance leave the possibility for the reader's imagination to turn to that which is outside time itself, maybe.

This is aided when stories stretch the imagination beyond the drab blur of trite familiarity when life seems stagnant—not for the purposes

133. Farrer in Henderson, "Austin Farrer," 46.

134. See "Mythopoeia," 88–89.

135. "Mythopoeia," 90.

136. "Mythopoeia," 87.

137. See Milbank, *Chesterton*, 167.

138. Kuyper, *Wisdom*, 159.

139. "Mythopoeia," 90.

140. "Mythopoeia," 90 (emphasis mine).

141. *Letters*, 288.

of escape, but to take hold of new freshness of life as time ticks on. "Life is . . . above the measure of us all," Tolkien wrote.[142] Thus, "we all need literature that is above our measure. . . . [Regardless of] Age I think we only are really moved by what is at least in some point or aspect above us, above our measure, at any rate before we have read it and 'taken it in.'"[143] Although in real life what we must do is not as clear-cut as stories illustrate, if readers take it in and value it with credence, *LOTR* becomes a progenitive bridge from Tolkien's creativity to readers that can awaken the religious sense and can encourage them further on into fullness of life in God.

142. *Letters*, 298.

143. *Letters*, 298.

Conclusion

"If art is a poetic parallel to reality, then Christian art is a poetic parallel to Christ's presence in the world."[1] Tolkien thought that fantasy presents the "most potent" and "pure" poetic parallel when sub-creativity derives literary credibility so verisimilar that it enchants readers to believe what they are being shown within the story.[2] Though it does not produce a physically real world, it is capital-*P* Poetry, and by virtue of its independent operations, a superior form of poetics that causes readers to imagine otherwise.[3]

But in what way is it superior? The climactic *mythos* of all time is the story of Christ whose incarnation, participation in history, sacrificial death for humanity, and resurrection mediate the ultimate salvific meaning. This was the Great Poet physically mediating through time and space to clarify God's supreme essence through the *mythos* of eternal *Logos* so that every personal narrative may be transformed into living and thinking otherwise. It is the greatest and perfect eucatastrophe that "rends . . . the very web of story, and lets a gleam come through" the dark shrouding over human experience, if allowed.[4]

If Christian *poiema* presents a poetic parallel to Christ's presence in the world, the literary belief it compels should present some form of an ontological encounter that nourishes individual being in a eucatastrophic way; otherwise, it is not truly a parallel. Encounters

1. Knippers, "Old Story," 68.
2. OFS, 60.
3. See OFS, 60.
4. OFS, 76.

through such secondary realities open doors that awaken the religious sense originated by God, yet this sense is awakened by the extra-mental world that mediates person-to-person creativity. Therefore, what readers experience as they witness the shaping of characters can become formative to personal experience.

In this study of how Tolkien's creativity brought *LOTR* into being, I have not concentrated on the intricacies of all the characters and motives. Neither have I highlighted plot themes to suggest why certain types of readers may or may not be affected by them. Rather, I have focused on the inherent capacity of Tolkien's mytho-*logos* to cohere with the religious sense all image-bearers share while respecting the fact that everybody has a "compost-heap" soil of their own lives. This allowed the discussion to focus on how and why *LOTR* mediates various mythic meanings into individual lives in unique ways.

I began demonstrating this in chapters 1 and 2 by discussing how poetics bring about intentional meaning through *poesis* via personal *logos*. When the sub-creator makes a new "thing in being," it forges an imaginative pathway by which meaning transcends through mytho-*logos* into readers. In one sense, meaning progenitively moves from the poet's mind to the reader's, which is a person-to-person ontological encounter. But we saw sub-creation as capable of becoming more affective when a transcendent divine mind permeates an orderly cosmos. If so, God can mediate truth to a person through this same pathway. God makes abstract meaning personably concrete through whatever instruments are chosen to mediate divine grace. This includes poetics.

Since my argument centers on analogically modeling God through personal creativity, I focused on how Tolkien maintained a parallel secondary reality as wholly other, with its own verisimilitude, narrative language, aesthetic nature, and spirituality. In the examples of Bilbo in *Hobbit* and Gandalf and Pippin in *LOTR*, we saw that Tolkien's narratives illustrate how these characters awakened to a cosmos more alive than they previously knew, something reaching them from beyond their present circumstances: for Bilbo, from the cozy comforts of homely life; for Gandalf and Pippin, from a place of near hopelessness. Only by understanding each narrative context can we comprehend that their imminent needs would only be satisfied when provoked by otherness apart from themselves because they were unable to meet these needs themselves.

If readers are affected by *LOTR*, I have contended this must be because Tolkien's mytho-*logos* prompts responses through meaning that transcends words. Tolkien's *poesis* engendered certain meanings in *LOTR* that awaken readers "to its own reality" in-and-beyond its textual frame. That is, poetic meaning operatively bridges imaginations to *LOTR* through the mythic effects stimulated by and permeating through the osmotic design of its *mythos*. Since Tolkien's ontological outlook was grounded in God who orchestrates all cosmic development through the substance and sustenance of Christ, his mytho-*logos* needed to portray an existing relation between divinity and created beings within *LOTR* analogously.

I also demonstrated how Tolkien injected meaning into the poetics of *LOTR* to awaken readers to the "old light" of God who remains ever-present. If readers "participate in the extra-mental reality words signify," they participate in *LOTR* in a parallel way to how they might participate in God through Christ. Each requires seeing at different stages of imagination. Through *Leaf by Niggle*, we were able to see how Tolkien reconciled investing so much time and sub-creative energy into a project without it being fruitless: God *can* draw readers through ontological encounters via human creativity to awaken the religious sense to reality and truth beyond the self.

In chapters 3 and 4, we learned different ways fantasy gives us lenses through which to imagine and noted that intelligent beings do this regularly. *LOTR* progenitively actuated Tolkien's imagery through narrative and language, the "peculiar message" of which lies in the integrity of his own personalized mytho-*logos*, the poetic meaning of which cannot be exactly imaged to other imaginations. Tolkien gave his own version of Faërie for others to envision in *LOTR*. In one sense, *LOTR* is as a stage play unfolding before our eyes. In a different sense, its mytho-*logos* is a mode of time-travel that transports us there to experience consciously.[5] Each sense describes different ways *LOTR* is disclosed to us. We experience feigned history concurrent with personal history, and as we experience it, we absorb it into our own without dislocation of ourselves from ordinary life. Although what happens within the story is not directly correlated with the details of our actual lives, we may find applicability to real-life situations after learning from and comprehending different contextual situations that may enlarge our own living narratives. The applicability of a work, then, stems first from the sub-creator's personal *poesis* before becoming finalized as *poiema*, "something said." When we look upon a stage play or

5. For a similar point, see Duriez, "Fairy Story," 19.

peer into another room, we are not inhabitants of the fantasy imaged, but observers of meaning placed there by somebody else.

Chapter 5 discussed how *LOTR* has ontic grounding in its own *logos* analogous to a Primary World cosmic order permeated by the transcendent God as interpreted through the lens of Christ. If God is involved in the cosmos with humanity, God can mediate divine meaning in purposefully personalized ways. Tolkien's mytho-*logos* utilized Eru, whose "presence" is only detectable based on what the narrative transsignifies. It is enhanced by the glimpses of the backdrop of Tolkien's mythological history, which sharpens how *LOTR* induces the Secondary Belief about the divine sensibility of Middle-earth's fairy faith under The One. An ontological encounter through such sensibilities can awaken what Giussani called the *religious sense*.

Chapter 6 directed attention to why Secondary Belief through Tolkien's mytho-*logos* is significant: it can awaken readers to the possibility of *the* transcendent God who is the ontic foundation to which all Primary Belief should be given. *LOTR* gives a new lens, a clean window to see participatory ontology in action. If it purposefully affects readers through an ontological encounter, it can then be a means through which the Judeo-Christian God awakens readers to the concrete sense of divine presence despite immanent frame assertions. Therefore, there is a recovery of an old reading of a world that is not actually lost but still exists.

The voices of Taylor and MacIntyre gave us an understanding for the chaotic-ness of the ontological unsteadiness many Western societies exude. *LOTR* effectively gives readers a cosmic imaginary without myriad competing cross-pressures and isms. Its mytho-*logos* provides steady ground through which good and evil are clearly discernible, and every time we read it, it is always the same world though it may generate new meaning for us. It never becomes confusing in subsequent readings. Though it initially strikes readers as complete and complicated, *LOTR* projects a lifelike interlacement of various threads through which character transformation happens by trial, disappointment, doubt, and loss, yet with hope.

Chapters 7 and 8 articulated how analogical participation through enchanting narrative can awaken readers to fullness in life now as they observe how characters persevere through their personal narratives amidst the greater narrative of life. Reading allows for porousness so that buffered selves may be affected even if they have raised defenses. The demand for more of Tolkien's world after *Hobbit* allowed him to develop and enhance his mytho-*logos* to a fuller extent in *LOTR* to give readers the nourishment they wanted. A subsistent principal causality is embedded in each text. Tolkien modelled this after his own divine sensibilities about Primary Reality through which God's miracles and magic are perceptible in everyday life. An embedded sense of analogical transcendence is preserved through the history, events, and characters participating in the secondary reality *LOTR* reveals. Instead of being theoretical or something to believe in, readers *experience* it analogically. If affected, they experience it porously and mythically because the poetic meaning operates in ways that engage imaginative intuition.

Human intelligence capably discerns that a green sun is possible in fantasy because the sub-creator's language has caused it to be believably imagined. Such is the way of sub-creation when "the medium disappears" and we are enchanted. The immaterial machinery of *LOTR* implies divine causality interlaced into the fabric of the world. Readers can sense this throughout the story. But this is different and perhaps more clear-cut than a divine mind might be perceived in Primary World experience. Therefore, readers awaken to what is true about Tolkien's fairy-story based on how his mytho-*logos* "telescopes" them into observing this close-up, because it gives a clean window through which to see Middle-earth. An ontic sense of grounding is perceptible through the contextual narratives of life of the hobbit characters that are subservient to wiser characters who are accountable to higher moral authorities. Each personally perseveres in the cosmic "soil" of Middle-earth by attaining some sense of fullness through teleological pursuits without ontic doubt.

I have accentuated how and why *LOTR* creates conditions of belief for ontological encounters that may mediate God's truth. Because Tolkien was a Catholic philologist who loved mythology, fairy-stories, God, creation, language, medieval literature, and meaning, all coalesced into his creative *mythos* to bring us *LOTR*. When reading the story, we are not experiencing Catholicism, philological science, and so forth, exactly, nor do we need to buy into all of Tolkien's beliefs and interests. He declared himself "most readily available *corpus vile*" to avoid this so that *LOTR* could be experienced freely without details about himself being a distraction.[6] When readers step to the threshold of *LOTR*, they come to an enchanted cosmic imaginary like, yet unlike, our world. Even if readers do not believe in an old cosmo-*logos* of Primary Reality, Secondary Belief

6. *Letters*, 231.

implies they actually *do* believe in some form of it within *LOTR*, though it is merely an echo of the actual cosmo-*logos* God has not withdrawn from. *LOTR* allows readers to witness character transformation happening concurrent with divine causality implicit in the narrative.

Tolkien's hope for his mythopoesis was to *perchance* mirror some likeness of the True through the lesser things of his fairy-story. This required engendering an experience akin to Christian perseverance such as the *Beowulf* poet who

> could hardly have been less aware than we that in history . . . and in Scripture, people could depart from the one God to other service in time of trial—precisely because that God has never guaranteed to His servants immunity from temporal calamity, before or after prayer. It is to idols that men turned (and turn) for quick and literal answers.[7]

LOTR's participatory realism challenges readers to face their living narratives in times of peace and trial. If we remember what was observed about *LOTR* in chapter 1—that it can cause one to require more, mediate divine presence, be a source of restoration, exude pervasive religious sensibility—all these observations acknowledge how *LOTR* can have real-world effects because it is exciting yet exhibits "real pathos"[8] through the adversity Tolkien's characters face. But in order for there to be a divine encounter, this remains in the hands of God, not the sub-creator since any sanctity inhabiting sub-creative works do not come from, but through, the poet. *LOTR* is a particular story that creates conditions for belief to enhance the possibility for any sort of ontological encounter through the text to awaken the religious sense in which readers might taste the sanctity of God.

This study belongs in the territory of the Tolkien scholars noted in the Introduction, each of whom were intent on illuminating how Tolkien's Christianity shaped his creativity in a way that readers may be affected by it. Caldecott stated people reread *LOTR* for "refreshment of soul,"[9] and Wood's students noted how reading *LOTR* made them "feel 'clean.'"[10] Further research could undertake a qualitative study about the details of such

7. "Beowulf," 44.

8. Warren Lewis, *Brothers*, 259. "Warnie" Lewis was C. S. Lewis's brother and regular Inkling. He wrote this after reading the manuscript nearly five years prior to *LOTR*'s publication.

9. Caldecott, *Power*, 5.

10. Wood, *Gospel*, 75.

expressions and their relation to some perceived mediation or restoration with divine or other sensibilities. A subsequent study might investigate how and why *LOTR* has specifically shaped and formed readers over time and compare this to formation of characters in the story.[11] There is also a frontier for examining Tolkien's conception of the imagination's power in relation to neuroscience. Further investigations could also explore how Tolkien's world affects readers directly through the text when compared to visual imagery cast by filmmakers.[12] An interesting part of this investigation might address how such findings compare to Christopher Tolkien's belief that *LOTR* films' "commercialization has reduced the aesthetic and philosophical impact of [it] to nothing."[13]

LOTR as a narrative text is significant because its mythic effects mediate meaning without confining it to allegories, opinions, science, or cinematic visualizations. These can limit free participation in mytho-*logos*. Reading fantasy allows for meaning to mediate from one being's creativity into another's, and this single source can affect various readers in particular ways. This is how myth always operates—freely, through the poetic meaning of sub-creation that links to individual imaginations. *LOTR* mediates a religious sensibility that gives rise to Secondary Belief presently, directly, and always parallel to Christ's presence in the world. Nobody knows exactly what God will do, but myth provides an understanding for how God might: by gracefully mediating gospel concreteness to readers in peace or trial and nurturing them on to fullness of life in Christ through divine mystery in the contexts of our individual living narratives.

The Introduction introduced how *mythos* is the medium of experience on which the rest of my argument depends: the notion of literary narrative's inherent power to mediate meaning into various narratives of life regardless of belief system. Throughout the book, I have examined how Tolkien's creativity in writing *LOTR* allows us to comprehend why his mytho-*logos* compels Secondary Belief. The presumptive basis for my argument is that every person is an image-bearer of God gifted with creativity from God. These shared characteristics allow intelligent beings to communicate and receive *mythos* in countless ways that may

11. A helpful source for this might be Shaeffer's, "Spiritual Formation."

12. Tolkien was open to such adaptations, so long as they were not "altered by the adapter's private imagination," especially with "needless . . . points of detail" (Scull and Hammond, *JRRT Companion*, 19).

13. Rérolle, "My Father's."

awaken the religious sense regardless of personal history. Because God has potentially predisposed all people to aspire after the divine, this capacity to enter into relation with God

> is in all men but every man, every human being develops his own consciousness of this religious sentiment according to his temperament, according to his background, according to his character, according to the circumstances that befall him. So may [sic] fables may be construed about the religious sentiment but they are not so different that the value ultimately inherent in all these fables is taken away, which is the religious sense proper. In all these fables the value of religious sentiment is affirmed.[14]

Giussani asserts a possible way for understanding how the inherent meaning of particular stories can affect the uniqueness of personal being whether the person claims to be religious or not. This encounter may be the "spark" people need to direct their attention outside themselves in search of salvation, which fairy-stories give only a foretaste.

In its most basic sense, I have provided a lens for seeing how encountering the poetic meaning of *LOTR* analogically awakens religious sensibilities that are only fully and truly satisfied by the Christian gospel. If mytho-*logos* mediates meaning that makes readers see clearly, think otherwise, experience excitement, or be deeply moved, *LOTR* is a conversation starter for how and why Tolkien's sub-creativity produces an echo of the concrete truths readers actually need to move further on in their individual narratives of life in God.

Like Niggle's Tree, *LOTR* is an organism whose life has not ended. Although Tolkien offered it up as completed *poiema*, the result of its capabilities to impact readers is in the hands of God. *LOTR* is the foremost Tree on a canvas that evidences much more, and when readers accept the invitation to venture into it, they may find their attention directed to something both in and beyond this experience that nudges them into awareness of the living presence of God. Such, at least, was Tolkien's hope.

14. Giussani, "Religious Sense and Faith," 1.

Bibliography

Abrams, M. H. *A Glossary of Literary Terms*. 8th ed. Boston: Thomson Wadsworth, 2005.

Anderson, Douglas A. Commentary to George MacDonald's *The Golden Key*. In *Tales Before Tolkien: The Roots of Modern Fantasy*, edited by Douglas A. Anderson, 21–22. New York: Del Ray, 2003.

———. Introduction and notes. In *The Annotated Hobbit*, by J. R. R. Tolkien. Boston: Houghton Mifflin, 1988.

———. Note on the Text. In *The Lord of the Rings*, by J. R. R. Tolkien. Boston: Houghton Mifflin, 1994.

Ashford, Bruce. "Jordan Peterson: High Priest for a Secular Age." *Gospel Coalition*, April 8, 2019. https://www.thegospelcoalition.org/article/jordan-peterson-high-priest-secular-age.

Bacote, Vincent E. Introduction to *Wisdom & Wonder*, by Abraham Kuyper, 23–29. Translated by Nelson D. Kloosterman. Edited by Jordan J. Ballor and Stephen J. Grabill. Grand Rapids, MI: Christian's Library, 2011.

Bailey, Derek, dir. *J. R. R. T.: A Film Portrait of J. R. R. Tolkien*. London: Landseer, 1996. https://www.youtube.com/watch?v=rNqVqzIxi3A.

Barber, Dorothy Elizabeth Klein. "The Structure of *The Lord of the Rings*." PhD diss., University of Michigan, 1965.

Barfield, Owen. *History in English Words*. Hudson, NY: Lindisfarne, 1967.

———. "Poetic Diction and Legal Fiction." In *The Importance of Language*, edited by Max Black, 51–71. Englewood Cliffs, NJ: Prentice-Hall, 1962.

———. *Poetic Diction: A Study in Meaning*. Middletown, CT: Wesleyan University Press, 1973.

Barron, Bishop Robert. "The Adventures of Classical Morality." *Word on Fire*, May 8, 2013. https://www.wordonfire.org/resources/article/the-adventures-of-classical-morality/461.

Basney, Lionel. "Myth, History, and Time in *The Lord of the Rings*." In *Understanding "The Lord of the Rings": The Best of Tolkien Criticism*, edited by Rose A. Zimbardo and Neil D. Isaacs, 183–94. Boston: Houghton Mifflin, 2004.

Bell, Anita Miller. "*The Lord of the Rings* and the Emerging Generation: A Study of the Message and Medium: J. R. R. Tolkien and Peter Jackson." DLitt diss., Drew University, 2009.

Bellah, Robert N. "Christian Faithfulness in a Pluralist World." In *Postmodern Theology*, edited by Frederic B. Burnham, 74–91. San Francisco: Harper and Row, 1989.

Bergmann, Frank. "The Roots of Tolkien's Tree: The Influence of George MacDonald and German Romanticism Upon Tolkien's Essay 'On Fairy-stories.'" In *Faerie, Fantasy, & Pseudo-Mediaevalia in XX-Century Literature*, edited by John Wortley, 5–14. Winnipeg, Canada: University of Manitoba Press, 1977.

Bernthal, Craig. *Tolkien's Sacramental Vision: Discerning the Holy in Middle Earth*. Kettering, OH: Second Spring, 2014.

Betz, John R. Translator's Introduction to *Analogia Entis: Metaphysics: Original Structure and Universal Rhythm*, by Erich Przywara, 1–115. Translated by John R. Betz and David Bentley Hart. Grand Rapids, MI: Eerdmans, 2014.

Birzer, Bradley J. "The Christian Gifts of J. R. R. Tolkien." *New Oxford Review* 68.10 (2001) 25–29.

———. *J. R. R. Tolkien's Sanctifying Myth: Understanding Middle-earth*. Wilmington, DE: ISI, 2003.

Bliss, Alan. Preface to *Finn and Hengest*, by J. R. R. Tolkien, v–ix. Edited by Alan Bliss. London: HarperCollins, 2006.

Bodleian Libraries. *Tolkien: Maker of Middle-earth*. End of Exhibition Report. Weston Library, June 1–October 28, 2018.

Boersma, Hans. *Heavenly Participation: The Weaving of a Sacramental Tapestry*. Grand Rapids, MI: Eerdmans, 2011.

Bowman, Mary R. "The Story Was Already Written: Narrative Theory in *The Lord of the Rings*." *Narrative* 14.3 (2006) 272–93. http://dx.doi.org/10.1353/nar.2006.0010.

Bratman, David. "Tolkien at the PCA." *Tolkien Society* (blog), April 12, 2015. https://www.tolkiensociety.org/blog/2015/04/tolkien-at-the-pca.

Brewer, Derek S. "*The Lord of the Rings* as Romance." In *J. R. R. Tolkien, Scholar and Storyteller: Essays in Memoriam*, edited by Mary Salu and Robert T. Farrell, 249–64. Ithaca, NY: Cornell University Press, 1979.

Brown, Colin. *From the Ancient World to the Age of Enlightenment*. Vol. 1 of *Christianity & Western Thought*. Downers Grove, IL: InterVarsity, 1990.

Caldecott, Stratford. "Over the Chasm of Fire: Christian Heroism in *The Silmarillion* and *The Lord of the Rings*." In *Tolkien: A Celebration*, edited by Joseph Pearce, 17–33. San Francisco: Ignatius, 2001.

———. *The Power of the Ring*. New York: Crossroad, 2005.

Candler, Peter M., Jr. "Tolkien or Nietzsche, Philology and Nihilism." Paper presented at the Centre of Theology and Philosophy, University of Nottingham, 2008. http://www.theologyphilosophycentre.co.uk/papers/Candler_TolkeinNietzsche.doc.

Carpenter, Humphrey. *The Inklings: C. S. Lewis, J. R. R. Tolkien, Charles Williams and Their Friends*. London: HarperCollins, 1997.

———. *J. R. R. Tolkien: A Biography*. Boston: Houghton Mifflin, 2000.

Casanova, Jóse. "Secular, Secularizations, Secularisms." *Immanent Frame*, October 25, 2007. https://tif.ssrc.org/2007/10/25/secular-secularizations-secularisms.

Catholic Church. *Catechism of the Catholic Church*. 2nd ed. Washington, DC: United States Catholic Conference, 1994.

Cavaliero, Glen. *Charles Williams: Poet of Theology*. Grand Rapids, MI: Eerdmans, 1983.

Chesterton, Gilbert Keith. *Orthodoxy*. Charleston, SC: BiblioBazaar, 2007.
Cohen, S. Marc. "Aristotle's Metaphysics." *Stanford Encyclopedia of Philosophy*, June 15, 2016. https://plato.stanford.edu/archives/win2016/entries/aristotle-metaphysics.
Curry, Patrick. *Defending Middle-earth*. Boston: Houghton Mifflin, 2004.
Curtis, Anthony. "Remembering Tolkien and Lewis." *British Book News*, June 1977, 429–30.
Davidsen, Markus Altena. "The Spiritual Milieu Based on J. R. R. Tolkien's Literary Mythology." In *Handbook of Hyper-Real Religions*, edited by Adam Possamai, 185–204. Boston: Brill, 2012.
Dawson, Christopher. "History and Christian Revelation." In *Dynamics of World History*, edited by John J. Mulloy, 263–73. 3rd ed. Wilmington, DE: ISI, 2002.
———. *Progress and Religion*. Washington, DC: Catholic University of America Press, 2001.
Dickerson, Matthew. *A Hobbit Journey: Discovering the Enchantment of Tolkien's Middle-earth*. Grand Rapids, MI: Brazos, 2012.
Di Fuccia, Michael Vincent. *Owen Barfield: Philosophy, Poetry, and Theology*. Eugene, OR: Cascade, 2016.
Dowie, William. "The Gospel of Middle-earth According to J. R. R. Tolkien." In *J. R. R. Tolkien, Scholar and Storyteller: Essays in Memoriam*, edited by Mary Salu and Robert T. Farrell, 265–85. Ithaca, NY: Cornell University Press, 1979.
Dubs, Kathleen E. "Fortune and Fate." In *J. R. R. Tolkien Encyclopedia Scholarship and Critical Assessment*, edited by Michael D. C. Drout, 214–15. New York: Routledge, 2013.
———. "Providence, Fate, and Chance: Boethian Philosophy in *The Lord of the Rings*." In *Tolkien and the Invention of Myth*, edited by Jane Chance, 133–42. Lexington: The University Press of Kentucky, 2004.
Dupré, Louis. *Passage to Modernity: An Essay on the Hermeneutics of Nature and Culture*. New Haven, CT: Yale University Press, 1993.
Duriez, Colin. *The C. S. Lewis Encyclopedia*. Wheaton, IL: Crossway, 2000.
———. "The Fairy Story: J. R. R. Tolkien and C. S. Lewis." In *Tree of Tales: Tolkien, Literature, and Theology*, edited by Trevor Hart and Ivan Khovacs, 13–23. Waco, TX: Baylor University Press, 2007.
———. "J. R. R. Tolkien for the Ages." *Sewanee Theological Review* 57.3 (2014) 321–41.
———. *The J. R. R. Tolkien Handbook*. Grand Rapids, MI: Baker, 1992.
———. *J. R. R. Tolkien: The Making of a Legend*. Oxford: Lion Hudson, 2012.
———. *The Oxford Inklings: Lewis, Tolkien and Their Circle*. Oxford: Lion Hudson, 2015.
———. "Sub-Creation and Tolkien's Theology of Story." In *Scholarship and Fantasy: Proceedings of the Tolkien Phenomenon, May 1992*, edited by Keith J. Battarbee, 133–50. Turku: University of Turku, 1993.
———. *Tolkien and C. S. Lewis: The Gift of Friendship*. Mahwah, NJ: HiddenSpring, 2003.
Dyrness, William A. *Poetic Theology: God and the Poetics of Everyday Life*. Grand Rapids, MI: Eerdmans, 2011.
———. "Subjectivity, the Person, and Modern Art: Theological Reflections on Jacques Maritain and Charles Taylor." *CrossCurrents* 63.1 (2013) 92–105.
Eden, Bradford Lee. "Elves." In *J. R. R. Tolkien Encyclopedia: Scholarship and Critical Assessment*, edited by Michael D. C. Drout, 150–52. New York: Routledge, 2013.

Evans-Wentz, W. Y. *The Fairy Faith in Celtic Countries*. Glastonbury: Lost Library, 1911.

Farrer, Austin. "Poetic Truth." In *Reflective Faith: Essays in Philosophical Theology*, edited by Charles C. Conti, 24–38. London: SPCK, 1972.

Fimi, Dimitra. *Tolkien, Race and Cultural History: From Fairies to Hobbits*. New York: Palgrave Macmillan, 2009.

Flieger, Verlyn. "Frame Narrative." In *J. R. R. Tolkien Encyclopedia: Scholarship and Critical Assessment*, edited by Michael D. C. Drout, 216–18. New York: Routledge, 2013.

———. *Splintered Light: Logos and Language in Tolkien's World*. Rev. ed. Kent, OH: Kent State University Press, 2002.

———. "Time." In *J. R. R. Tolkien Encyclopedia: Scholarship and Critical Assessment*, edited by Michael D. C. Drout, 647–50. New York: Routledge, 2013.

Flieger, Verlyn, and Douglas A. Anderson. "Editors' Commentary." In *Tolkien On Fairy-stories*, edited by Verlyn Flieger and Douglas A. Anderson, 85–121. Exp. ed. London: HarperCollins, 2008.

———. "The History of 'On Fairy-stories.'" In *Tolkien On Fairy-stories*, edited by Verlyn Flieger and Douglas A. Anderson, 122–58. Exp. ed. London: HarperCollins, 2008.

———. Introduction to *Tolkien On Fairy-stories*, edited by Verlyn Flieger and Douglas A. Anderson, 9–23. Exp. ed. London: HarperCollins, 2008.

Flieger, Verlyn, and Tom Shippey. "Allegory versus Bounce: Tolkien's *Smith of Wootton Major*: An Academic Debate between Verlyn Flieger and Tom Shippey." In *Green Suns and Faërie: Essays on Tolkien*, by Verlyn Flieger, 165–78. Kent, OH: Kent State University Press, 2012.

Fonstad, Karen Wynn. *The Atlas of Middle-earth*. Rev. ed. Boston: Houghton Mifflin, 1991.

Fradd, Matt. "What Are the Four Causes of Aristotle? How Do They Apply to Your Five Ways?" Episode 56 of *Pints with Aquinas* (podcast), May 8, 2017. 27:23. https://podbay.fm/podcast/1097862282/e/1494309600.

Freeman, Austin M. *Tolkien Dogmatics: Theology Through Mythology with the Maker of Middle-earth*. Bellingham, WA: Lexham, 2022.

Garth, John. *Tolkien and the Great War: The Threshold of Middle-earth*. Boston: Houghton Mifflin, 2003.

———. *The Worlds of J. R. R. Tolkien: The Places that Inspired Middle-earth*. London: Frances Lincoln, 2020.

Gilliver, Peter, et al. *The Ring of Words: Tolkien and the Oxford English Dictionary*. Oxford: Oxford University Press, 2006.

Giussani, Luigi. *Religious Awareness in Modern Man*. New York: Crossroads Cultural Center, 1998. http://static1.1.sqspcdn.com/static/f/297809/11810109/1303254582793/religious+awareness+in+modern+man.pdf?token=c5fmnvriz9jfq3mwh%2ffsrunc8ok%3d.

———. *The Religious Sense*. Translated by John Zucchi. Montreal: McGill-Queen's University Press, 1997.

———. "The Religious Sense and Faith." *Communio* (blog), February 4, 2011. http://communio.stblogs.org/The%20Religious%20Sense%20and%20Faith.pdf.

Godzieba, Anthony J. "The Catholic Sacramental Imagination and the Access/Excess of Grace." *New Theology Review* 21.3 (2008) 14–26.

GoodKnight, Glen H. "An Enlargement of Being." *Mythlore* 11.3 (1976) 9, 28.

Grant, Patrick. "Tolkien: Archetype and Word." In *Understanding "The Lord of the Rings": The Best of Tolkien Criticism*, edited by Rose A. Zimbardo and Neil D. Isaacs, 163–82. Boston: Houghton Mifflin, 2004.

Gregory, Brad S. *The Unintended Reformation: How a Religious Revolution Secularized Society*. Cambridge, MA: Harvard University Press, 2012.

Hammond, Wayne G., and Christina Scull. *"The Lord of the Rings": A Reader's Companion*. Boston: Houghton Mifflin, 2005.

Helms, Randel. *Tolkien's World*. Boston: Houghton Mifflin, 1974.

Henderson, Edward. "Austin Farrer: The Sacramental Imagination." In *C. S. Lewis and Friends*, edited by David Hein and Edward Henderson, 35–51. Eugene, OR: Cascade, 2011.

Hooper, Walter. "Tolkien and Lewis: An Interview with Walter Hooper." In *Tolkien: A Celebration*, edited by Joseph Pearce, 190–98. San Francisco: Ignatius, 1999.

Howard, Thomas. "Sacramental Imagination." *Christian History* 22/2.78 (2003) 23–24.

Jacobs, Alan. "Fantasy and the Buffered Self." *The New Atlantis* 41 (2014) 3–18.

———. *The Narnian*. San Francisco: HarperSanFrancisco, 2006.

Jeffrey, David Lyle. "Tolkien as Philologist." In *Tolkien and the Invention of Myth*, edited by Jane Chance, 61–78. Lexington: University Press of Kentucky, 2004.

Johnson, Kirstin. "Tolkien's Mythopoesis." In *Tree of Tales: Tolkien, Literature, and Theology*, edited by Trevor Hart and Ivan Khovacs, 25–38. Waco, TX: Baylor University Press, 2007.

Jones, Diana Wynne. "The Shape of the Narrative in *The Lord of the Rings*." In *J. R. R. Tolkien: This Far Land*, edited by Robert Giddings, 87–107. Totowa, NJ: Barnes & Noble, 1984.

Karukoski, Dome, dir. *Tolkien*. Los Angeles: Chernin Entertainment; Fox Searchlight, 2019.

Keller, Timothy. *Every Good Endeavor*. New York: Dutton, 2012.

Kerry, Paul E., ed. *The Ring and the Cross: Christianity and "The Lord of the Rings."* Vancouver, BC: Fairleigh Dickinson University Press, 2013.

Kilby, Clyde S. "Meaning in *The Lord of the Rings*." In *Shadows of Imagination: The Fantasies of C. S. Lewis, J. R. R. Tolkien, and Charles Williams*, edited by Mark R. Hillegas, 70–80. Carbondale: Southern Illinois University Press, 1969.

———. "Mythic and Christian Elements in Tolkien." In *Myth, Allegory, and Gospel*, by Edmund Fuller et al., 119–43. Minneapolis, MN: Bethany Fellowship, 1974.

———. *Tolkien & the Silmarillion*. Wheaton, IL: Harold Shaw, 1976.

———. "Tolkien as Scholar and Artist." *Tolkien Journal* 3.1 (1967) 9–11.

Knippers, Edward. "The Old, Old Story." In *It Was Good: Making Art to the Glory of God*, edited by Ned Bustard, 67–86. 2nd ed. Baltimore, MD: Square Halo, 2006.

Kocher, Paul H. *Master of Middle-earth*. Boston: Houghton Mifflin, 1972.

Koterski, Joseph W. *An Introduction to Medieval Philosophy*. West Sussex: Wiley-Blackwell, 2009.

Kreeft, Peter J. *The Philosophy of Tolkien: The Worldview Behind "The Lord of the Rings."* San Francisco: Ignatius, 2005.

Kuhl, Rand. "Owen Barfield in Southern California." *Mythlore* 1.4 (1969) 8–10.

Kuyper, Abraham. *Wisdom & Wonder: Common Grace in Science & Art*. Edited by Jordan J. Ballor and Stephen J. Grabill. Translated by Nelson D. Kloosterman. Grand Rapids, MI: Christian's Library, 2011.

Lauro, Reno E. "Beyond the Colonization of Human Imagining and Everyday Life: Crafting Mythopoeic Lifeworlds as a Theological Response to Hyperreality." PhD diss., University of St Andrews, 2012. http://hdl.handle.net/10023/3207.

Lee, Stuart D., and Elizabeth Solopova. *The Keys of Middle-earth: Discovering Medieval Literature Through the Fiction of J. R. R. Tolkien*. Hampshire: Palgrave Macmillan, 2005.

Lewis, C. S. *The Allegory of Love: A Study in Medieval Tradition*. Oxford: Oxford University Press, 1958.

———. "Bluspels and Flalansferes: A Semantic Nightmare." In *Rehabilitations and Other Essays*, 135–58. Folcroft, PA: Folcroft Library Editions, 1973.

———. *Collected Letters*. Edited by Walter Hooper. 3 vols. London: HarperCollins, 2000–2006.

———. "The Dethronement of Power." In *Understanding "The Lord of the Rings": The Best of Tolkien Criticism*, edited by Rose A. Zimbardo and Neil D. Isaacs, 11–15. Boston: Houghton Mifflin, 2004.

———. *The Discarded Image*. Cambridge: Cambridge University Press, 1976.

———. *English Literature in the Sixteenth Century, Excluding Drama*. Oxford: Oxford University Press, 1973.

———. *An Experiment in Criticism*. Cambridge: Cambridge University Press, 2013.

———. "First and Second Things." In *God in the Dock*, edited by Walter Hooper, 278–81. Grand Rapids, MI: Eerdmans, 1970.

———. "The Gods Return to Earth." In *The QPB Companion to "The Lord of the Rings,"* edited by Brandon Geist, 31–35. New York: Quality Paperback Book Club, 2001.

———. "Imagination and Thought in the Middle Ages." In *Studies in Medieval and Renaissance Literature*, 41–63. Cambridge: Cambridge University Press, 1998.

———. "Myth Became Fact." In *God in the Dock*, edited by Walter Hooper, 63–67. Grand Rapids, MI: Eerdmans, 1970.

———. "Professor Tolkien's 'Hobbit.'" *Times*, October 8, 1937, 10.

———. "Transposition." In *The Weight of Glory*, 91–115. San Francisco: HarperSanFrancisco, 2001.

Lewis, Warren Hamilton. *Brother and Friends: The Diaries of Major Warren Hamilton Lewis*. Edited by Clyde S. Kilby and Marjorie Lamp Mead. New York: Ballantine, 1988.

Lindbo, David, et al. "Know Soil, Know Life." In *Know Soil, Know Life*, edited by David Lindbo et al., 1–13. Madison, WI: Soil Science Society of America, 2012. http://dx.doi.org/10.2136/2012.knowsoil.c1.

Lindley, John, and Thomas Moore, eds. *The Treasury of Botany*. London: Longmans, Green, 1889.

Lobdell, Jared, ed. *A Tolkien Compass*. Chicago: Open Court, 2003.

Long, Josh B. "Two Views of Faërie in *Smith of Wootton Major*: Nokes and His Cake, Smith and His Star." *Mythlore* 26.3 (2008) 89–100. https://dc.swosu.edu/mythlore/vol26/iss3/7.

López, Antonio. "Growing Human: The Experience of God and of Man in the Work of Luigi Giussani." *Communio* 37 (2010) 209–42.

"*The Lord of the Rings* > Editions." *GoodReads.com*. https://www.goodreads.com/work/editions/3462456-the-lord-of-the-rings.

MacDonald, George. "The Fantastic Imagination." In *The Complete Fairy Tales*, edited by U. C. Knoepflmacher, 5–10. New York: Penguin, 1999.

———. "The Imagination: Its Function and Its Culture." 1867. *George MacDonald Society*, March 27, 1999. https://www.george-macdonald.com/essays_sermons/the_imagination.html.

MacIntyre, Alasdair. *After Virtue*. 2nd ed. Notre Dame, IN: University of Notre Dame Press, 1984.

MacQuarrie, John. "Natural Theology." In *The Blackwell Encyclopedia of Modern Thought*, edited by Alister E. McGrath, 402–5. Cambridge, MA: Basil Blackwell, 1993.

———. *Principles of Christian Theology*. Rev. ed. London: SCM, 1977.

Madsen, Catherine. "'Light from an Invisible Lamp': Natural Religion in *The Lord of the Rings*." In *Tolkien and the Invention of Myth*, edited by Jane Chance, 235–47. Lexington: University Press of Kentucky, 2004.

Maritain, Jacques. *Art and Scholasticism and the Frontiers of Poetry*. Translated by Joseph W. Evans. Notre Dame, IN: University of Notre Dame, 1935. https://maritain.nd.edu/jmc/etext/art.htm.

———. "Concerning Poetic Knowledge." In *The Situation of Poetry: Four Essays on the Relations between Poetry, Mysticism, Magic, and Knowledge*, by Jacques Maritain and Raïssa Maritain, 37–70. Translated by Marshall Suther. New York: Kraus Reprint, 1968.

———. *Creative Intuition in Art and Poetry*. New York: Meridian, 1955.

Markos, Louis. *On the Shoulders of Hobbits: The Road to Virtue with Tolkien and Lewis*. Chicago: Moody, 2012.

McAleer, Graham. "All Valid Law Is Analogical." *Law & Liberty*, November 16, 2015. http://www.libertylawsite.org/book-review/all-valid-law-is-analogical.

McGrath, Alister E. *C. S. Lewis: A Life*. Carol Stream, IL: Tyndale, 2013.

———. *Heresy: A History of Defending the Truth*. New York: HarperOne, 2009.

———. *Nature*. Vol. 1 of *A Scientific Theology*. Grand Rapids, MI: Eerdmans, 2001.

———. *The Open Secret: A New Vision for Natural Theology*. Malden, MA: Blackwell, 2008.

———. *The Order of Things: Explorations in Scientific Theology*. Malden, MA: Blackwell, 2006.

———. *Theory*. Vol. 3 of *A Scientific Theology*. Grand Rapids, MI: Eerdmans, 2003.

McIntosh, Jonathan S. *The Flame Imperishable: Tolkien, St. Thomas, and the Metaphysics of Faërie*. Kettering, OH: Angelico, 2017.

McIntyre, John. *Faith, Theology and Imagination*. Edinburgh: Handsel, 1987.

Milbank, Alison. "Apologetics and the Imagination: Making Strange." In *Imaginative Apologetics: Theology, Philosophy and the Catholic Tradition*, edited by Andrew Davison, 31–45. Grand Rapids, MI: Baker Academic, 2012.

———. *Chesterton and Tolkien as Theologians: The Fantasy of the Real*. London: T&T Clark, 2008.

———. "Tolkien, Chesterton, and Thomism." In *Tolkien's "The Lord of the Rings": Sources of Inspiration*, edited by Stratford Caldecott and Thomas M. Honegger, 187–98. Zürich: Walking Tree, 2008.

Mills, David. "One Truth, Many Tales." *Christian History* 22/2.78 (2003) 20–22.

Murray, Robert. "A Tribute to Tolkien." *Chesterton Review* 28.1/2 (2002) 173–76.

Noble, Alan. "How Stories Unsettle Our Secular Age." *Gospel Coalition*, February 4, 2019. https://www.thegospelcoalition.org/article/stories-unsettle-secular-age.

Norwood, W. D. "Tolkien's Intention in *The Lord of the Rings*." *Tolkien Papers, Mankato Studies in English* 2 (1967) 18–24.

Oden, Thomas C. "Without Excuse: Classic Christian Exegesis of General Revelation." *Journal of the Evangelical Theological Society* 41.1 (1998) 55–68.

Oliver, Simon. *Creation: A Guide for the Perplexed*. London: Bloomsbury T&T Clark, 2017.

———. "Nouvelle Théologie, De Lubac & Radical Orthodoxy." *Timeline Theological Videos*, September 14, 2012. https://www.youtube.com/watch?v=UgTnc_JJXcw.

Olsen, Corey. *Exploring J. R. R. Tolkien's "The Hobbit."* Boston: Houghton Mifflin Harcourt, 2012.

Ordway, Holly. *Tolkien's Faith: A Spiritual Biography*. Elk Grove Village, IL: Word on Fire Academic, 2023.

Oxford English Dictionary Online [OED Online]. Oxford: Oxford University Press, 2019.

Pask, Kevin. *The Fairy Way of Writing: Shakespeare to Tolkien*. Baltimore, MD: Johns Hopkins University Press, 2013.

Pearce, Joseph. *Tolkien: Man and Myth*. San Francisco: Ignatius, 1998.

Pereira, Leon. "Morals Makyth Man—and Hobbit." In *Tolkien's "The Lord of the Rings": Sources of Inspiration*, edited by Stratford Caldecott and Thomas M. Honegger, 171–85. Zürich: Walking Tree, 2008.

Pettersson, Ninni M. "The HoMe-Texts in Chronological Order." *Mellonath Daeron—The Language Guild of the Forodrim*, March 27, 1998. http://www.forodrim.org/daeron/md_hmch.html.

Plummer, Robert L. *Forty Questions About Interpreting the Bible*. Grand Rapids, MI: Kregel Academic, 2010.

Polkinghorne, John C. *One World: The Interaction of Science and Theology*. West Conshohocken, PA: Templeton, 2007.

Poythress, Vern S. *Chance and the Sovereignty of God*. Wheaton: IL, Crossway, 2014.

———. *In the Beginning Was the Word: Language—A God-Centered Approach*. Wheaton, IL: Crossway, 2009.

———. *Redeeming Science: A God-Centered Approach*. Wheaton, IL: Crossway, 2006.

"Professor J. R. R. Tolkien: Creator of Hobbits and Inventor of a New Mythology." In *J. R. R. Tolkien, Scholar and Storyteller: Essays in Memoriam*, edited by Mary Salu and Robert T. Farrell, 12–14. Ithaca, NY: Cornell University Press, 1979.

Przywara, Erich. *Analogia Entis: Metaphysics: Original Structure and Universal Rhythm*. Translated by John R. Betz and David Bentley Hart. Grand Rapids, MI: Eerdmans, 2014.

Rateliff, John D. *Mr. Baggins*. The History of "The Hobbit" 1. Boston: Houghton Mifflin, 2007.

———. *Return to Bag-End*. The History of "The Hobbit" 2. Boston: Houghton Mifflin, 2007.

Reilly, R. J. *Romantic Religion: A Study of Barfield, Lewis, Williams, and Tolkien*. Athens: University of Georgia Press, 1972.

Rérolle, Raphaëlle. "My Father's 'Eviscerated' Work—Son of Hobbit Scribe J. R. R. Tolkien Finally Speaks Out." *World Crunch*, December 5, 2012. https://www.worldcrunch.com/culture-society/my-father039s-quoteevisceratedquot-work-son-of-hobbit-scribe-jrr-tolkien-finally-speaks-out.

Resnick, Henry. "An Interview with Tolkien." *Niekas* 18 (1967) 37–47.

Rutledge, Fleming. *The Battle for Middle-earth: Tolkien's Divine Design in "The Lord of the Rings."* Grand Rapids, MI: Eerdmans, 2004.

Ryken, Leland, et al., eds. "Mountain." In *Dictionary of Biblical Imagery*, 572–74. Downers Grove, IL: IVP Academic, 1998.

Sapir, Edward. *Language*. Mineola, NY: Dover, 2004.

Sayer, George. "Recollections of J. R. R. Tolkien." In *Tolkien: A Celebration*, edited by Joseph Pearce, 1–16. San Francisco: Ignatius, 2001.

Sayers, Dorothy L. *The Mind of the Maker*. San Francisco: HarperOne, 1987.

Schwartzel, Erich. "How Amazon Turned 'Lord of the Rings' into the Most Expensive Show of All Time." *Wall Street Journal*, August 26, 2022. https://www.wsj.com/articles/amazon-lord-of-the-rings-expensive-11661482048.

Scull, Christina, and Wayne G. Hammond. *The J. R. R. Tolkien Companion and Guide: Reader's Guide*. Boston: Houghton Mifflin, 2006.

Sebanc, Mark. "J. R. R. Tolkien: Lover of Logos." *Communio* 20 (1993) 84–106.

Shaeffer, Adam Brent. "Spiritual Formation in Tolkien's Legendarium." PhD diss., Durham University, 2017. http://etheses.dur.ac.uk/12325.

Shippey, T. A. "Another Road to Middle-earth: Jackson's Movie Trilogy." In *Understanding "The Lord of the Rings": The Best of Tolkien Criticism*, edited by Rose A. Zimbardo and Neil D. Isaacs, 233–54. Boston: Houghton Mifflin, 2004.

———. "Creation from Philology in *The Lord of the Rings*." In *J. R. R. Tolkien, Scholar and Storyteller: Essays in Memoriam*, edited by Mary Salu and Robert T. Farrell, 286–316. Ithaca, NY: Cornell University Press, 1979.

———. "A Feeling for Language." *Christian History* 22/2.78 (2003) 14.

———. "Interview with Tom Shippey." In *The QPB Companion to "The Lord of the Rings,"* edited by Brandon Geist, 17–20. New York: Quality Paperback Book Club, 2001.

———. *J. R. R. Tolkien: Author of the Century*. Boston: Houghton Mifflin, 2002.

———. *The Road to Middle-earth*. Rev. and exp. ed. Boston: Houghton Mifflin, 2003.

Siewers, Alfred K. "Tolkien's Cosmic-Christian Ecology: The Medieval Underpinnings." In *Tolkien's Modern Middle Ages*, edited by Jane Chance and Alfred K. Siewers, 139–53. New York: Palgrave Macmillan, 2005.

Simpson, J. A., and E. S. C. Weiner, eds. *Oxford English Dictionary [OED]*. 20 vols. 2nd ed. Oxford: Clarendon, 1989.

Sire, James M. *The Universe Next Door*. 4th ed. Downers Grove, IL: InterVarsity, 2004.

Smith, James K. A. *How (Not) to Be Secular: Reading Charles Taylor*. Grand Rapids, MI: Eerdmans, 2014.

Smith, Thomas W. "Tolkien's Catholic Imagination and the Uses and Abuses of Tradition." Paper presented at the Catholic Imagination Lecture Series, Villanova University, Villanova, PA, December 2004.

Snyder, Christopher. *The Making of Middle-earth*. New York: Sterling, 2013.

Spirito, Guglielmo. "The Influence of Holiness: The Healing Power of Tolkien's Narrative." In *Tolkien's "The Lord of the Rings": Sources of Inspiration*, edited by Stratford Caldecott and Thomas M. Honegger, 199–210. Zürich: Walking Tree, 2008.

Steiner, George. "Oxford's Eccentric Don." *Tolkien Studies* 5 (2008) 186–88. http://dx.doi.org/10.1353/tks.0.0001.

Strelzyk, Yvan. "Chronology of the Translations." *Elrond's Library: Translations of Tolkien All Over the World*, n.d. https://www.tolkienguide.com/archive/ElrondsLibrary/Chrono.html.

Suárez, Francisco. "Types of Efficient Causes." *Alfred J. Freddoso*, n.d. https://www3.nd.edu/~afreddos/courses/527/create03.htm.

Taylor, Charles. "Buffered and Porous Selves." *Immanent Frame*, September 2, 2008. https://tif.ssrc.org/2008/09/02/buffered-and-porous-selves.

———. *The Language Animal*. Cambridge, MA: Belknap Press of Harvard University Press, 2016.

———. *A Secular Age*. Cambridge, MA: Belknap Press of Harvard University Press, 2007.

———. *Sources of the Self*. Cambridge, MA: Harvard University Press, 1989.

Tolkien, Christopher. Foreword in *The Return of the Shadow*, by J. R. R. Tolkien, 1–7. Edited by Christopher Tolkien. Boston: Houghton Mifflin, 2000.

———. Foreword in *The Silmarillion*, by J. R. R. Tolkien, vii–ix. Edited by Christopher Tolkien. 2nd ed. Boston: Houghton Mifflin, 2001.

———. Introduction to "The Notion Club Papers." In *Sauron Defeated*, by J. R. R. Tolkien, 145–54. Edited by Christopher Tolkien. London: HarperCollins, 2002.

———. Preface to *Beowulf: A Translation and Commentary Together with Sellic Spell*, by J. R. R. Tolkien, vii–xiii. Edited by Christopher Tolkien. Boston: Houghton Mifflin Harcourt, 2014.

———. "*The Silmarillion* (by) J. R. R. Tolkien: A Brief Account of the Book and Its Making." *Mallorn* 14 (1980) 3–5, 7–8.

Tolkien, J. R. R. *The Adventures of Tom Bombadil*. In *The Tolkien Reader*, 7–64. New York: Ballantine, 1966.

———. "The Annals of Aman." In *Morgoth's Ring*, edited by Christopher Tolkien, 47–138. London: HarperCollins, 2002.

———. "The Appendix on Languages." In *The Peoples of Middle-earth*, edited by Christopher Tolkien, 19–84. London: HarperCollins, 2015.

———. "Beowulf: The Monsters and the Critics." In *The Monsters and the Critics and Other Essays*, edited by Christopher Tolkien, 5–48. London: HarperCollins, 2006.

———. *The Book of Lost Tales, Part 1*. Edited by Christopher Tolkien. New York: Del Ray, 1992.

———. "English and Welsh." In *The Monsters and the Critics and Other Essays*, edited by Christopher Tolkien, 162–97. London: HarperCollins, 2006.

———. Excerpt from *Tolkien in Oxford*. *BBC 2*, March 30, 1968. http://www.tolkienlibrary.com/press/814-Tolkien-1968-BBC-Interview.php.

———. "'Genesis of the Story' Tolkien's Note to Clyde Kilby." In *Smith of Wootton Major*, by J. R. R. Tolkien, 85–87. Edited by Verlyn Flieger. Ext. ed. London: HarperCollins, 2015.

———. "Guide to the Names in *The Lord of the Rings*." In *A Tolkien Compass*, edited by Jared Lobdell, 155–201. La Salle, IL: Open Court, 1975.

———. *The Hobbit*. Boston: Houghton Mifflin, 2001.

———. Interview with Denys Gueroult. *BBC Radio 4*, January 20, 1965. BBC Author Archive Collection. https://www.bbc.co.uk/programmes/p021jx7j.

———. "The Istari." In *Unfinished Tales of Númenor and Middle-earth*, edited by Christopher Tolkien, 388–402. Boston: Houghton Mifflin, 1980.

———. "The Later Quenta Silmarillion, Phase 1." In *Morgoth's Ring*, edited by Christopher Tolkien, 141–99. London: HarperCollins, 2002.

———. *Leaf by Niggle*. In *Tree and Leaf* in *The Tolkien Reader*, 87–122. New York: Ballantine, 1966.

———. Letter to Joan O. Falconer. January 24, 1965. Department of Special Collections and University Archives, Marquette University, Milwaukee, WI. Quotations reproduced with permission of the Tolkien Estate.

———. Letter to Nancy Smith. December 25, 1963–January 2, 1964. Department of Special Collections and University Archives, Marquette University, Milwaukee, WI. Quotations reproduced with permission of the Tolkien Estate.

———. *The Letters of J. R. R. Tolkien*. Edited by Humphrey Carpenter. Boston: Houghton Mifflin, 2000.

———. *The Letters of J. R. R. Tolkien*. Edited by Humphrey Carpenter. Rev. and exp. ed. London: HarperCollins, 2023.

———. *The Lord of the Rings*. Boston: Houghton Mifflin, 1994.

———. "The Making of Appendix A." In *The Peoples of Middle-earth*, edited by Christopher Tolkien, 253–89. London: HarperCollins, 2015.

———. "Manuscript B." In *Tolkien On Fairy-stories*, edited by Verlyn Flieger and Douglas A. Anderson, 206–96. Exp. ed. London: HarperCollins, 2008.

———. *A Middle English Vocabulary*. Mineola, NY: Dover, 2005.

———. "Mythopoeia." In *Tree and Leaf*, 85–90. London: HarperCollins, 2001.

———. *The Nature of Middle-earth: Late Writings on the Lands, Inhabitants, and Metaphysics of Middle-earth*. Edited by Carl F. Hostetter. Boston: Mariner, 2021.

———. "The Notion Club Papers." In *Sauron Defeated*, edited by Christopher Tolkien, 145–327. London: HarperCollins, 2002.

———. "Of Lembas." In *The Peoples of Middle-earth*, edited by Christopher Tolkien, 403–5. London: HarperCollins, 2015.

———. "Of the Rings of Power and the Third Age." In *The Silmarillion*, edited by Christopher Tolkien, 285–304. 2nd ed. Boston: Houghton Mifflin, 2001.

———. "On Fairy-stories." In *Tolkien On Fairy-stories*, edited by Verlyn Flieger and Douglas A. Anderson, 27–84. Exp. ed. London: HarperCollins, 2008.

———. "On Translating Beowulf." In *The Monsters and the Critics and Other Essays*, edited by Christopher Tolkien, 49–71. London: HarperCollins, 2006.

———. "The Quest for Erebor." In *Unfinished Tales of Númenor and Middle-earth*, edited by Christopher Tolkien, 321–36. Boston: Houghton Mifflin, 1980.

———. *The Return of the Shadow*. Edited by Christopher Tolkien. Boston: Houghton Mifflin, 2000.

———. "A Secret Vice." In *The Monsters and the Critics and Other Essays*, edited by Christopher Tolkien, 198–223. London: HarperCollins, 2006.

———. *The Silmarillion*. Edited by Christopher Tolkien. 2nd ed. Boston: Houghton Mifflin, 2001.

———. "Sir Gawain and the Green Knight." In *The Monsters and the Critics and Other Essays*, edited by Christopher Tolkien, 72–108. London: HarperCollins, 2006.

———. *Sir Gawain and the Green Knight, Pearl, and Sir Orfeo*. Translated by J. R. R. Tolkien. Boston: Houghton Mifflin, 1978.

———. *Smith of Wootton Major*. Edited by Verlyn Flieger. Ext. ed. London: HarperCollins, 2015.

———. "Smith of Wootton Major Essay." In *Smith of Wootton Major*, edited by Verlyn Flieger, 111–45. Ext. ed. London: HarperCollins, 2015.

———. "Tolkien's Draft Introduction to *The Golden Key*." In *Smith of Wootton Major*, edited by Verlyn Flieger, 89–96. Ext. ed. London: HarperCollins, 2015.

———. *Tree and Leaf* in *The Tolkien Reader*, 2–112. New York: Ballantine, 1966.

———. *The War of the Ring*. Edited by Christopher Tolkien. Boston: Houghton Mifflin, 2000.

Tolley, Clive. "Tolkien's 'Essay on Man': a Look at *Mythopoeia*." In *A Hidden Presence: The Catholic Imagination of J. R. R. Tolkien*, edited by Ian Boyd and Stratford Caldecott, 43–59. South Orange, NJ: Chesterton, 2003.

Torrance, T. F. *Reality and Scientific Theology*. Edinburgh: Scottish Academic, 1985.

Turner, Allan. "A Theoretical Model for Tolkien Translation Criticism." In *Tolkien in Translation*, edited by Thomas Honegger, 1–30. Zürich: Walking Tree, 2003.

Turney, Wayne S. "Notes on Naturalism in the Theatre." *Wayne S. Turney*, n.d. https://web.archive.org/web/20080514174112/http://www.wayneturney.20m.com/naturalism.htm.

University of Nottingham. "Introduction to Medieval Books: Decoration and Illumination." *Manuscripts and Special Collections*, February 2011. https://www.nottingham.ac.uk/manuscriptsandspecialcollections/researchguidance/medievalbooks/decorationandillumination.aspx.

Unwin, Rayner. "Tolkien and His Publisher: A Forty-Year Relationship." *Logos* 10.4 (1999) 200–210.

Ward, Graham. "How Literature Resists Secularity." *Literature & Theology* 24.1 (2010) 73–88. http://dx.doi.org/10.1093/litthe/frp057.

———. "Narrative and Ethics: The Structures of Believing and the Practices of Hope." *Literature & Theology* 20.4 (2006) 438–61. http://dx.doi.org/10.1093/litthe/frl057.

———. *The Politics of Discipleship*. Grand Rapids, MI: Baker Academic, 2009.

Ward, Michael. "The Good Serves the Better and Both the Best: C. S. Lewis on Imagination and Reason in Apologetics." In *Imaginative Apologetics: Theology, Philosophy and the Catholic Tradition*, edited by Andrew Davison, 59–78. Grand Rapids, MI: Baker Academic, 2012.

Warner, Michael, et al., eds. Editors' Introduction to *Varieties of Secularism in a Secular Age*, 1–31. Cambridge, MA: Harvard University Press, 2010.

Weiner, Edmund. "Tolkien and the Aesthetics of Philology: A Talk Given to the Oxford Tolkien Society, Taruithorn, on 6 March 2015." *Philoloblog* (blog), March 23, 2016. http://philoloblog.blogspot.co.uk/2016/03/tolkien-and-aesthetics-of-philology.html.

West, Richard C. "The Interlace Structure of *The Lord of the Rings*." In *A Tolkien Compass*, edited by Jared Lobdell, 77–94. La Salle, IL: Open Court, 1975.

"What Color Is the Sun?" *Stanford Solar Center*, n.d. http://solar-center.stanford.edu/SID/activities/GreenSun.html.

Willard, Dallas. "Language, Being, God, and the Three Stages of Theistic Evidence." *Dallas Willard Ministries*, 1992. https://dwillard.org/resources/articles/language-being-god-and-the-three-stages-of-theistic-evidence.

Williams, Rowan. *Grace and Necessity: Reflections on Art and Love*. London: Continuum, 2006.

———. Series Introduction to *George MacDonald: Divine Carelessness and Fairytale Levity*, by Daniel Gabelman, v–vii. Waco, TX: Baylor University Press, 2013.

Wolf, Mark J. P. *Building Imaginary Worlds*. New York: Routledge, 2012.

Wolterstorff, Nicholas. *Art in Action*. Grand Rapids, MI: Eerdmans, 1980.

Wood, Ralph C. *The Gospel According to Tolkien: Visions of the Kingdom in Middle-earth*. Louisville, KY: Westminster John Knox, 2003.

Yandell, Stephen. "'A Pattern Which Our Nature Cries Out For': The Medieval Tradition of the Ordered Four in the Fiction of J. R. R. Tolkien." *Mythlore* 21/2.80 (1996). https://dc.swosu.edu/mythlore/vol21/iss2/57.

Zaleski, Philip, and Carol Zaleski. *The Fellowship: The Literary Lives of the Inklings: J. R. R. Tolkien, C. S. Lewis, Owen Barfield, Charles Williams*. New York: Farrar, Straus, and Giroux, 2015.

Index

www.ingramcontent.com/pod-product-compliance
Lightning Source LLC
LaVergne TN
LVHW050618100826
845148LV00011B/1645

9781725271982